THE PARTING GLASS

THE PARTING GLASS

GINA MARIE GUADAGNINO

ATRIA BOOKS

New York London Toronto Sydney New Delhi

An Imprint of Simon & Schuster, Inc.
1230 Avenue of the Americas
New York, NY 10020

This book is a work of fiction. Any references to historical events, real people, or real places are used fictitiously. Other names, characters, places, and events are products of the author's imagination, and any resemblance to actual events or places or persons, living or dead, is entirely coincidental.

First Atria Books hardcover edition March 2019

ATRIA BOOKS and colophon are registered trademarks of Simon & Schuster, Inc.

For information about special discounts for bulk purchases, please contact Simon & Schuster Special Sales at 1-866-506-1949 or business@simonandschuster.com.

The Simon & Schuster Speakers Bureau can bring authors to your live event. For more information or to book an event, contact the Simon & Schuster Speakers Bureau at 1-866-248-3049 or visit our website at www.simonspeakers.com.

Interior design by Jill Putorti

Manufactured in the United States of America

10 9 8 7 6 5 4 3 2 1

The Library of Congress has cataloged the Touchstone edition as follows:

Names: Guadagnino, Gina Marie, 1982– author.
Title: The parting glass / Gina Marie Guadagnino.
Description: First Touchstone hardcover edition. | New York : Touchstone, 2019. |
Identifiers: LCCN 2018013998 (print) | LCCN 2018016652 (ebook) | ISBN 9781501198434 | ISBN 9781501198410 (hardcover) | ISBN 9781501198427 (pbk.)
Classification: LCC PS3607.U216 (ebook) | LCC PS3607.U216 P37 2019 (print) | DDC 813/.6—dc23
LC record available at https://lccn.loc.gov/2018013998

ISBN 978-1-5011-9841-0
ISBN 978-1-5011-9843-4 (ebook)

For Anthony:

It's not exactly "Clouds," but I hope it will do

When you are entrusted with secrets in confidence, remember that this may be done, and is often done, under doubt, or at least suspicions may arise afterwards; and if you, by inadvertence or vanity, give cause for such suspicions, your credit and character will henceforth be forfeited and lost. . . . For go where you will, the character which you have made for yourself will be certain, sooner or later, to follow you.

—*The Duties of a Lady's Maid*

In some families, there are secrets on which the welfare, and perhaps the very existence of the persons concerned may depend.

—*The Duties of a Lady's Maid*

WASHINGTON SQUARE, 1837

It was Thursday again, and once more I was courting misery with both arms open wide.

"Thank you, Ballard, that will do," Miss Charlotte Walden said, and, bobbing a curtsy, I showed myself quickly from the room. The heavy oak door shut solidly, with a soft click following as the lock was engaged. The Argand lamps threw but dim illumination along the heavy carpet lining the hall, casting flickering shadows amongst the birds and flowers woven there. I made my way along the muffled corridor to the door that led into the servants' stair. On the landing was the door to my own narrow chamber. I pressed myself to this barrier, one ear flat against the wood. Through the door, I could only just make out the muffled scrape of the window opening in the room beyond. It was all so faint, in the faded light on the landing, almost dreamlike. I let my forehead rest against the door, my eyes closed. I strained for the sound of the bed, imagining its creak coming through the door as a whisper once, twice, again.

Quick footfalls broke my reverie, and I lurched from the door as Mrs. Harrison came up the stair. I froze, my ears still straining, but the heavy oak was my mistress's shield. One hand went up involuntarily to see my hair was straight, and I nodded to the imposing housekeeper.

"Miss Ballard. Is it not your night off?"

"Yes, Mrs. Harrison, mum."

"Is Miss Walden abed and all your duties discharged?" she asked, her face placid, her tone bland.

"Indeed they are, Mrs. Harrison."

"Then I see no cause for you to linger when you might very well go."

"Yes, thank you, mum."

Beneath Mrs. Harrison's critical eye, I hurried down the back stairs to the kitchen. I stopped on the landing to arrange my face into a mask of tranquillity before I faced Cook.

"Night off, Miss Ballard?" the big woman asked, as though she didn't already know the answer.

"Yes, Mrs. Freedman, mum."

"Bit of a snack for you then, child." She gestured at a small parcel with the knife she held. "Right then, off with you." Mrs. Freedman, brusque with everyone, always took the time to show me kindness in her own harsh way. She was under no obligation to feed me extra on my night off, but she often did it anyway, suspicious in that chronic way of cooks that I was not adequately fed unless she was doing the feeding. "All skin and bones, that one," I heard her mutter as she returned to her chopping. "See you bundle well, child," she said, raising her voice again. "It's turned snowy again."

I huddled into my wool mantle, tying my bonnet firmly under my chin. No mitts or gloves had I, but only Charlotte Walden's muff from four seasons ago, the fur patchy and worn near to the skin. Thus attired, I nodded farewell to Cook and slipped out the kitchen door. I made my way down the snowy cobbles to the gate at the end of the mews, should anyone be watching from the windows, then doubled back along the other side of the block and ducked inside the street door to our own carriage house. The horses nickered softly, cold air gusting down the row of stalls from the open door. Moonlight and streetlamps lit my way across the flagstones to the Waldens' coach, black and hulking. The door stuck a little as I opened it and crawled in to sit on the floor. I breathed in deeply the smells of the carriage house: sweet hay and oat mash, worn leather, brass polish, and the musky scent of horse. Such aromas as had clung to my father. I opened Cook's parcel to nibble at my portion of bread and cheese, listening to the wind rattle the shutters. Licking my fingers, brushing the crumbs from my skirt, I settled in to wait.

It was nearly pitch dark when Seanin arrived, the streetlamps having guttered low. I had dozed off with my head on the carriage seat, but woke at once when he touched my arm. In the wan light, he smiled, his eyes gleaming. I smiled back, took his glove, and let him hand me down from the coach like the lady I'd never be. Softly, so our boots wouldn't ring on the flagstones, we slipped out the carriage house's front door onto the street. A clock struck one over at St. Mark's as we made our way east out onto Broadway. A sudden gust as we rounded the corner threw me off-balance; I moved into the proffered circle of his arm, huddling close against him. A light snow fell, swirling in eddies over the cobbles, and I gripped his arm to keep from slipping on the shell of ice formed over the street. The houses and shops that lined the way were dark, silent, and we had gone several blocks south before we saw lights dancing behind curtained windows and either of us dared speak.

"Have you eaten?" he asked me quietly in Irish.

"I have," I whispered back. "Have you?"

"I ate. But I'm not yet satisfied." He smiled wickedly; I shoved him, grinning in spite of myself.

We crossed over Houston and down to one of the narrow side streets, a swell of light and noise rising to meet us as we came to Lafayette. Warm light and capering shadows thrown from the windows of public houses and dance halls stained the snow, a mix of song and laughter escaping from behind the doors.

The Hibernian stood on Mulberry Street, on a block crammed full of public houses and a handful of the more respectable sorts of brothels. Like its neighbors, it catered almost exclusively to Irish, though one might find the rare Italian or Prussian who'd wandered north out of the Sixth Ward, the borders of which were still confined to the south. It was already all Catholics then in Mulberry Street, but the Hibernian was full of lilting voices from every corner of the island. Here, broad Galway vowels rubbed up against rapid Belfast chatter and clipped Dublin drawl. And from behind the bar, his heavy brogue booming over the din, reigned Dermot John O'Brien, proprietor and publican, who nodded to us as we entered. We nodded back, weaving our way through the patrons packing the place.

At a cramped bench in the back, I waited while Seanin sidled up to the bar. When he returned, he held two mugs in each hand, foam streaming down the sides. I had slipped off my bonnet and mantle, my face flushed from the heat of the room, and, reaching for one of the mugs, gulped down half its contents in one swig.

"Easy now," he said, speaking English this time. "It'll go straight to your head."

"Fuck it, Johnny," I said, using his English name. I took another swallow, having by now dropped the posh accent I adopted in the

Waldens' home and slipping back into my native brogue. "Just because you're buying there's no call to be an ass."

He spread his hands in a defenseless sort of gesture that I had been growing lately to despise. I turned my eyes back to my ale, scowling. He was always a great one for ruining a moment.

My temper up, we drank then in silence; the amber firelight from the hearth seemed to suffuse the amber liquid in my mug. From time to time, I saw him nod or say a word in acknowledgment of other patrons, men I recognized as friends of his, but I kept my eyes firmly on my ale, refusing stubbornly to meet anyone's gaze. At last he sighed loudly.

"What now?"

He shrugged with exaggerated casualness. "Might go greet the lads, if you weren't feeling social."

"It's all the same to me."

"Grand," he said, clinking his glass cockily to mine and sauntering into the press toward a knot of his cronies.

I relocated to the bar in the hopes of engaging Dermot in a lengthy discourse on Seanin's many faults, but the bustle kept him moving up and down the counter, too busy refilling mugs with ale and topping off glasses of whiskey to do more than keep my own mug filled and shrug apologetically at me as he moved on to less sullen patrons. I counted seven rounds before the room began to blur and sway, the light and laughter swirling like the gustings of snow that still fell, before a sudden smack of cold stung my cheeks. Seanin was holding my shoulders firmly as I retched in the alley behind the Hibernian, the icy wind sobering. I shook his arm from my shoulders, pushing past him back into the pub. Weaving between the scattered remaining patrons, I made my way to the stairs at the back of the bar, sketching a rough salute to Dermot as I passed him. He reached out to steady me as I swayed, but I waved him off, leaning heavily against the wall for balance. I descended, making my way past the casks and kegs to a double pallet spread out by the hearth. I could hear Seanin hurrying behind me, and sat, legs splayed, waiting for him on the pallet. My braid had come down, uncoiling over my shoulder, which I noted in a detached sort of way as I allowed him to remove my boots and stockings. I bent forward, nose to my knees, and waited for him to unbutton me enough to slide my frock over my head. I felt his fingers clumsily picking at the knots in my stays, and moved to help him unlace me. I was shivering then, clad only in my thin shift, lying back onto the pallet, my eyes closed as I listened to him move about the room. I heard him building up the fire, felt him sit heavily onto the pallet beside me, pulling the layers of blankets up around me to stop me shivering. I rolled over on my side and took his hand, pressing it gratefully to my cheek. I squeezed his fingers, inhaling the perfumed hair oil of Charlotte Walden, who, only hours before, had lain with him in her bed.

Seanin retrieved his hand, brushing a stray hair back from my face, and saying in Irish, “There now, little Maire. What did I say about all that drink?”

“Hell with it, Seanin,” I said in our father’s language. “There’ll be time to regret it all in the morning.”

“Go to sleep, Sister,” he whispered, kissing my brow before heading back up the stairs, but I was already drifting off.

Whatever may be told you, therefore, by your mistress, should be kept inviolable, though she does not particularly enjoin secrecy.

—*The Duties of a Lady's Maid*

It had been just over a year ago that Charlotte Walden had met my eyes in the mirror and asked, "Where do you go on your nights off, Ballard?" and I had invented an aunt who lived in Essex Street. The question wasn't wholly unexpected, and the Hibernian was in the general direction of Essex anyway.

I listened attentively as she asked me to leave the window of my closet room ajar. Charlotte Walden had never left her nursery; it had merely been made over as she came of age, and when her nurse moved out of the tiny adjoining room, a governess had moved in. The autumn of Charlotte's coming out, I had been hired and it had been made over yet again, the little closet now reserved for her lady's maid. It had been the closest thing I had to a home for nearly two winters by the time she made the request. It was cramped, with space enough only for a narrow bed and my trunk, one door leading to Charlotte's bedchamber, the other door leading to the servants' stair. The tiny window, just wide enough for a lean man to climb through, looked out into the mews. Thick ivy crept up the bricks, providing ample handholds, and I thought later, as I looked out the window, that the little room could not have been better designed for such clandestine purposes.

I listened, I nodded, I murmured "yes, miss," as though it was the most natural thing in the world. As though she had asked me to hand her a stocking or find her glove. *Of course, Miss Walden. I'd be happy to help.* The next Thursday, I did as I was bade, and then listened outside the door on the landing as my brother shimmied through the window to fuck my mistress. I tried to listen to their muffled talk, imagining his smooth compliments, her halfhearted protestations. I listened for the silence of their first kiss. I listened for the swish of silk slipping over her shoulders, to the creak of the bed as they fell against it, to the rhythm of them making love. I thought I heard her moan and cry out, so soft, so soft. And what sounds the oak door robbed me of, I could imagine well enough.

When it was over, I was waiting for Seanin in the carriage house, as though it were any other Thursday night, and we walked in silence to the Hibernian. I could smell her on him: the lavender-scented oil I brushed into her shining hair, the musk of her underarms, the heavy, earthy scent from between her legs. I wanted to ask if she'd wanted it. I wanted to ask if her lips were soft beneath his own. I wanted to ask if she'd bled, and when she'd cried if it had been with pain or joy, and what she'd said to him after it was over. I wanted to ask a thousand questions burning in my heart, but I was ashamed and asked nothing at all. It was Seanin's fault, with his hangdog face, looking pleased and embarrassed both, so I dared say not a word. When finally we reached the Hibernian, I let him stand me round after round until I staggered into the back alley and was sick into my hair. We slept back to back that night, but the smell of her rose off him in warm waves, curdling my stomach. I heaved myself up the stair again and went out back to retch in the alley until there was nothing left but bile, then retched that up too. Dermot found me there, shivering and barefoot, and made me eat a few handfuls of clean snow. He picked me up in his arms as though I were a babe, and carried me back down to my pallet in the cellar. Once he had settled me, he shook Seanin till his teeth rattled.

"I don't know what's between you two, and I don't care to either. But if you ever let your sister get that sick and grieved again, you can find another goddamn floor to sleep on."

I wept silently as Seanin apologized over and over until, satisfied, Dermot took himself back upstairs. When he crawled to the pallet, Seanin was tender enough, wiping away my tears, asking how he'd grieved me. But what could I have said? My questions stayed unasked, and his stayed unanswered.

We'd never spoken of it again.

In the morning, we rose before first light to make our way back to the Waldens' stately house in the Square—Seanin back to being Johnny in the carriage house, and I to Charlotte Walden's bedchamber. I tidied things quietly as my mistress slept, removing all trace of her nocturnal doings and misdoings, erasing my brother from Charlotte's life. But not entirely, for the next week, she asked me to keep the window open again, and the week after that, and the one that followed, until she no longer need ask, for I did it without being told.

Week after week the window was left ajar, until it became a ritual, like the Mass I never took now in fear I'd be thrown out for popery. It was a ritual to bathe and wash her hair, to anoint her with scented oils and dress her in lace and silk. A ritual in which I knew not if she was priestess or sacrifice, only that to touch her, to make her ready, was a sacred thing. I took great care with her, Charlotte Walden. But also I took care to show her no more or less attention than before, to be no more or less familiar. I took care that she should never feel awkward, or unsure of me. I treated her like a treasure, the perfect creature that she was.

With Seanin, I said nothing. We resumed our weekly walk to the Hibernian, our routine—a few rounds of ale, pleasantries exchanged with his cronies, and him footing the bill—until one Thursday I realized an entire year had spun by and, bleary with ale, the bitter words poured forth from me in a torrent.

"You've ruined her."

Seanin looked up from his circle of mates, surprised. He had been saying something about the upcoming elections that I hadn't been minding, and I had interrupted him. Giving his companions a forced smile, he took me by the elbow and propelled me to the corner by the alley door. I glanced back over my shoulder at the knot of men we'd left behind and their wary, knowing looks. Seanin spun me around to face him, hissing, "What call have you got to bring her into it?"

"She's ruined, I say."

"She's rich, how could she be ruined?"

"Not that kind of ruined. Morally ruined. She'll have to marry someday, and then they'll know." I shook my head, suddenly terrified. "Oh god, they'll know."

Seanin patted my arm, awkwardly. "It could have happened riding."

"She scarce ever rides, Johnny."

"She rides every week."

"That's not the sort of riding that'll do such a thing. She trots the palfrey once around the park."

"She spends enough time in the carriage house."

"And you should tell her to stop. They'll notice someday. The way she looks at you."

"Ah, she never says a word to me." His light tone had taken on an edge of annoyance.

"Her eyes say it loud enough." I pleaded, unable to make him understand the danger they were both in. "They'll realize it was you. Or one day you'll get caught."

"Go on. They won't catch me, I'd be out the window again before they could."

I clutched at his arm. "It's a horrible risk."

"I said I'd be fine."

"Well, what about her? Think of her if you won't think of yourself. She's been good to me, Johnny. She doesn't deserve—"

"What? What don't she deserve? I love her, Mar, and she loves me."

His words cut me then, though I couldn't quite say why. Certainly I had known, must have known that she loved him, for a well-bred lady like Charlotte Walden doesn't go fucking her groom unless she's convinced that it's love. Perhaps it hadn't occurred to me until just then that Seanin loved her back.

"Listen to you," I said, with all the contempt I could muster. "She's just a fine bit of stuff to you, and you know it. So cut the tripe and let her be."

He should have been angry—I had been trying to make him angry just then—but he shook his head with an expression of vehement earnestness. "It ain't tripe, Mar. Jesus, I swear it ain't. I love her. God help me, but I do."

"Seanin, you're my only kin left living," I whispered in Irish. "Don't I love you too? And if you should be caught, they would surely hang you, and just as sure I'd die too for the grief of it."

"Go on," he said, much louder and in English.

"It can't last, Johnny," I said, squeezing his hand.

He squeezed mine back and said softly, "I know it."

"Then end it," I pleaded. "Now."

He bit his lip, considering. "No."

"Fuck you, Johnny," I whispered, pulling my hand out of his.

He grabbed my arm, hissing, "Keep that fucking window open, drink your fucking ale, and say no more about this, Mar."

I threw the contents of my mug right in his goddamn face and stalked out into the snow. I spent an hour howling my rage in the alley behind the pub, sobbing until my cheeks were red and blotchy, until snot ran down my face with the tears.

I hated them both.

A year had spun by and every Thursday, I blunted my jealousy on Dermot's ale until it mellowed into misery, and this became my state, waking and sleeping, from which I mourned the love they'd found.

> She who indulges in all the excesses of such a place, is not one whom we should expect to behave well when at home.
>
> —*The Duties of a Lady's Maid*

Seanin shook me gently awake and we dressed in dark and silence. My head rang, my tongue tasted of cotton and sick. I followed Seanin upstairs to find Dermot had left coffee and eggs and rashers on the potbellied stove for us. As Seanin fixed us plates, I poured the coffee. Seanin tucked in with a fair vigor, but it was ashes in my mouth. By the time Dermot came back in, shaking the slush from his overcoat, Seanin was building up the fire and I was washing the dishes in a basin of melted snow.

"You're green again, Maire," he said by way of welcome. He stomped his boots to clear them of snow, in an unaccountably good mood for an hour before daylight.

"Ah, go on now," Seanin said. "'Twas her night off."

Dermot shook his head at me, tsking in mock chagrin. I said nothing, just handed over our wages for him to lock away into the strongbox he kept in the back room, safer than a bank, and surer for two Irish orphans.

"Will you have a belt for the road, Mar?" he asked, and, when I looked up, eyes glassy, he chuckled. "Hair of the dog?"

I managed a narrow grin. "Sure I ain't so green as all that now. Keep it for me till next week?"

He slapped me on the back, and I nearly retched again. "Ah, there's my good lass," he said, and I wasn't sure he meant it was good of me to refuse a belt on a workday, or he was glad I wasn't as distempered as I looked. He pecked me hard on the cheek and said, "Hm, we'll have roses there yet, or something duskier, I'll warrant." I smiled weakly. It was never a good sign when Dermot turned tease. It meant he had something on you.

We trudged back through the snow in the blue light before dawn.

Charlotte Walden's room was dark. Her bed was of a newfangled design without hangings, but once I kindled the fire, I could see well enough to pick my way across the room, gathering clothing as I went. I always inspected the carpet carefully; once, I'd found a wooden button, clearly from Johnny's shirt, and, after secreting it back to him, had boxed his ears for carelessness. Today, I found no trace, save for a stiffed flannel I grasped with distaste, using the corner of my apron as a barrier.

From the bed, Charlotte stirred, and I paused, not daring to move, my arms laden with her night rail and her dressing gown. I watched as Charlotte rolled over, her breath a sigh, and settled into the blankets once more. Limbs melting, I fled to my closet, pressing my back against the door. I forced myself to breathe through the throb in my head, forced my shaking hands still. Through the door, I heard Charlotte stir and sit up, the ringing of her silver bell cutting through the lingering effects of my intemperance. I pressed my hand against the coolness of the windowpane, and then to the back of my neck, delaying as long as possible.

"Yes, miss?" I asked, tucking the Irish away as neatly as her dressing gown, and adopting a tonier accent.

"Good morning, Ballard," Charlotte Walden murmured.

"Shall I ring for your tray, miss?" I asked, pulling open the curtains. The wan light of snow flurries sifted into the room.

"What time is it? Yes, I believe I . . ." The finely pointed chin wavered. "Perhaps a . . . bath first?" Charlotte looked guiltily at the press of white against the window. I raised my eyebrows, but she nodded, resolutely. "Yes. I couldn't possibly face today without a bath."

I rang for water.

Sponging the creamy skin of Charlotte's back, I fumed. It was unlike her to be quite this careless. Ordering a bath on a February morning when she'd only just had one two days ago was bound to cause talk belowstairs. Agnes, the scullery girl, was probably complaining to all and sundry, no doubt lamenting to Grace Porter, Mrs. Walden's pinch-faced maid. Charlotte shivered as she rose, water sheeting down her pale, jutting hips. I folded her into a flannel, pressing the cloth into her skin, feeling the contours of the slim body beneath. I slipped a wrapper over the narrow shoulders, ushered her to the dressing table to run fingers and comb through the shining auburn hair.

The Waldens were Scots, going back several generations now, but the breeding showed true in Charlotte's hair. A century and more of genteel downtown addresses and crystal stemware and taffeta and silk melted away to some godforsaken highland crag in the wildness of her deep, ruddy locks. The hours I spent, taming her hair with lavender oil—good, you know, for curls—and brushing it until it shone before knotting up the wildness at last into a decorous coil of braids against the nape of her neck. With nimble fingers, I pinned her tresses into submission before tucking a final ornamental comb into the arrangement.

There was a timid rap at the door. Charlotte lay propped on the chaise longue in her dressing gown, a blanket tucked about her knees. Millie, the head housemaid, was holding Charlotte's breakfast tray. She craned her head to see into the room, but I blocked her view with my body and took the tray with an icy "That will do, Millie," before shutting the door in her face.

Charlotte ate delicately. Cook had sent up two soft-boiled eggs and a plate of toast. Forbidden by her mother to drink coffee, Charlotte took chocolate instead, gazing out the frosty window as she sipped. Upon Mr. Walden's death, his daughter had taken to having a tray sent up, rather than sit alone in the empty dining room, an arrangement that, though highly unorthodox, excused Cook; the butler, Mr. Buckley; and myself from the trouble of dressing and feeding Charlotte in style each morning.

I set her empty tray on the table in the hall and rang for someone to come and take it away while I helped Charlotte into her shift and stays. I presented her with a celadon morning dress, which she accepted with almost no consideration of the matter. Her eyes held a faraway look, and it was plain that her mind was, if not miles away from the room in which she stood, then across the mews in the loft above the carriage house.

Once I had seen my mistress buttoned and on her way to the parlor, I saw to the bed, dabbing delicately at a telltale stain on the sheet with a damp piece of potato before tossing this last bit evidence into the fire. I sprinkled lavender water to mask whatever traces of the earthy, horsey smell of my brother might rise from the sheets: a night specter, dispelled with the dawn. Surveying my handiwork with satisfaction, I settled myself into a tufted chair by the fire and began picking a bit of trim off one of her last season's gowns. I knew

I ought to take my work down to the kitchen and put on a show of sociability, but, still feeling indisposed, I could not face the heat and noise and bustle. The snowy blue light from the window and the deep amber glow of the fire suffused the silent room. My eyes blurred, the tiny rows of stitches fading in and out of focus, until at last the pearl-handled sewing knife slipped from my fingers and sleep overtook me.

Raised voices roused me.

I stood, the room lurching, sleep crusting my eyes. I blinked, rubbed my face, and was staring stupidly at the fire as Charlotte Walden burst into the room, pink cheeked and furious. She slammed the door, glared at me, and rubbed her eyes indelicately with the back of one hand.

The door opened behind her to admit Mrs. Walden. She took in the room, took in her daughter's sulk, my flushed face, and said to me, "Leave us, Ballard," in a tone that brooked no disagreement.

I fled to the kitchen.

Cook, Grace Porter, and Mrs. Harrison were sitting around a teapot while Agnes chopped parsnips.

"Well now," said Cook, motioning for Agnes to fetch me a cup. "What's got the missus so crabbed up at our princess?"

I sat at the kitchen bench and shrugged. "Miss Porter would know better than I."

Grace Porter sniffed. She was a weedy thing, of later middle years, and had been Mrs. Walden's maid since before she was twenty. It was a point of pride for her that, in all her years of faithful service, she had never disturbed Mrs. Walden by having any beaux come calling. She tossed her iron-gray head. "I'm sure I've no more idea than yourself, Miss Ballard," she said, as though I had insulted her.

"*I* was not cloistered in Miss Charlotte's room. What on *earth* could she possibly have wanted a bath for on a day like today?"

"That's right," Cook said. "Hasn't Agnes got enough to do without getting all that water boiled up? We've still Saturday's dinner to plan, to say nothing of tonight."

"And me with all them carrots to do," Agnes whined. "I ain't half-done with the parsnips."

Cook slapped her hand against the table. "And complaining will make it go all the faster, I suppose?"

"No, Mrs. Freedman, ma'am. Sorry, ma'am."

I sighed, doing my best to play the put-upon servant. "Feverish in the night, woke up in such a sweat, you know. Well, nothing would do for her but to bathe."

Grace Porter sipped her tea. "I would have sponged her instead."

"Now then," Mrs. Harrison said mildly. "I would not have ever suspected you, Miss Porter, as one inclined to gainsay one's betters."

Grace had dignity enough to blush at that, saying, "Certainly not, Mrs. Harrison."

Mrs. Harrison deigned to pour. "No more so Miss Ballard, I daresay."

I studied Mrs. Harrison out of the corner of my eye, unsure, as always, what she might think of me. Certainly, I knew she had not been particularly keen to take me on, and I had never felt secure that she was convinced of my character. She gave me plenty of rope, that was certain, but Johnny said it was only to see how much it took for me to hang myself.

My reverie was broken by Charlotte Walden's bell. I thanked Cook for the tea and took my time answering the summons. The back stairs seemed steeper today for my aching head, and I paused to catch my breath before stepping through the door that led back into the hall.

Charlotte's door was ominously open. It was plain that Mrs. Walden had only recently vacated it. Moving carefully, I took in the wreckage of the room. All in all, it was more mess than destruction. The shepherdess figurine, beloved of Charlotte's youth, lay in pieces on the floor. Pillows had been flung in disarray, a pot of pomatum overturned on the rug, but still lidded and not yet leaking. My mistress was at her dressing table, dabbing a wet cloth to her puffy face. Her mother had vanished.

"For pity's sake, Ballard," Charlotte said, her voice low and steady. "Get it all out of my sight." I began collecting pieces in my apron, her eyes boring into my back.

If you cannot keep your own secrets, why should you suppose that another will be more cautious?

—*The Duties of a Lady's Maid*

At supper that night in the kitchen, I spilled the pepper pot—our old signal, well worth the withering words from Cook—and saw Johnny nod once out of the corner of my eye. The hours dragged, as I combed out Charlotte's hair, tucked the brazier at the foot of her bed, and waited for my mistress's reflection in the dressing table mirror to nod dismissal. I went into my little closet, extinguished the candle, and lay fully dressed on the bed, waiting. The hours ticked by, until, near midnight, I heard the soft *tock* of an acorn hitting my window. I looked down into the small alley between the row of town houses and the carriage houses, empty, save for the slanting moonlight. But I knew he was there. I wrapped myself in my wool shawl, and slipped on stockinged feet out the back door of my tiny room and down the hall to the kitchen stairs.

Moving through the Walden house was a simple matter, complicated only by Agnes, who slept by the kitchen hearth in winter. A little gust of cold air as I opened the door made her stir, but no more.

Outside, the snow soaked right through my stockings, freezing my feet straightaway, but my path to the carriage house went unnoticed. In the doorway under the eaves, Seanin was waiting.

He looked troubled, as well he might. "Well?"

"She rowed with the missus this morning. Pillows flung, stuff broken. A right tantrum. I think she knows."

"What, the missus?"

I nodded.

"How could she?"

"Herself ordered up a bath this morning."

He snorted. "Ah, go on. 'Tis just a bath."

"Aye, and she had one earlier this week. It looks queer."

Seanin blew on his fingers, chuckling. "You kept me out of bed over a fucking bath? Ah, Mar, you're getting soft as shite."

I shoved him. "This ain't a game. This is life or fucking death. I think you should skip this week. Just to be safe."

"Ah, you'd like that, wouldn't you?"

I stiffened. "What the fuck is that supposed to mean?"

Seanin looked away. "Nothing."

I grabbed his arm. "No. What did you mean?"

"Nothing, I said." He took me in, shivering, my shoeless feet, and gathered me into his arms. "Ah, Mar, look at you, *a mhuirnín.* Go back to bed. You'll catch your death out here. Look, I'll be careful, I swear."

"I don't like it." I rested my head on his shoulder. "Johnny, it'd break my heart if they should discover you. Will you not have a care?"

"Go on," he said with a smile. He took my hand and squeezed it. "They could've been rowing about any old thing. I know you're afeared. And you're a good lass to give me warning. I mean it, I'm grateful. I shouldn't've spoken harsh to you. I've no wish to be caught, Mar, truly, but there's no cause to stand out in the cold and make yourself ill over it. I know my business well enough."

I shrugged, reluctant to let go his hand. "You promise you'll be careful?"

"I do. Go on, now. Back to bed."

He kissed my forehead, and I went silently back into the house.

It was Thursday again, and as Seanin handed me down from the Waldens' carriage, I resolved to keep my head and my temper. I tucked my hand into Seanin's arm, and we made our way down Broadway in high spirits, singing scraps of songs our father had sung off-key when he thought he was alone with the horses. We were still laughing when we arrived at the door of the Hibernian, breathless and merry.

There were rarely other women at the Hibernian, and those who wandered in were mainly stargazers. Now and again, it was possible to find a group like the merry foursome clustered tonight in one of the bay windows: two working lads and a pair of lassies they admired, come to woo in all the privacy the din and clatter of a public house could offer. Consequently, there had been, my first evening at the Hibernian, a smattering of comments, insinuating whispers, and, as I hung back in the corner by the hearth, a man with a leer who put hands upon my person in a most unwelcome manner. I shrieked, tossing my ale into the offending party's face, bringing the now-empty mug down on his pate in fury. The man shook his head, momentarily stunned, then snarled, lunging at me. Seanin was by my side in an instant, interposing himself between my would-be assailant and me. There was a flurry of fists, a clamor of voices, as one man and then another joined the resulting brawl, and I would have thrown myself into the melee to aid my brother had Dermot not snatched me back by the waist and pulled me from harm's way as I howled in rage.

The fight was over nearly before it began, at any rate. Seanin had held his own, and, with the help of a few of the brawlers who had taken his part, tossed the offending party out the public house's door before declaring loudly that anyone else in the Hibernian who cared to address his sister would be wise to address themselves to him first.

I had questioned Dermot on the queerness of this American custom later as I dabbed at Seanin's split eyebrow before attempting to stitch him up; at home, it had not been uncommon to see in the pubs fond husbands with their wives, or knots of girls come in after their shifts in the shops or dairies to sip a pint and make eyes at the errand boys and farriers' apprentices in the hopes of getting a husband. There would be new mothers there, drinking porter with babbies at the teat, and weary widows, come down for their drop of whiskey. Dermot's own mother ran our local back in Donegal Town, and it'd have been a daring lad indeed to tell her she ought to do otherwise.

But though the clientele was Irish, the unspoken rules of the New World prevailed, and no respectable woman would have come into the Hibernian on her own, a notion that made me laugh.

"But where *do* the women go if they want a pint?"

"American women don't usually drink ale," Dermot said. "Or at any rate, they aren't meant to enjoy it. They put it down as something only foreigners do."

"Well, where am I meant to do it, if I'm not to do it here?"

Dermot shrugged with a nonchalance belied by the gleam in his eye as he replied, "In a grocery," and then proceeded to roar with laughter as I expressed, at length, my refusal to do any such thing. I was too green yet in New York to know what a grocery was, and it amused Dermot to no end to hear my ignorant, Old Country notions about what it must be like to sip a drop amongst the turnips and the cabbages. In the event, the results of that evening's brawl had been that friendless Seanin O'Farren had become Johnny Prior, acquired a few instant comrades, and, as the benefit of their collective influence and Dermot's reign over the Hibernian, I had never again suffered insult in the establishment. Every now and again, emboldened by my example and Johnny's stout defense, they would bring along a sister or cousin, knowing that I would be there to provide female company.

It was one of these stalwarts who greeted us upon our arrival, breaking free from a garrulous quartet to clap Johnny on the back and bow ludicrously over my hand. Daniel Quigley had been one of the first of the Irish rabbits to dive into Johnny's inaugural fray at the Hibernian, and had, in the interim, become his closest friend. Upon learning my occupation, he took to greeting me as Lady Mary, trotting out his flawed impression of Bond Street manners and simpering upon my entrance—a tactic that by turns infuriated and delighted me, depending upon my mood. Tonight, however, I was in high spirits and took Quigley's standard freak with good grace, allowing him to chivalrously bully a pair of drovers from their place by the fire for my benefit and pluck a mug from Johnny's hand to offer it to me with absurd fanfare. Settling himself next to me, forcing Johnny to stand, he assumed a ridiculously erect posture and began to pay me extravagant court.

"Lady Mary," he began, putting on a mincingly aristocratic accent that in no way concealed his natural Dublin lilt. "Thank the lord you are come! I was just engaged in a most trying conversation with O'Mara and MacBride as to the quantity of lace on ladies' collars this season, and I fear we could resolve nothing without your expertise!" The two lads he named inclined their heads with momentary seriousness, and then snickered into their ale.

I rolled my eyes, swatting away his charade with my free hand and declaring airily that, as it was my night off, lace collars were of no consequence to me, and I would thank him to allow them to remain outside the confines of the Hibernian. This produced a far heartier laugh from him than was seemly, and my smile grew a bit fixed. Quigley's elaborate and obvious pretenses with me made me uneasy in a way I could not quite articulate. It was thoroughly clear that the attention he insisted upon paying me was, in truth, unromantic and farcical, and I never felt with him the underlying menace a young woman sometimes has when she doubts the honorability of a man's intentions. Quigley meant me no harm—he was, on the rare occasions that Johnny should not be by my side, a most reliable defender from insult or insinuation. But there was something too polished and knowing in his manner with me, and I suspected strongly that it was because Quigley was privy to Johnny's affair with Charlotte Walden. Moreover, I was sure that my brother had revealed more than my complicity in these proceedings—I was positive he had also revealed my misgivings, and, from them, Quigley had somehow divined my jealousy. I had no proof, of course. The entire act might have meant anything, and the days when it failed to amuse and instead ignited my fury, I was convinced it was nothing more than the mockery a brother might use to torment his sister, such as Johnny had engaged in with me in our younger years. Tonight, however, Quigley dropped his put-on voice and absurd queries straightaway and began an amusing tale about a woman who had alighted from her carriage on Great Jones Street and mistaken Quigley for one of her new footmen, berating him at length for being in the street out of his livery. He was a gifted storyteller, was Quigley, and he had me laughing merrily in moments.

Seeing me thus engaged, Johnny caught my eye, nodding approvingly as I laughed at Quigley's predicament, and turned away in conversation with O'Mara and MacBride. I noticed that they were joined by several other men, and spared a moment of warmth for my brother. Even back home on the estate, he had always been a favorite with the grooms and the kennel boys, attracting a knot of admirers in the servants' hall, who hung on every word of his stories. He was so like Da in that way: genial and well liked. It was no wonder he had won over everyone from Charlotte Walden to the lads in the pub. Tonight, instead of my falling into bitterness and jealousy that I did not share such qualities, the ale buoyed me and my pride in my brother, and, from the corner of my eye, I watched him speaking earnestly before turning back and giving my full attention to Quigley's tale.

It was cozy by the fire; I was four or five rounds in—still upright but no longer clearheaded, and feeling a general sense of satisfaction with the world around me. Quigley had excused himself a moment before and gone to Johnny's side, and, as I raised my mug to my lips, I found it empty save for a scum of froth on the bottom. I pulled myself to my feet, the room wavering as I rose, and thought for a moment about my options. I could make my way to the bar for a refill and bend Dermot's ear awhile. I could join the cluster of lads by Johnny, but the thought of standing idly and ignorantly by as they talked of politics was dull enough to dampen my fair mood. I chose instead to end the evening before things could grow sour, and left my mug on the end of the bar to make my way unobserved down the stairs and put myself to bed.

In the dark, cool cellar, the smell of hard-packed earth and malt rising up around me, I could still hear the din from upstairs. My head swam a bit with the pleasant rise and fall of voices, and I thought for a moment that it could always be like this, if only I could forget Charlotte Walden and remember that my brother and I were here—in this country, in this city, in this public house—because we had made a vow to stay together, and that everything we had done since arriving three years ago had been in service of that vow. But even this thought brought my desire for her rushing to the foremost part of my mind, and I went to sleep in a wash of longing, punctuated by a dull, throbbing ache in my gut.

I woke in the morning, my brother's arm draped protectively over my shoulder, prickling with sweat from Johnny's hot, rank breath against the back of my neck and plagued with a nether cramping that meant my monthly courses had begun.

> Desire nothing but what is within your reach; for if your desires are unreasonable you may be certain of disappointment.
>
> —*The Duties of a Lady's Maid*

Charlotte Walden took to her bed with laudanum whenever she had her courses, a habit she had inherited from her mother. I could not be certain if it was necessity or imitation that drove her to her bed, or if she merely relished the excuse to withdraw from society. Cook would make her beef tea, and she would lie about with the curtains half-drawn to dim the room, watching the shadows move across the wall. Sometimes she'd embroider, or read, or sometimes embroider whilst I read aloud to her. So long as it was *Godey's Lady's Book* or the like, I would do just fine. If it were Edgeworth, or Austen, or Radcliffe, it would be slower going, and she would be rather quickish when correcting me. I was a fair hand with *Pickwick* serials, too, which hardly gave me any trouble at all. I think she knew reading didn't come naturally to me, though she would never shame me with pointing it out. She had read all those novels herself a thousand times or more, but she would never read anything new when she was poorly. I asked her why, once.

"What if," she said, choosing her words with excruciating leisure, "what if I took up a new book, and it should not be comforting?"

"Comforting, miss?"

She waved her hand, dismissing some idea from the air. "If there should be something that disturbed my mind? Something that took hold and gave me a fright? No, not a fright. An uneasiness, perhaps." She looked and saw no comprehension had taken root in me. "Suppose I were to read something new and I should be troubled by what I read when I was already so unwell?"

I nodded, though, not being much of a reader myself, I had no notion of what she meant.

"Come here, Ballard." She was holding out her narrow white hands to me. I settled on the edge of her bed and took them into mine. They were cold; I closed my warm fingers over hers. "When I am unwell," she said, her voice low, "I want all those familiar things that buoy my spirits. Beef tea and favorite books. You by my side. I could not bear to be disturbed in the mind when I am already so low, do you see? I should never sleep a wink, I should be so anxious. That is why I must have you by, my dear Ballard, my succor."

After that, I hardly left her for a moment when her monthlies came. I used to leave the door of my closet open so that she would know I was near. I bathed her face in her lavender water, I made her the sweet, milky tea her nurse used to make. Sometimes in the night, when she whimpered, I would sing softly to her and stroke her hair until she slept. When Grace Porter and I passed one another in the hall, our arms full of fresh flannels, we would nod and roll our eyes in mutual sympathy, but where Grace dawdled in the kitchen, I hurried back to Charlotte Walden's room to rub her sore back or dab oil of verbena on her temples. She was my only care, though, being so long in her company, I nearly always had my indisposition when she had hers, as women sometimes do when they are so much together. My own courses never seemed to cause the cramps and fever of Charlotte Walden's, though once when the ache seemed greater than usual, I took myself a drop or two of her laudanum to help me to sleep. It was not unlike being very greatly drunk and foggy in the head, though I found my dreams that night to be vivid, I could not remember them again in the morning.

Should her indisposition fall on a Thursday, I would forgo my night out, sending Johnny off to the Hibernian without me. When we had first come to the Waldens' house, this had seemed to gall Johnny. But after a year or so, a change appeared to come over him, and he had become more sanguine about his nights out alone and, somehow, more purposeful. I supposed that Dermot or Quigley had knocked some sense into him, or introduced him around, for, as time wore on, I noticed that instead of his merely tipping his cap to some of the other regulars upon entering the Hibernian, more and more men greeted him by name and came to stand by him and talk in low, intent voices. On his Sunday afternoons off, he no longer asked after my whereabouts, which suited me fine, but instead went off with his new mates to speak fervently about politics and practice voting—an insipid and alcohol-fueled bit of playacting that always made me glad I was a woman born and exempt from such absurd goings-on. At such times, I was engrossed in my own doings, thinking nothing of Johnny's preoccupations, except that I was grateful they kept him out of my hair. My rare Thursdays alone with Charlotte became precious, and my private Sundays remained my own affair.

It was on such a rare, sweet Thursday that Charlotte rang for me after I had undressed for the night. I had already put her in her bed and was preparing to climb into my own when I answered the summons. In the flickering light of the candle I held aloft, she looked pale, her white skin one with the sheet, and made even paler by the firelight glinting in her hair.

She raised herself up and held out one hand to me. "I shall not sleep tonight, Ballard," she said. "I have been filled with such fearful thoughts that I am afraid to dream."

"There now, miss," I said. "Will you have some laudanum to ease your sleep?"

She shook her head, trembling a little, and drew me down onto the bed. "Please don't leave me tonight, Ballard," she said plaintively. "Will you be my succor tonight? My comfort?"

I nodded mutely, scarcely daring to draw breath. She pulled back the blankets and made room for me to join her. I blew out my taper and settled myself under the coverlet. I had lain on her bed before, but never under the blankets with her. The closeness of her made me lie stiffly, though I longed to take her in my arms.

In the dark, I stared at the pale curve of her shoulder beneath her white night rail. Her back was to me, and her braid curled over her shoulder. Though the blankets were up, she shivered delicately, and I carefully drew her to me, slipping one arm beneath her head and draping the other about her shoulders. She took my hand in hers, brushing her lips against my knuckles as she relaxed, the curve of her back forming to my own curved form. She snuggled down against me, the stray hairs from her braid tickling my cheek, and I closed my eyes, filled with the warmth of her. I barely slept that night, so filled with the novelty and delight of holding her cradled in my arms that I was kept wakeful with joy. She kept curling further and further back against me until I was very nearly off the bed and obliged to gently navigate her back toward the center, but I didn't care. In the morning, just before she woke, I crept quietly from her bed to dress in my own room. I could not keep from smelling my arms, which were scented with her hair oil, as Johnny's often were. All day, whenever I lifted my arms, the scent came wafting up, making me weak and giddy.

But that night, as I dressed her and helped her under the blankets, I looked at her expectantly and her eyes grew clouded when she dismissed me in a firm sort of tone. I waited until she was asleep, lying quietly alone in the dark before creeping softly into her room to watch her. I took her hand in mine, raising her palm, smooth and unblemished as a child's, to my lips, marveling at the softness of her skin. She sighed and stirred, and I froze, waiting with her palm still pressed to my lips as she settled back into a deeper sleep. Gently, I laid her hand down upon the counterpane and crept back into my little closet, consumed with longing for her. My own bed seemed all the narrower and colder that night, and I woke in the morning no better rested than from my sleepless night before.

Those days I spent alone with her, she was all I could think about, every moment standing next to her, bathing her, dressing her, coiffing her hair, and the air between us seemed to crackle like the air during a storm, just before lightning strikes. At night, I would lie in my bed and replay all the things we had said to each other that day—and did she think me clever, or good? And did she lie abed thinking of the things I'd said that made her smile, and when she slept did she, as I did, dream of our eyes meeting in the mirror as I braided her hair? I knew she did not. If she dreamed of stolen looks, or the accidental brushing of hands, it was Johnny of whom she must dream, not me. I went to bed with the smell of her on my hands, and lay staring at the finial on the ceiling, until finally her perfume drove me to lick the scent off my fingertips. Slowly, silently, barely daring to move, I ran my hands across my breasts, slipping beneath the blankets. There, I worked the linen of my shift up my legs, over my hips, and slid my fingers into the down between my legs. Closing my eyes, I imagined her lying over me, her lips brushing mine. I imagined what it would be to kiss her, and the thought of brushing her lips with my tongue made me tighten in anticipation. I held my breath, picturing her as she rose from her bath, her auburn hair cascading about her shoulders, the curls wrapping naughtily around her pert nipples. My breath caught as my fingers worked the soft, wet place between my legs, and I imagined breathing in the scent of her. The pleasure of it, of giving myself over to thinking of her that way, of imagining her lips on mine, of picturing my hands wandering over the softness of her skin, brought a moan to my lips. The wet ache of my need began to overwhelm me, and I plunged my two fingers into the quavering place inside me as my longing for her crested and broke.

With the sweetness of release came a sadness, and I lay there, sticky-fingered and shamed, still besotted with pining after her. My fingers left slick trails along my legs as I pulled them back up toward my face to smell her perfume again, now coated in my own musky odor. I groaned softly, my satisfaction gone as quickly as it'd come, and rolled over onto my side, shimmying my shift down. I closed my eyes and let sleep take me, but my dreams were full of her.

> You may say, indeed, it would be better were the temptation not thrown in your way; but in many situations it is unavoidable, and in all it is requisite to be very guarded and cautious in those particulars.
>
> —*The Duties of a Lady's Maid*

With every form of comfort I took against my passion for Charlotte there came a pang, for, through the course of her affair with my brother, I had found some succor of my own. There had been one night when, Seanin being knocked up with a bad cold, I had gone by myself to the Hibernian. It had been late summer then, and the affair between my mistress and my brother had been at its height. I was feeling foul and put out, for I had been first obliged to listen to Charlotte Walden's vague laments and pouts and then obliged to listen to Seanin's more specific ones, and was sick to death of the both of them. The heat of the day still lingered on the cobbles, and my clothes had grown damp and clinging in the humid air as I trudged down to Mulberry Street. All along the street, the doors and windows of the public houses were thrown open to catch some slight breeze, and the air was heavy with the odors of sweat, piss, and spilled beer. From the upper windows, gay girls lounged, fanning themselves languidly or calling saucy remarks across the street to each other, occasionally pausing in their gossip to address the passersby. Men stood in small knots outside the tavern doors, their shirtsleeves rolled back, arms bare to the elbow. A few had taken off their hats, fanning florid, streaming faces as they laughed and called to the women above, bargaining in merry tones.

The heat had made me cross, and I pushed irritably past the knot of men blocking the way into the Hibernian, snapping back as they catcalled and made grabs at my skirt. They were regulars, of course, and so were only sporting with me, for by this time my face and Johnny's were familiar sights. They laughed good-naturedly enough at my salty retorts and let me past with no trouble, but I was soured on their mirth, and was pulling a face by the time I gained the bar.

The Hibernian was packed, and Dermot had to shout for me to hear him over the din. "Where's himself then?"

"Knocked up."

"Shouldn't you be nursing him?"

I shook my head. "Ain't supposed to fraternize with the Irish horse groom, am I?"

He nodded. "Right so, lass. Aye, I'm coming," he hollered to another group clamoring at the bar, before turning momentarily back to me. "If it gets too much for you, you just nip downstairs as you please, aye?"

I nodded back and took my mug. None of Johnny's usual crowd had arrived, not that I was in much of a mood for Quigley's teasing or standing on the fringes as they talked about the glories of the Democratic party. To add to my irritation, there was nowhere to sit, and so I slipped out the side door to the alley. Here, the roar of the bar and the calls from the street echoed dimly from the walls, so I took a sip and closed my eyes. The alley was all in shadow and a sight cooler besides. I breathed in deeply the smell of stale beer, the hot, thick scent of summer, and tried to let my anger melt into the cobbles underfoot. There were a few casks and hogsheads along the wall, and I clambered up onto one near the door. From this perch, I leaned my back against the cool bricks of the building and drank deeply.

The light had faded and I was near to draining my mug when I heard the alley door bang open and shut as a shrill voice cried out, "Piss, shit, cunt, fuck, goddamn!"

I looked down from my barrel to the author of this tirade and saw a girl near to my own age, who stomped her foot with some passion. She was very small with delicate, doll-like features and a pretty face that she had screwed up into a scowl so severe that on her sweet mien it was almost comical. Her skin was the color of strong tea and weak cream, freckles sprinkling her upturned nose like currants scattered in a cake. The boot she had stomped belonged to a tiny foot, and her gown was cut high to show her slender ankles and the swell of her calf beneath silk stockings. Her show of leg was matched by the bareness of her arms and the tightness of her bodice, which had been laced to great effect, and her small, high bosoms peeked over the lace edge. Most remarkable of all was her hair, which had been set with sugar water and hung in stiff, perfect ebony ringlets against her cheeks and coiled into twists that rose above her neck.

I laughed at this stream of profanity, issuing, as it did, from such a dainty creature, and she looked up in surprise.

"Lord!" she cried. "You gave me such a start!" Her voice was all of the broad vowels and crisp consonants of the tonier parts of London, and, as she spoke, she held one little hand theatrically to her bosom.

"Not half the one you gave me," I said, still looking down at her, and she laughed a merry, tinkling laugh.

"I should think!" she said, smiling. "Oh, but I promise I don't speak so harsh all the time, but only when I am most terribly vexed."

"And what made you so vexed just now?" I asked.

She laughed again and shook her head, her stiff curls scarcely moving. "La, it is nothing, only a bit of business didn't come off quite as I'd hoped. I'll be well presently. I say," she said, changing the subject suddenly, "have you got a light?"

I hadn't, and I said so, but she shook her head. "Never mind." She rummaged a moment in her reticule, which was beaded gaudily, until she found a man's monogrammed cigarette case. From this she plucked a single cigarette, then, raising her eyebrows suggestively at me, she disappeared around the corner and out into the street in front of the tavern. She reappeared a moment later, crossed one arm under the other, and regarded me thoughtfully as she puffed.

"It's a sight far too hot in there for me, and you look so cool up there," she said.

"There's room enough for two," I replied, and she dimpled prettily as I helped her up. She held out the cigarette to me, and I shook my head.

She looked steadily at me. "What are you doing up here, anyway?"

I shrugged. "I don't much care for the crowds. Truth to tell, I just wanted to drink in peace."

The girl made a face. "Would you rather I go?"

"No, no." I laughed. "Sure, I couldn't send you off like that to be vexed again, could I? Besides, it ought to do me good to entertain someone who's been in a fouler mood than myself tonight."

She laughed again, and I discovered I rather enjoyed the novelty of amusing someone. "You're a queer one, now." She stuck out her hand at me and we shook like gentlemen, which tickled me exceedingly.

"Liddie Lawrence," she said by way of introduction.

"Mary Ballard," I replied automatically, and she snorted.

"It isn't either. That's no Ulster name."

"You've a good ear," I said, avoiding the question she'd left unasked.

She shrugged, smoke pluming out from her nostrils. "It's all part of the profession," she said. "So then, ahem, Mary Ballard from somewhere in the north—or is it northwest?—of Ireland. I don't suppose you'd like to stand me a drink?"

In the time since I've come into this country, I've spent almost no money on myself. Miser that I am, I take my clothing allowance from Charlotte Walden and turn my wages over to Dermot O'Brien for safekeeping. I was reared to expect so little, and I am frugal. I do not read for pleasure. I do not care for frippery or sweets. I do not write letters. I do not attend the dance halls. I do not give to charity. I do not, in short, have a taste for any thing that money can buy, save, as by now I've made clear, I have a fair mouth for spirits, and Johnny mostly buys the rounds ever since we came to our understanding about Charlotte Walden. I do not stand drinks to people I don't know, and I do not, on the basis of principle, particularly care for whores. It is not a distaste based on moral grounds, but it is only that I must look down on those who cannot live by their wits and must trade on their own flesh. There has always seemed to me something very sorry in not being clever enough for any trade but lying on your back.

Yet I could find nothing contemptible in this frank, cheerful girl, who looked at me with her head cocked to one side, her stiff curls hanging rigid against her neck. She smiled at me, and there was nothing in it artful or fast. There was nothing in it that I could hate, the way I always seemed to hate those who were cadging me for something. In spite of myself, I smiled back. *What the hell?* I thought.

I had refilled our mugs several times, and by now the Hibernian was overflowing. A session band had formed; heat and light and music poured from the open door into the alley, and we sat still perched atop the hogshead, our arms linked about one another's waists like sisters. We swayed and sang along with the crowd inside as they bellowed through tune after tune. They were singing now "The Mantle So Green," which my father had loved, and so I knew all the words, though Liddie did not. She swayed back and forth with me, her head coming to rest from time to time on my shoulder, chiming in with her sweet, high soprano on the refrain at the end of each verse. The night was still hot, and the places where she leaned against me made my skin prickle pleasantly.

The song ended with a great gale of cheering—evidently there was no shortage of veterans in the crowd that night—and I pulled her closer so that our foreheads were touching. We smiled at each other, and I gazed deep into her dark eyes.

"Now then, Mary Ballard," she whispered. "Do you think you'd like to kiss me?"

I swallowed, my tongue darting nervously over my suddenly dry lips. She leaned toward me, her breath warm, her eyes half-closed. She tasted of ale and smoke. Her mouth was soft; her tongue slid between my parted lips. My arm tightened about her waist and I pulled her closer still. My pulse quickened, and I felt suddenly weak with need. I could not breathe for wanting her, and my kisses grew more urgent as I ran my hands along her sides. It was awkward, for we still sat side to side, and I pulled her up onto my lap, whereupon I discovered that I could from this vantage kiss her bosom quite freely. I felt her heart beat faster beneath my kisses, and she laughed hoarsely.

"Come now," she said in a throaty whisper, edging off my lap. "Is there somewhere we can go?"

I rose and let myself down from the hogshead before lifting her down. Even with the great mass of her petticoats, she seemed to weigh almost nothing at all. I took her hand and started for the door of the tavern, but she held back. I smiled back at her and drew her into the circle of my arm. Thus steering her, I maneuvered us to the cellar stairs.

The air was humid and smelled of malt as we made our way down into the dark. Dermot had banked the fire, and the only light came from the moon streaming in at the high windows. She held my hand, and I led her toward the pallet Johnny and I normally shared. She slipped her bare arms about my neck and fell to kissing me again, and I felt myself grow slick with desire. Her high, firm breasts were pressing against my chest, and she was laced so tight I could feel every breath she drew. She was unbuttoning me as she kissed me, and I fumbled furiously with the buttons at the back of her frock. We laughed between kisses as we strove to undress one another, and at last she stepped away from me to shed her frock in a movement quick and practiced. Our eyes had adjusted to the dark by then, and in the dim blue light I drank in the sight of her. She still wore her corset and her boots and stockings, but she wore no shift, which was terribly daring and stirred me. I drew her close and began to pick at the knots of her stays. She protested, but I kissed her neck and she began to relent. I slid the thing down over her hips and pulled her down to my pallet. She reclined gracefully, and I lifted each foot to remove each boot and each stocking. Her skin shone dully in the moonlight, and she propped herself up on one hand, regarding me with a wicked, knowing grin. She gasped when I buried my face in her cunt.

I had, of course, many times imagined what such an encounter might be like with Charlotte Walden, but all of the tenderness, the slow and gentle caresses I had envisioned were lost with Liddie in the flurried, frenzied tumult of our joining. I had brought myself to pleasure and release time and again thinking of Charlotte, and felt, time and again, the secret self-loathing such actions must bring me, but Liddie, in spite of my raw and terrible need, was as generous to me as I think I was rough with her. She was skilled in the use of both her fingers and her tongue, and as she took me to the brink of pleasure and beyond, I cried out gratefully.

We lay together afterwards, sticky and hot, our joined flesh wet with sweat. Her curls were stiff against my chest and shoulder. I stroked the bare skin of her narrow waist contentedly. She smiled up at me.

"Who is Charlotte?" she asked, all innocence.

I stiffened. "What do you mean?"

She propped herself up on one elbow to look at me. "You murmured the name. Who is she?"

I shook my head, prepared to deny such a thing, but when I opened my mouth to speak, no words would come out. I felt then the tears welling up at the corners of my eyes, and I covered my face in shame. Liddie gathered me into her arms, and I wept for a time on her breast while she stroked my hair, which had come quite undone during the evening's exertions. "There now," she said gently. "It's all well. You needn't fret." She held me until my tears subsided, then wiped my face with the corner of my petticoat.

"There now," she said brightly. "I've had cullies who've cried before, but you're a first." She stood and looked at me again with her head cocked to the side. "All to rights now?" I nodded. "Good then," she said, and began to dress.

"Will you . . . will you not stay?" I asked, uncertainly.

She shook her head as she shimmied into her corset. "The publican was looking at me queerly. It wouldn't suit. Will you lace me, Mary? Nice perk to fucking a lady's maid, as they'll know how to dress you after. It's been an age since I've had anyone about to do up my stays for me. I ought to have found one of you girls out ages ago."

"How could you possibly know I was a lady's maid?" I asked, trying to be indignant, but laughing a little in spite of myself.

Liddie shrugged. "You've got a neat hand for corset laces, and you're wearing a frock that was fashionable two seasons ago. Good quality, but darker where you've picked off the trim. Came from your mistress, I'll warrant. What?" She laughed as I stared at her with frank admiration. "You have to have an eye for this sort of thing in my line. I can tell anyone's profession, for how else will I know if they're game, or if they can pay?" I must have looked crestfallen at this, for she cupped my cheek in her hand and smiled at me. "Now, now, Mary Ballard. It isn't every day a girl like me finds someone quite like you. I suppose I like extending you the compliments of the house." She kissed me again and then sat to lace up her boots. "Come visit me sometime? I keep a room in Chambers Street, number eighty-two."

"All right," I said, becoming shy of her. The headiness of the beer and of kissing her had worn off, and I took her hand. "Liddie, I—"

She laughed and shushed me. "Never done it with a gay girl before? Or with a colored girl? Or with anyone at all but yourself? Never mind, Mary Ballard." She rose and drew me to her for another lingering kiss. "Get to bed now, girlie, for your mistress will want you again in the morning, and you musn't go to her reeking of cunt." I watched her skirts swish as she ascended the stair, and then lay back on my pallet to think over the entire mad adventure in the moments before sleep took me.

> Be upon your guard, in the strictest manner, against such gossiping, either as a reporter or a listener, as nothing will sooner tend to destroy both your character and your peace of mind.
>
> —*The Duties of a Lady's Maid*

By the following Saturday, Charlotte's indisposition had passed, which was well, for the household's preparations for the ball Mrs. Walden held every year in honor of St. Valentine's Day had begun. She herself had been married to Mr. Walden on the day some three and twenty years ago, and it had been his custom, when alive, to celebrate their anniversary thusly. Though she had abandoned the tradition during her period of strictest mourning, Augusta Walden had revived her St. Valentine's Day ball a few years before Charlotte had come of age. In the days and weeks before the ball, Mrs. Harrison and Mr. Buckley were directing the house in a flurry of preparations. The house did not have a ballroom, and, on the occasions when Augusta Walden hosted dances, the whole of the second floor was transformed for that purpose. The great double doors of the salon were drawn open on one side, and those of the music room drawn open on the other, and, together with the broad second-floor landing onto which they both opened, made up the dance floor. Number seventeen Washington Square North was significantly broader than its neighbors, having been built on a double lot, and in it Augusta Walden's visions of a fashionable address and genteel living had been realized. The house, while not so grand as those of the Astors and Jays on Art Street, or the Grahams on Bond, was still the most magnificent of those situated upon the Square and, when opened to capacity, boasted the largest assembly space.

Grace Porter and I stayed chiefly out of the way as Mr. Buckley directed the footmen, Eben and Eugene, in the movement of furniture from its accustomed spaces to one of the spare bedrooms on the third floor. The only item that would remain was, of course, the pianoforte, for not only was it impossible to shift but the musicians would need the use of it. After sniffing with considerable volume over the state of the transformation, Grace insisted I adjourn with her to the kitchen, where she might hold forth on matters more important than the removal of the rugs and the laying of Holland.

The kitchen was full of no less activity as Cook gave herself over to the preparations for the impending festivities. The accompanying supper was her chief concern, and Grace and I were enjoined to help ourselves to the tea she had just set to brew and then, for the love of god, leave her alone. We took ourselves to the other end of the table, where Johnny and Young Frank, Cook's son, the stableboy, were sitting before a tray of bread and coffee. They rose in deference as we approached to sit. I inclined my head, and Grace gave a rapid nod, saying, "Mr. Prior," and then turning her attention to me fully. I gave her only half an ear as she rambled on about airing gowns and polishing jewels, so intently was I focused on Johnny, who was listening to us. He seemed, I thought, more engrossed in Grace Porter's diatribe on curling papers than he ought, and when she was not looking, I rolled my eyes meaningfully at him. He gave me a discreet half shrug before gesturing to Young Frank their departure, and still Grace prattled on. I watched him out of the corner of my eye as he made his exit.

It was nearly an hour and a full pot of tea later that I was able to legitimately excuse myself to the privy, as Grace paused for breath between sentences. As I made my way back, Johnny was leaning on the open half door of the carriage house, looking far too nonchalant for my comfort. He nodded to me, less formally than he was wont. "It seems that you've a great many preparations to make, Miss Ballard," he said, grinning broadly.

"It seems that *you* have been very attentive to *my* duties, Mr. Prior," I retorted, wrinkling my nose. "I had not thought you should care so very much over the details of a lady's toilette. Indeed," I said, "I thought your interest in the subject almost unnatural."

"Indeed?" he echoed. "I hardly thought anyone but you should notice a groom's interest in any subject under discussion with the household so unsettled."

I looked quickly around to ensure that we were unobserved before leaning close and, dropping my posh accent, asked in an undertone, "What are you on about, Seanin, you git?"

He went red, mumbling, "Just wanted to know what color she was wearing."

"What color? Why on earth should you care about such a thing?" I asked, baffled, and he scowled shamefacedly—an expression that brought instantly to mind the rare times Da had switched us in our childhood and wrung my heart. I shook my head at him fondly. "It's blue, right so? She's wearing feckin' blue."

His face lit up and he squeezed my hand wordlessly before retreating inside the carriage house. I chewed my lip as I took myself back indoors, puzzled over why he was behaving so imprudently. It was nearly a relief to return to the kitchen and find Grace ready to resume her lecture on the importance of our preparations, as if she had never paused at all.

When I had been first engaged as Charlotte's maid, Grace Porter had taken it upon herself to explain the significance of the occasion while stressing in a way altogether too fervent for my comfort that, despite the connotations of sainthood in the holiday, the celebration was in no way connected to any popery.

It was now three seasons that Charlotte Walden had been out, and it was clear by her third St. Valentine's Day ball that Mrs. Walden felt it time that Charlotte settle on a husband of her own.

"You do not," she had been prone to repeating my first year of employment, "want to have yourself engaged by the end of your first season. Some women view it as a great success, but there is something rather cheap about attaching yourself so soon, you know. It makes it look as though you are desperate to make a match, and that, of course, will not do. It is best to come to some sort of understanding by the end of your second season so that you might have a declaration by the start of your third and let your wedding be *the* event at the end of it." Charlotte had very clearly been the belle of her first season, and had had two or three notable proposals, which she had declined respectfully at her mother's bidding. While it was generally expected that she would make a match her second season, Mrs. Walden's aspirations were thwarted, as they so often seemed to be, by the escapades of her half sister, Prudence Graham.

Thaddeus Graham was a banker of substantial wealth and somber reputation. His wife had died young, and it was only when his daughter Augusta married Lawrence Walden that he engaged in the sole caprice of his life. Finding himself quite alone in his Bond Street mansion, he set about on a single-minded mission to seduce one Miss Sabrina Clemons, his daughter's dearest friend. The folly of his suit elicited the whispers of derision that might be expected when a widower pays court to a girl his own daughter's age, but these whispers were nothing to the clamor in every drawing room when Sabrina Clemons actually accepted his hand. The fruit of this unlikely union was Prudence Graham, who had been born a mere eighteen months after her own niece, Charlotte.

Prudence Graham would have been a sensation in her own right, if only for the circumstances of her parentage, which bordered on scandal. That she was a pretty girl who merely grew prettier with time certainly enhanced her allure. Though society might speculate, Mrs. Walden and the latest Mrs. Graham displayed their daughters together, one auburn and one dark, to striking effect. The two girls played together, they sang together, they rode together, and tormented a governess together. In the course of their intertwining lives, there were but two ripples to disturb the smoothness of their friendship.

The first had occurred early in their childhood, many years before I had come across the ocean. It was told to me in whispers when I first came into the household by Grace Porter, who still felt the slight as though it had happened only the day before. When Charlotte was five and Prudence was three, Thaddeus Graham's young wife persuaded him to back her brother Josiah in a mining venture in India. Through her pleading, he purchased a stake in a hole in the ground, sight unseen, on the other side of the world. If the drawing rooms had whispered when Sabrina Clemons married Thaddeus Graham, this was nothing to the fevered pitch the gossip reached when he parted with half his fortune on her brother's whim. For almost a year, rumors of ruin and imminent destitution hovered about the Graham residence, which, it was said, had been twice mortgaged in that twelvemonth alone. So it probably goes without saying that all of New York sat back in shock when the news of diamonds came.

Within the span of a week, Prudence Graham went from being a pretty child with mismatched parents on the precipice of impoverishment to being the greatest heiress of her generation. Her dowry portion was now rumored to be more than quintuple that of her half sister, Augusta, which had been considered jaw-dropping in its day, and it was said that Charlotte, as Thaddeus Graham's only grandchild, stood to inherit a tidy portion as well. Of the impact of this windfall on Augusta Walden, however, there was no word, for old Mr. Graham had given her portion over when she was married, and it seemed unlikely she should have another cent.

Consider, then, the impression this story would have made on a girl like me when first I arrived at the Waldens' house. I was at that time so grateful for the roof over my head and the clothes on my back that I could not yet see how a few dollars more or less in the bank should be the cause of so much family rancor. It was not until I actually met Prudence Graham that the full import of the matter hit me.

As I have said, the year I began maiding for Charlotte Walden was the year she had come out. In the month that followed her debut, she came to be considered quite the belle, and in consequence Mrs. Sabrina Graham deemed it wise to remove to Paris for the whole of the season and most of the following summer. It was not, then, until the Grahams returned the following autumn that I first met Miss Prudence.

Prudence Graham would have been called a great beauty many times in her youth, but I tell you in all fairness that it wasn't quite so. She was very pretty, in her own way, but she was never really what one might term beautiful. Her eyes were far too large for her face, which I would dare to call elfin. Slighter than her niece, she was delicately built with a pointed chin and long face that made her seem smaller than she was. Her hair was dark and very heavy, waved but not curled, and the great, black profusion of it made her face seem even paler and narrower than it was. She cut a very striking figure to be sure, but I could not, in justice, call her a beauty. The difference, I suppose, between my opinion and that of her admirers was that I never wanted her money.

There were plenty, however, who did, and when the season opened with the coming out of Miss Prudence Graham, there were few altogether who could see past the elegant French frocks and Indian diamond mines to realize that she was not, in fact, the beauty of her age, as well as the heiress of it. That honor, I felt, still belonged to her niece. Still, determined that her daughter should not be outshone by the brightness of her sister's diamonds, Augusta Walden made sure the girls continued to exhibit together. They played together, and sang together, and rode together, just as they had when they were young. Only this time, the stakes were much, much higher.

Unlike their mothers, Charlotte and Prudence took the circumstances of their supposed rivalry in good grace. They still linked arms, like sisters do, at each ball, and took afternoon constitutionals in the park, which occasioned the second ripple: Johnny. Where Charlotte was more retiring, Prudence Graham was social in the extreme, prone to chatting familiarly with anyone she encountered, from her father's friends to her niece's groom. When the two belles rode together, considerations of rank played no part in the avidity with which Prudence questioned Johnny about horse breeding. Johnny had eyes in his head and sense enough to know he trained the horses of the beauty of her generation, and, though he answered Prudence carefully, it was not she to whom he began directing himself. Charlotte Walden was always courteous to him, but it was clear, before Prudence Graham drew Johnny out, that she had never noticed him, beyond to thank him for handing her up. Which, I ought point out, had rather been the plan. But as her aunt found more frequent opportunities to involve the two into her rambling conversations, Charlotte began to spend more time in the carriage house than might be considered necessary for her weekly ride.

It was autumn then, and the leaves in the Square had gone from green to gold, just tipped with red. The days when the militia did not march, Miss Walden and Miss Graham frequently showed themselves to advantage by taking a turn along the parade grounds. They were crossing north of the Square when a hackney came careening round the corner. There is, of course, no way to tell what spooked the horses, but, by the time the young driver had got them under the rein again, Miss Walden had shoved Miss Graham out of harm's way and got a dirty gown and a twisted ankle for her troubles. I was in the kitchen when we heard Johnny bursting through the front door upstairs in a gust of crisp autumn air, and her cradled in his arms, looking pale. Behind them came Miss Graham, her bonnet gone quite askew, her face all streaked with tears, and speaking with such breathless rapidity that it was impossible to know what she said. I never knew how Johnny came to be watching in the street that day, nor how he went so nimbly—almost between the horses' legs, Miss Graham would later swear—to pluck my mistress from the cobbles and sweep her up the stairs and into the house.

I never thought of it at all until months later, and then I knew what I had never suspected: that Johnny kept his heart as close and closed as I did my own. Damn him. I can only think how it went in the interval, between the time when Charlotte, at last clean and dressed, her pretty ankle bound up by the doctor, had me summon Johnny up from the carriage house to her own room. And I, all unsuspecting of what was to come, took him there almost by the ear, hissing admonishments of politeness and courtesy—as if he intended otherwise!—as I led him up. I remember so little of that interview, save that Johnny was nervous, and how I was ashamed of the beads of sweat that crept along the edges of his brow until I remembered that, in this house, he was nothing to me. Only the Irish groom who had come to work here a week after myself. Practically a stranger.

Yes, that was the second ripple, for in those moments when Charlotte Walden thanked my brother in her low, sweet voice, some transaction, invisible to myself, was made, and thereafter she never cared if Prudence Graham had more beaux than herself, for Charlotte Walden had fallen in love with Johnny.

Have you ever seen a girl dance her way through a season looking for a husband? There is something sharpish-knowing in her eye, and, when she is filling her dance card, you can see her weighing the consequences of her choices. To whom should she bestow the honor of the quadrille, and to whom might she give the quiet privacy of the waltz? Is it altogether wise to grant two dances to he who asks when she is not quite sure of his intentions? The girl who is dancing her way to the altar must consider these things; she must calculate. But the girl who has already reached an understanding may simply dance. She may be freer with her favors; she is secure, and she might be quite as careless with her dance card as she pleases, for, saving the dances she will always give to her intended, the rest of her night is of little consequence.

That was how Charlotte Walden became, after she let Johnny into her bed. The only difference was that her beloved could not claim a single dance from her; he was not even allowed in the house. He never stood back appreciatively to watch her whirl, admiring the neatness of her figure, or straining to catch a glimpse of ankle. No. That was me. From the fringes of the hall, I watched with Grace Porter and any other number of ladies' maids, as our mistresses minced and spun, and Charlotte made every impolitic choice that her dance card would allow. I watched as Grace wrung her hands in imitation of her own mistress, who stood by as match after match slipped through her daughter's careless fingers. There were no more proposals that season, for who could be encouraged in pursuit of a girl whose dreamy mien suggested her affections were otherwise engaged?

There are girls who, when at the end of the night they are unlaced and brushed and combed, will sigh into their mirrors, thinking over the hard, strong hands at their waists, the pressure of another's palm against their own, the whisper of a compliment paid as they flew across the polished floor. Charlotte Walden sighed as well: for the man who was not at the ball.

It would not do to think for a moment that Mrs. Walden had not noticed something amiss, and I was forever in expectation that she would cipher out the cause. She would have to have been a proper fool not to realize her daughter's affections were misplaced, and that the source of all her sighing was not to be found in the ballroom. Grace Porter, who lived and breathed on such scraps, was only too happy to share her mistress's theory as we sat and sewed one morning while the ladies made their calls. There had been a Prussian baron her first season, whom Charlotte had been advised not to accept, the precariousness of Germanic politics being what they were. And this had gone very hard with my mistress, who had declined two other proposals in as many months, and been rather taken with him at the time. Still, when the moment came, she declined his offer gracefully, though she did not speak with her mother for days afterwards. It was all so neat, so tidily packaged, that I lost no time in readily agreeing that it was the likeliest case, and Grace nodded wisely, and I knew that Johnny was safe.

Yet, though Johnny was safe, Charlotte was not; for an heiress, unmarried, cannot go carrying on with her groom forever when there are expectations that she make a grand match. Charlotte and her mother had been left well provisioned when Mr. Walden was carried off by the influenza, but the money was not inexhaustible, and soon or late Charlotte was meant to marry into affluence greater than her own. Her portion of the estate could not be touched until she was wed, at any rate, and, as freely as Mrs. Walden might spend on frocks and balls, it was all an investment with great expectations of return. And so it was, midway through Charlotte Walden's third season, that her mother's campaign, begun in earnest, carried on through exasperation, grew desperate.

With the eye of a woman who has known only wealth to be attractive, Augusta Walden had, at the start of the summer, laid out an enormous sum toward Charlotte's wardrobe for the coming season. That summer, I had joined Charlotte in the carriage as we made countless trips to Marguerite Beauchamp's boutique on Broadway. There, Augusta Walden joined the renowned dressmaker in lively debates regarding the colors and fabrics best suited to Charlotte's graceful frame and auburn hair. I sat on a stool in the corner as Marguerite and her assistant, Claire, pinned and draped and fussed, holding bolts of fabric up and swathing them over Charlotte's bare petticoats while my mistress stood, bored, impassive, and patient in the face of such ado. Then, too, were there visits to the cobbler and the milliner, though Augusta Walden was far more content to allow Charlotte to wear last season's vestments outside of the ballroom. Bodices were very low-cut that year, and

I well recall she had ordered two new corsets to accommodate this newly fashionable plunge.

All this, however, was nothing to the sole visit on which I accompanied them to the jewelers. It had previously been Augusta Walden's policy that, as she had not had any new jewels during her years as a debutante, her daughter needed none. While concessions had been made during Prudence Graham's debut, Charlotte had previously been content to wear out the limited contents of her jewel box, augmented only by a few loans from her mother. Regrettably, the family rubies looked ill when worn against Charlotte's hair. They had come to Mrs. Walden through her mother, the first Mrs. Graham, as part of her dower portion. At last it was decided that the versatility of pearls would do, for of course Augusta Walden could not bear to see her daughter wear diamonds. There was also a sapphire brooch, very fine, and a set of matching combs, for blue looked well against Charlotte's auburn, and her gown for the St. Valentine's Day ball was to be of that color.

Grace Porter joined me to help put away Charlotte's finery when it was at last delivered. I watched as she ran her appraising fingers over the lace and flounces, as she fingered the beads and rubbed the slippery taffeta. She sat and watched me hungrily as I shined my mistress's new gems with vinegar and ran a soft cloth against the pearls. You mustn't think Grace personally covetous; she merely lived on reflected glory. She should not have known what to do with such gems herself, but she fair lived for the notion of fastening them onto her mistress's throat and wrists. She longed for the days when she could dress Augusta Walden as finely as I now dressed her daughter, and I found myself caught up in her enthusiasm. She showed me how to wrap the sapphires in squares of silk to prevent them jostling and scratching in the jewel box, and she taught me to warm Charlotte's pearls against my own skin to bring out their luster.

I had dressed Charlotte for countless balls since she had come out, but, on the evening of the St. Valentine's Day ball, I took extra care. I oiled her hair with *huile antique* and brushed it until it looked like burnished copper. I papered the sides while I braided and coiled it in the back, securing the coil with the sapphire combs. Her shoulders I sponged with buttermilk, brandy, and alum and rubbed them so that her skin glowed creamy white before helping her into her chemise and lacing her into one of the new corsets. The whalebone creaked slightly as I ran the cording through the brass eyelets, and I thought with secret pleasure that I was the only one who ever saw her like this, that the periwinkles embroidered on her stays were for my benefit and mine alone. I paused to take her in: the swell of her bosom above the sateen edging, and the gentle curve of her hip below. It was almost a pity to cover it with her crinoline and coats before at last sliding the Egyptian blue taffeta gown over her head and buttoning up her back. The gown hung from her shoulders, a layer of paler blue lace along the sloping neckline, and below it on her arms were embroidered bands that gave way to the round puffed sleeves then in vogue. The high-waist bodice nipped tightly in before falling away into a profusion of pleats, just brushing the floor. I wrapped her as carefully as I now unwrapped her jewels, and, like the glittering brooch on her bodice, my mistress shone.

> If you have any personal attractions, and most young women have something that is agreeable or pleasing, beware of the least approach to familiarity with any of the gentlemen . . . should you so far gain the affections of any of the young gentlemen as to induce him to marry you.
>
> —*The Duties of a Lady's Maid*

It must not be supposed that Charlotte did not have suitors while she loved Johnny. There are always those who appreciate a lady with a cooler eye, a stiller heart. Of these, two such gentlemen had, in Charlotte's third season, begun to pay her court in earnest. The first was Lord Robert Deane, fifth Baron Muskerry. The second was an American named Elijah Dawson. I did not particularly care for either of them.

Lord Deane had come to New York the previous spring with the purpose, it was said, of marrying an American heiress. Though he talked often of his ancestral home, it was rumored that Springfield Castle was badly in need of repairs, and that the fourth Baron Muskerry's gambling debts had made the necessary refurbishments impossible. Though he was far too urbane and well regarded in society's drawing rooms to be considered a fortune hunter, it was still worthy of note that, while eager, the baron could hardly be considered ardent. With a show of respectful formality, he had begun securing Charlotte Walden's waltzes early in the season and had invited her driving more than once. Both Charlotte and her mother had been to dine with him at his hotel, and he had squired them twice to the opera.

On the subject of his suit to her daughter, Grace Porter told us, Augusta Walden was of two minds. It would be a fine thing to be the mother of a baroness, Augusta Walden had concluded, and, while Charlotte's inheritance was substantial enough to support a failing barony for a generation or two, Mrs. Walden would have rather seen her daughter ally her great fortune with one of its like. It was therefore widely conjectured in the kitchen that Augusta Walden was merely encouraging Lord Deane's suit as a means of creating jealousy in Elijah Dawson.

Elijah Dawson's blood was far redder than his rival's more aristocratic blue. The son of a Hempstead plantation owner, Mr. Dawson had lost both father and brothers when a fire broke out on the property in '14 and become heir to the family estates at the tender age of seven. His country rearing at the hands of his grandmother had rendered him soft-spoken and frequently reserved, though his reserve seemed to melt away when he took Charlotte into his arms on the ballroom floor. Often I had observed the brightness in his eyes as he watched the grace with which my mistress flew across the floor. He had asked her three times for the waltz, which she had granted, and I could not tear my gaze from his hand resting gently but firmly at her waist.

Quite naturally, I detested him.

Of Mr. Dawson's credentials, Augusta Walden was far more effusive. His grandmother, the formidable Geraldine Dawson, had insisted upon his education at Columbia College, and this familiarity with the City of New York disposed my mistress's mother to him greatly. It was Augusta Walden's considered opinion that Long Island was a rustic wilderness, practically a frontier, and had it not been for the civilizing influence of an education in the city, I do not think she would have considered Mr. Dawson's suit at all. That he had returned frequently from his plantation showed, in her opinion, good judgment, and, while she could not see herself settled at such a remove from the city as Hempstead Plains, she held no such compunctions about her daughter's future. That Elijah Dawson rented a house on Great Jones Street added to his many charms. The Grahams, in recognition of his suitability even for Prudence, had invited him to dine, and Charlotte had noted later to me how full of quiet praise he had been when she and her aunt sang. His one fault appeared to be his indirect manner, for, though he seemed eager enough to press his suit to Charlotte at every assembly at which they met, Augusta Walden had thus far failed to secure him for even a single dinner.

It was with this failure to bring Elijah Dawson into her home that Augusta Walden began plotting to assure his acceptance of her invitation to the St. Valentine's Day ball. That the invitations themselves were exclusive—the Walden family's ball was considered one of *the* events of the season—was not, on this occasion, considered allure enough to ensure Mr. Dawson's attendance. Augusta Walden's campaign, therefore, consisted of, in the days following her footman's delivery of the invitation, conspiring to intersect with the poor man and, stopping him in the street, to force an acceptance from him with all the charm a society dam can bring to bear.

I remember a fairy story from my childhood, about a knight or warrior who was trying to reach the battle, and a great fairy queen disguised as a lovely young maiden who stood in his path. When the knight paid her no heed, she swore she would do everything in her power to stand in the way of his battle, and she turned herself into an eel and a wolf and a cow to try to get him to stop and show her the respect she was due. Finally, she took the form of an old crone, and, blocking his path, made him acknowledge her and grant her his blessing. It was this story I recalled as Charlotte told over her mother's travails while I brushed out her hair for the night. Da used to say how it was a mark of the knight's goodness that he could not be turned aside by beauty or force, but was compelled by his honor to show respect for a humble granny. Over this story I would worry like a loose tooth, for it meant to me that honor was a weakness, if it made a person so easy to compel. I was troubled that I could not remember how it ended.

Looking at Elijah Dawson now, standing against the edge of the assembly in the makeshift ballroom, his face set stoically, I followed his gaze to where Augusta Walden stood speaking with her father across the room. Though long since past her mourning period, Augusta Walden honored the memory of her husband by donning a ball gown of black velvet. Her mother's rubies were fastened in her dark hair, and a massive square pendant of the same gem hung at her throat. The contrast of her dark hair and gown made her skin seem unearthly pale, against which the rubies showed like drops of blood. I suddenly recalled the rest of the fairy story that had troubled me before. The queen had changed her shape to take the form of a raven, and watched the knight on the field of battle. She circled high above until she saw him mortally wounded, then came to perch upon his shoulder until he died of his wounds. I shuddered, suppressing the urge to cross myself at such a grim recollection. Mr. Dawson hardly looked like a knight or warrior; he looked like a scholar or a minister or something else genteel and dull and serious. Such a man hardly seemed fair prey for a fearsome queen like Augusta Walden, bent on marrying off her daughter.

I must here remark that I have always thought anyone laboring under the delusion that women are the weaker sex is unfamiliar with the field of battle that is a society ballroom. For the ballroom is not the place of leisure and frivolity it purports to be. The music is there, I've always felt, to drown out the drums of war.

Let us begin with the principal warriors—the debutantes. With their ladies' maids acting as their faithful squires, the armor they don must surely compare to the maille and plate worn by the knights of old. Beneath the silk and taffeta, the insubstantial gauze, are whalebone and horsehair, cordage and steel. Every demoiselle has been laced tight, wasp-waisted above the gracious swell of her skirts, her stays stemming her in. The curved bell of her gown, made possible by her corded crinoline and three or four more petticoats, hangs ponderously from her hips. Even her arms, though bare below the elbow, are encumbered with sleeve plumpers, filled with feathers. She is girded for battle beneath the clothes the gentlemen see, the gentle slope of her shoulders rising above the layers of fabric that weigh her down. Atop her head, the precarious Apollo knot, filled with feathers or decked in jewels, strains her neck, and her throat is wrapped in beads. Thus laden, she is meant to smile as she glides through the room, the thrusts and parries of each conversation and dance dealt with grace and dignity.

And who is orchestrating these forays onto the field of *amor*? Why, the old generals, their mamas and grandmamas, the veterans of a thousand such campaigns. Grouped together along the fringes of the room—never huddled, for one does not huddle when surveying one's domain—their feints are subtler still. No less bedecked than the young ladies in their care, no less intent on those matrimonial objects, theirs is no longer to smile or simper for the gentlemen themselves. They vie behind the scenes. A word dropped here, a hint or suggestion there—she's looking pale, she dined with him, he lingered long at tea—a whiff of scandal on the wind. With a well-turned phrase, alliances are made, reputations ruined, fates sealed.

The gentlemen, eligible bachelors, thinking that, because it is theirs to ask, they hold all the cards, have no notion of the machinations, the artifice of all that lies beneath. They see vacant, lovely faces; they see innocence and purity. They see what the women want them to see. Little do they suspect the gears behind the faces that they meet are churning, churning, churning.

Lord Deane was able to secure the opening quadrille with Charlotte, while Mr. Dawson, with a fervor of which I had not suspected him, wrung from her a promise of, by my count, his fourth waltz this season. Mrs. Walden seemed pleased with this arrangement, and, from our place behind the screens along the wall, Grace grinned at me with yellow teeth. I smiled back, as thin-lipped as politeness would allow at her sallow grimace, and turned my attention to Charlotte.

Candlelight is always flattering, particularly with the soft gleam of ball gowns and gems, but Charlotte looked radiant, as if lit from within. She was assuming her place to lead the quadrille—taking the role of the hostess, for Mrs. Walden never now danced. Her features looked as composed as Grace's were anxious, and, though all eyes were on her, she held herself naturally, with none of the self-conscious stiffness so often seen in girls her age. As the music played, she and the baron began the intricate steps, and I began to wonder at her placid comportment, for her partner was not her equal.

Lord Deane danced badly, perhaps suffering from the misconception that simply being of the gentry made him genteel. His steps were too high, his tempo was off, and he danced with alarming little kicks and flourishes that suggested an inflated notion of his abilities. Not a few suppressed titters flitted through the room at his performance. Grace turned to me, bald disapproval on her face, and tsked disparagingly. I rolled my eyes, and we turned back to the display in time to see the baron's bootheel catch on the hem of Charlotte's gown. I watched in horror as time seemed to slow down and Charlotte stepped quickly away before he could remove his foot. The sound of her gown tearing surely could not have been heard above the music, but, whenever I think back, I seem to hear it anyway, drowning out the clarinet, the flute, the pianoforte, and the bass. The seam between the skirt and the bodice gaped, revealing Charlotte's corset and her outer petticoats. My mistress froze, the dance faltered, and all eyes turned to her where she was exposed. Charlotte colored, then fled.

Grace jabbed me with her elbow. "Go!" she hissed, and I dashed for the stairs.

What I would particularly caution you against, however, in this respect, is giving advice when you are not asked, or thrusting your opinion upon your mistress, whether she seems desirous of having it or not.

—*The Duties of a Lady's Maid*

By the time Charlotte gained the door to her room, I was ready with my sewing basket, unspooling a length of blue silk and threading my needle with it. Charlotte, red-faced and breathless, caught sight of me and smiled her relief.

"Oh, Ballard, bless you!" She was by my side in a moment, grasping my hands and forcing me to drop the needle and thread. "I might have known! Did you see it? Did everyone see? How bad is it?"

I squeezed her hands and smiled at her. "Be easy, Miss Charlotte. Stand stock-still, and I'll do what I can."

"Oh, bless you, Ballard," she said again, as I ducked to retrieve the needle. Threading it at last, I jabbed it into a pincushion, which I handed to Charlotte. She took it obediently, and stood with her arms held out from her body as I began to unbutton her from behind.

I slid one hand along her back, worming between the heavy taffeta layer of her gown and the lighter taffeta of her petticoats, the backs of my knuckles sliding up against the laces of her stays, pressed against the contours of her waist. Holding the material taut, I examined the tear.

"Well?" she asked, her arms uncomfortably akimbo, looking back over her shoulder expectantly.

"He's done his work thoroughly, miss," I said. "Shirred the seam, for it was cross-stitched here, and the fabric along it's frayed. I can tack it back together and it should hold for now. There's just enough seam left to hide it, I think."

She leaned back, arching her white neck toward the ceiling and sighing as deeply as her stays allowed.

"Thank you, Ballard. I suppose I shall have to send for Marguerite's girl?"

"More than likely, miss. It should be reinforced with another piece of taffeta, and Mademoiselle Claire will certainly do better than I."

"Well, do what you can, Ballard."

As I bowed my head to the work, the fire glinting off the fine weave, there was a rap at the door, which flew open before Charlotte could answer. A swirl of skirts dashed into the room, depositing itself on the chaise longue with unexpected grace. Charlotte twisted to see the interloper, and I stabbed myself in the hand with the needle.

"Lord!" I heard from the other side of the gown. "It has turned quite grim down there, you know. Though it was hardly impressive before—what *is* Augusta on about, to hire musicians and then force them to play so insipidly?"

Charlotte made a face. "Is no one dancing? Mama will never speak to Lord Deane again."

"The question, Lottie," said Miss Graham, who was of course the only person in the world with enough ill grace to enter the hostess's bedroom during a ball, "is whether *you* will ever speak to him again."

I peered at her from around Charlotte's skirt. Prudence Graham's gown was a silk brocade of rich burgundy hue, which had been adorned with jet beads. Her heavy dark tresses were caught back with combs that had been inlaid with diamonds, and that same stone glittered from her earbobs and wrists as well. She shone so it bordered on vulgar, even to my eye.

"La! I could kiss him!" Charlotte said, at which Miss Graham actually looked shocked for once in her own rather shocking life. Charlotte smirked at the expression on her aunt's face. "Oh, Prue, for pity's sake, you know I wasn't talking of that! I'm only grateful he got me out of waltzing with Mr. Dawson, yet again."

"Yes, well, if Augusta insists on having them play the waltz as though it were a dirge, I can hardly fault you."

Charlotte shifted from one foot to the other. "What would you have them play?"

"I wouldn't," Miss Graham said, absently flicking the jet beads on her daringly narrow sleeves. "I had rather play myself."

"Tosh," Charlotte said, more intent on her aunt's gown than on her words. "You always say that. Who in heavens let you do those sleeves? It wasn't your mama."

Prudence looked up with a grin. "Like them? They're *très français.* No one's wearing those plumpers anymore this season—they've gotten so big now it's impossible to play."

"You mean no one's wearing them to a salon or to dinner. *Did* Grandmama Sabrina let you?"

"Don't be absurd. I had a word with the sempstress after. Mama does adore French fashion, but after all . . ." She trailed off meaningfully.

"She might adore French fashion," Charlotte said. "But she detests your Viennese sensibilities."

"Now, then, there's a notion," Prudence said. "You might, just might, be more inclined toward dancing the waltz if Augusta would let them play Schubert."

"Not if I was dancing with Mr. Dawson."

"I fail to see exactly what you find so objectionable about Mr. Dawson."

Charlotte shuddered delicately, and I found my fingers once more imperiled by the needle. "Have *you* waltzed with him?"

"No such luck, and more's the pity." Prudence sighed.

"Pity me, rather," said Charlotte. "His eyes, the way he *stares* at me!"

"I'd be flattered, myself," said Prudence carefully.

"But he looks at me with such intensity! I hardly think it's flattering to be so baldly assessed," said Charlotte, a chill creeping into her voice.

"Perhaps you simply don't care for the assessment," Prudence teased. "Come now, he's rich and handsome, and, moreover, dear Lottie, he's the right age. Every other beau Augusta's thrown at you has been far too old. Including Lord Deane, whom you seemed so eager to kiss a moment ago."

I swallowed hard, keeping my face a mask of composure. The baron and his eagerness had caused me no few sleepless nights. It had occurred to me before that any suitor of Charlotte Walden's who might have an ear for my lilt if he heard me slip was a dangerous prospect indeed. Mrs. Walden, as I had said, was not at all averse to the idea of titled son-in-law, though Charlotte feigned indifference to the prospect of marriage altogether. Before Johnny, it had been a different matter, and I had been subjected to many an hour of hearing her and Miss Graham sigh over this or that gentleman that had paid them compliment.

Charlotte tossed her head. "Lord Deane is not yet forty. And besides, my mother's taste in beaux runs along only one line. She has made her intentions for my future quite clear, Prue, and it is for me to say yes or no only in the particulars."

"Which are?"

Charlotte colored, which I am afraid she never did prettily, for her Scottish came out and she went somewhat blotchy about the cheeks. "I should not wish to leave New York," she said in what I'm sure she thought was a careless sort of way.

Miss Graham was not fooled. She smiled thinly and replied, "Yes, well, I'm sure there are things you would miss terribly. For myself, I've been longing to go back to Europe, but Mama won't let me go as far as East Hampton until I've accepted a proposal. Now you, I think, would be happy if you could accept the *nearest* offer, wouldn't you, Lottie?"

I realized I had been holding my breath and inhaled sharply as the edges of my vision began to blur.

"Ballard?" Charlotte looked down over her shoulder at me. "Is it very bad?"

"No worse than I thought, miss," I replied, finishing the last stitch and tying off the thread. "Only, I should think that you'll need to call for Miss Marguerite's girl straightaway tomorrow. It ought to hold for tonight, but it cannot last forever, you know. After all, Miss Charlotte, nothing lasts forever, and you ought to remedy what you can."

She looked at me sharply, and I met her gaze as blandly as I was able. "Will that be all, Miss Charlotte?"

She narrowed her eyes. "Why, yes, Ballard. Yes, I think that's quite enough." She turned to Miss Graham. "Well, then, Prue. I suppose we ought to salvage the evening for Mama, hadn't we? Ballard, do me back up? Quickly now."

Prudence Graham rose, her arm out to her niece in a rakish, masculine way when her eye caught something on Charlotte's dressing table we both had missed.

"Hullo," she said, snatching up a nosegay of bachelor's buttons, tied with a bit of white silk. "Who sent you this?"

Charlotte's eyes widened, and she turned to Prudence with a look of innocence and said, "I've no idea," before taking her aunt firmly by the arm and leading her from the room.

> I advise . . . that you do not stay till a late hour, when drunkenness and revelling are at the height.
>
> —*The Duties of a Lady's Maid*

The sound of a rollicking polka—what Miss Graham would have called "low music"—reached me from the stair. I stood at the turning, suddenly too weary to slide back to my place behind the screened-off landing, from where I could watch Charlotte and her mother making assurances to their guests that all was well. It was only nine o'clock, and it was three hours yet before supper would be served. The idea of standing on the landing with Grace while my legs cramped up seemed too exhausting to contemplate. Instead, I made my way down to the kitchen in the hopes of tea. Peals of laughter and raised voices rose up to meet me, as I discovered the room packed with drivers deep in their small beer, Mrs. Freedman shooing them impatiently away from the table. Agnes and Liza were flitting back and forth, hefting platters and tureens, while Millie attempted to organize the drivers and keep them from being underfoot. They ignored me as I passed along the wall, lifting my cloak from its hook by the door and ducking out into the mews.

A few coachmen were lingering along the kitchen wall, smoking and talking amiably, and these lifted their hats to me as I passed by on my way to the privy. My boots crunched on the fresh snow, and the bracing cold rallied my spirits. I walked from the kitchen door down the mews to Fifth Avenue before turning back. As I approached the kitchen door, I looked up at the Waldens' carriage house. There, backlit from the loft window, stood Johnny. He was not looking down to me in the mews, but, following his gaze, I saw that he was staring into the Waldens' brightly lit second floor. As he shifted, light fell over his features and I could see a bright blue bachelor's button pinned to his lapel. I paused, momentarily tempted to shout up to him for being a fecking fool, but ended instead by laughing. Blue. She's wearing feckin' blue. The git. Gritting my teeth, I went back inside to wait until I should be required again.

> Your time, while you are in place, you must remember is not your own. You have agreed to give it up to your employer for the money, board and lodging, for which you bargain. It is therefore no less dishonest than actual pilfering, to be indolent and neglectful in the services required of you, as by so doing, you are evidently guilty of fraud and gross misdemeanor. Nothing will sooner attach to your character and render you disliked than careless and slovenly habits, and nothing will be more against your own comfort, both in keeping you always in a bustle, and in delaying and confusing every thing you have to do.
>
> —*The Duties of a Lady's Maid*

The advantage to waiting up for the Waldens was that they were both then late risers, and the whole house got a bit of a lie-in, except for Agnes, of course. I lay abed, studying the plaster wreath affixed to my ceiling and wondering, not for the first time, what earthly purpose it served and why such a bit of frippery had been installed in a nurse's closet. I supposed it was laurel, for the leaves were longish, and I knew of no other leaf used in wreath making, excepting perhaps holly. Outside it was snowing again, and the dim winter light filtered through the thin baize curtains that hung before my tiny window, leaving half my laurel wreath in shadows. I was never one for lying about the way Charlotte and Mrs. Walden seemed to, and though it was many hours before I would need to attend to my mistress, I rose and dressed myself and slipped down the back stairs to the kitchen.

Walking into the kitchen was like slipping into a warm bath, for it was baking day, and the smell of new-made bread enveloped me as I came in. Agnes stoked the fire while Cook tied herbs to a roast. Four loaves were cooling on the sill, and I knew there would be four more in the oven, for Cook always made them in batches of eight. None of the housemaids were down yet, but the pantry was open, and from within I could hear Mrs. Harrison and Mr. Buckley rowing in their quiet way. They rowed quite frequently, though they did it in such a still, sedate sort of manner that you would not realize they were rowing if you were not listening to their words. This morning, they were having a terribly polite go at each other over the state of the apple bin. I looked at Cook, who rolled her eyes and cocked her head sharply at me. When I came close, she said in an undertone, "The missus is sick of apple tart, yes indeed she is. And here it is, only February and months yet before we'll have anything new. We didn't put up half as many cherries as last summer, and the peach crop wasn't nearly as good. I tell the missus every year to send up for peaches from Georgia like she used to when my Frank was still living, but she never does."

I nodded, not really hearing her, for I did not care at all if there was tart with dinner so long as we were fed. She nodded back in a knowing, conspiratorial way. "Those loaves should be cool enough to slice, if you're peckish. Breakfast won't be but another hour, so there's a girl."

I almost never came over peckish, since I came into this house where meals were regular, though, when I'd first come, I ate like a creature starved. Mrs. Freedman thought me skinny still. She was very generous, far too, with her portions for me, and so I obliged her by slicing myself a bit of the heel. As I stood by the fire, chewing it slowly, Grace Porter came bustling in, a flannel in her hand. She nodded sharply to me and to Cook.

"Mrs. Harrison?" she called in her thin, shrill voice. "Mrs. Harrison?"

Mrs. Harrison and Mr. Buckley emerged from the pantry. Mrs.

Harrison looked cool and appraising as ever, but Mr. Buckley looked rather hot around the collar. "Yes, Miss Porter?" Mrs. Harrison said, sounding somehow withering instead of weary.

"Mrs. Harrison, you must speak to Agnes and Liza. This is not to be borne!" Grace said, her voice cracking with rage as she held out the flannel. We all peered in at it, and there was a faded rusty stain, sure enough. Grace held it far from her, like some noxious thing, grimacing in distaste. "Suppose I had handed it to Mrs. Walden? It is only Providence that they were misfolded, or I should not have noticed until it was too late." She shook the offending item at Mrs. Harrison, who took it gingerly by the corner and held it out to Agnes, who was cringing in the corner like a beaten cur.

"Agnes, who is responsible for adding the bluing? Is it yourself, or is it Liza?"

Agnes, twisting her apron in her hands, as though she had been accused of murder, burst into tears and buried her face into the twists. Mrs. Harrison chucked the flannel at her feet in disgust.

"I trust we shall not be treated to a recurrence of these proceedings?"

Agnes blubbered something into her apron, and somehow managed to bob a curtsy with the thing still over her head. I could only imagine what wonderings of admonishment were in store for Liza when she was done lighting the fires. She was only second housemaid, and, though you couldn't say her star was on the rise, she was at least not so wretched a creature as poor, sniveling Agnes. The whole kitchen seemed to bristle with Agnes's shame, and it was all I could do not to stare about me at so many fools for whom a bit of an old stain was now to be the gossip of the morning.

My superior sentiments did not last long, for Grace Porter, deprived of the drubbing she so clearly felt Agnes deserved, turned her pale, critical eye on me and cried, with all the horror such a turn entailed, "Why, Miss Ballard, you have broken your bootlace."

I looked down, and, yes, the frayed bit that always rubbed against the loop holes had snapped at last. I looked stupidly at Mrs. Harrison, who sighed and said, "Is this not your second bootlace this month, Miss Ballard? You are quite out of your allowance, I am afraid, unless you wish to purchase one against your salary?"

"No need," said Grace Porter. "I haven't used my allowance in two months. Miss Ballard may take one of mine."

What followed was the dullest showing of Grace Porter's magnanimity and my gratitude, whereupon a bootlace was procured and my frayed one removed and replaced, and much was made over Grace and her goddamn sharp eyes and her goddamn sense of generosity.

There were days when things like apple tart and clean flannels and bootlaces drove me mad, for I felt sometimes on those days the immensity of my life, and the briefness of it, and how the bulk of it had been built of apple tart and flannels and bootlaces, and then my heart beat very fast, and my face grew hot, and I felt as though my hands were grown huge and thick and heavy, like warming pans heaped with coals. I could feel it coming on me now, that wave of heat, and I excused myself to the privy.

The wind whipped up the snow, and I picked my way carefully across the slick cobbles. It was cold inside the privy; my breath came quickly in smoky puffs. I counted the puffs of breath, willing myself to think only of the numbers, and of nothing else. The heat slowly left my body, my hands shrunk to their normal size. I quieted my breathing, putting my hands to my face. Though calmer, I was not yet ready to face the kitchen, and instead made my way to the carriage house.

Johnny and Young Frank, the stableboy, were feeding and watering the horses, and right away the smells of hay and dung and leather soothed me something marvelous. I was always that way around the horses, for they were the smell of Johnny now, as once they had been the smell of Da. It had been too many years now that he was gone for me to picture his face quite as clearly as I used, but the smell of him stayed sharp in my memory. I walked directly to Charlotte's sweet-tempered mare, who had come to lean over the opening of her box. I stroked her velvety nose, taking pleasure in the softness. Out of the corner of my eye, I saw Johnny making his way down the aisle. I stiffened as he approached me.

"Miss Ballard," he said in a low voice.

"Mr. Prior," I replied, in soft tones.

He eyed me carefully. "May I assist you, Miss Ballard?" There were, of course, rather stringent prohibitions about any of the housemaids making bold in the carriage house, and though there might be some leeway for Miss Charlotte's maid were it her riding day, on a snowbound morning someone surely would mark it odd. Young Frank, still at the other end of the stalls, was looking at us curiously.

"She's a darling, isn't she?" I asked, not raising my eyes. "So gentle. So obliging. So lovely and soft. How you must enjoy your time with her."

"To whom do you refer, Miss Ballard?" he asked, an edge to his voice.

"Why, to Angelica, of course," I said, still caressing the horse. "Goodness, but to whom else should I refer?"

Johnny made a noise that was equal parts exasperation and mirth. I went on tranquilly rubbing Angelica's nose, and, at length, Johnny produced a carrot from his pocket.

"She likes her treats, does this one," he said, pressing it into my hand. "I meant to give it to her myself, she being the good lass you say, but perhaps you might care to?"

I held the carrot flat in the palm of my hand, offering it to Angelica. Her lips, thick and velvety, tickled, and her blunt teeth scraped gently against my skin as she gobbled it up. I brushed my damp hand against my skirts before resuming my caresses. "Indeed," I said softly, for Young Frank was coming nearer. "It is kind of you to let me, though any young miss will appreciate a posy from an admirer."

"And you admire her?"

I shrugged, not meeting his eye. "You might say that. Though my familiarity with her could never rival your own."

"A creature like her," Johnny said, "and you'd be a fool not to admire her. She's lovely to ride."

"What?" I said, startled.

"I said she's lovely to ride. She's always eager for it, very willing creature, and a steady gait. It's an absolute pleasure to be atop her."

"Are we still speaking of Angelica?" I asked, my cheeks glowing crimson.

"To be sure," Johnny said, his eyes bright with mischief. "To whom else could I be referring? Is there anything else I can do for you this morning, Miss Ballard?"

"Thank you, Mr. Prior, but I was just passing by."

"Passing by? I see." Young Frank was approaching with water for Angelica now. Johnny stepped out of the way to allow the stableboy egress, and I backed away from both of them.

"I shall take up no more of your time," I said, my cheeks still blazing. I left in a hurry, knowing Johnny would be puzzling over why I had come and wondering why I had started such a conversation. Let him think it was his goddamn bachelor's buttons.

The heat of the kitchen closed in over me, and, after my exchange in the carriage house, I no longer felt soothed. Sweat prickled my neck, collecting at the base of my hairline, and I thought I should stifle in the thick, close air. The smell of baking bread, which always cheered me, now filled my nose and was like to smother me. I closed my eyes, wishing I could stop up my ears, for Grace Porter *would* go on after poor Agnes, who was defending herself in a whining tone. I sat very still indeed, fearing that if I moved it would be to dash Grace's head against the flagstones, or Agnes's, or my own. Not Cook or Mrs. Harrison said a word, and I knew I must not either, but sitting there I thought they would drive me mad between them. And then—like music!—Charlotte's bell was ringing with such vigor that I stood in a rush and upset my untouched teacup.

She was sitting on the thick-piled rug next to her bed, the chamber pot on the floor next to her. The color was all drained away from her face, her hair stained with sweat, her skin gleaming with a fine sheen of it. I paled myself, for I had never seen her so unwell, and was by her side in a moment, to help her back to her bed. She began to rise, never speaking a word, but before I could get her upright, she was back on her knees again, retching. I held back her hair where it had come loose, thinking of the times Johnny had done as much for me, then pushing the memories ungratefully away. She sat up at last, breathless, and tears at the corners of her eyes. I rubbed her back, feeling her shoulders heave beneath the fine linen of her night rail.

"Ballard, I—" she began when she had caught her breath, but I hushed her. She rubbed her lips with the back of her hand, a small brown smear coming away on her pale skin, and that nearly set her to heaving again. I took a cloth and dipped it into the ewer by the washbasin to clean her hand and bathe her face. She sat propped up against the side of her bed while I crouched beside her and took her white face into my hand. When she was neat, her skin cooler, I slipped her arm around my shoulder to get her to rise. She stood, then leaned against me hard, both her arms around my neck, her loose auburn curls falling on my face, and I breathed in sharply the scent of her. She buckled in my arms, and I thought she might fall again, but I managed to maneuver her onto the bed.

"There, there, miss," I murmured as I tucked her in. "Shall I bring you some beef tea then? Or some bread, new baked?"

She shook her head weakly. "No, nothing. I am afraid I have a head, Ballard." She smiled, her lips thin and tight. "I should be ashamed, I suppose, but Mr. Dawson *would* keep handing me champagne."

"Hush now," I said, for her words came thickly and cost her something to form. "I shall find something to tempt you. You lay still now."

She smiled up at me again, and I slipped down the servants' stair back to the kitchen. Grace had gone away again, and Agnes was sniffling by the hearth. The rest of the household were at breakfast; Johnny looked up sharply as I came in. Cook nodded to me.

"Up already, is she, Miss Ballard? Well, child, you sit and have a bite while Agnes fixes her tray."

I shook my head. "Miss Walden is poorly. Perhaps an egg posset this morning, Agnes."

"Poorly? What, again?" asked Agnes.

Mrs. Harrison sniffed. "Miss Walden does not wish to be poorly, I'm sure. Well, but sit and eat a moment, Miss Ballard, while Agnes boils the water." She rose, her keys clinking softly against her skirt. "I believe we have a very fine chamomile that might serve, if she is poorly," she said, going to unlock the caddy.

I sat and helped myself to a slice of bread and butter, but left the rashers untouched, for Charlotte would not like the smell of them on my breath. Millie whispered something to Liza, who tittered and caught the attention of Mr. Buckley.

"Is there something amusing, Liza?" he asked, and that wiped the smile off her face fast enough.

"No, sir," she said, stealing a sidelong look at me that I did not much care for. She and Millie were rising to go just as Agnes was finishing my tray. I followed them into the corridor and stepped on Liza's skirt, holding her back.

"Hey, hey!" she cried, and I kicked at her. She gave a little yelp, though I could barely feel her through her petticoats, and knew she was only surprised.

"What was that now?" I hissed at her.

She scowled. "I ain't going to say a word, anyhow."

I stepped on her foot. "I saw you looking at me. What's that you've got to say that you're too ashamed to say to my face?"

Liza pulled her foot out from under mine and huffed, "Only that she's got caught out at last, and serves her right."

I stepped back. "Caught out?"

"You heard me," Liza said. "Everybody knows it. She can't have gone on about it as long as she has without getting caught out. Won't nobody say it before you or before Miss Porter, but we all knows it just the same."

"Gone on about what, exactly?" I said, and Liza looked surprised by the chill in my voice.

"Why, the way she and Miss Graham go on. You or me was to tipple like that and they'd toss us out in the gutter, but them being ladies nobody says a word. Well, it shows you what comes of it.

Always a head in the mornings after a party, hasn't she? Takes her breakfast tray like a married lady in her room. That ain't proper."

She stood, fixing me with a look both smug and frightened, proud at her boldness and fearful of what her honesty might cost. I narrowed my eyes at her. "I had not realized, Liza, that you had become an expert on propriety. Perhaps, with your newfound airs, you might ask Mrs. Harrison to be promoted to something more promising than the bluing."

She bit her lip then, for, as I had imagined, she had been taken to task in the time that I had been in with Charlotte. I just narrowed my eyes and said, "Get on with you," and watched her scurry off. I felt my knees weaken when she was gone, and it was only that I was still holding Charlotte's tray that I managed to keep upright. Relief washed through me, and I thought, *We are still safe, we are still safe,* in time with my tread up the stair.

Charlotte seemed a figure of wax, lying motionless against the pillows in the exact posture that I had left her. Her lids fluttered as I came in with her tray, but she did not open them. She sniffed delicately.

"What have you brought, Ballard?" she asked without opening her eyes.

"Mrs. Harrison has sent up some chamomile, very fine stuff, miss."

Charlotte raised her lids and sighed as though the thought of chamomile was terribly trying.

"It will do you good, miss." She was regarding me with suspicion. "You needn't touch anything but the chamomile, Miss Charlotte."

She nodded once, and I set the tray down on her nightstand, pouring out some tea before coming over with the cup and saucer. I sat myself down on the edge of the bed and held the cup to her lips. She sipped very slowly.

"There now, miss, can you hold it yourself? Good, good. Let me bathe your face again."

Charlotte held the cup listlessly in her lap while I poured some water from the ewer into the basin and added a few drops of oil of verbena. I looked at her over my shoulder. With her auburn curls spread out against the pillow behind her and her porcelain face, she looked like a doll. "Take a sip now, Miss Charlotte." She obeyed woodenly, reinforcing the image. I returned to the bed with a damp cloth and pressed it gently against her temples. She caught at my fingers with one hand and squeezed them tight.

"My dear Ballard. You are so good to me."

She held my fingers in hers, so close to her face that her breath, foul with her sick and sweet with the chamomile, warmed them. I wanted to reach out and stroke her cheek and kiss her and tell her that all would be well, and in some madness I think I began to lean in when she squeezed my fingers again and released me.

"I think you had better tell my mother I shan't be able to join them for dinner," she said.

I raised my eyebrows sharply, but said only "Oh, really now, miss, I shouldn't think that needful. I daresay Mrs. Walden hasn't even risen yet."

She favored me with a thin smile. "Oh, very well, you can tell her later. I don't blame you when she's bound to make such a stir." Her eyes darted back to the tray. "What else did Mrs. Freedman send up?"

"Some hot milk with an egg beaten in."

Charlotte sighed again, very deeply. "I suppose I shouldn't disappoint her by sending it back untried."

"Just a sip, miss," I said, holding the cup to her lips. She drank a little down, smiled, and took the cup on her own. "Not too quickly now," I cautioned. I sat next to her as she took alternating sips of the tea and the egg posset, so very slowly finishing them both. After she was done, I rose to take the tray back to the kitchen when she plucked at my sleeve.

"Oh, don't leave me, Ballard!" she cried, looking suddenly more fretful than I'd seen her. "Suppose it doesn't stay down?"

I left the tray outside the door and pulled the bell. Agnes would be in a pout over all the extra work, but it was no concern of mine. Agnes had exasperated me enough for one day, and it was not yet ten. *Fuck Agnes,* I thought as Charlotte held her arms out to me, and I came and settled onto the bed next to her. She nestled herself in my arms, and I rested my chin atop her head.

"Please," she whispered, "please just stay here with me. I don't know why I should be so unwell."

I shushed her gently. "Now, now. It's that Mr. Dawson should be ashamed of himself."

Charlotte gave a weak little laugh. "He's not a bad sort, I suppose."

I made a face. "I'm sure he's a very fine gentleman, miss."

"I suppose," she said. "Mother has been dangling me before him all season, and I suppose I could do worse, but it galls, Ballard, to let her drive me like a lamb to slaughter."

I forced a brittle laugh. "Slaughter, miss? I had not thought the prospect of marriage so grim."

She blushed furiously and said, "No indeed, I had not thought but that I should marry, of course. I should merely like to be the one who decides, in the end."

I stroked her hair. "We are not all so lucky as to choose our fates, miss," I said. "Mrs. Walden wishes only to see you comfortable and settled. If not Mr. Dawson, miss, then who?"

She let the weight of my words hang for a moment and then said softly, "I don't particularly care to speak of Mr. Dawson, Ballard."

"Then," I said, quite relieved, "let us speak no more of him."

We lay there in silence for some time, and by and by Charlotte's breath slowed and she became slack and heavy in my arms. I lay back against the pillows, hardly daring to breathe lest I mar the sweetness of her weight against me. In the end, my arm went numb, and I carefully slid it out from under her. She stirred a little as I arranged her against the pillows and returned to my needlework in my customary chair by the window. Though she might wish to fall asleep in my arms, I knew better than to risk the coldness or shyness she was wont to display upon waking up in them.

By the afternoon, Charlotte had recovered herself and decided she would go down to dinner after all. It was just as well, for the Grahams were expected, and Mrs. Walden would not countenance entertaining even her own family without Charlotte in attendance. I had the right of it anyhow, for when Mrs. Walden did finally rise, she had a head as well, or so I surmised from Grace, who was as protective of her mistress's indisposition as she was put out by it. I was fastening a cameo on Charlotte when Mrs. Walden made her first call on her daughter.

There were many things I could say about Grace Porter; she was a prude and a bore and a busybody, but she was an unimpeachable lady's maid. Augusta Walden looked positively regal in her gown of emerald velvet. Grace had decked her in amber beads and tortoiseshell combs and powdered every suggestion of a line or shadow from her face. I was always a little afraid of her, even though I well knew the effect was achieved through hours of artifice. Still, the temperature of the room lowered by degrees when she entered it. Charlotte and I both looked at her in the mirror as she prepared to speak.

"I received Mr. Dawson's card this morning," Mrs. Walden said, brandishing it. "I have invited him to dine on Monday next." The words were spoken calmly, without a hint of the threat or a challenge that must be inferred. I looked to the carpet, half-expecting she had thrown a glove.

Charlotte's smile did not quite reach her eyes as she replied, "How lovely. Do order a game course, for he is an avid hunter, you know."

Augusta Walden narrowed her eyes, immediately suspicious of such pliancy in her daughter, but when no biting second remark followed, she nodded, allowing herself a small, satisfied smile. "An excellent notion, my dear."

When she left, Charlotte caught my eye in the mirror. "Well," she said, frank relief suffusing her features, "that was painless enough."

We laughed. In the mirror I watched our two red mouths, our two sets of white teeth, unladylike and wide.

Charlotte was in very fine spirits when she came up to bed. From the kitchen, I had heard her and Miss Graham exhibiting on the pianoforte. Charlotte Walden had a very fine voice, a smooth and low alto, while Prudence Graham's was a high and lilting soprano. It was Prudence who tended to play, her long, thin fingers fluttering nimbly over the keys. Sometimes when Grace and I would watch them from beyond the fringed curtain that separated the parlor from the dining room, I would see her close her eyes and become so lost in the music emanating from her fingertips that she forgot to sing. Such lapses would, of course, occasion much good-natured teasing from her mother and sister, and Miss Graham would then be obliged to blush and say what a ninny she was, but there was something wounded in her eyes and pitying in Charlotte's that gave me pause. To Grace Porter, such lapses were merely evidence of

Charlotte Walden's superior accomplishments, as she would never be silenced on the subject when we were back in the kitchen, but I could not but feel for the girl. Were she any common miss, she might have been in a way to play more, but for the heiress of the Graham diamond mines, music must be forever relegated to one of the many accomplishments—with riding, and needlepoint, and languages, and dance—that were all calculated to attract a husband.

I have always thought it was the most bitter injustice that gentlemen of means are encouraged to develop those talents in which they show promise, for these accomplishments are but an ornament to their attractions in society, while a young lady of means diminishes her worth when she seeks to cultivate a particular talent. Those skills or arts, which only serve to heighten a gentleman's appeal and showcase his industry in practicing them, become a liability for a young lady, for such industry smacks of occupation or, at best, unmannerly exhibitionism—neither of which society will tolerate in the female sex. Worse, the level of knowledge and skill such demonstrations of mastery must reveal is telling of those unfeminine qualities—education and ambition—which no marriageable young lady of good family would think to betray. Prudence Graham might speak of her admiration for Liszt—just then coming into vogue—or his mentor Beethoven—still shocking to New York society matrons—if she could bear to do it in the prosaic terms in which any young lady with an appreciation of the musical arts might be acquainted. That she was incapable of doing so without praising the merits of those composers' techniques insinuated a mastery or, worse, an intimacy with contemporary composition that many of her set found unsettling, if not distasteful.

Charlotte Walden did not herself indulge in her aunt's passion for music. She was a lovely and accomplished singer, and, as such, harbored a tempered admiration for modern composition. She was well informed enough to converse fluently with Prudence on her aunt's singular passion, and gifted enough to follow the accompaniments in which Prudence delighted, but there was lacking in her execution Prudence's curious loss of self in the performance. I well knew what it was to feel so deeply and be denied.

There was something musical still in Charlotte's tone as I undressed her, and I put her to bed satisfied that Mr. Dawson and his liberality with the champagne had done my mistress no lasting damage. Thus it was that, two mornings later, I awoke with a start in my little closet as I heard Charlotte tumble out of bed and retch again into her chamber pot. I stood in the doorway, my shawl thrown over my shift, as she looked balefully up at me, her eyes red-rimmed, her knuckles white. I was at her side in a moment, snatching a flannel from her washstand and dabbing at her lips, pouring her cool water. Dawn's thin light was edging its way in through the gap in the curtain. Charlotte shuddered helplessly as I guided her back into her bed, tucking the eiderdown under her chin and smoothing the stray curls from her forehead. She sunk back to sleep almost instantly, but I was too worried for her health, which had been growing so fragile all winter, that I dressed and went belowstairs. Charlotte did not ring until nearly nine, and, when I brought up her tray, she devoured the contents. I examined her as she ate, but her eyes were bright and her cheeks rosy, and so I dismissed her indisposition as a freak.

It was not until the pattern had gone on for over a week that I began to suspect. When, on Sunday, I heard the now-familiar splash of her sick, I roused myself, and, realizing that my monthlies had come, made to blot up my spot of blood before throwing on a wrapper and attending to my mistress. Once I had helped her back into bed, I took more care in arranging my rags before making myself neat and dressing. I noted to myself to ensure I had extra flannels on hand for when Charlotte's blood came, as it always did, a day or so after mine. By Tuesday, however, when Grace came into the kitchen intimating Mrs. Walden's indisposition, I went cold, for now it was two days gone by and Charlotte showed no signs of bleeding. I thought then with a chill of her retching, of her rosy skin, of the fact that I was lacing her stays looser though she had not yet bled. A fear shot through me. It could not be. It could not be. Was there some other cause that kept women from their courses? Could there be any reason, anything other than the one that filled me with such fear? The kitchen fire became suffocating; I could not think. My face felt suffused with flame.

When Charlotte rang, I bolted up the stairs.

She had been ill again, though a week of the habit had wearied her to it. She passed the back of her hand over her lips, grown chapped now. Her cheeks were flushed, her eyes feverishly bright.

"I think, Ballard," she said, easing herself into the tufted chair, "perhaps it is time I asked Mother to send for Dr. Carlyle. I cannot remember last when I was so indisposed."

"Miss," I said softly, "your mother is in bed with her courses."

Charlotte frowned. "That is very strange, for does she not usually take to bed when I do?"

I settled a blanket over her knees, tucking it around her legs as I chose my next words with care. "It is most unusual, miss, for I cannot think of a time when you were not abed at the same time. Indeed—forgive me, Miss Charlotte—but I cannot wonder if your indisposition has . . . stayed your courses, somehow?"

"Stayed them?" said Charlotte. "Why, I know of no malady that stays one's courses."

"I would not call it a malady, miss. Perhaps . . . some other affliction."

"Some other affliction . . ." she said wonderingly, and she froze, the roses fading quickly from her cheeks. Her eyes, as she fixed them on me, were quite wild. Before us was the breach we'd neither of us attempted to cross before this moment; the unspoken secret lay yawning between us. I did not trust myself to speak, and held my two trembling hands out to her. She took them and I knelt before her, so close, so close, and I felt her pulse throbbing in her slender wrists.

"You know?" she whispered hoarsely.

"I know it all, miss."

"Ballard," she said. "Ballard, what have I done?"

"Oh, miss," I sighed.

"I have been such a fool, Ballard. Oh god, I've been such a fool."

"No, miss, no," I said, roughly wiping away the tears that had sprung to my eyes. "It's him that's to blame."

Charlotte groaned. "Oh, Ballard, I am ruined!" She tossed her arms about my neck and, shaking, commenced to weeping softly. I stroked her back, and she slid down from the chair and I cradled her as she wept in my arms there on the floor. I buried my face in her hair and let myself weep into the auburn waves coming unbound from her braid, the scent of her hair oil perfuming my tears. And we sat there, joined in misery, for what could I do now to comfort her?

At last, I said, "He would marry you, you know."

Charlotte laughed bitterly. "Marry me? My god, Ballard, do you expect me to be the wife of a stable groom?"

I shuddered at the harshness of her words. "No, of course not, miss."

She sniffed, sitting up, her arms still twined in mine. "Do not mistake me, Ballard. I love him. Yes," she said vehemently when she saw the look on my face. "Oh yes, I love him. But I never did intend to marry him." She shook her head ruefully, tears streaming down her cheeks. I reached up and wiped them gently away. "I begin to think I never knew what I intended. Oh, he was clever, and he seduced me, but I let him because I wanted him to. I gave up my virtue and my pride for him. I was willing to be his whore."

"Oh, miss!" I cried, shocked by her words. "You mustn't say such things."

"Why not, Ballard? It is nothing less than the truth. I was his whore, and I have reaped a whore's wages. That is the matter, and I cannot change it."

I sighed. "You cannot change it. But you might yet undo it."

She looked at me sharply. "What do you mean?"

I wet my lips. "There are ways of casting it off."

"I do not know, Ballard," Charlotte said. "I could not be seen calling a midwife."

"There are other ways, I think," I said. "There is someone I know who could give me the answer."

"What if they can't?"

I sighed. "There's no use in thinking about such a thing until that time comes. This person will know what to do. But if she doesn't, I suppose you shall have to sing again for Mr. Dawson, and something very sweet this time."

> If you wish to be happy, avoid all such [tales of love and adventure], for they will only fill your fancy with vain images, and make you hopelessly wish for miraculous events that never can happen.
>
> —*The Duties of a Lady's Maid*

Each month since the summer I had taken my Sunday afternoons off and gone down to Chambers Street. Each time, I half-hoped and half-feared Liddie Lawrence would be from home, and each time I sunk gratefully into her proffered arms. My first visit, I was awkward and afraid, sitting politely on the edge of the chair she offered, talking woodenly of the weather. She did not allow me to suffer long.

"Now then, Mary Ballard," she said merrily, "do you really care at all if it is very warm for the season, or did you not come here to fuck me again?" She rose up from her seat and took me by the hand. "For you see, I don't care to talk about the weather. I had much rather you kiss me." She led me to the divan, where we made love slowly and languidly in the afternoon heat.

Afterwards, she posed me naked on the divan, unpinning my hair, arranging it carefully, and cautioning me to stay very still before taking up a chair across the room. She made me watch, unmoving, as she pleasured herself with a rapid, practiced hand until my breath came quickly and I was moaning for her again. She took her time, letting her nimble fingers tease and play with me until I was begging her to finish me. She laughed at my shocked expression when she licked her fingers clean.

But in the perfumed arms of Liddie Lawrence, I learned as much of pain as I did of pleasure. Though she would take no coin for her services, my visits to Liddie cost me dearly, as, in her sweet and terrible way, she exacted from me the story of my great love for Charlotte Walden.

Do you know what a whore will cost you, when you seek her embraces to quell the memory of another? It is nothing more or less than this: the tenderness of your own heart. When you are filled with need and longing, she will take it from your body, and, thinking that your body is now free of it, you will not notice that it has filled up your heart. And so, to free yourself from the need and longing, you will go to her again, that she might bring your body the warmth and solace it so craves. Sated, you shall think you are cured, but the longing in your heart, which cannot be satisfied with the caresses of another than she who inspired it, will grow. It will fester. Then, with each visit, your heart will ache and harden more quickly, until the needs of your body are a trivial thing and the needs of your heart burn and consume. A whore will fill the needs of your body until you are spent, but she cannot help you spend the longing in your heart. I paid with all the naïve tenderness that I had, and each time I kissed Liddie while dreaming of Charlotte, my heart grew more and more callused. In this way, she gave me the armor I needed to continue on in that house, watching my mistress fall more deeply in love with my brother every day.

Do not think I was ungrateful to Liddie, or that I was not fond of her. For years, I had ached with the shame and need of desiring Charlotte Walden, and in Liddie I found the sweetness of release. But each time I visited her, I left more and more callused, for it was not her for whom I burned, and my love for Charlotte had blossomed and flowered and grew thorns that wrapped around my heart. It was not long before Liddie had the whole story from me, and I think that my pain and longing brought her pleasure, for often she would make me tell over my passion for Charlotte as she undressed me, kissing my neck and breasts so that I might continue to talk, and, when she moved my hands to her body, I would find her already wet and willing, though I had done nothing but recite my sorrows.

Her life, as I slowly learned of it, was so different from my own in every way. Olivia Lawrence had been born in the same London brothel as her eighteen-year-old mother. It was an exclusive establishment that catered to gentlemen of "exotic" tastes, though none of the patrons seemed wise to the fact that their "Oriental Lilies" and "Abyssinian Princesses" were often Londoners born and bred. Georgiana Lawrence's grandmother had been imported from Bermuda, and, while the current proprietress of the house would have been shocked at the notion that she considered any of her courtesans slaves per se, it was clear that she felt the residents were all her property to one degree or another.

Georgiana Lawrence had been three years at the trade when a Mr. Arnold of the Theatre Royal struck a bargain with the Lady Abbess for Georgiana's services backstage. Drury Lane was eager to retain its temperamental Macbeth, who, of late, seemed far more interested in taking late-night gallops through London on his stallion, Shylock, or romping with the tame lion cub he kept in his dressing room than he did in arriving for his performances on time or sober. He talked endlessly of wishing to tour America—when not half-drowning himself in the most convenient decanter of brandy. Mr. Arnold, charged by the trustees with keeping the theater's most lucrative leading man happy, sober, and treading the boards, had decided that the surest way of ensuring that the wayward actor focused on the theater was to capitalize on one of his less reckless eccentricities and install a courtesan in his dressing room for the run of the production.

Georgiana proved to be a perfect solution to management's problem. Her striking looks being enough to satisfy the actor's desires for the "exotic," and she being creative enough in her seductions to retain his interest, the arrangement was deemed so salubrious to all parties that it continued past the run of *Macbeth,* and, before a twelvemonth was out, Georgiana found herself playing Desdemona to his Iago, Ophelia to his Hamlet, and Juliet to his Romeo, all from the comfort of his dressing room. By the time he had transformed yet again—this time to Timon of Athens—she was growing, as the Earl of Gloucester in *Lear* might have said, round-wombed, and had, indeed, a child for her cradle ere she had a husband for her bed. Not that she had been expecting a husband; Edmund Kean was already married.

"Edmund Kean?" I asked, incredulous. "You're saying you're the natural daughter of Edmund Kean?"

"Oh," Liddie said brightly. "You've heard of him?"

"Of course I've heard of him! You might well ask me if I've ever heard of Shakespeare himself!"

Liddie rolled her eyes. "Well, it's only you've never seemed to notice when I mention Shakespeare at all, and you said yourself you never visit the theaters. How was I to know if you knew who Edmund Kean was?"

"It's my job to know what's in vogue, and that generally means more than necklines. My mistress is very fond of the theater. Did you ever see him perform?" I asked. "I'd be mad to if it was me."

"I saw his Henry V at Drury Lane back in 'thirty," she said. "And his Othello in 'thirty-three. That was his last role, you know. He was onstage with his son."

I covered my mouth with both hands, thrilled. "You saw him and Charles Kean? Your brother, you mean? Was there, that is, could you see any resemblance?"

She snorted. "First of all, I was in the balcony, and not much in a position to examine features. Secondly, I take after my mother almost entirely. And anyway," she went on as I made a wry face, "I couldn't say with any certainty if I was his natural daughter or not. He was hardly my mother's only patron during that time. Mr. Arnold paid her well, of course, but he never said it was an exclusive engagement. So it could have been anybody, I suppose. Though Mama always did like to think it was him. She was very fond of him, of course."

Georgiana had named her daughter after the countess in *Twelfth Night,* as Kean had hoped—in vain—that Drury Lane might let him play Malvolio. "Tragedies," he had told Liddie's mother balefully, "they only ever want to let me play tragedies. They never realize that dying is easy; comedy is hard."

Though discarded by Kean during her pregnancy, Georgiana's reputation had been made with his patronage. "Mama," Liddie said, "was ever after a very great favorite with the actors and the opera players. The ones who fancy girls at all, I mean. It's not just the likes of Kean who have a taste for a bit of something exotic, you know. And the poets! You should see the lines they wrote her. She kept them all, every phrase, be they well or ill turned. 'My dusky rose,' 'thou ebon idol,' 'oh, maiden of the moonless night!' You'd not believe," she said, taking a drag from her cigarette and rolling her eyes expressively, "how many ways there are to say 'black' when you're a poet. Lord, what fools these mortals be!"

Liddie had been raised as the pet of the brothel, often dressed up as a miniature lady and called upon to declaim for gentlemen waiting for their chosen paramours to become available. She could read as well as any lady, and far better than I could myself. Like her mother, she had a taste for Shakespeare, and owned a battered copy of his complete works that had been her mother's parting gift before she had come over the sea. Liddie had joined her mother's profession early, the stage, of course, being off-limits owing to the color of her skin. Though growing as popular amongst the patrons as her mother had ever been, Liddie hoarded her earnings until she had enough to buy passage to New York, and a fresh start, just over a year ago, that she might not have to whore her entire life under the Abbess's overbearing thumb.

"What happened?" I asked, as we lay together by the fire.

She shrugged, the coverlet slipping down and exposing her shoulder. "I'm willful, I suppose, and I like being my own mistress. Life was easier in the brothel, but my time—my life—was never my own. I rowed with the Abbess, and she made things harder for me, till I could not bear it. There are ways," she said wryly at my uncomprehending look, "that brothel life can be easier or harder. Who they have you go with. What you get for it in return. I wasn't biddable, and Lady Abbess likes the girls biddable. I thought it would be easier to set up here than in London. I'm an independent sort, and isn't that why people come to America, after all?"

"No, I mean, after you got here, what made you go back to stargazing?" I pressed.

An unreadable expression slid across Liddie's face, her features blurring for a moment before solidifying into a blank mask. She had sat up, and was looking at me solemnly. "What do you mean 'go back to stargazing'?" she asked.

I was sitting up now as well, and suddenly found I could not quite meet her eyes. "You'd said you wanted a fresh start . . . I thought you meant . . . that is . . ." I looked up at her, helplessly. "I mean, you never really wanted to do . . . all this!"

Liddie raised an eyebrow appraisingly. "You certainly didn't object to 'all this' a moment ago, did you?"

"I only meant—well, but you're clever! You could do anything you liked!"

"And what makes you think," Liddie said very slowly, "that I am not doing exactly what I like?" I opened my mouth and then shut it again, my cheeks aflame. Liddie snorted; it was an ugly sound. "That's queer. I never did peg you for the sort that objected to a woman's pleasure, seeing as you've no qualms about taking your own."

I was silent, my stomach curdling in shame.

"Tell me, Mary, why I should prefer another trade? Even if I had the patience for needlework, I don't much fancy going stitch-blind by the time I'm thirty. I could try my hand at maiding, but, and no offense meant, Mary" (I winced at that), "but the wages don't seem worth all the bother. You might not care overmuch for my profession, but I can't see how you stomach yours—running hither and thither at another woman's whim with barely ever a moment to yourself." She got up, wrapping the coverlet about herself and leaving me bare, pulling one of her cigarettes from her reticule and lighting it on the lamp. "I've no inclination for any trade at all, save the one I was born to, and, without the Lady Abbess fussing the life out of me, it isn't such bad work. I can pick myself who I'll have without the Abbess's orders. I make enough to keep my own quarters and save a bit, and one day when I have enough I'll open a brothel of my own. Keep the girls gently, too. No, it isn't such bad work, after all, no matter what you might think of it."

I had always thought that no one could choose whoring if they'd wit enough to do anything different, but Liddie had turned this notion of mine deftly on its head. She sat on the divan, looking down at me, still naked on the rug before the fire. She took a drag and crossed one leg over the other expectantly.

"Here is the part, Mary Ballard, where either you decide you're too good to keep a whore's company and find your way to the door, or you find a damn good way to say pax instead."

I took a slow breath in, pulling myself up onto my knees. "There's another perk, you know, to fucking a lady's maid."

"And what is that, might I ask?"

"In service," I said, uncrossing her legs and pulling the coverlet from her, "we learn to grovel very prettily."

After that, we hadn't quarreled over something as irrelevant as the benefits or drawbacks to either of our professions again.

As I had taken Liddie into my confidence, she took me into hers. In our afternoons together by the fire, she told me stories of her first few months, how dirty and rough New York had seemed after her life growing up in Mayfair, and how she'd learned the way and flavor of New York's streets, and how she'd made do to see herself over the rough patches of her arrival.

Liddie had ambition, and a determination to see her ambitions through, that I couldn't help but admire. She had taught herself reckoning, and kept an account book to track her earnings. She routinely observed the better brothels in the area, and now and again bribed the porters—with coin or with her person—to tell her the quantities of provisions for that month, how many times the midwife had come, and various other daily details of running such an establishment. She had a separate account book in which she tallied the estimated costs of her own future brothel, and had calculated that she would be stargazing herself for only five or six more years before she had earned enough to cover the opening costs. For someone like myself, who had never thought to want so much from life, let alone map out the way to such achievements, her grit was impressive indeed, and, with growing respect, I told her so.

She shrugged. "What vision I possess, I have inherited from my mother. She helped me save to come here, and it would be a poor repayment if I did not achieve everything I set out to do. She helped me put away everything she could, though she wasn't keen on staying with the Abbess herself, either. I can't forget that."

"Do you never hear from your mam?"

"Of course, now and again. The news is always three months old by the time it reaches me, but we do write regularly. She finally left the Abbess's house only a month or so after I came out to New York. Found a patron. A swell, a proper gentleman, who keeps her as a ladybird. Not one of her poets, but one of those who fancies himself a patron of the arts. She holds salons now—imagine!" She rolled onto her back, smoke pluming from her nostrils. "I do miss her, you know. When I've my establishment, I just might write and send her passage to come over to help me in the business. She'd like that, I think."

I lay back on a velvet pillow, running my hand absently against the nap, thinking of the people I'd left behind in Donegal, wondering if any of them ever spared a thought for Seanin and me. The house where we'd grown up, the only home we'd ever known, had come to seem so cold and alien by the time we saw the last of it. The faces we'd known all our lives, warm and welcoming, were turned against us when we left. If any of them spared a thought for either of us, it was more likely to be to mutter a curse and spit at the sound of our names. Then Liddie, with her uncanny way of sensing when I was troubling, nuzzled her lips against my neck, and slid a comforting hand between my legs.

Yet, after I had been with Liddie, it was worse, for, having tasted the pleasures of her flesh, I could not but imagine Charlotte Walden held in such similar embraces with my brother. Would her breath catch as Liddie's had? Would her head loll back, a lazy smile on her lips as Seanin thrust inside her? Could she, too, be caressed and cajoled into such acrobatic poses as Liddie held me? Often, I had pictured her in bed, which had been torment enough to me, but now I must imagine her pressed up against the wall next to her bookcase, bent over the ottoman, kneeling up against him in the tufted chair. The more enthusiastic Liddie became in our lovemaking, the more vividly I could imagine Charlotte's. When next I came home, these ordinary images—a pillow askew in the chair, a book out of place on the shelf—filled me with such bitter longing that I thought I must claw out my own eyes to stop from seeing them, or else go mad. I soon grew glad I could not visit Liddie above once a month, for I could hardly bear to look at Charlotte Walden again when I would come home. *Look what I have done, for wanting you,* I would think. *Look at what I have become. Look at me.* She never did.

> What crowds of drunken men are there, who will hardly suffer a modest girl to pass along unmolested! . . . what bold and impudent women, who ought not even to be looked at but with a sigh of pity or a frown of disapprobation!
>
> —*The Duties of a Lady's Maid*

I lay abed, fully dressed, waiting for the house to darken and quiet. The clock in the square tolled eleven before I rose and slipped from the house. I tiptoed through the mews, taking care my boots should not ring out on the cobbles, and, keeping to the shadows, I made my way down to the familiar house on Chambers Street.

It was a long way to walk at such an hour, and I took care not to be seen, for there were rough men about. I skirted west, beyond the gaslights and noise of Broadway, taking the long route west through the village, and three quarters of an hour later finally arriving down to the block of Chambers Street that Liddie called home.

I looked up from the street to see a light burning in her rooms, and so I tossed a handful of pebbles at her window. A few moments later, her face appeared in the casement, and she looked down frowning. I caught her eye, and she gasped. I saw her turn away, and I melted into the shadows of the building opposite to wait. Presently, the door opened and I turned away as I heard a man, angry and brusque, bustle from the building, knocking over a pile of empty crates with some vigor before marching away down the block. I slipped into the door he had left ajar and made my way up the narrow stair to Liddie's rooms.

She was seated on the divan, enveloped in a silk wrapper with her hair set in those stiff curls upon her shoulders. She was adding leaves to a teapot, and looked up at me with a curious expression on her face.

"Well now, Mary Ballard," she said. "I do not know if I should be pleased to see you, for I have just sent away someone very important for your sake. I hope you haven't come only for a taste of my quim."

I remained standing in the doorway. "I came because I did not know to whom else I might turn, and because it is a matter that could not wait until my next Sunday off."

She raised her eyebrows and motioned me to the seat opposite her, which I took gratefully after my long walk, though I left my bonnet pointedly on. She poured the tea and offered me a cup, looking at me over her rim as she sipped.

"I scarcely know where to begin," I said. "But you must know I should not have come had this not been a matter of some urgency."

Liddie laughed bitterly. "Never mind, I think I can guess. Indeed, I can think of only one thing so urgent that a fortnight's hesitation might further mar."

I drew back. "Then you know what to do?"

She had set her face into a grim smile. "Of course. I've done it a time or two myself." She looked at me hard. "I hope it was worth it, anyway. Who was he? A footman? The butler? You hardly seem the sort who'll bend for any of the roughs who hang about the Hibernian."

I set down my teacup and rose. "I think perhaps that we are at cross-purposes, Olivia Lawrence. I'm sorry I troubled you so late at night. Perhaps I should have known better than to interrupt when you were busy entertaining."

Liddie sat back in her chair, her wrapper falling further open and showing the swell of her breasts beneath. "You needn't be so high and mighty," she said with great disdain. "'O world, how apt the poor are to be proud!' In your condition, you might consider that you're past a whore shaming you."

I shook my head. "I am going now. Good night, Liddie."

"Wait," she said, hesitating. "Wait. Don't go. I'll help you. Good lord, Mary, I'm many things, but I'm not heartless." She looked at me, her face a cipher. I remained silent, and she shrugged at me. "I haven't got any on me just now, but I will get it for you."

I sat back down. "Get what, exactly?"

"It's a tea. Pennyroyal and cohosh. Mind you, it won't be pleasant, but it's meant to be a great deal better than the other way. I wouldn't know. The tea has always been enough for me. It'll cost three dollars."

"Three dollars!" I started, but she shook her head.

"The compliments of the house are over, I'm afraid," she said. "A castoff never comes cheap. It'll take me a day or two to get it. Can you come back on your night off?"

I nodded. "Thank you, Liddie."

Her lovely face twisted into a scowl as she drew the wrapper tight across her chest. "Well, I suppose it happens to the best of us."

The cool night air rippled through me as I stepped from the warmth and light of Liddie Lawrence's rooms and back into the gloom of the street. A fog had risen during our brief interview, and, grateful for the protection it gave, I hurried back to Washington Square to sleep for a few brief hours before sunrise.

The next day I spent worrying over the three dollars, which I could have got from Charlotte easily enough, I suppose. I had never spoken to her of money before; I could not even be sure she knew what my wages were. I could certainly afford to part with three dollars from the generous eighteen I got every month, though some cold part of my heart whispered that Johnny had rather pay than me. In the end, though, embarrassment over the role I had played in their liaison shamed me to silence, and I could not bring myself to ask either of them.

Charlotte had said nothing to me of averting Johnny's visit—what, I suppose, was the worst that could come of it now?—and so on Thursday, once I had finished my duties for the night, I hurriedly accepted my wages from Mrs. Harrison, my bread and cheese from Cook, and my cloak from Agnes, who had ironed it earlier in the day. I left four small stones in a perfect square on the floor of the Waldens' coach, my sign to Johnny that I had not waited but gone on ahead, and slipped out of the mews and on down to Chambers Street.

Liddie's rooms were locked and there was no answer when I rapped impatiently at her door. Furious at her, I sat down and was obliged to wait nearly half an hour in the dark hallway before at last she arrived. I heard her sharp, rapid footfalls as she came up the stair, and I scrambled to my feet, cheeks pink with the rage that had built in me as I waited. Yet, of course, I still needed Liddie and the parcel I prayed she had brought me, so when she came over the landing I said nothing.

She started when she saw me. "Oh," she cried. "I had not thought you would be so early."

"Have you got it?" I asked, and she wrinkled her nose at my businesslike tone.

"Inside," she said, gently pushing me away and turning her key. I waited in the doorway as she lit the lamps and disappeared into the bedroom. She returned with a small package wrapped in brown paper. "Have you got the money?" she asked.

I took the three dollars from my reticule and passed them over to her. She handed me the package, looking at me curiously. "You brew it into a tea," she said. "There is enough there for six doses. You drink two cups a day until your bleeding comes. There'll be some cramping and some sickness, so you'd best keep the chamber pot nearby. If the blood doesn't come in three days' time, well, I got the tea from a woman in Pitt Street who does a neat bit of crochet and lacework, if you take my meaning. She lives at number seventeen, on the third floor. But the tea has always been enough for me."

I nodded, not meeting her eye.

"If you like, I can brew you a cup now, so you'll see the proper proportions?"

"No, thank you all the same. Is there anything else?"

She thought a moment. "You had better tell your mistress you've got the flux, or that you have your monthlies, and you'll need to keep abed. It'll last as long as your courses usually last. Do be sure you have rags enough, for it'll be more blood than you're used to, and very dark colored. Don't mind it if you see any lumps or clots, that's meant to happen. Mary! You've gone green."

She motioned me to a chair and bent over me in concern for a moment before she suddenly reached out and grabbed my breast, squeezing hard. I gasped in pain and slapped her away. She stood up, rubbing her sore hand and grinning ruefully.

"Now, then," she said. "What's your game, Mary Ballard?"

"What are you on about?" I shrieked. "Christ almighty, that hurt!"

"You little ass," she said, sitting opposite me. "I thought it was for you!"

"It is," I said stubbornly.

"You're a poor fucking liar," she said, taking a cigarette from her reticule and moving the shade from the Argand lamp to light it. "If you were far enough gone to know it, your teats'd be rock hard and a great deal larger than they usually are. Trust me, for wouldn't I know? Come now, then. Who's it for?"

"Who the fuck'd you think?" I said bitterly.

Liddie puffed smoke angrily from her nostrils. "Well, he finally stuffed her up then? And here's you having to sweep up the mess? Ha! That's fine, then. Just fine."

"Oh, be quiet Liddie." I sighed. "I liked it better when you were angry with me."

"You're a fucking martyr," Liddie said. "The way you let them treat you like shit."

I rose. "I'm grateful to you, Liddie," I said, and turned to go.

Liddie leapt from her chair. "No, now, I can't let you go like that!" She wrapped her arms around me, holding her cigarette at length away from my hair, and kissed my cheek. "Come, Mary, don't be angry at me. Truly, I am sorry for the way I acted before. A bit jealous, I suppose. How's that for stupid?"

I squeezed her back. "It's all right," I said. "I didn't want you to know."

"Why ever not? I've nothing but compassion for you, you know."

I sighed. "That's just it, Lid. I don't want your compassion. It was simpler for me to have you be stern."

Liddie drew back and regarded me sadly before standing up on her tiptoes to kiss my forehead. "You're a good woman, Mary Ballard," she said softly. "You're a sight too good for all this shit."

I smiled as I squeezed her hand, and turned to go.

> Take care, therefore, never to brood over resentment which may, perhaps, be from the first ill-grounded, and which is always inflamed by reflecting upon an injury, real or supposed.
>
> —*The Duties of a Lady's Maid*

From Liddie's I took myself directly to the Hibernian, wrapping my shawl against the coolness of the night. The cobbles were slick, for a light mist fell, and I picked my way cautiously around puddles as I went. In the chill and the moisture, I could have been back in Donegal Town; only the smells were wrong. There, though the buildings were close and huddling, the scents of horse and sheep, of turf fire and spilled ale, of the sharp salt wind blowing its winding way in from the sea all mingled. Here, as I drew closer to the Five Points, the smell of chamber pots, offal, and the sick-sweet reek of slaughter houses ran together with the dank, brackish smell of the rivers and the bay. The wind was yet chill, its breath running a clean sigh through the miasma of the city.

I had never made the walk from Liddie's to the Hibernian before, and as I hurried past the side streets coming up from downtown, I heard a whistle or two from doorsteps and alleys as I passed. I wrapped my shawl tighter and kept my face straight ahead, paying these dubious compliments no mind. There will always be the rougher sort of man who will think a girl alone is gay, and that he might speak whatever discourtesies he pleases as she goes by. From the shadows, I heard voices calling out to me lewd suggestions of what their owners would like to do if they could get their hands under my skirts. I felt my cheeks burning as I tried to ignore them, bustling along, wishing that my brother was by my side.

It was well before midnight when I arrived, but I was tired and felt grateful to see warm golden light streaming from the Hibernian's door. Dermot nodded to me as I entered, and, seeing none of Johnny's usual companions about, I made straight for him at the bar.

"You're a sight earlier than I've seen you in a year or more now," he said, pouring off a mug for me. "Where's himself now?"

"Ah, he'll be along," I said. "Sure and why should I wait on him always when I've you for company, Dermot?"

He shook his head. "Ah, Mar. You've always kept your own counsel, the two of you."

I met his eye. "And there's things then, Dermot O'Brien, that don't bear repeating, for the truth is there's no profit by it."

"That's the truth," he said. "But don't think I don't know the look of her that's in over her head, Mar. You're a hard one to read, but, aye, that much's plain. You'll always have me ear, lass, if ever you find need of it."

I laughed, tried not to wince at the forced sound. "Ah, go on, Dermot. You'd not want to hear me complain of maiding in so sweet a cut as you found for me."

There was no trace of mirth in his face as he replied, "I'll not force your counsel, Mar, but you'll always have me ear." He turned to the tide of patrons swelling the bar, eager to spend their recently paid wages. I turned to my beer, though Quigley and MacBride arrived soon after and joined me at the bar. MacBride had brought his sister, Annie, a kitchen maid at one of the new estates off the pastureland up by Fourteenth Street, who rarely ventured so far down into the city proper on her nights off. I had met Annie a time or two before, since she had come out from Londonderry last year, and liked her well enough. She was just seventeen and she meant to be head cook someday. I liked her ambition, liked to hear a girl who'd been born on a country estate—same as myself—speak so knowledgably of the five French sauces she was learning to make. It was a relief to hear about Annie MacBride's simple worries and wonder to myself how sauce could "break" and say a silent prayer of thanksgiving that when, in my line of work, something broke, I could generally mend it with a needle and thread. Or, the thought intruded, a packet of tea. Ruthlessly, I forced myself to stop thinking of Charlotte for just one evening and turned my attention back to Annie, her eyes bright and cheeks flushed with ale.

When Johnny came in, an hour later, I nodded stiffly at him, drained my mug, and wordlessly maneuvered Annie MacBride to a bench closer to the fire and away from the knot of men who had gathered around our brothers. I could listen to Annie's cheerful chatter, but the thought of keeping up a pleasant veneer around Johnny at the moment was more than I could countenance. It was cozy in the corner, and I was grateful to be out of the way.

Annie was practically nodding on my shoulder by the time MacBride came to collect her home. I said farewell, and, noting that Johnny was still otherwise engaged, headed down to our pallet in the cellar. The damp air was chilly and the fire was dying. I built it back up before undressing, settling myself into the warmth of the blankets, staring at the flickering flames until I was overcome by sleep. I never heard Johnny come down the stairs, nor stirred when he got under the covers beside me.

> Your situation as a confidential upper servant, will often bring you into conversation with your employers, and if you have a pleasing and affable manner, they will have you more with them than may perhaps be proper for you.
>
> —*The Duties of a Lady's Maid*

It took all three days for Liddie's tea to work. It smelled bitter and foul, an impression confirmed by Charlotte Walden, who shuddered and made faces as she bolted it down. The first two days went by with no change in Charlotte's state, but on the evening of the third day she was stricken with cramps that set her doubled over and retching. The blood came a day later, dark and clotted as Liddie had predicted, and I grimly mopped her brow as I watched Charlotte cast forth my brother's child. Charlotte set her teeth and whimpered in pain, shivering with the flux that racked her slender frame. It was the flux that saved her from suspicion, though I feared as I watched her shudder over her chamber pot that it should kill her. Cook sent up basins of the clear broth that were all Charlotte could swallow, and Agnes took down the befouled chamber pots, replacing them with clean ones. I measured out tincture of peppermint with a dropper, mixing it into warm water for Charlotte to sip in between bouts. Feverish and aching, she would allow no one in the room save myself.

By the fourth day of purging, Mrs. Walden wished to call for the physician. Looking in briefly at her daughter, who lay moaning on the bed, she motioned me to follow her into the hall.

"Her symptoms, Ballard," Augusta Walden said, her voice sharp as ever, not quite matching her eyes, bright with worry. "Are they worsening? You have been a most attentive nurse, but I wonder now if I ought to send for Dr. Carlyle."

I considered this, chewing my lip in concern. Liddie had said that the castoff would take as long as Charlotte's courses typically took, and Charlotte was often abed for a week. Surely the doctor would know right away what was amiss? But what if something truly was amiss and the flux that accompanied the purge was weakening her even more than she let on? The weight of responsibility rendered me dumb, and Augusta Walden stared at me in my nervous silence, gripping her hands together so tightly her knuckles went white. I licked my dry lips and at last came to a decision.

"Let us see how she fares tonight, mum," I said. "If she is not better in the morning, then should you send."

She nodded crisply and turned away. I crept back into Charlotte's room to keep my grim vigil.

I barely slept that night, helping her to the chamber pot when it was needful, bathing her face when she lay still. By dawn, though, her fever had broke, and by midmorning the flux was ebbing. When evening came, it seemed the worst of Charlotte's malady at last was over, and I came to realize what terror had gripped me only when I began to feel it subside. As I tucked her into bed that night, her skin cool, her cramps subsiding, I gave a silent prayer of thanksgiving. *We are safe, we are safe, we are safe.*

The first night after Charlotte's illness subsided that I was able to join the rest of the household staff at supper, Johnny knocked over the pepper pot. Hours later, I stood in the dark of my little closet, debating with myself whether I would go or no. I was still dressed but still undecided when I heard the *tock* of Johnny's acorn against the glass, and with weary feet I slipped down the back stair to him. The house was dark, and, as the weather warmed, Agnes would be sleeping in the laundry, so I passed easily through the kitchen and out the door.

Even in the half-light of the moon, Johnny's face was lined with worry. His eyes were sunken, shadowed. He gripped my arm and pulled me into the shelter of the stable's eaves.

"Well?" he asked hoarsely.

I made a face. "She'll live."

"Christ, Mar—" he began, but I cut him off, pulling my arm from his grasp.

"Fuck, Johnny," I hissed. "Did you keep me out of bed for this?"

"Mar," he whispered brokenly, gripping my shoulders. "I was half-dead my own self with worry. There was talk belowstairs—"

I went stiff. "What kind of talk?"

He licked his lips and looked nervously toward the empty mews. "Cholera." I nearly laughed aloud in relief, and he dug his fingers into my shoulders, shaking me. "In God's name, what's the matter with you, Mar?" I laughed helplessly, and he shook me harder.

"Take your hands off me," I said, struggling against him. "Christ, what a fool. It wasn't cholera. She's resting easy now, Johnny."

He eased his hands from my shoulders, taking a great, shuddering breath. "When can I see her?"

I snorted. "Always thinking with your prick, aren't you? Used to have a sight more sense. You can see her when she's well enough to see you, and until then you stay the fuck away from her."

"Damn you, Mar," he said. "What've you got to be so stern for? I don't want to hurt her."

"Keep your voice down, you damn fool. It's a sight too late to fret about hurting her now, isn't it?"

He drew back from me. "When did I ever hurt her? Mar, did she say I did?"

I stared at him, his eyes wide in his hangdog face, and I shook my head. "She didn't," I said evenly, "say anything."

His face went slack with relief; he reached for my hand but I pulled away. "I'm tired, Johnny," I said. "I've been up nursing her for three nights now, barely slept a wink myself, living in fear of losing her. Let me go to bed."

"Aye, aye," he said distractedly. "I'd not thought—"

"You never do," I said, and, pulling away, I slipped back across the alley and into the house. I shut the kitchen door quietly and turned around to find Mr. Buckley standing in the door from his pantry, in his cap and robe.

"I say, Miss Ballard," he hissed loudly, his whispered voice ringing on the flagstones. "What on earth are you doing out-of-doors at this time of night?"

I froze, icy fingers closing over my heart before a sudden terror and inspiration propelled me toward him, clutching at the front of his robe. He started back, reeling from the impact as I fell against him.

"Oh, Mr. Buckley!" I cried. "I was in such a fright! There was a terrible large rat in the privy, sir!"

"Now then, Miss Ballard," he said, stepping back from me and straightening his robe. "It's only a rat. What on earth were you doing in the privy at this time of night?" I colored deeply and looked down, and he coughed a bit and said, "Well, never mind that now, never mind. I'll have Eben set one of the mousers on it in the morning."

"Oh, I wish you would, sir," I said. "It was a nasty creature, and I was nearly scared out of my wits. Thank you, sir." And, bobbing a curtsy, I fled up the stairs, leaving Mr. Buckley alone in the dark kitchen below.

> Pride that dines on vanity, says another proverb, sups on contempt: it neither promotes health nor eases pain, while it is certain to create envy and hasten misfortune.
>
> —*The Duties of a Lady's Maid*

It was Thursday again, and Charlotte, still weak from her ordeal, had not dined out all week. I brushed her auburn hair until it shone, rubbing oil into the ends so that they would not split or fray. I helped her into the bed, smoothing the sheets over her, and shut the door. She had said nothing to me, and so I had left my window unlocked, though it irked me to do so. I waited on the floor of the carriage, picking idly at my cheese for only about a quarter of an hour before I heard Johnny open the stable door. We walked in silence for several blocks; I stole glances at him, his face screwed up, his hands jammed into his pockets.

We said nothing until we were nearly to Mulberry Street, and then, just outside the door of the Hibernian, Johnny turned on me.

"What the fuck was the matter with her, Mar, if it wasn't the cholera?" he said fiercely. "She looked weak as water, but she wouldn't tell me a word."

I turned to go into the tavern. "If she hasn't told you yet, it's not for me to say."

He grabbed me roughly and shoved me up against the wall. "Goddamn it, Mar!" he growled. "I'm weary to death of all your sniping and your snideness. If you have something to tell me, you'd best fucking say it."

"Take your hands off me! I'll not say a fucking word! Why should I answer to you, you fucking git? Sure and I've done enough for you and her, more than you'll ever know, and do I have to answer to you for it all too?"

"Goddamn it, Mar! Either talk sense and do it now, or shut the fuck up."

"Go to hell, Johnny!" I said, and he struck my face. I cried out and went for his eyes, and he howled as I sunk my nails into his flesh. He flailed back blindly, and his balled fist connected with my nose. I felt something give and crack, and then the hot, metallic tang of blood filled my mouth. I pushed him over and we were down on the pavement, my fingers still going for his eyes, when I felt strong arms lifting me away from him. I kicked uselessly at the air as Dermot hauled me bodily into the alley.

"Mother of Christ, let me go!" I wailed, but the words came out broken and garbled, and Dermot sat me down heavily on an upturned crate. Men's raised voices echoed from the street as the pub's regulars came out to gawk at the disturbance.

"For fuck's sake, Mar," he said, taking out his handkerchief and handing it to me. I mopped at my face uselessly, for the thing became sodden in a matter of moments, and Dermot went in through the alley door to fetch a flannel from the bar. He held my face up to the light that spilled from the open doorway, turning my head roughly this way and that, and then, before I could protest, he had locked my head into the crook of his arm and was giving my nose such a wrench that I screamed out. He released me, and I ran questing fingers over my nose, out of which blood and snot were flowing freely. He inspected me, then nodded once, satisfied. "Should mend clean now."

I glared up at him balefully. “Why'd you pull me off?”

Dermot wiped his brow. “You were in a fair way to sink your nails into his eyes, and there's folk here that wouldn't have taken too kindly to that.”

“Don't take your meaning.”

“I mean”—Dermot sighed—“that while you've been drinking yourself sick and gadding about with that colored streetwalker—oh, aye, I know all about that—your brother's been talking more than horse rearing and politics. He's been making some friends who mightn't care to see you gouge out his eyes, and I mean more than Quigley and O'Mara and your other wee man there.”

“MacBride,” I said automatically, rubbing at the blood on my face and succeeding only in smearing the sticky mess about further.

“Aye, MacBride, right so.” He looked down at me. “Look here. You're a right mess, Mar. I'll bring some hot water down the cellar, eh? Get yourself clean.” He held out one of his hands and hauled me to my feet. “Boyo'll be sleeping elsewhere tonight.”

I let him guide me down the cellar stairs to my pallet, and waited dully while he brought me a basin and his shaving mirror. I was a pretty sight; both eyes had begun to ring in a ghastly greenish purple, with sticky smears of blood covering my nose and chin and mouth. Blood had run down my neck and dripped from my face and stained the neckline of my dress. Upon inspection, I found the stains had begun to seep into my shift, so I took both dress and shift off and soaked them until the water ran red, and I had to stand at the head of the stairs wrapped in the coverlet and holler up to Dermot for a fresh basin. He brought it quick enough, and a pint glass of whiskey besides, which he cautioned me to drink slowly. I rinsed and wrung my frock and shift, hanging them before the fire to dry, and sat sipping my whiskey and staring into the flames for a while before Dermot came down holding a set of his shirtsleeves and an old moth-eaten wrapper. He turned his back while I dressed, and then, sitting next to me on the pallet, our backs up against the brick wall, he produced a bottle of whiskey, which we sat and passed back and forth between us in silence.

At last he said, "I told you both when this first started I didn't want to hear about the cause." He looked at me and nodded at my surprise. "Oh, aye, I know well enough that whatever this foolishness is has been going on for well nigh over a year now."

I sniffed, which rather hurt in light of recent events. "How'd you know it was the same foolishness, then?"

Dermot shrugged. "'Cause since then, he's always buying the drinks, and 'cause that's around the time you started puking out back in my alley. Before that, you could always hold your liquor. I've got eyes, Mar. He's guilty about something, and you're angry about it, and, fools that you both are, you're sniping and rowing with each other instead of talking it out like civilized creatures. He's hurt you bad, Mar, that much is plain, but for all he knows he hurt you, he doesn't know how he's done it. Isn't that the way of it?"

I sighed impatiently and made to speak, but he held up a big hand and said, "I still won't press to know the cause, if you're unwilling. It's just there's only so much watching you can do when a lass makes up her mind to drown and will not clasp on no matter how much rope you throw her."

I shrugged. "Then, aye, that's the way of it, and if he can't see how he's hurt me he's a bigger fool than I ever dreamed of."

Dermot passed the bottle back to me. "Hadn't you better tell him then, if he'll not see it on his own?"

"Fuck that," I said, taking a swig and handing the bottle back to him. "Besides, it's bigger than the two of us, and it isn't mine to sort him out. Thanks for everything, Dermot."

He rested a hand on my shoulder and nodded. I lay down on my pallet and drifted off.

> You should strive to subdue in your mind all idle repining that it has not been your fate to be placed in such a rank, and that Providence, undoubtedly, for wise purposes, has ordered it otherwise.
>
> —*The Duties of a Lady's Maid*

I have memories, of course, from the steerage hold on the ship *Peregrine,* though I have learned, over the years, to push that hell down into the darkest recesses of my mind, where it belongs. There was seasickness, naturally, and scurvy as well, and no end to the reek of sick and shit, which sloshed about the floor. As a scullion and a groom in a big house, we were hardly what you would call gently reared, but even a life of blacking grates or mucking stalls was no preparation for the cramped, dark bunk on which we huddled while the sea pitched and heaved. All around us, voices cried out in the dark, praying for God to deliver us from the fickle ocean, punctuated by wailing, feral cries, and, sending shivers of horror down my spine, the keening for the dead. For death lurked all around us in the dark, as people died of empty bellies, of vermin, of disease. We survived, as others did, by divesting the corpses of what food or valuables we could before they were sewn into shrouds and tossed into the maw of the sea. I would dream at night on my foul bunk that I, too, had been sewn into a canvas tube and dropped down into the ocean. The water would fill my lungs, blackness would fill my eyes, and I would be screaming as Seanin shook me awake. Much of the voyage seems to me now as a fever dream—distorted and nightmarish and with no respite on waking.

When at last we disembarked, the land rose up in a sickening wave and I fell facefirst onto the muddy cobbles of New York. Mrs. Boyle's watered silk morning dress, which Seanin had pilfered from the laundry for me to wear on our journey, was now fetid and crumpled, torn and spattered with the grime from the street. Seanin scrambled to my side, and in helping me to rise was nearly struck himself as a carriage clattered by, splashing filthy water on us as it passed.

It was Seanin who found the shabby waterfront inn where we spent our first night in America, but it was I who nicked us new clothes from the laundry and dragged him into skipping out on the bill in the early hours before dawn. Seanin's shirt and pants were a bit larger than was fitting, but I fairly swam in the broad taffeta monstrosity I had stolen. I cursed bitterly the poor light in the hall and the slippery temptation of the fine taffeta as I pinned and hiked the wretched frock as well I could before we shimmied out the window and off down the stable roof. Having inquired as to our route the day before, we walked the two miles straight up through the Sixth Ward, all innocent of the geography of our new home. It was July, and the still, humid air was thick with the rank smells of fish, rotten meat, human sweat, and excrement. In the pale light before dawn, we made our way through the ward, the streets quiet as, from within the ramshackle buildings, the residents had just begun to stir.

The day broke on us cutting across Spring Street toward the Hibernian's perch on the corner of Mulberry. Seanin kept looking back over his shoulder nervously, as though he expected to be clapped into irons at any moment for the stolen clothes on his back.

The Hibernian was closed, of course. Seanin licked his lips nervously and said, "We ought just come back later, Mar."

I shot him a withering look and began pounding on the door, the bolt and chain rattling as I did.

"Quit it, Mar!" he said, trying to pull me away.

"Fuck it," I said, still banging. "I'll not stand about in the street all morning, nor walk back through that blight we just come through."

A roar issued from inside the tavern, and I left off my assault on the door as, through the thick, green glass, we could make out a figure approaching. The chain was pulled back, the bolt pulled, and a furious-looking man dressed only in his nightshirt glared balefully down at us.

"For fuck's sake," he bellowed. "What're you on about, you wee mad bitch?"

I stared up at him. "Sure and I expected better welcome from Colleen O'Brien's son."

His eyes went wide, and he shook his head, snorting. "You'll not be those snappers from up Ballyboyle Manor? It's barely daybreak! Get in, get in with you!" He ushered us into the tavern, shuffling behind the bar and pulling two mugs of ale and setting them out on the counter, running his hand through his hair. "Christ, but it's early for a tale of woe. Sit and have a drink. A fellow'll need his trousers and his wits both to deal with the likes of this shite."

He shambled off up the stairs, muttering darkly to himself, and Seanin turned to me. "Do you suppose he'll help us?" he asked.

I shrugged. "You're the one what had Colleen write him."

"The way Colleen keeps on, you'd think the sun shone out his arse."

"Well, he don't seem to have taken a shine to us, that's certain."

"She's the only person left to help us who knew someone in America. And I told you not to keep up that banging."

"Seanin O'Farren! Will you keep your fecking self still while I sort out the angle here? You give me a pain."

Seanin shrugged and took a swig or two of liquid courage while I sipped slowly, a plan forming in my head.

"The break of day comes at too early an hour to contemplate business best conducted in shadow." Dermot took up his customary place behind the bar and regarded us skeptically. I was sure we made a sorry pair. "Well, now then." He ran his hands again through his thick, graying hair. "So it's work you want, eh?" He chuckled, rubbing the sleep from his eyes. "Don't know what kind of coin for what manner of work you're used to in the Old Country, but this town ain't for the soft."

I tossed my head with a confidence I did not feel. "There's none's as called us soft before. If there's work to be had, we can do it. Meself and me brother too. We're used to hard work up at the big house on the estate."

"Well, it's plain you're used to dirty work," he said wryly. "What can you two do?"

I chewed my lip a moment, calculating, before replying in the ubiquitous, mumbling lilt of the underclasses, "I were a lady's maid at the Boyles' big house in Donegal. And me brother were head groom."

He chuckled at the audacity of this, as well he might. "Go on. You never were."

It had been an absurd claim, but his casual refutation of it infuriated me into stamping my foot at his laughter. I raised my chin, and, breathing in deeply, took the time to look him in the eye and hold his gaze before putting my plan into action. "I was the personal maid to her ladyship, and dressed her hair, and drew her bath, and laced her stays, and buttoned her gowns, and every other goddamn thing." My voice had changed, the heavy country accent that came naturally to me melting away and taking on the clipped, respectable qualities of the ton. I'd straightened my posture, holding myself erect, and adopted a look of mild disdain for the public house in which we all stood.

Dermot raised an eyebrow, his only outward concession to any shock he felt at this transformation. "Christ, lass. Where'd you learn to do that, then?" I said nothing. It was the result of hours of work and careful study—a contributing factor that had landed me in the scrape that sent Seanin and me over the sea. "And you, lad? Can you do it as well?"

Seanin shook his head mutely.

"Well, any good with horses, even?"

"Oh, aye, sir. Done nothin' but, m'entire life." He was turning his cap nervously in his hands.

The publican chuckled. "Right then, I'll be the judge of that. But you'll keep your mouth shut and your ears open until you learn how to talk more like herself, right so? We'll not need to erase your accent altogether, only iron it out a mite, if you take me meaning?"

It was plain from the expression on Seanin's face, looking bewilderedly to me then back to Dermot, that he did not.

Raising his glass toward me, Dermot said, "Your sister has the right of it. There's not much sympathy for the Irish here, you'll find. This town's run by Prods of all stripes, and if you want to get ahead, you'd do well to keep the country out of your voice as best you can." He took a meditative sip of his pint. "Might not be the worst thing in the world to change your names, either. Show up calling yourself O'Farren and they'll never hire you on, so."

"Oh, aye, sir."

I elbowed Seanin in the ribs, but not unkindly. "You don't say 'aye' in American. It's 'yes,' you feckin' fool."

"Well now, Lady Muck," said Dermot, clearly amused by this exchange. "Did your last mistress write you a character?"

"Lost it on the ship." I fell to chewing my lip again, playing for time, but Dermot said nothing, all too clearly waiting to see how I meant to account for myself. "Supposing," I said, not quite meeting his eye, "if you knowed of a scrivener, I could write her ladyship for another?"

Dermot said nothing. He poured himself a pint as he studied us carefully. I kept my features schooled, though I burned with shame, knowing how he must see us. My collarbones stood out too sharply against my skin, which had turned sallow in the ship's hold. My lips and knuckles were red and raw. My eyes were sunk in my face, which I knew had grown pinched, and the bit of flaxen hair that protruded from my bonnet was dirty and lank. He looked from me to my brother, who was, if anything, bonier and more unkempt than myself. His skin was gritty beneath his obviously pilfered clothes, which, though rumpled and ill-fitting, were still new and clean.

None of these contrasts escaped Dermot, who jerked his head toward me. "Where'd you find that gown, then?"

"'Tis mine," I declared boldly, hardening my jaw with a mindless determination.

Dermot snorted. "'Tis now, sure enough. But I didn't ask that. I asked where you found it."

"And I told you. It's all me own. *My* own. I made it. Made it my own self."

"Sure, you never did. I could fit two of you in there."

I shifted uncomfortably. "Fit me just fine in Donegal."

Seanin stepped forward. "We didn't eat much on the ship."

"Well, once you've scrubbed, we'll sell it to the Yiddishers down in the Sixth Ward and find you something more fitting. By now you've surely spoiled it with your lice. It'll want boiling to make it fit again."

I wrapped my arms across my bosom. "You'll not have me gown!" I said shrilly.

"Don't be a fool, lass. That's a lady's gown, and you ain't hardly a lady. You'd look a right blowden showing up in a gaud like that. It'll not do to have them think you're a thief straight off." He shook his head. "Aye, you're a stubborn one, and no mistaking. Can't think why you didn't thrive up at the big house with gumption like that."

I went pale, ducking my head and scowling, and Seanin, showing the first sign of backbone I'd detected in him since we disembarked, slipped a protective arm over my shoulders and said coldly, "That's no concern of yours."

Dermot's eyebrows shot up again, but he spread his hands and shrugged his compliance. "Well, and you'll thrive here, ambition like yours. You're sure you've a mind to go back into service, though?"

"What'd you mean?" Seanin inquired.

"Only," he said, a bit more gently than he'd been speaking, "that if there were something in service that didn't suit, you're not bound to it. There's other manner of work, if you want it."

I raised my eyes to his again and said in the posh voice I'd taken pains to cultivate, "I want to be a lady's maid, sir, and nothing would please me more than your assistance in finding a situation that would suit."

He chuckled at this. "Fair enough, lass. Fair enough. And you, lad?"

Seanin tightened his grip around my shoulders. "I'll not be parted from me sister. We'll have positions in the same house, like as we had back home."

"Well, lad," the publican said. "You're in America now. This is your home."

Our first night in Dermot's cellar, I lay freshly scrubbed and dressed in a clean if threadbare shift, pillowed in Seanin's arms. Dermot had made up a pallet for us by the hearth, and, unused to the humid night air, we lay together atop the blankets, grateful for the slight coolness now belowground. The grate was cold, and by the moonlight slanting in from the high windows, I peered around the room at the vaulted ceilings, the casks and hogsheads piled up between the pillars and along the walls. The smell of warm malt made me think of Colleen O'Brien's pub in Donegal Town, and I wondered if Dermot ever wandered down here on sleepless nights to breathe deeply the smells of his childhood. The thought made me tremble and huddle closer to Seanin, who was snoring gently beside me. It was curious that he did not smell like himself, like Da had, of horse and leather, but instead the queer aroma of the lye soap Dermot had insisted we scrub with came off him. I thought of the position we might get, if we might be allowed to share a bed, for I had never slept alone before, and now, in this strange, bustling city, the thought of passing a night without my brother by my side filled me with sudden terror. Back at the big house, Mrs. Boyle's maid had a room of her own; was it the same for ladies' maids in America? Or would I share my chamber with another maid? I shivered at the thought, unsure if it would be worse to sleep alone or what might come of lying again beside a girl I did not know, and, rolling over, Seanin pulled me closer. His breath smelled of ale, a little foul with sleep, and the familiarity of his hot breath against my cheek soothed my panic but filled me with nostalgia. We had come here for a better life, one where we could remain side by side. What if that should not be possible here, any more than it was in Donegal? I had thought myself done with tears, and, as my eyes welled full of them, silent sobs racking my frame, Seanin woke. He blinked at me in sleepy concern, brushing the damp from my lashes.

"It's over," he whispered. "We're here. Safe. Together."

"Together," I repeated.

"Together. And I swear," he said, holding me tight, "there's no one and nothing that can come between us. We'll never be parted."

> Nothing is more disliked in a servant, whatever may have been the previous familiarity, than this unbidden giving of opinions and advice.
>
> —*The Duties of a Lady's Maid*

Dermot wrote a note from my "aunt" to Charlotte Walden in a curling and feminine hand explaining that I had taken a fall and was unwell. I protested, for I was uneasy about Charlotte's condition, but Dermot held up his shaving glass so that I could see the patchwork of bruises blossoming, and I consented to spend the day lying on my pallet with a side of beef fairly smothering my face to take down the swelling. In the afternoon, between the lull of the dinner set and the regulars who came in after work, Dermot came to ask if I needed anything, and I broke down and had him send for Liddie.

"For then," I said thickly, "if you know all about her, I might as well have some comfort out of it."

Dermot shook his head. "I don't care if you're a tribade, Mar. That's between you and the Lord, and I don't doubt but that the Lord has other axes to grind, so. But it won't do to be whoring with that colored London wench."

"Ah, go on. She's only a friend."

"Oh aye." Dermot snorted. "A bosom friend, I've no doubt."

I propped myself up on one elbow and regarded him as critically as I could from my one good eye. "What is it exactly you object to? The colored part? Or the whoring part? For there's nothing you can say I'll take kind to on the former, and as far as the latter part goes, I can promise there's never been a penny passed between us."

"Sure and close as you've been, d'you reckon you could fit a penny to pass between you?" he muttered. But he sent for her anyway, and, as the tavern above filled up with the scraping and stomping of work boots, I heard her light heels tripping down the stairs. I lay still on my pallet and heard her stop before me. I lifted the corner of the steak off my eye and saw her looking down at me, her hands on her hips. She snorted and came to sit beside me in a flutter of petticoats.

"Well, now, let's have a look," she said, lifting the beef away and setting it on a plate. I saw her eyebrows shoot up in concern as she took in my mottled visage, but she forced a smile and bathed my face in cool water. "Gracious, aren't you a sight?" she asked, shaking her head, and she gently brushed out my hair. She helped me dress into my shift before easing me back into Dermot's wrapper, and she set to plaiting and coiling up my hair. I was feeling nearly human again as she inspected my rumpled gown where it still hung by the fire.

"Shall I press it for you?" she asked. "I could run up and get an iron from the publican."

"Don't trouble yourself," I said. "Come and lay with me awhile and we'll talk."

"Oh, it won't be a moment. I'll set the iron on the fire while we talk," she said, and disappeared up the stairs. I heard her voice at the head of the stair, shrill and questioning, before she dashed back down to me, her face ashen.

"I must know," she said, hushed and agitated, "if you will see a visitor."

"A visitor?" I asked. "Who in hell would be visiting me?"

"A man," she said, dropping her voice even lower. "His name is Johnny Prior."

I nearly laughed, though the pain in my face would not permit it. "That eejit," I said. "Right then, I'll see him."

For the first time in our acquaintance, Liddie looked shocked, but she said nothing when she led Johnny in. I sat propped up on the pallet, leaning against the wall as he approached, hat in hand and looking crestfallen. He had narrow welts around his eyes from where I'd dug in my nails, but he looked otherwise unscathed. He was limping a bit, favoring one leg, I noted with satisfaction, and he seemed properly horror-struck when he saw my face.

"Oh, Christ, Mar," he said, dropping to one side of the pallet. "I didn't mean it, I swear."

"Ah, go on," I said gently. "You'd been spoiling for a fight."

He stiffened. "So'd you."

I shrugged, uncertain as to whether I had just forgiven him. Over his shoulder, Liddie stood with her feet planted and her arms crossed. I looked up at her and then meaningfully at the stairs, but she shook her head ever so slightly. I switched to Irish. "What'd you want then, Seanin?"

He looked surprised, glancing quickly over his shoulder at Liddie, whose face flashed annoyance at the change I'd just effected. "To see how you are, of course."

"Ah, I'll live. Sure, and you should see the other fellow."

He snorted, running his fingers gently over the scratch marks. "Aren't we a pair, then?" He shook his head ruefully. "We can't go on like this, Mar. You can tell me what I've done to make you hate me so, but . . ." He trailed off, looking down.

I took his hand in mine. "I don't hate you, Seanin. Truly, I don't."

"She was sore worried about you," he said, meeting my eyes at last. "It was all the talk in the kitchen."

"Was she now?" I said softly. "I wouldn't have thought."

"It's about her, isn't it?" he asked. "Why you've grown so harsh and cold with me. I always knew it was her, though I'd not thought that was why. You're . . . fond of her, after . . . your fashion, I know. It was plain how you . . . admired her. But's not like you could ever love her the way I do."

I let this aspersion go, piqued by his own declaration. "Do you? Are you, I mean? In love with her?"

"I am."

I shook my head. "That won't be enough in the end. She can't marry you, Seanin."

"Not as I am now, I know it. Someday, perhaps—"

"Don't be daft, Seanin. She can't marry you and she can't bear your children, either, unmarried as she is."

He shrugged. "I wouldn't ask it of her."

"Good," I said, hesitating a moment. This was as good an opening as I was likely to get. "Because she hasn't."

He looked confused. "I know she hasn't."

"No," I said slowly, "I don't think you do. She can't bear your child. She would be ruined."

"I know that."

"So she didn't do it."

"Didn't do what?"

I drew a deep breath and said my next words very slowly. "She didn't bear your child."

His hands were shaking in mine. I swallowed.

"She wouldn't," he whispered. "She never would."

"She did," I whispered back. "And I helped her to."

He stood, drawing his hands from mine. "You bitch," he said. "You perfect goddamn bitch."

I scrambled to my feet. "You only just said—"

"To hell with what I just said." He cut me off. "You helped her murder my child."

"You're a fucking fool," I said wearily. "She couldn't bear your child, and I saw to it she didn't have to."

He shook his head, and, when he spoke, his voice was cold. "I'm through with you, Maire. I'm through with you, and I'm through with her. Between you, you've cut out my heart." He turned to go.

"For Christ's sake," I said in English. "See reason!"

"Fuck yourself and all your reasons." He spat. "Fuck yourself and everything you've brought on me, Maire O'Farren." And he pushed past Liddie up the stairs.

I slumped, shaking and shaken, and Liddie rushed to my side. Her hands were cold as she gripped mine. "Jesus fucking Christ," she whispered, her voice quavering. "How the fuck do you know Johnny Prior, and how'd you come to talk Gaelic with him?"

Tears had begun to ooze from the corners of my eyes, burning their way down my swollen cheeks. "He's my brother," I whispered back. "He's my twin brother."

Liddie's jaw dropped. "Jesus Christ," she breathed. "I knew Ballard wasn't your real name, but fucked if I ever thought you were related to the likes of Johnny Prior."

I dabbed at my tearstained face, the import of her words slowly dawning, and looked Liddie squarely in the eye. "And how do you," I said, "know the name Johnny Prior?"

She blinked, disbelieving. "Oh Christ, Mary. You're in for a shock."

> The wise look forward to misfortunes, and prevent or provide for them before they come.
>
> —*The Duties of a Lady's Maid*

In her line of work, Liddie Lawrence knew better than most what streets were safe to walk alone at night. Though she relished her own independence, it came at a price, and, like so many other street-walkers, Liddie had found it prudent to take precautions. It seemed that every other week the croakers were reporting the death of another light-skirts—she clucked her tongue, reading of Helen Jewett, bludgeoned to death, her body burnt in her own draperied bed. She did not ply her trade amongst the potentially more respectable cullies in the Third Ward, where she lived. The merchants, clerks, and lawyers might represent repeat custom, but there was too much risk of being followed home. She never went stargazing in the Sixth Ward, naturally, and the brothels upon which she hoped to someday model her own were in the Tenth and the Fourteenth. Upwind of the miasma that still hung over the now-filled Collect, north of the merchant district, were the dance halls and public houses lining the Bowery. It was here she made her rounds before making her way back down to Chambers.

She was completing her circuit one early summer night, too chilly for June, coming down Mulberry Street, when she saw flames fanning south from the Sixth Ward. Amidst the cramped, fetid blocks of the Sixth Ward, where the buildings leaned together like drunkards holding each other upright, fires were as common as dirt, and there was no shortage of that either. With a foot or less between the buildings, flames spread quickly, consuming whole blocks sometimes before the fire brigades could arrive and complete their pugilistic competition over access to the pumps. With no desire to be caught up in the rush of the brigades, Liddie had paused to reconsider how far east she should alter her route when the clang of alarm bells began. A door in the building closest to her swung open with a slam, and a group of men poured out, talking rapidly in Gaelic. They clustered in a knot in the street, speaking harshly, some pointing urgently downtown to where the blaze could be seen, flames licking the night sky. She pressed herself into a darkened doorway, observing the men quietly. She thought she recognized one or two from her route—impossible to tell for sure at this distance, in the dark. One man was talking over the crowd, waving his hat emphatically, his fair hair shining in the moonlight. After a moment, he had the other men nodding in agreement. They swept past her in a rush, pulling on hats and coats, shouting to one another as they hustled south toward the conflagration. The door they left open behind them, creaking ajar on its hinges. She stepped out of the shadows and moved to shut it, noticing the Celtic cross carved into the heavy wood. As the door swung shut, she caught a glimpse of the room beyond, where a single candle guttered on a table, against which leaned a small cache of rifles.

She stopped, her hand on the door, her fingers tracing the grooves carved deep into the wood. The clanging from the belfry above her drowned out the shouts as men ran toward the blaze, but not the uneasiness in her heart—what were so many guns doing inside a church? A door slammed nearby, and she jumped, jerking her hand back from the carved wood.

Rattled, she turned east, going south only when she reached the Bowery again. At every intersection, people were turning out of the pubs and houses in an effort to see the fire, and as she came closer to where the flames were rising, the crowds grew thicker. The further south she went, the warmer the air grew, thick with smoke and the press of bodies, men and women running in both directions. She hurried on, hoping to skirt the worst of it. The ground rumbled as fire trucks clattered past down side streets, horses whinnying in fear. Passing Pell Street, she felt a rapid gust of hot wind, and suddenly she was knocked off her feet when the blast issued from a nearby building as the flames consumed it. She hit her head when she fell, blacking out for a moment. Her eyelids fluttered, and the world around her came alight in a hideous, incandescent blaze. Pushing herself to sit upright, she realized that her hands were scraped and bleeding, and one knee throbbed. She staggered, her ears ringing, and was promptly sick on the cobbles. The heat bore down upon her in waves, and she knew she must rise up and run, but in her pain and terror she could not move. Flames licked the building in front of her. All about, figures raced, silhouetted in the fire, their mouths open in silent screams she could not hear for the pounding in her head.

A hand was tugging on her arm. She looked up, dazed. He was staring down at her, shouting something, but she could make no sense of his words. His face was streaked with soot and grime, but she recognized him as the fair-haired man who'd come racing from the church, shouting to his fellows in Gaelic. He was speaking English now, she knew that somehow, though her head ached and her ears rang and his words meant nothing to her. She reached for him with her other hand, and he hauled her to her feet, pulling her up from the cobbles, and, with him half-supporting her, they staggered together out of the street as the fire brigade pulled up, the ringing of hooves the first sound she properly heard. The man left her leaning on a hitching post as he dashed back toward the blaze.

She clutched at the post, the roar of noise about her slowly penetrating through the fog in her head. She stared in fascinated horror as men flung buckets of water at the blaze, figures seeming to hurry in and out of the wall of flame. A group of them appeared to be waving their limbs frantically together, until her watering eyes were able to make sense of the scene, and she realized that there was a melee. Firemen and tattered workingmen and swells off the Bowery were brawling, spending equal energy on gaining control of the pump and on pummeling one another. Liddie, who knew the value of territory and boundaries, thought perhaps she had an inkling as to the cause, though she might have no agreement with or stake in it.

A shadow was coming out of the knot of bodies bustling by the fire wagon, a man breaking away from the melee, running toward her as shouts rose up behind him. With him surreally backlit by the flames, she barely realized it until he was upon her. The fair-haired man grasped her hands. His brow was split and bleeding, and his eyes were wide with fear. He was shouting something at her. Dimly, she realized he was asking her for help. "Hide me!" And the part of her brain that was still working took his arm in a firmer grip and began directing their steps south to Chambers Street. Hell broke loose behind them.

She led him up the narrow steps, recalling vaguely that she never let the cullies know where she lived, and then feeling an absurd reassurance that he was not a cully. She fumbled with the chatelaine chain until she managed to fit the key into the lock, and ushered him into her dark room. She felt her way to the lamp, fumbling hopelessly with the lucifers, her scraped fingers clumsy. Gratitude flooded her when he took the matches gently from her shaking hands and lit the lamp himself before collapsing on her chaise. She sat down on her bed, staring at him in numb relief. She did not remember falling asleep fully clothed.

It was full dawn when she awoke. The man was still snoring gently on the chaise, and her stays cut cruelly into her breasts. She stumbled about the bedroom, unlacing her boots and pulling them off impatiently before she poured water from the small ewer on her dressing table into a washbasin. She regarded her reflection critically. There was a nasty bruise on her forehead, and her lip was split. The greatest damage was to her hair, the carefully set sugar curls crushed, her braids coming down, the pins lost. She stripped to her shift and began to bathe her face. She didn't hear him rise over the splashing water.

When she turned, he was standing in the doorway, staring at her. She stared back blandly, aware her figure was plainly visible beneath the sheer gauze of her shift. He swallowed, his gaze resting on her bosom.

She broke the silence. "You rescued me." He nodded. She reached down to pull up her shift.

"Don't."

She stopped, raising her eyebrows at him.

"I mean, you don't have to do that. I have . . . that is . . ." He looked away, blushing furiously. "I mean, you rescued me too." His heavy accent betrayed him as native to the northwest of Ireland. His voice was thick, clotted with smoke.

She shrugged. "I only brought you back here."

"Aye," he said. "That's what did it. And I thank you for it." He rummaged in his trouser pocket and brought forth a coin, pressing it into her hand. "Hold on to that now. If you ever find things going arseways with one of my people, do you show them that and tell them Johnny Prior gave it to you, and there's none as'll trouble you."

She looked at the coin in her hand. It wasn't currency. On closer inspection, she saw it was a tin medal, embossed around the edges with the words *Friendship, Unity, and Christian Charity.* "Johnny Prior. That's you, is it?"

" 'Tis," he said.

She held out her hand. "Liddie Lawrence, at your service, Mr. Prior."

He took her hand and pressed his lips to it. "Are you, then?" he said softly.

She shrugged. "It's my profession, being at men's service."

"I see. Well," he said, "if, in the course of your service, you find yourself in need of . . . shall we call it recourse? You just show 'em that token there. And in return . . ."

"In return," Liddie said slowly. "And what if anyone shows me a token like that one . . ."

"Maybe you'll show them some kindness for my sake?"

Liddie nodded. "I may at that."

"Clever lass." He pulled on his jacket, moving toward the window to peer out at the pavement below.

"Well?" she asked.

"Clear as day," he said. "That's me off, I suppose. We'll meet again, to be sure."

"To be sure," she repeated wonderingly, showing him to the door.

"Be well, Liddie Lawrence."

"Safe travels, Johnny Prior."

After he was gone, she examined the small medal. With an awl, she bored a hole through the middle and strung it on a chain. She slipped it around her neck, tucking the medal into her bodice, and wondering what magic this token might work.

It didn't take long before she began to feel the effects of her newfound association. In the week that followed, she noticed a surge in custom. Then the cully with the Kerry accent—a regular, with the flat on Elizabeth Street—got rough with her one night. A pert remark of the sort he generally fancied set him off, and his hands closed on her throat. She clawed at his fingers, and suddenly he stopped. She rubbed her neck, shouting hoarsely at him, calling him a dirty prick.

"Right, right, I didn't know," he said, backing away as she advanced angrily. "Only don't be telling Johnny Prior, aye?" To her amazement, he paid her double. It was only afterwards that she realized that, in the struggle, the tin medal had come free from her bodice, and lay exposed on her breast.

A month after the encounter, the bruises on her neck finally faded, she arrived home one night to see a strange man leaning on the wall next to her door, flipping a coin and catching it again, one-handed.

"You'll be Lawrence, I reckon?" he asked as she approached.

She smiled tightly. "Who's asking?"

He caught the coin again and flashed it to her, holding it between his thumb and middle finger—his forefinger was missing at the knuckle. In the dim light of the Argand lamp, she could just make out the inscription: *Friendship, Unity, and Christian Charity.* The man grinned. "Name's Quigley. A friend of a friend, you might say."

"Oh, indeed?" she said cautiously. "And what do you require of my friendship, Mr. Quigley?"

The man pocketed the coin, still grinning. "Sure it'd be pleasanter to discuss up in your rooms, eh?"

When it was over, she lay in her bed, wondering if he would leave her anything for her trouble. He didn't keep her in suspense for long.

"You'll be having it ready?" he said, smiling pleasantly at her as he pulled on his braces.

She blinked. "Having what ready?"

He seemed as surprised as she was. "Why, five percent, of course." He took in her expression of incomprehension. "Of your earnings. Johnny said you'd have it ready?"

She sat up, furious. "I agreed to no such thing!"

Quigley pointed at the medal, which hung between her bare breasts. "Under his protection, aren't you? Haven't had any of the lads raise a hand to you or the like since you've been wearing it?"

Liddie pulled the medal from around her neck and tossed it at him. "Tell him he can keep his protection," she spat. "I was doing just fine on my own before he started protecting me."

He tossed it back, discomfort suffusing his features. "Sure, I'm partial to my throat. Hard to sip a pint with it cut, aye? Tell him yourself, lassie. You're a fine bit o' stuff, Lawrence, but you ain't worth the risk."

"And where would I find him to take up the matter?" she asked through gritted teeth.

"The Hibernian, on Mulberry. He's there Sundays and Thursdays." The man rubbed the back of his head, looking sheepish. "But I'll be needing the money, lassie. It's worth more than my life to go back to him empty-handed."

"No." She shook her head firmly. "I agreed to no such thing."

He laughed. "Aye, you did when you put that thing around your neck. Come now, lassie. Five percent of your take."

"I said no."

"Aye, I heard you," he said almost gently. "But I'm thinking you'd not care for the alternative to handing it over."

Her eyes narrowed. "What's that now?"

Quigley rubbed the back of his head sheepishly. "It ain't personal, you know. 'Tis just my job, see? But it's either you turn over Johnny's cut or I rough you up a bit."

"What's 'a bit'?"

He sighed, then, looming over her, took her roughly by the arm with one hand, grabbed her little finger with the other hand and twisted it sharply. She screamed, and he released her to cradle her hand, the finger bent out from the palm at a sickening angle.

"You bloody bastard, you complete fucking bastard!" she howled as he donned his hat and coat.

"Told you 'tweren't personal," he muttered. "I expect I'll be seeing you Thursday night. Come by after two or so. He should be free by then. I'll show myself out."

At two o'clock in the morning on the following Thursday, she was just finishing her circuit, her finger splinted and wrapped, the medal clutched firmly in her good hand. The crowd at the Hibernian had begun to thin. He was sitting at the bench closest to the fire, with Quigley sitting beside him. He looked up as Quigley elbowed him in the side, and raised his glass to her, gesturing for her to sit. She seated herself and placed the medal on the bench between them with a cold *thunk*. She pursed her lips, and he looked at the medal, smiling.

"Dermot," he called. "Get my friend Liddie a round."

She allowed a small, tight smile to play upon her lips. "Thank you, but I'll not be staying. I only wished to return this item, of which I am no longer in need."

The big barman came from behind the counter, holding out a mug to her and favoring her with a scowl before returning to his place. Johnny gestured for her to drink up, but she held the mug stiffly in her hands, staring obstinately. Johnny smiled.

"Suit yourself, lassie. Now, what's this I hear about you making poor Quigley here break your finger?"

"Go fuck yourself."

He spread his hands. "Have you not had an easier time of it, wearing my medal? Less trouble for you, I'll wager."

"I didn't ask for your protection, and I'll be damned if I'm going to pay you for a service I didn't ask you to provide," she said, clenching her jaw. "Take that filthy thing back and leave me be, will you?"

Quigley, who had positioned himself behind her, pressed his broad hands on her shoulders. Johnny leaned back and regarded her thoughtfully. "Now, lassie, that's what I call a rare mistake. 'Tis terrible dangerous on the streets, you know. Be a real shame if a pretty thing like you should come to harm. Come now, lassie, be reasonable."

"It would have been far more reasonable if I'd never taken you in that night," she scowled.

"Be that as it may," he said. "Now pick up that medal, put it back on, and expect Quigley on the first and third Monday of each month, there's a good lass?"

She snatched the medal, shrugging Quigley's hands off, and stormed out, the sound of their laughter ringing in her ears as she fled.

When the appointed day came, she arrived home to find Quigley leaning against her door again. She sighed, pushing past him into the hall and marching up the stairs. Inside her chambers, she handed him a small leathern purse, which he counted out with a smile. "Right so, lassie. There's the cash, but your hospitality's a bit lacking tonight."

She stood, hands on her hips, and stomped her foot. "And what further satisfaction can you have tonight?" she asked, falling back, as she often did in times of exasperation, on the familiar Shakespearean quotations of her childhood. His grin was his answer, and Liddie Lawrence learned that night that Johnny Prior's medal could not protect her from everything.

Three months of Mondays later, bruised and sore, she rose from her bed on a Tuesday morning, deciding enough was enough. He could have his bloody money, or Quigley could take it out of her in flesh, but damned if she'd subject herself to both. The latter wasn't part of the agreement anyway. She wondered if Johnny even knew. She remembered the way he'd stammered and his face had reddened, that first morning after the fire when she'd pulled up her shift, and ground her teeth in fury.

That Thursday, she marched to the Hibernian, intent on having her say. It was a breezeless night in early September, the air still, flies harassing her as she walked determinedly past the reeking miasma of the Sixth Ward and up to the pub.

Quigley was inside, along with a few of the others she'd come to recognize. Maguire, one was called. And her Kerryman, O'Mara. She scanned the room, but there was no sign of Johnny Prior.

"Knocked up," said Quigley, over the din. He held her arm, and not gently either. "What'd you need to see him for anyway?"

"Mind your own business," Liddie said tartly, and Quigley laughed good-naturedly.

"Darlin', you *are* my business."

She stormed out to curse in the alley, amidst the privacy of the hogsheads, starting in fear as ringing laughter met her curses. She never thought to equate the fair-haired girl laughing on the hogsheads with the fair-haired man who was extorting her. Not even the Donegal accent—so similar in cadence to the one she had expected to hear that night—had sparked any connection in her mind. Exhausted and furious, she took her pleasure with the girl from the alley to remind herself that she was still her own mistress, and that there was still unexpected sweetness in her life.

As we lay together on my pallet on the floor of the Hibernian, I listened to Liddie's account of my brother in wonder. I'd had no notion of what he talked about with his mates, or what he did once I was too blind drunk to stand. I listened to her talk of Quigley, his brutal ease with her body, and I felt ill. How many nights had he kept my company, so studious of my virtue, after taking Liddie by force? I knew, too, that my brother had spoken with MacBride and O'Mara and Maguire and Riley and the others about "organizing things" in some vague way obscure to myself. I knew they were political—most men here in America were—and I knew that, being Irish and political, they all voted Democrat and occasionally engaged in fisticuffs with Whigs and nativists; that was expected of them. But in my sorrowing rage over Charlotte Walden—it was always, I thought furiously, over Charlotte Walden—it had never occurred to me that Johnny and his mates might be doing much of anything at all besides being friendly with others of our countrymen, voting and fighting for whomever Tammany had decreed. The thought of my brother presiding over a meeting at St. Patrick's with a cache of guns made my blood run cold. The thought of him part of a group of men that could offer badges of protection—and all such a thing entailed—turned me pale.

"How many more?" I finally asked. "Like you, I mean?"

Liddie sighed. "Whores? Or businesses?"

I started. "Come again now?"

She rolled over onto her back, settling her cheek next to mine. "It's not just streetwalkers. They've brothels, of course. Then there's a fair few pubs, some of the groceries, most of the boardinghouses—that's all in the Sixth Ward, you know—and I think two of the dance halls on the Bowery. One of the girls I know who does her route along Houston says they even have a theater, but I've never seen a sign of it."

"They, they, they! But, Liddie," I asked, "who are *they*?"

She shrugged, discomfited by my upset. "Why, the Order, of course. Who else would I mean?"

"What Order?"

"Are you Irish or aren't you?" She laughed nervously. "Lord knows you've more of a nose for quim than for politics, but I would have thought even you would know about the Order." I stared at her, all uncomprehending. "The Ancient Order of Hibernians. Republicans, you'd call them, back home?"

"The Ancient Order of Hibernians?" I asked. "Surely not? Were they not just the lads who'd banded up to protect the churches after the nativists were burning them the past two summers?"

"They're Catholics, certainly, banding together against the Orange-men and the Whigs and the nativists," Liddie said. "And it did all start after those fires, I'm told. They started holding meetings to protect Irish businesses. That's what got them together. But, well, people tell things to whores. After, usually, when they're feeling talkative. So I've gathered there's a bit more to it than protecting churches and taverns."

"Like what?"

"I've heard tell they're raising money—all that protection money, of course, but donations from the churches they protect as well—to send back home to the anti-Unionists in Ireland."

"Anti-Unionists," I mused. "What, you mean like the separatists who want to break with England?"

"Isn't that what all Irish are after? A sovereign nation of their own?"

I shook my head. "I couldn't say. It's what Robert Emmet wanted, sure enough. Da used to talk of the Rebellion sometimes, but it wasn't a thing we'd discuss openly back on the estate. The Boyles, them that ran the estate, Ballyboyle it was called ("Of course it was," Liddie muttered), Mr. Boyle used to say that it was their own parliament Irishmen were so keen after. That there would be one day the same rebellion the British faced in America if they denied the Irish a voice in Parliament."

"That may be," Liddie said. "But the rebellions don't grow out of the ground overnight like a pack of Phoenician soldiers, do they?"

"A pack of *what*?"

"Cadmus? Tsk. Never mind," she said, waving her hand impatiently, as was her wont when I failed to cotton to one of her literary references. "The point I'm making is this; to start a rebellion, you must have arms and ammunition. It takes more than rhetoric to fight for freedom; it takes tactics, does it not? But arms and ammunition cost a pretty penny, and the Irish haven't had so much as a whiff of spare cash for nigh on three hundred years."

My mind reeled as I thought in a flash of Ballyboyle: the stately white stone manor house, set back from the manicured drive; its tapestried halls; the rows of silver candelabras that always wanted polishing; the sparkling crystal chandeliers that must be lowered once a week for dusting; the gleaming oaken floors, rubbed bright with wax. It was the epitome of wealth and privilege and luxury, the inhabitants thereof a species removed from those who toiled and suffered most under British rule. The thought that they might part with a single shilling to support a cause that could risk in the slightest their fragile way of life was laughable. But when I had lived there, I had always thought of my brother and me as part of that life, as fixed and firm as the flagstones on the hearth. I tried to imagine anyone who had come up on the estate as a radical patriot and failed.

"How did Seanin get involved with that lot?" I wondered aloud. "There was nothing like that in our upbringing."

"Seanin?"

"Johnny." I shook my head, wondering what good our pseudonyms would do us anymore. "It doesn't matter now. I don't know how he came to be part of such a lot, is all."

"What other lot is there for the likes of him?" Liddie asked, rummaging in her reticule for a cigarette. "You might do that posh voice you put on betimes and pass yourself as something else, but your brother looks Irish, acts Irish, and sounds as Irish as they come. The nativists have been taking a harder line with the foreigners, and wouldn't I know? It's either join up with your own kind and brawl together for your share of the scratch, or . . ." She shrugged, pausing a moment to light her cigarette from the fire. "They want money and they want to brawl with the nativist gangs. You know, stake out their territory, like you read in the penny dreadfuls. Brickbats and lead knuckles and all that. Johnny Prior's a fair enough hand at it—you don't rise to captain if you aren't, after all."

"Captain?"

"There's probably a Gaelic word for it." She shrugged again. "But I don't know what it is. Chief of his division of the Order. He must have cracked his share of skulls too, as there's a fair few nativists who've taken a dislike to him over the past year. I gather he's not very popular with the firedog brigades on account of him cutting out the eye of a fireman back when he was starting out. There now!" she cried, for suddenly I was shaking. She wrapped her arms around me, saying, "It will be well," until my shaking subsided. But all her talk about Johnny and the Order had so unsettled me that I felt as though the ground beneath me had fallen away, and I'd lost my brother over Charlotte, and now to the Hibernians, and nothing would be well ever again.

> Sickness, danger, and adversity, usually level distinctions of rank; but you must never forget that you are a servant, nor assume the airs and the consequence of a gentlewoman so long as you are in the pay and at the command of another.
>
> —*The Duties of a Lady's Maid*

By Saturday morning, I persuaded Dermot to allow me to return to the Waldens' house. Having used Quigley as a go-between to make it clear my brother would have been gone already, we had concocted a story to tell, featuring Johnny as the villain, should our ruse about my taking a fall prove flimsy. Arranging my hair in Dermot's shaving glass, my face still blooming with ugly bruises, I steeled myself for the scrutiny that was sure to come. I practiced deception in that household every day with my posh voice and studied manners—what was one more lie to the many I had already told to get and keep my place? Yet my fingers trembled as I tied my bonnet under my chin.

Dermot was waiting at the top of the stairs with a dram of whiskey. "You needn't go back, Maire," he said. "Not if you don't want to. You were only ever there because they were hiring for posts where the two of you could be together."

I took the whiskey from him, bolted it, and handed the vessel back to him with a weak smile. Dermot shook his head and escorted me out onto Mulberry Street to hail a hackney. He pressed a few coins on me, handing me up himself and giving the driver directions. It was strange, rattling along the cobbles as we ran up the

Bowery, for I had certainly never thought to pay for the extravagance of such a conveyance. Stepping down, I waited until the hack had rattled off before hobbling around to let myself in through the servants' entrance in the mews. There was a thin layer of slush on the cobbles, and I took care to knock it from my boots as I pushed my way into the kitchen.

There was a cry and a gasp, and I was enveloped in Cook's strong arms before I had taken two steps into the room. In the face of her bustle and energy, I felt faint. I heard someone call out, "Oh, catch her," and everything blurred away into darkness.

When I came to myself a moment or two later, I was in the arms of Mr. Buckley, who was supporting me into Cook's rocker. Mrs. Harrison was taking my cloak and shawl, and Cook was pressing a mug of beef tea into my hand. Agnes was sobbing with her apron over her head, her back to me.

"Good lord, girl," Cook said. "It's more than a fall that did that to you."

"Now, now, Mrs. Freedman," said Mrs. Harrison briskly. "There will be time enough for that later. Have you a length of cheesecloth? Very good. Agnes, put some water on to boil. Quickly now, girl, leave off that wailing. Mr. Buckley, I daresay you might help Miss Ballard to my own chamber, if she's still unsteady on her feet? No, no, Miss Ballard," she said as I tried to protest. "I shall meet you there directly."

She turned and directed her energies to ordering about the kitchen staff as I availed myself of Mr. Buckley's proffered arm and allowed myself to be escorted to Mrs. Harrison's room. No sooner had Mr. Buckley made me comfortable in the chair by the fire than Mrs. Harrison herself entered, bearing the tea tray, some cheesecloth, and a pot of salve. Closing the door firmly behind the butler, she pulled the ottoman up before me, and dipped the cheesecloth into the salve before daubing it delicately onto my face. She did not meet my eyes, but kept her gaze fixed upon the bruises to which she ministered.

For a time, neither of us spoke, until at last she broke the silence. "You will have the goodness, Miss Ballard," she said, very softly, "to permit me to remark it strange that our head groom should give notice suddenly on the very afternoon that Miss Walden's maid sends word that she is too indisposed to come home from her night off. It seems quite strange indeed that he should have come to us rather worse for the wear when you yourself, Miss Ballard, should present yourself back to us in such sorry condition. It rather beggars belief to consider that two such occurrences are merely coincidence."

I swallowed, but said nothing. Mrs. Harrison sighed. "Child," she said, this time exasperated. "Will you kindly tell me why John Prior beat you, and why you so obviously attempted to claw his eyes out? For I shall be in a rather bad humor if you attempt to deny it, you know."

I pursed my lips. "He's given notice, you say?"

Mrs. Harrison nodded. "Given notice and cleared out, and if he thinks he's likely to get a character from Mrs. Walden after departing in such a state, he is sorely mistaken. So, Miss Ballard," she said, eyeing me critically, "there is rather little chance of him coming back." Still, I hesitated, and she said, "Come now, child. From the moment he came into this house, you have been cold to that man. Will you not tell me why?"

"I did not care," I said in a low, hard voice I had practiced with Dermot, "for the way he spoke to me." I looked up, squarely meeting her eyes, and had the pleasure of seeing surprise flicker momentarily across her features. "I'd no wish to speak ill of the man whilst he was under this roof, but I tell you plain, that Prior was never the name he was born with."

The color drained from Mrs. Harrison's face. "Whatever do you mean?"

I shook my head. There was no going back now. If Johnny had lost his character, if he had gone to his friends at the Order, I could do worse than to blacken his name in the Walden house. "You will not know, Mrs. Harrison, by nature of your breeding, the various accents of the Irish. I think I may safely confess to you that, while I was in Dublin, as a maid, it was not always my privilege to associate with the better parts of society. You will understand that I do not wish to dwell upon that unhappy time, but after those misfortunes, I can, with justice, recognize the tones of the lower orders. Mark my words, Mrs. Harrison. That man was born a Papist and a farmer."

She shook her head, her cheek still pale. "A Papist!"

"I could never suffer him to speak so freely to me as he did, nor so freely as I heard him speak to Miss Walden. But it is not in my nature to criticize others, and so I held my tongue."

"But why should he beat you then, Miss Ballard, unless you threatened to expose him? And how did he come to find you on your night off?"

I scowled darkly. Why could not the woman leave off with her questions? I took a breath and began the tale Dermot and I had cobbled together, based on the falsehoods I had already told, and praying it might ring true. "Perhaps you are aware, mum, of my aunt who lives in Essex Street, with whom I stay on Thursdays?" Mrs. Harrison nodded. "Well, I was foolish enough to indulge my cousin, she is just fourteen, who wished to go to one of the Punch and Judy Shows down in Paradise Square. She was like to worry my aunt to death with all her pleading, and at last I said I should accompany her. It was as we were leaving the area that we encountered Mr. Prior, who, it was clear, had been in his cups." My words came quickly now, the story tumbling out unbidden. "He addressed me, and I acknowledged him, but liquor had loosened his tongue, and he made so bold as to say several impertinent things to me. I could not abide that he should be so free with me, and me with my young cousin present, and so I told him if he did not cease to address me in such a manner, I should have no choice but to tell Mrs. Walden that he was not all he pretended to be. Lord! How he cursed then, and struck my face, and I did my best to defend myself. I do not know what should have become of me had the fracas not drawn the attention of a drover who pulled him off of me and bore my cousin and me home." Here I made myself begin to weep, though it hurt my face, and the ointment Mrs. Harrison had rubbed onto my skin got into my eyes and stung. "I nearly fainted in fear I should have to return and see him here, for as they were pulling him off of me, I heard him swear he'd beat the life from me if I should say what he had done." The tears were flowing freely now, and my shoulders shook as I wept. Through my fingers, I could see Mrs. Harrison looking, by turns, indignant and concerned. She patted my shoulder awkwardly before going to her night table and producing a bottle of brandy. She poured it into my tea and pressed the cup into my hand. I sniffed, and looked up, allowing a calculated shock to show through my weeping. "Oh, Mrs. Harrison, I couldn't take spirits!" I cried.

"Now, now, Miss Ballard," she said, crisply. "You drink that and it will brace you up. You've had a trying time of it, and no mistaking. Just this once won't hurt."

I took a sip and remembered to make a face, as ladies do. I looked up at her, and she seemed annoyed by my reticence. Meekly, I brought the cup to my lips and took a swallow, making a show of schooling my features. She nodded.

"That's better," she said. "Now, you've nothing to fear from Mr. Prior, for he'll never be welcome in this house again. I shall speak to Mr. Buckley directly."

"Oh, bless you, Mrs. Harrison," I said, taking her hand.

"Come, child," she said, helping me to rise. "I'll see you to your room. You come to me twice a day for more of that ointment. Once when you wake, and once before you retire for the night. It's rare luck that brute didn't break your nose, but it seems straight enough."

"I think he did. My aunt straightened it for me, and I was in a faint."

She clucked her tongue and patted my hand. "Well, if I'm any judge, it should mend clean. Now then, child, I think you'd better have a rest. I'll tell Miss Porter she'll need to attend to Miss Walden again this evening. We'll give you some time to recover."

Mrs. Harrison had put me to bed in my own room, dosing me once more with brandy, which this time she had doctored with Charlotte Walden's laudanum. I slept that night straight through the pain that had kept me wakeful the previous two. In the morning, I woke to the sound of Charlotte stirring, and, throwing on my wrapper, knocked gently as I entered her chamber.

She was sitting up in bed, and her face, when she saw mine, went a paler shade of white. I hurried to her side and took her hands, which she held out to me, and squeezed my fingers tight.

"He's gone," she breathed, and my heart sunk, all warmth at her tender looks gone instantly cold. I pulled my hands abruptly from hers, confusion flickering across her features.

"Of course," I said, not troubling to keep the bitterness from my voice. "It's him that concerns you, isn't it?"

"Ballard, what has come over you?" she asked.

"You cannot know, miss," I said quietly, "how little he deserves you."

Her face darkened. "Say rather how little I deserve him! Oh, that our last interview should have been so marred by that which I had not the courage to tell him!"

"And yet there is much he has been too coward to say to you."

"Coward! What can you mean, Ballard?"

I sighed. I felt as though I were forever sighing, forever in a state of constraint and exasperation in which these two I loved had me bound. God pity all fools and lovers. And yet, though I wanted in my heart to hate Johnny for the fool that he was, I could not bring myself to hurt Charlotte by tarnishing her memories of him. "You must know," I said slowly. "That he loved you very much. He told me so, many a time."

"What cause had he," she said, her eyes growing wide, "to speak of me to you?"

"I waited for him every night after . . . it was over. We walked together, and sometimes he would speak of you."

"I never asked," Charlotte said, her voice edged like flint, "how you knew it was him."

I moistened my lips nervously. Lies had come easily when I was speaking to Mrs. Harrison, as of course they must, but with Charlotte it was different. I had a chance to write Johnny out of both of our lives, but I would not let myself take it. I pressed my lips together and made my choice. "He is my brother."

She paled. "Your brother? But how?"

This time, my words tumbled out slowly. "We knew I should not get work as a lady's maid if it was known I was born Irish, and he could not learn to drop his accent so well as I. It was the only way we could think to find the work we had done in Ireland. To stay together."

"Your brother," she said wonderingly, peering keenly into my face. "Yes, I see it now, the resemblance. I had not noted it before."

"People see what they wish to see, miss."

"That is so." She sighed. "I find each day new ways I have been a fool, Ballard." She looked up suddenly. "Or is it Prior, after all?"

I stiffened. Names have power, Da used to say when he told us all the old tales at night before we slept. Knowing a person's true name gives you power over them, and the name Mary Ballard had been as armor to me here. Only Dermot and Johnny knew my true name, and though I loved Charlotte with all my heart, she already possessed such considerable power to hurt me. I felt her staring at me, but could not meet her eyes.

When she spoke, her voice was gentle and low. "I will not force your confidence," she said. "I shall still call you Ballard if you wish, you know."

I looked up into her sweet, earnest face, and found, in the end, that there was almost nothing I could deny her. I was already in her power, and, bewitched, I gave her one last terrible hold over me. "O'Farren, miss. Maire O'Farren. But I'd thank you to please call me Ballard, for there's none in this country that knows me by another name, save two."

"Who is the other? Your aunt?"

I snorted. "I haven't got an aunt, miss. On nights off, I sleep in the cellar of a tavern to the north of the Sixth Ward. The publican's mother was a friend back home."

"It is very strange," she said, "that you should know everything about my life, and what little I know of yours has been but fiction." She shook her head when I would have protested and said, more gently still, "I do not blame you, Ballard, for it has been a necessary fiction, and, had you not told it, I should not have had the sweetness of yourself and your brother in my life. For in spite of all, it has been sweet. Oh, Ballard," she said, taking up my hands again. "Do you suppose I shall see him again?"

I shook my head, not trusting myself to speak at first, and, when I did, I chose my words with care. "I suppose it might be possible, miss, but I would not set your heart upon it. When we parted, he said it must be for good."

"For good! But you are his sister!"

"We came to harsh words about you, miss. Harsh words and blows."

"My god!" she cried, raising a hand to my mottled cheek. "Did he do this to you? For my sake?"

"I would not say, miss, what was not mine to tell, and we fought. When at last I confessed the truth, he could not accept what we had done, and said that he was finished with us both."

Charlotte groaned. "Would that I had the strength to tell him myself!"

"He would not see reason, miss."

"Even still. I could not have foreseen he would react with such . . . brutality. Not him. Not my Johnny." She reached to touch my face again, and when I flinched she pulled her hand away, as though burned. "I would not, for all the world, have had you suffer more than you have already for my sake, Ballard. Nor would wish you to be severed from your only family on my account."

"It is not on your account, miss," I said. "It is through his own pride, which will not countenance the notion that you cannot be his wife and bear his children." She would have protested, but I went on. "It is his pride that is hurt, miss. To save it, would you have given yourself up as ruined? Would you buy his pride with your reputation?"

"No," she said, the flint creeping back into her voice. "I could not have sunk myself to be my own groom's wife. It would not be my reputation alone with which I paid, but my family's. With my mother's. With Prudence's. Oh, it is all very romantic to throw one's pride away for love, but it is something else again to sacrifice one's family on the altar of such a passion. I could never do such a thing. For all that I love him, I must let his memory go."

When she was done speaking, there were tears in her eyes, and I dabbed them away with the sleeve of my wrapper. She moved into the circle of my arms, her auburn head resting on my shoulder as she wept softly.

"If only we could have gone on like that forever," she said, her breath warm against my neck. "If only I could have had one more night with him. Oh, Ballard, if only it hadn't all come to an end."

I stroked her hair, breathing in her scent, saying nothing.

A good temper, indeed, is every thing, for you cannot expect your superiors to conform to your whims or humours, and your employers have too many concerns of their own to put up with your vexations.

—*The Duties of a Lady's Maid*

In consequence of Charlotte's flux and protracted illness, Augusta Walden had postponed the dinner with which the family had been engaged to Mr. Dawson. Charlotte, still not up to making calls, had spent much of the week closeted in her room, and I hovered in close attendance, grateful that her malady excused me from the sidelong glances in the kitchen. My face, mottled with bruises, eased from purple to green to yellow under Mrs. Harrison's care. I had noticed a distinct change in the housekeeper's demeanor as she sat with me, daubing my skin with salve. Her grim coolness melted a little, and her gentle hands seemed almost tender as she ministered to my hurts. One could not call her warm or motherly—she remained far too imposing a figure for any sentiment so familiar—but I felt far more kindness from her quarter than I had since my arrival three years ago. I suppose Johnny's drubbing had convinced her at last of my story and my character, for, on those occasions when I did find myself in the kitchen, she often took pains to draw me into the privileged conversations it was her wont to hold with Cook and Grace Porter. They were company, at least, though without Johnny the house seemed hollow somehow. Just knowing that he was somewhere about the place, in the carriage house or the kitchen, had been a comfort to me, and, when I thought on it, I could not recall a time in my life when I was not certain that he was by.

There had been a blacksmith, Ned Gallagher, in Donegal Town, who'd lost his leg below the knee. He wore a wooden peg, older than I was by the time I knew him, which he had been known to absently reach down and scratch before his fingers encountered the wood and, his face grown sheepish, he would withdraw his fingers slowly. "After all them years," he'd say, a touch of wonder in his voice, "I can still feel it itching." That was what it was like, once Johnny had gone. A missing limb I couldn't scratch. A phantom ache.

Determined to bury Johnny's memory, Charlotte Walden seemed transformed overnight. There was something cool and sedate about her now, as though a fever had broken, and the mad dreams of her illness melted away into quiet convalescence. The gentle, level calm that had marked her ballroom demeanor now pervaded her hours, sleeping and waking.

On the first day that she was at home to callers, she was visited by Prudence Graham. I was passing by the landing window when I saw her coach standing out front, odd in itself, for well I knew how lengthy Prudence's calls to her niece could be, and the Grahams' coachman was a familiar enough sight in our kitchen. Quietly, I slipped down the front stair to listen to their voices, muffled behind the sitting room door. What passed betwixt them I could not say, but they spoke in low and rapid tones, tension clipping their words, until finally I heard the rustle of skirts and a creak of boards as one of them rose. I backed away from the door just in time for it to burst open as Prudence Graham pushed past me and let herself quickly out the front door. I stood in the hall, looking first through the door of the sitting room, where Charlotte Walden sat, her face smeared with tears; then out the front door, watching Prudence as she ran, bonnet in hand, into the waiting door of her carriage.

That night, Charlotte and her mother supped in and retired early, each to her separate room. Augusta Walden's imperious composure had been ruffled by Charlotte's malady, and in her dealings with her daughter she had adopted a manner of gracious solicitude that, if it could not be called warmly affectionate, could at least be termed kind. Charlotte, meanwhile, had grown so meek with her mother that supper, devoid of the veiled barbs that normally peppered the meal, was an altogether bland affair. We had barely finished in the kitchen when Mr. Buckley reappeared to announce the ladies' withdrawal, and I took the back stairs two at a time, a last spoonful of pudding unswallowed in my mouth, to race to my closet next to Charlotte's room and compose myself before I was called for.

My mistress rang, and, taking a deep breath, I opened the door.

Charlotte Walden sat in the tufted chair before the fire, one wrist drooping over the carved wooden arm, a wan smile on her lips. Her other hand rested gently on her stomach, over the spot from whence Johnny's child had recently been displaced. The flames from the grate lent her lingering pallor a rosy hue, and her eyes seemed too large in her drawn face. She gestured me closer and held out her hands to me, and, eagerly, I took them, kneeling at her feet.

"It is early yet," she said. "I am weary, but I am not tired. They are two different things, have you noticed? Will you sit and sew with me, Ballard?"

"Of course, miss," I said, fetching her sewing basket before retrieving a dress in need of hemming from my closet. I drew up the footstool near to the hearth so that our feet were almost touching, and, smiling, we both bowed to our work in companionable silence.

The fire crackled merrily, and I thought how snug, how happy we were and how content I might be if only we could go on like this, she and I, and then, when weariness overcame us, I might lie beside her and rest my fair head against her auburn and wind my arms about her. Not even to kiss or caress her, but just to have her sleeping in my arms at night, and wake to the sight of her in the morning, would have been enough. And though often, before, such thoughts had made my heart ache and race all at once, tonight the notion soothed me. I began to hum a cheery tune, and, before long, Charlotte joined in. I looked at her from beneath my lashes, the soft half smile on her face, the play of the firelight against the gleam of her hair. Her lids were lowered so I should not have known they were open at all had she not been still employed at making quick stitches, and it was no small surprise to me when she suddenly looked up and caught my eye. With a grin, a flash of mischief so rare, of late, across her face, she broke out in a robust whistle of the tune, and I looked openmouthed at her. I could not have said what shocked me more—that she would have known the air, which, cheery as it was, was a bawdy music hall number, or that she was whistling it quite tunefully. When she ended on one last trilling note, I put down my stitching in wonder.

"Oh, well done, miss, very game!"

She inclined her head graciously and smiled very smugly, her eyes alight for the first time in weeks. "And now that I've exhibited, let's hear you have at it, Ballard."

I shook my head in protest. "Oh, I couldn't, miss. For whistling maids and crowing hens are neither fit for God nor men." We laughed, and Charlotte whistled a scrap of a hymn, and that set us to laughing all the harder.

"Now you, Ballard, now you," she said.

I flushed crimson, pleased and embarrassed, wondering what tune I should choose, when everything dear about that moment was shattered with a knocking coming from within my closet door. The spell was broken, and the bright mirth that had suffused Charlotte's face faded white as she quaveringly bade the knocker enter.

It was a rare moment when I was ever glad to see Agnes's broad, dull face. This moment was absolutely not one of them.

As she entered the room, her eyes darting furtively about, as though she feared to tread in such a hallowed chamber, I saw the shadow of disappointment that flickered across Charlotte's face, and thought it must be mirrored on my own. Of course it had not been him. How on earth could either of us have considered such a thing? Agnes, in her goddamn taint of misery, had sapped the first flush of warmth and closeness I had shared with Charlotte Walden since I helped her cast forth my brother's child, and all the things I had allowed myself to imagine as we sewed grew dim and faded. I thought then that hope was a terrible thing, perhaps even the worst thing in the world. For hope can burn at one's heart until it's consumed with ash, and one can cling to hope like a wasting sickness. And when hope lives long past when it should have died, there is no feeling emptier.

Charlotte regained her composure first, all her mirth subsumed in that quiet, porcelain-cool calmness in which she had spent the past week. She regarded Agnes, who had fallen to twisting the corner of her apron in her hands, with a relative dispassion. I, on the other hand, glared at the interloper with banked fury smoldering in my eyes. How dare the chit creep up the stair and through my chamber?

"Well?" asked Charlotte, in an impressive imitation of her mother.

"Begging your pardon, miss," Agnes whined nasally, "I wouldn't dare enter for the world, but she told me I must, and so, only please don't tell Mrs. Harrison I come into your rooms like this?"

Charlotte looked at me, raising her eyebrows, and I lost all patience. "In God's name, Agnes, what are you nattering about?"

Agnes's fingers were twined about her apron so tightly her knuckles had gone white. "Miss Graham!" she said. "She came tapping at the kitchen window, and she said I mustn't be seen. She's wanting to see you, Miss Walden."

An expression of annoyance flitted over Charlotte's mask of calm. "Ballard," she said. "Please see to this?" And I bustled Agnes out of the room and into my closet.

"What are you on about?" I hissed, shutting the door. "Coming up to Miss Walden's chamber like that! Have you gone mad?"

"It's Miss Graham that's gone mad," Agnes moaned. "Didn't want to be announced. Wanted me to take her up the back stairs straightaway."

"Well, and where is she now?"

Agnes looked down. "I couldn't very well let her up without asking the young mistress."

"Agnes! Where is Miss Graham now?"

"Bottom of the stairs," Agnes mumbled.

"You left Prudence Graham, the heiress Prudence Graham of the Graham diamond mines, my mistress's aunt, Mrs. Augusta Walden's half sister, cooling her heels at the bottom of the servants' staircase?" I struggled to keep my voice down. "You witless ninny!"

Agnes had by now begun to cry, and I hushed her, pushing past the wretched creature to hurry down the back stairs. Sitting on the bottom step, her ankles peeping out from beneath an evening gown and a wrap too light for the chill weather, sat the heiress of her generation.

"Miss Graham," I whispered, and she swiveled her head to me with a start.

"Ah, Ballard, is that you?" she asked in an undertone.

"Will you have the goodness to come with me, miss?" I extended my hand, helped her to rise, and led her up to my chamber. The stiff taffeta of her skirts sounded unnaturally loud as it brushed against the narrow stairwell's walls, and I cringed at the echo of that rustling. We passed Agnes, still sniveling on the landing, before making our way into my room. I rapped gently at the door to my mistress's chamber and opened it when we heard Charlotte softly call, "Come in."

Charlotte Walden was sitting in her customary chair by the fire, but she had clearly taken pains to arrange herself to her best advantage. She had draped her skirts to hang carefully over the edge of the chair, and had taken the pins out of her braid, which lay over one shoulder. She was sitting up very straight, much more formally than she had been when I left her, and she had taken up a complicated piece of embroidery—not the trimming I had left her working upon. It was artful, what she had done, all calculated to show herself as comfortable and at ease, yet accomplished and in control. She took her time looking up from her embroidery, as though her aunt was shown into her bedroom through the servants' stair every night of the week. My neck prickled, as Charlotte Walden would not ordinarily have gone to so much trouble to convey such an image to her dearest friend and confidante.

Prudence Graham took two steps into the room and looked back over her shoulder at me before turning to look at Charlotte. Charlotte's face remained emotionless and still as she peered over her aunt's shoulder to me. "That will be all, Ballard, thank you." I closed the door as quietly as I might.

"What'd she want, then?" Agnes asked from the doorway, and I shushed her, waving her from my room. She tripped noisily out onto the stair, wiping her nose with the back of her hand, and I put my hands on either side of the doorjamb as I fixed her with my stoniest glare.

"You'll tell no one of this, understand me?" I said, and she nodded. "Prudence Graham was never here. You never saw her. Do you understand?" She nodded again, sniffling. "Good. Get you down to that kitchen, then." She turned to go. "Oh, and Agnes?" She turned back, her dim eyes expectant. "If you ever come into my chamber again, I'll have you out on the street, see if I don't." I had taken her candle, and though she stared at it in my hand, wetting her lips nervously, she could not bring herself to ask for it back. I fixed her with a stony gaze, and she turned to feel her way cautiously down the dark stairs.

Once she was gone, I stood in the doorway for a moment, deciding the safest course of action. To creep back into my closet and listen at the door was to risk the creaking floorboards and disturb the tête-à-tête in Charlotte's room. To remain on the landing was to risk Mrs. Harrison or one of the housemaids finding me. I opted to edge my way along the wall and back into my tiny chamber, closing the door gently behind me. From here, I crawled across my bed to be closer to the sound of voices drifting from Charlotte's room. Prudence Graham spoke in low and careful tones, and, holding my breath, I was able to make out the two girls' conversation.

". . . and I would not force your confidence, Lottie, but if something has changed between us, if I have given offense, would you not tell me? For you were never wont to be so cool with me."

"As I told you earlier, Prudence, I have been ill, and I should think I might be allowed to recuperate in my own time without you flying at me."

"Good heavens, Charlotte, permit me my finer feelings. I certainly never fly at you."

"Yes, I suppose that's one thing you and Mama have in common. When you needle, it's with far more elegance than someone with my hysterical disposition."

"I wish you wouldn't throw up Augusta at me, or put her words in my mouth. I can't help having her for a sister any more than you can for a mother, and I'll thank you to remember that it's nothing to me if you marry or no."

Charlotte sniffed. "For a subject that is nothing to you, it must occupy your thoughts greatly, as you have had the indelicacy to broach it with me twice in one day. Gracious, what an uncomfortable change it must be for you to consider my matrimonial prospects superior to chattering endlessly about your precious Beethoven!"

I could hear the rustle of taffeta as Prudence settled herself on the floor. "Lottie," she said. "What is the trouble? Why do you speak to me this way, to wound me so? 'Indelicacy'? As though we had never spoken of such things before, or shared the most cherished yearnings of our hearts? You have changed this past year, for never until now has your heart been hidden from me, but I have gone on with perfect faith you would confide in me in time."

"There is nothing to confide," said Charlotte coldly.

"If you must scorn my confidence, have the goodness then not to insult my intellect. I have said I will not force your confidence, but I want only to know if you are withholding our former intimacy to punish me for some offense, for I swear I do not know what I have done!" Prudence's voice cracked.

Charlotte hushed her. "You'll wake the house. You've done nothing, Prudence, and I confide nothing because I have no wish to tell over the troubles of my heart. For my heart is troubled now, and the object that had occupied it removed. I will say no more. I have no wish to dwell on my grief."

"Better grief than such coldness! Grief I can help you mend."

"Huh. And I suppose you think Mr. Dawson the proper balm."

"Do you?"

"*Will* you leave off about Mr. Dawson! Why does nothing else seem to occupy your mind?"

"Because he has spent the entirety of your illness talking to me of you!"

There was a brief silence, and I wished fervently that I could see Charlotte's face as she took in this declaration. When she spoke again, however, it was in such a coldly ironical tone as to wipe away whatever emotions might have arisen. "Indeed?" she asked. "My, my Prudence, was it so terribly dull to speak of me being ill when you could have been discussing the symphony? I do apologize for depriving you of more scintillating conversation."

"If you think," said Prudence, her voice wavering, "that I could dismiss your illness so callously . . ." She trailed off a moment before collecting her thoughts and beginning again. "He came to dine with us again this evening, and I might have turned the conversation to whatever I liked, but I could not deprive either of us of the chance to seek solace in our mutual concern for you. We talked of you, Lottie, because we both of us love you, do you not see?"

Charlotte replied, "Oh, I see! You love me so well that you cannot wait until I am fully recovered before inflicting him upon me. Between you, you have decided it already, have you?"

"What power have I to compel you, Charlotte?" Prudence asked, wounded. "I am not Augusta, dictating to you. I wish only for you to be happy, as you once were!"

"That is impossible, now."

"Is it impossible to be happy with a man who thinks of nothing but you?" Prudence asked. "When we spoke this evening, he wanted nothing more than to hear if I had seen you and how you fared. He asked—" And here her voice cracked. "He asked if you had spoken of him, or if there was anything he could send you to make your convalescence more pleasant."

Charlotte's laugh chilled me. "It would have been more pleasant not to have been ill in the first place. Surely even you could understand that!"

"Even I!" said Prudence wonderingly. "I, who have expressed only love and concern for you! I, who have prayed every night you might be well! And this is how I am thanked for my solicitude."

"If only you knew," Charlotte said bitterly. "How solicitous I have been, you might think—"

There was the sound of a door opening and closing heavily down the hall at this, and I darted unceremoniously into my mistress's chamber to toss Charlotte her dressing gown, point to her bed, blow out her candle, and snatch Prudence Graham from off the floor where she sat at my mistress's feet and hustle her into my closet. From beyond the door, I could hear Charlotte vaulting into her bed a few moments before Mrs. Walden began to knock at her daughter's door.

Putting my finger to my lips, I motioned Prudence to be still as Charlotte feigned sleepiness to bid her mother enter. Their voices low, I could hear her mother's queries, Charlotte's quiet reassurance, and the sound of Augusta Walden closing the door behind her. When her footfalls had echoed away, Prudence and I peeked our heads into the dimness of Charlotte's bedroom. She peered at me from her bed, her skirts ballooning suspiciously from under the coverlet.

"Please see Miss Graham out," she whispered, and I nodded, taking my unlikely guest by the arm and leading her down the back stairs. Agnes was nowhere to be seen, and we crossed the kitchen silently before stepping together out into the mews. I drew my arms across my chest against the chill.

"Shall I get the carriage for you, Miss Graham? Or hail a hansom?" I asked, trying to be as solicitous and natural as my mistress would wish me to be.

"No, indeed, I shall walk. The hour is late, and the sound of hooves on the cobbles wouldn't do."

"What, alone, miss?" I said, for while I would not have thought twice of walking abroad myself at such an hour, I could hardly expect Prudence Graham to do it.

She shrugged, her diamond earbobs swaying. It struck me then how very hardy and practical she was behind her fine, elfin features, and she reminded me quite suddenly of Liddie. It seemed strange that I had never noticed it before, nor how much more delicate Charlotte's sensibilities were, for all she was the less ethereal-looking of the two. "Thank you for your assistance, Ballard," she said. "You have been most gracious this evening." And she strode purposefully off into the dark.

Having spent the days after my altercation with Johnny at the Hibernian, I forbore to take my night off the first Thursday following my return. Instead, I spent the evening sitting quietly in the kitchen with a cup of tea while Mrs. Freedman told me stories about her girlhood and mixed dough for the next day's baking. Meandering, good-natured stories, commonplace and comforting, sprinkled generously with advice on culinary technique. She reminded me of Da, training a skittish yearling: her low tones soothing. She talked of everything and nothing, interrupting her own tales to remark upon the ingredients she was adding, or the proper technique for kneading, before resuming as though she had never digressed. The table was covered in a fine dusting of flour, which was liberally smudged on her cheeks and apron. She drew absently in the flour dust, abstract spiral patterns that called to my mind the carvings you might see sometimes on the old monument stones back home in Ireland. As she went on drawing and erasing, her voice rising and falling, I felt lulled into the comfort of Mrs. Freedman's kitchen, and when my head began to nod, she shook me gently by the shoulder and sent me up to bed.

The following Thursday, Charlotte abed for the night, I made my way down the stairs to the kitchen. Mrs. Freedman, who was assembling the ingredients for her baking, looked up as I descended.

"You all finished for the night?" she asked. I nodded assent. "Then you best dress warm. The breeze's picked up again, and you don't want to catch a chill so soon after you've recovered."

I lingered at the bottom of the stair, my hands behind my back, pressed against the wall. "I wasn't so sure I'd go out tonight," I said, almost shyly. "If it's getting breezy again."

Mrs. Freedman turned to look at me, her hands on her hips. "I didn't peg you for the type who'd let a little breeze stand in her way. It's all well and good to rest up when you're needing rest, but if you let every stir of air keep you in the house, when you do finally set yourself outside again, you'll be blown off course. Not," she said, as I bit my lip, "that I mind your company. But you're too young to hang about my kitchen for fear of what you'll find if you head out-of-doors. Now, don't you think that aunt of yours must be missing you?"

"Yes, ma'am," I said, fetching my cloak.

"Then there's biscuits in the basket on the table, and a bottle of buttermilk for your aunt besides." She raised her brows at me. "And you see you get that basket back to me tomorrow morning, hear?"

"Yes, Mrs. Freedman."

"Young Frank is off down to Broadway later, if you've a mind to wait for him," the cook said carefully. "I'm sure he wouldn't mind escorting you as far as Houston if you're minded to the company."

God help me, but I actually considered letting a beardless boy squire me south of Washington Square, but then the fear that, in his gallantry, Young Frank might offer to bring me directly to my non-existent aunt's door held me back. Besides, she was right. I couldn't hang around the Walden kitchen forever. Instead, I met her eyes and shook my head determinedly.

"Good girl," she said, cocking her head at the door. "Now get."

I stood on the back steps into the mews, pausing for a moment with indecision. There was no one to wait for in the Waldens' carriage house. Liddie would be out making her circuit at this early hour. Screwing up my courage, I tramped down to the Hibernian.

Though light streamed from the windows and a fair crowd could be seen inside, the Hibernian felt deserted to me. The few men I thought I recognized turned aside when I entered, avoiding my eye. The rest were strangers, some who leered at me as I made my way toward the bar, some who ignored me altogether. It felt strangely like my first night, three years ago, and in my displacement and disorientation, I wondered if it was possible to live those three years over again, away from the Walden household, with my brother by my side.

Dermot approached me, a full mug ready in his hand. "Wondered if I'd see you tonight," he said, his voice husky.

"Ah, go on," I said, favoring him with a genuine smile. "If you're still pouring for me, you'll not keep me away."

He folded my narrow hands into his big ones. "There's my best lass. Ah, Maire, I've done wrong by you, I see that now."

I squeezed his hands. "I'll not hear that sort of talk from you, Dermot O'Brien. You've been a true friend to me these three years, and I'll hear naught against you, not even from yourself."

"Might not feel that way once we've had a bit o' time to sort things out," Dermot said gruffly. "How does this suit you? Ale's on me today, and when this place clears out, we can talk a bit, aye?"

"Aye, that'll suit grand," I said, releasing his hands. "I'm not bothered, Dermot. Whatever it is you need to say to me, I'm not bothered a bit."

He nodded, his eyes growing hard as he stared around the room behind me. I turned around. The patrons of the Hibernian, either openly or covertly, had their eyes fixed upon us. I lifted my chin, staring round the room, and Dermot's hand reached over the bar to squeeze my shoulder. The low rumble of voices had hushed. I sniffed audibly and turned back to the bar, draining my mug.

"I'll have another now, Dermot," I said loudly, bringing the mug down with a bang.

"Right so, lass," Dermot replied, filling it with ale. "There'll always be another pint ready for you here at the Hibernian." He turned blandly to the next customer, and I stood there, slowly sipping my ale. It was cool; my cheeks burned. It was the longest drink I ever had in my life, save for the one that came after it, and then the one after that. No one spoke to me, save Dermot, who came to refill my mug, and, as the night drew on, chat with me about terribly ordinary things: the weather, the price of ribbon, the fact that there were so many carriages nowadays that you could hardly walk down the street without being mired in shit. When the last patron had left, Dermot threw the bolt on the door and had me pull a bench up to the fire while he went for a bottle of whiskey.

We sat, sipping the amber liquid in silence a moment before Dermot spoke at last.

"You'll wonder, I suppose, how it is I'm a bachelor all these years, seeing as how I'm my own man with my own business and handsome as the devil himself to boot." He grinned rakishly at me, offering me the bottle.

"I had always wondered, now that you call it to my mind."

"Truth to tell, I was in love once," Dermot said. "Tiny slip of a thing, auburn-haired she was, come over from an estate in Meath. Never been off the estate her whole life, and scared to death of every noise and ruckus in the city. Didn't have your gumption, Mar, that's for certain. She was staying in the basement of the boardinghouse next to Trinity for nearly a week, and every day she'd come by with three or four other lassies to see if I had heard of any work for them. I thought maybe by and by she'd grow more used to the place, maybe less frightened. Ah, she was a sweet thing! A kinder, gentler soul I've never met. Sure, she was wasting away here downtown, her nerves jangled over every little thing. So finally, I found her a position up in the north of the island in Harlem Heights. I thought the country might put her in mind of home, and do her some good."

"And she liked it so well she stayed there and you've never heard of her since?"

"No."

"Or, no, let me guess. She married a farmer and bore his children and lived happily all her days?"

"No."

"Well, what then?" I asked. "Why didn't you fetch her down again and woo her properly?"

"She hanged herself on Michaelmas Eve, nine months to the day after she arrived."

I stared at Dermot, and Dermot stared at the fire. "Jesus fucking Christ," I whispered, crossing myself.

"I've spent years," Dermot said quietly, not looking at me, "wondering if it was my fault. If it was being there—and it was I who found her the position, she'd not have been there but for me, make no mistake—but if it was being there, so far away from her own people, that made her do it. Or if she would have done it wherever she'd ended up."

"I'm that sorry, Dermot," I said softly, slipping my hand into his.

"Her name was Maggie McArdle," Dermot said. "She's been gone seven years and more now, God rest her, and you'll wonder besides why I'm telling you about her now." I nodded, not trusting myself to speak. "Well, it comes to this. There isn't a day that goes by I don't think about Maggie and wonder if, when I thought I was doing what was best for her, I wasn't laying the path that sent her straight to hell. And I've done my best for you and for your brother, but I don't know that I've done you any better service, seeing the state things have come to, and I only hope I haven't made as terrible a botch of things this time around."

"Dermot," I said carefully. "You'd better start explaining things, for you're beginning to frighten me."

Dermot retrieved the bottle from me and poured himself another before he began. "You'll mind how when I pulled you off himself that there'd be those as wouldn't care overmuch for it if you clawed out his eyes?"

"That'd be the Order, I suppose," I said, staring at my drink.

Dermot snorted. "Aye, sure enough. I knew that light-skirts of yours was deeper in it than she'd let on."

"Not so deep," I said with a rueful laugh. "Possible now the Order was deeper in her."

Dermot chuckled. "Aye, men do like to talk once the deed is done. Like as not she doesn't know the true ins and outs, but what she does know is more than's good for her."

"But you're going to tell me." It wasn't a question.

"Oh, aye," he agreed.

"She told me," I said slowly, "that they were doing more than protecting the churches. She said they were protecting Irish businesses. For money. And that the money was going to buy guns and ammunition to be sent back to the Republicans and anti-Unionists in Ireland."

Dermot shook his head. "Aye, that's so. And, as I figured, more than is good for her, and sorrow on the fool who told it all to her."

"She said she saw a cache of guns at St. Patrick's one night, and Seanin was there," I said. "She's clever, and she pieced it all together. I don't think anyone told her outright."

"Then I suppose she's safe enough," Dermot considered. "If no one but you and I know how much she's privy to, there's none as'll trouble her, and now that your brother knows about the two of you, he's like enough to leave her alone."

"And what about you?" I asked. "Are you part of the Order too?"

"I am," Dermot said. "But not the way you're thinking of, the way Seanin is. That's a young man's game, brawling and carrying on the way they do. Nor do I pay protection the way the other alehouses and shopkeepers do. But when you're raising the kind of capital they do, you need a way to filter it through the proper channels, so. It doesn't do for a groom or a drover or a bricklayer to be buying up their own arsenal. Doesn't do for a publican either, when you come to it. But there's all types going in and out of an alehouse, and there's always money passing hands. So there's all types coming and going here, and every coin they have in the bargain."

"You're a go-between."

Dermot looked affronted. "You might as well call me a pander," he said. "Go-between indeed! Why do you suppose I call this place the *Hibernian*?"

My eyes went wide. "Then what on earth are ye—"

"I don't run the Order, and I didn't found it either," he said, interrupting me. "It's part of something far older, far deeper back home in Ireland. But I did my part in summoning together the parties at St. James last year, for there's not a man of them that hasn't passed through this alehouse. And I do keep this branch of it organized, so far's the Democratic party is concerned, sure enough. There's more to it than protection money and gun running. That's just the part your bit of skirt traced out. You don't have a group like that running that wide a racket in the city without Tammany's blessing. And I make sure we have that. Your brother may be a big man on the streets, but he's never the ward boss."

"And you are!"

"I am. I keep things sweet between the Order's *taisechs* and Tammany. We came to an understanding last week. He and his'll be drinking elsewhere from now on," Dermot said, taking a meditative sip of his whiskey. "I've introduced him around, and there're plenty of Irish doors open to him now."

"Where will he go?" I asked.

Dermot looked at me, considering. "I think perhaps it's better if you don't know. He's better at making his way than he was three years ago. Better at a lot of things. And if he's looking to cut ties with you, well, I'm not."

I could feel the tears forming in the corners of my eyes, and blinked them rapidly away. Dermot discreetly refilled my glass.

"It seems," I said carefully, "that all the men talk here is politics. Well, I suppose if you've got the vote you might very well go on and on about it. And from what I've seen, half of being political is thrashing the other side on Election Day."

"And every other day in between," Dermot said, rolling his eyes.

"But it strikes me that the other half is having the right alliances." I took a swallow of liquor. "Seems to me that my brother makes a better ally than I do."

"His lot isn't the only strong arm in the ward," Dermot said. "They're not even the only strong arm that drinks here, as you'd know if you came here any other day than Thursday. And besides, I'm not lacking for allies, lassie, on either side of the herring pond. But for all that, I've very few true friends. It took courage, coming back here tonight. It took courage to come banging on my door like a wee mad thing those years ago. I admire courage, Maire."

I closed my eyes. "And you're certain it isn't just headstrong foolishness?"

"There's that too," he said. "Did I not say you were mad?"

I smiled, opening my eyes again. "You did at that. Ah, Dermot,"

I said. "You are a good friend to me. And I'm proud to be a friend to you."

"And you aren't angry at me for what I've done for your brother?" he asked. "For helping him rise in the Order?"

"Go on," I said. "How could I be angry with you? Liddie said it was the only way to get ahead for someone like him, and I'd be a fool indeed to be angry at you for helping him get ahead."

"You know that's not what I meant," Dermot said. "There's ways to rise without taking up a brickbat or putting on lead knuckles. Precious few for an able-bodied lad like Seanin O'Farren, but I have the ear of enough Tammany Democrats that I maybe could have found one."

"Tell me," I asked. "If you had, do you think, truly, it would have stopped him from joining the Order?"

"Stopped him? No." Dermot scratched his head. "Redirected him, maybe. But after the fires two summers ago, your brother was a changed man. He was here almost every night of the week, sneaking out late, until he and his lot started meeting up at St. Patrick's maybe a year back. That's when they formed this branch of the Order, banded up all the small groups together. You see, Tammany doesn't mind the protection take—they get a cut, of course—and there's none of them as minds the brawling. But Tammany would rather the money was staying in the city, and it's not. The Order has a branch in Boston, and they've even had something to do with the coal miners in Pennsylvania. But they have a finger in every Irish pie this side of the Atlantic, and your brother is one of those who's always looking to see how they can be of benefit back to those on the other side."

"He would never have come here if it wasn't for me," I said. "Of course he's always looking back at Ireland. If there'd been anywhere else for us to go, any opportunities at all, we'd not have come here."

"I'll not have you blaming yourself. It's my fault he's got involved, and it's down to me he rose as far as he did. Your brother," Dermot said, stirring the embers of the dying fire, "as I was saying, was a changed man after that first fire. He and the lads had brawled a time or two with the nativists, but this was something else again. A pack of those rabbits down from Ward Eight were threatening to set fire to the rectory at St. Patrick's. He ended up down in the Five Points when the rioting got thick there."

I bit my lip. I had heard, of course, of the rioting and unrest in '35. We had been in New York for only a year, and that June the Waldens had been in Saratoga Springs, making their annual pilgrimage to the Grand Union. Seeing the newspapers, I had been wild with worry about Seanin, who had remained behind in the city, but when we returned he had seemed whole and sound, save for a split lip, already on the mend. A common enough injury, I had never asked how he came by it. Truth to tell, I hadn't wanted to know. But curiosity overtook me now, and I looked Dermot squarely in the eye, saying simply, "Tell me."

Seanin O'Farren was not entirely clear on how he came to be lying facedown in the filth and muck of Orange Street, a nativist rabbit's boot pressed against his neck. One moment, he'd been drinking with O'Malley and MacBride at the Hibernian, and the next he was near to drowning in the two inches of horse piss and spilled slops that coated the sloping streets while his assailant's hobnail boot cut into his flesh. The moments in between—the newsboy who brought word of St.

Patrick's rectory on fire, the mad scramble for cudgels and torches, the riotous march that had somehow brought him down into the Sixth Ward—seemed a dream. A blurred glimpse of jumbled images, already half-forgot. There was only *now,* and *now* it was imperative that he pull his nose and mouth from the sludge in the street and throw off the crowing bastard above, intent on bashing his skull in.

From somewhere very far away, he heard Quigley give a hearty *"faugh a ballagh,"* and the rabbit's weight shifted slightly as he turned his head toward the sound. It was subtle, but it was enough. Seanin grabbed the bastard's ankle with both hands and tugged, sending the rabbit sprawling. Gasping, he rolled over to the man, momentarily stunned, and gripped him by the greasy soap locks, wrapping his fingers in the rabbit's hair and using this handhold to bash the man's head against the filthy cobbles. The rabbit twitched and was still, stunned.

Seanin pulled the cudgel from the unconscious rabbit's hand and rose, wiping his face with a dirty sleeve, succeeding only in smearing the filth. He tasted iron, the bitter, metallic flavor of his own blood, overlaid with the reek of the excrement and filth that had recently filled his nostrils. The street was a battlefield, Irish and nativists grappling in silhouette as the flames from behind the church illuminated the scene. Somewhere, a fire wagon's bell clanged, announcing its approach, and it was any man's guess if the arriving company would set to work in putting out the flames or join the nativist rabbits against their Irish foes.

The church, god forgive him, was the least of Seanin's concerns just now. The street teemed with fighting men, each side doing its damnedest to savage the other, and Seanin waded into the thickest part of the fray instinctually, without pausing to consider a plan of action, but with only an inarticulate desire to take part in the savagery. Tightening his fist around his newly acquired cudgel, he raised the instrument and brought it firmly down on the head of the nearest rabbit, turning to meet the next foe before the first man had finished crumpling bonelessly to the ground. The weight of the thing in his hands reverberated with the impact as it connected solidly with another rabbit's head, his arms quavering with the effort of keeping the cudgel in his grasp. A feral glee welled up in him as he brought it down upon a third man, and in this state of bloodlust, he was blind to the fact that the swath of rabbits he was felling had attracted the attention of another of their ilk, who crept up behind him and jabbed a dirk into his side.

Stung, Seanin whirled, the blade still lodged between his ribs, and brought the cudgel across the rabbit's face, satisfaction blooming across his own features as the man's face caved obligingly in with a splattering of blood and a splintering of teeth and bone. He plucked nervelessly at the handle of the dirk, pulling it out and shoving his hand against the slice. Blood flowed freely against his hand, and he wondered absently if the blade had cut anything vital. If he was a walking dead man. That would be a shame, he thought in a detached sort of way as he raised his hand from the wound to wield the cudgel again. It would be unpleasant not to see his sister again. He felt the skin rip as he brought the thing to bear on yet another foe, and wondered if she would break the ruse they'd maintained to claim his body.

The shouts of the men, the sounds of metal and wood hitting flesh, the screaming of the fire horses at last arrived seemed muted and dull. His arms ached from swinging the cudgel, and then went numb. Time slowed, and there was suddenly no moment before this one, his face covered in shit and sweat, his hands slick with blood.

He had always been here on Orange Street, wounded and wounding, the heat of the flames warming his back. He would always be here. The stars were muted in the light from the blaze, but they prickled Seanin's eyes: the last thing he saw before collapsing in the street.

He awoke on the floor of the Hibernian. Scattered around him, a handful of men bled into the sawdust on the floor. His shirt was off and someone had bandaged the wound on his torso; every part of his body was sore. Moaning, he heaved himself upright, and a man in shirtsleeves who had been attending to one of his wounded mates turned at the sound.

"O'Brien!" the man called, and Dermot came clattering up the stairs, a bottle of whiskey in one hand, a pail of soapy water in the other. The man nodded at Seanin before turning back to his prone patient, and Dermot came over to help him up. Once he was seated on the floor, his back to the wall, Dermot poured him a mug filled to the brim with whiskey.

"For the pain," Dermot said, putting the stopper back in the bottle. "Yon Sweeney there"—the man in shirtsleeves cocked his head at the sound of his name—"Sweeney stitched you up. Says you'll mend fine, and a finer nick than Sweeney I know not, so you'll do."

"Glad to hear it," Seanin said, still dazed. He took a hefty swig of the whiskey, which helped his dizziness not at all.

"By all accounts, you acquitted yourself well," Dermot said, seating himself beside Seanin. "Very well indeed. So well, in fact, there's some of the lads looking to put a stop to all these riots that would see you and your mates do more in that line to prevent such things from occurring."

Seanin scrubbed a hand over his face. "More of that hell?" he asked. "Christ, Dermot, do y'know what went on out there?"

"That I do," the barman said wearily.

Seanin paused for another bolt of the whiskey. "There's knowing," he said. "And then again there's knowing. And now I know."

"What do you know, lad?"

Seanin told him. With the blood of his body and the filth of the street drying stiff on his trousers, the words tumbled out of him. Slowly at first, then gaining momentum, then—

"And when I woke, I was here," Seanin said. "Dead to the world while the finest nick you've ever known sews up the slits in me. And you want me and the lads to go out seeking that?"

Dermot refilled the whiskey, which had run low. "Well, lad," he said mildly. "Never did figure you for a coward, for all it's always been your sister with gumption."

Seanin scowled. "Aye, my sister. The one who can put on a voice and take off Ireland and never think twice about it. She always finds a way to get what she wants. To rise."

"And that's her way. Fine enough way, for a slip of a thing like her. But you'll never rise by the same path, Seanin."

Seanin shook his head. "Well, you're right enough about that. But she wouldn't have to take that path if she could do what she does and use her own voice plain enough. Or worship in her own church on Sunday. Dermot," he said suddenly, "is the church standing, still?"

"Flames never touched it," Dermot assured him. "Our boys had the water pumping away, to be sure."

"And what if it's this tavern next time?" he said. "Or what if one of them bastards hears us out on the street? I brought her here to protect her, but being Irish is no protection in this town, not from the likes of them."

"Then it sounds to me like you should meet up with those lads," Dermot said. "They're talking about taking a stand. And, sure, lad, isn't that why you're here after all? To make a better life?"

"That's so," Seanin said. "I've seen that there's more to life than the way I've been living it."

"Then get to living, lad," Dermot said. "Get to living."

It was the small hours before I made my way down to my pallet in the basement, and, though I had only a few hours to sleep before I must return to Washington Square, I found my mind too full of Dermot's story to seek my repose. With great prodding on my part and great reluctance on his, he had slowly revealed how Seanin had begun organizing the protection ring to keep Irish businesses safe from nativist gangs and Know-Nothings. I closed my eyes, but saw only Dermot's pleading face, asking me to consider Seanin's intentions, and I cursed myself for not considering them sooner. Seanin would have grappled at any chance he got to make something more of himself; was he not in love with the beauty of her generation? I was a fool to think he'd be content sneaking in and out of her bed, love's thief in the night. *Perhaps someday,* he had said, and I had never thought for a minute he was doing anything that might make "someday" a reality. More fool, I. Seanin O'Farren planned to get to living, and those plans included the woman he loved and the money to keep her. I wondered, excluded from and ignorant of his plans, where that left me.

> You should therefore obey directions with alacrity and cheerfulness, and not look sulky or mutter because those do not exactly accord with your own particular notions.
>
> —*The Duties of a Lady's Maid*

As the first thaw eased its way onto the island, the chill of Johnny's absence began to fade from the house on Washington Square. There was a new groom, Mr. Vandeman, engaged before Easter, having been recommended to the household by the ever-solicitous Mr. Dawson, and having passed deepest scrutiny from Mr. Buckley upon his hire. Young Frank, the stableboy, was grumbling in the kitchen that he should be passed over, and Cook rapped him sharply on the ear with a wooden spoon for gainsaying Mr. Buckley's wisdom in passing over a sixteen-year-old for the position. Grace Porter and I smiled into our teacups from across the room as Agnes tended to the wounded ear while Cook fumed.

"Aren't you ashamed of yourself, whining before Miss Ballard and Miss Porter, when you got no right to any station in this house except what you earn in it?" Cook left off brandishing the wooden spoon momentarily to stir something on the stove before turning and waving it menacingly at the pair, tiny, savory droplets scattering on the flagstones. "And don't you be getting any ideas up, Agnes, just 'cause that boy's making up to you with his hurt ear. He's a sly one, and I should know it. Just like his old daddy was."

"My daddy was good enough to be the Waldens' groom," Young Frank grumbled. "Seems like I ought to get a chance."

"Your daddy was twice your age before he ever came north, and thrice your age before old Mr. Walden hired him. He'd been breaking horses all over Georgia since he was a mite. How many horses've you broke?"

Agnes said something to Young Frank in an undertone that made both of them laugh, and Cook shot them a glare. Agnes excused herself, and Young Frank was left alone on a stool by the hearth, looking quite forlorn indeed.

"My father was a groom as well." The words were out of my mouth before I knew it.

Young Frank looked up, surprised, as well he might be. I had never addressed him directly before; he was always with Johnny. Cook looked at me queerly from the corner of her eye but said nothing.

"He started out in the stables when he was a lad, and he worked his way up. He was made head groom by the time I was still a little girl. There was no one gentler or trustier with horses. The old master used to say there was no one who could train a team like him. But he worked at it for years, you know. His whole life he did nothing but train horses."

Young Frank swallowed. "My daddy, too. When I was small, he used to take me up to the fields in Harlem with him to watch him break horses."

"Maybe you could ask Mr. Vandeman to let you help?" I smiled encouragingly.

"I'm sure he would," Grace put in unexpectedly. "After all, Mr. Dawson recommended him, and I feel certain that a man who came with Mr. Dawson's stamp of approval would have the whole household's best interests at heart."

"Yeah, maybe I should ask him." Young Frank brightened. "I'd like that."

"Then you best shake a leg back to the carriage house and be where he can see you," said Cook, her hands on her hips. Her son leapt from his stool, pecked her hard on the cheek, and, grinning at me, dashed out into the mews, slamming the door behind him.

Cook shook her head, sighing as she turned her attention back to the stew.

"It's that age. It's tragedy one minute, and sunshine the next. Lord, if I wasn't trouble too in those years, always sighing after something. Boys have it easier, I expect. Something to do with all that energy. Least I wasn't crying at the drop of a pin like that Agnes." She pursed her lips. "Impossible to train. Tears if you give her the slightest word. I declare, that girl'll be the death of me."

I heard a distinct sniff from the shadow of the stair, and it was clear Cook heard it too, for she raised her voice, saying, "And unreliable! Never around when I need her!" There was a scrape and a scuffle and Agnes fell over herself into the room. Grace, in a remarkable and hitherto unprecedented show of actual human decency, set down her teacup, rising and excusing herself. I followed, the sounds of Cook scolding the girl echoing up the stair behind us.

The changes wrought by Johnny's departure extended throughout the house. Mr. Dawson had become a regular fixture in the Waldens' parlor, and at the dinner table as well, as Charlotte, sobered by how close she had come to ruin, began at last to heed her mother's matrimonial urgings. Upon Charlotte's full recovery, Mrs.

Walden had closeted herself with her daughter in the drawing room for hours, and Liza—waiting, she claimed under Mrs. Harrison's withering look, to do the dusting—had lingered outside the door and heard it all. The merits of becoming Baroness Muskerry were laid out, debated, and abandoned in favor of the Dawson estates and their substantial income. For once, the ladies of the house were in agreement; a title, however grand, that could be maintained only on Charlotte's annuities was a precarious investment for any future issue in Mrs. Walden's opinion, while Charlotte remained adamant that she should not wish to emigrate.

Grace Porter sniffed derisively at Liza's recital, closing it with her considered opinion that it was rank brazenness to listen at doors, and her declaration that she would trim her new bonnet in her own quarters until supper before exiting the kitchen with sanctimonious dignity. Cook snorted after she was gone.

"Jealous she couldn't break the news herself, I expect," she said. "There now." She turned to Liza, who looked both pleased and stricken. "There's not a one of us that wouldn't have done the same, girl, least of all Miss High-and-Mighty Porter."

Mrs. Harrison inspected her keys, something like mirth creeping at the corners of her mouth, and said, "Oh really, Bertha, don't encourage the girl."

"You go on and have yourself a good laugh, Jane," said Cook, "if you haven't forgot how. Now, I think Liza's brought us news worth celebrating."

"Celebrating?" inquired Mr. Buckley. "Whatever exactly would we celebrate?"

"Just like a man! Why, the fact our princess won't be leaving the country!"

"Now, now," said Mr. Buckley. "I would think that's a little premature. After all, she hasn't married Mr. Dawson yet."

I laughed outright at this, bitterness mingling with amusement. "Indeed, Mr. Buckley, you must be the only man in New York who thinks that Charlotte Walden couldn't marry any man she sets her cap on."

Mr. Buckley sputtered a bit at this, but the knowing looks of every woman in the kitchen stifled him before he could give voice to his indignation.

> Another requisite of attention is, an observant eye to every thing that you see done; and if you are not perfect for want of practice, try your hand at it privately till you are.
>
> —*The Duties of a Lady's Maid*

In the month that followed Charlotte's resolution to secure her place in society as Mrs. Elijah Dawson, I would have been hard-pressed to say who was wooing whom. Mr. Dawson's visits were marked by an increase in Charlotte's musical repertoire; as fast as he brought her gifts of sheet music, she had the songs memorized. The tulips and lilacs he brought her were arranged carefully on the side tables in Mrs. Walden's best crystal vases. Young Frank was kept busy currying Charlotte's palfrey, Angelica, for, though she did not relish riding, she accepted Mr. Dawson's invitations to join him on horseback with alacrity.

In addition to his morning calls, Mr. Dawson seemed to have developed an almost preternatural sense of when Charlotte could be found taking a turn in the Square. More than once, she had gone out with Prudence to take in the spring air and returned with Mr. Dawson, who had fortuitously happened upon the ladies and insisted upon squiring them home. Invariably, he would return with them flanking him to the Walden residence, one auburn and one dark, one sedate and one agitated.

Indeed, Mr. Dawson's increased presence in the Walden home seemed to drive the Grahams from it. While Prudence and Charlotte had once exhibited in the music room together, it soon became obvious that Mr. Dawson's after-dinner conversation had but one object. Prudence Graham's face took on a pinched and sour look as she watched Mr. Dawson's attentions focus on her niece, and, rather than endure the slight, invitations to the Grahams began to return declined. Now Mr. Dawson himself played upon the pianoforte while Charlotte sang, and Mrs. Walden filled the void left by her family around her table with Jays and Astors to witness courtship's triumph.

The entire household was seized with anticipation for Charlotte; Grace Porter even took the opportunity to listen ignobly at the dining room door between courses one night, to the great annoyance of Mr. Buckley and Eben, until Mrs. Harrison at last banished her to her parlor for the remainder of the meal. Liza and Millie found every possible occasion to bustle quietly but industriously in and out of the hall past the sitting room when Mr. Dawson was paying court, and we hung upon each word of their reports. It seemed Charlotte Walden's suitor spent hours conversing with the object of his affections and her mother, taking great care to cultivate Augusta Walden's esteem along with her daughter's.

He needn't have bothered. I hardly had to linger in halls to learn how my mistress felt about Mr. Dawson and his suit. There were no secrets anymore between Charlotte and me; in the weeks and months of Johnny's absence, the warm intimacy of that night by the fire bloomed and deepened as I became her truest confidante in Prudence's absence. Charlotte and Augusta Walden were both determined to ensure a proposal from Elijah Dawson by season's end, and it would have taken some paramount scandal to have deterred them from this object.

Determination was one thing, but enthusiasm quite another.

Charlotte had given Mr. Dawson no reason to doubt her interest in his suit, and Augusta Walden had contrived many times to allow them the privacy needed for a declaration. Still, he persisted in his interminable suit, as cautious and circumspect as ever he had been before the ball. Charlotte thought of nothing else but enduring his modesty until his proposal, and I nodded while she listlessly told over the details of his wooing.

"The periwinkle muslin this morning, Ballard. Mr. Dawson likes me best in blue."

"I enjoyed the opera this evening. I suppose it is a blessing I am fond of music, for he keeps a box, and attends every production of the season."

"Not dove-colored taffeta, Ballard. Mr. Dawson called me pale when last I wore it, and worried over me all evening."

"Indeed, miss?" I asked in concealed exasperation at this last, for this was not to be the first or last occasion that Mr. Dawson's opinions of Charlotte's gowns had caused me some concern. Her lemon ball gown with the cream and gold lace trim had made her seem sallow. The fawn poplin day dress with the coffee braid had been called mousy. Unsurprisingly, though, it was his reaction to her new Brunswick green riding habit that troubled me the most.

"Mr. Dawson says I have a very fine seat when I ride. It is well to know he is a kindly liar," Charlotte said, frowning at her reflection as I eased the velvet jacket from her shoulders. "Perhaps, though, Ballard . . ." She trailed off, hesitating, and I could feel the discomfort she could not seem to voice. "Perhaps it will be warm enough to wear my navy twill next time. The one from last season? I do not think Mr. Dawson favored my habit."

"Did he not, Miss Charlotte?" I inquired blandly, inwardly

seething that yet another item must be banished from Charlotte's repertoire. "I will own, the skirt is rather wider than your navy twill, but I do think it quite lovely when it is draped properly."

"I believe it was not so much the quantity of the fabric to which he objected as the color," Charlotte said, still frowning. "He said the Brunswick made such a contrast with my hair that it looked far too red. Almost . . . almost Irish, he said." My mistress had the grace to blush.

I murmured something about having her navy twill habit ready the next time, eager as ever to soothe her disquiet, and inwardly reminded myself that I must not let my accent slip lest Mr. Dawson suspect me. After all I had sacrificed to stay by Charlotte's side, it would not do to be dismissed now. Perhaps, I reasoned, it was merely a manner of speaking—but I vowed to take care in the event it was not. It was impossible to know, after all, what thoughts churned behind Elijah Dawson's placid veneer.

Perhaps it is very strange, but in the wake of all that had befallen, it was some time before it occurred to me that I had had but little opportunity to observe the man who now occupied Charlotte's attentions, if not her affections.

Studying over the little notebook where I made record of what Charlotte had worn, and before whom, wondering a little frantically if perhaps a grayish lavender might satisfy Elijah Dawson's mania for blue, I happened to think of that esteemed suitor's valet. I had no notion who the man might be—old or young, knowing or naïve—but it occurred to me in a flash that, whoever he was, it was unlikely he was studying the contents of his master's wardrobe and agonizing over the lack of variety his master's intended had indicated in his choice of cravats. When it came to it, I had very little notion of Mr. Dawson himself, for all Charlotte might tell over his reactions and qualities at the end of each day, besides the sense that he was not to be pleased unless he had ordered things just so. If Charlotte suggested a duet, he had no compunctions about critiquing her choice in favor of his own. If she should propose a route to ride, he was ready with a more suitable alternative. I had had no opportunities to observe him closely, and what I could say of him, aside from being a careful and captious suitor, was, I suppose, in fact, praise for his valet. He was clean-shaven, save for neatly barbered side wings, and his straw-colored hair was always parted sharply to the side and sparingly macassared. He favored dark frock coats with fawn-colored trousers, when not in riding breeches, that is, and, aside from his equal appreciation for music and the equestrian arts, I knew nothing more of the man.

There was little information to be gleaned from Charlotte, who seemed to take her suitor's constant comments about her pallor and appearance in stride. When I had prepared Charlotte for bed each Thursday night, her milky skin had grown rosy and her green eyes bright. On those nights, her voice had fairly shaken with joy, her excitement palpable. I had hated those nights, hated her heated anticipation of my brother with a jealousy that writhed and seethed below the surface of my placid features. Now, all light had gone out of Charlotte. She confided the details of Mr. Dawson's growing regard for her with all the vim of a reluctant schoolboy's recitation. My heart, once full of spite toward her lover, grew heavy with borrowed sadness. I did what I could to buoy her: this new, sedate, and spiritless Charlotte.

When it finally occurred to me that there was now one in this household who must know, if not Mr. Dawson himself, then the man's valet, I made haste to this source of information. Surely, I thought, if I could but glean insight into Mr. Dawson's mind, I could help Charlotte put an end to his interminable courtship and settle her for once and all.

Mr. Vandeman had worked hard to ingratiate himself with the household since his arrival. Young Frank's timid suggestion that the southern pastures of Harlem made for a fine place to break the yearlings was rewarded with the offer to assist that Young Frank had so coveted. Mr. Vandeman had squired Millie and Liza to a Bowery music hall one night, and he always seemed ready to assist Eben and Eugene in the heavier household tasks. He took pains to praise Cook's dishes, and he even managed to put in a kind word for Agnes. In an effort to prove that I held no prejudice against all grooms, I had made myself civil with the man, but Grace Porter, despite her great respect for Mr. Dawson's recommendation, remained stalwartly unimpressed. As a result of Grace's aloofness, I had yet to have the opportunity to speak with the man at great length.

Thus resolved, I made directly for the carriage house, grabbing an apple from the kitchen bin on my way out into the mews. There was a light drizzle, and I strode quickly over the cobbles to duck inside. The carriage house was warm, smelling of sweet mash and musky horse. I went immediately to Charlotte's palfrey, Angelica. I had avoided the stable since my brother's departure, and found suddenly that I had missed my visits there, however rare they might be. Angelica, now spoiled by Young Frank with frequent attention, came eagerly to the side of her box, whickering expectantly. I laughed aloud at the lovely creature and her expectations, holding out the apple I had brought for her. It was gone in two bites.

"She's gotten greedy." A low voice came from behind me. I turned a pleasant smile on Mr. Vandeman.

"She works so hard," I said, wiping the mare's spittle on my handkerchief.

He laughed. "Well, she's no dray!"

"That's true enough. Though before Mr. Dawson began to pay Miss Walden court, she was idle more often than not."

Mr. Vandeman patted Angelica's neck. "It's not good for them to be idle," he said. "They're meant to run, see. This little girl should have seen a good deal more exercise before."

"Then it is well you are here now to attend to her properly," I said. "We are grateful for Mr. Dawson's reference."

"As am I," he said.

"The city must seem so close to you after living in the country."

"True, true, but I'd come here enough times to know what to expect. And, naturally, I'm grateful to Mr. Dawson for helping me to the position. Salisbury Park is a fine estate, as fine a one as you'll find on the Island, I believe, and I'd spent my whole life there, but there was no room to rise."

"How fortunate, then, that Mr. Dawson was able to recognize your talent and ambition and help you to make the most of it!"

"Well, I've known him since we were both lads," Mr. Vandeman said. "Mr. Elijah, as he was then, he always had one eye on the stables, see? Riding and hunting—it was him that taught me to shoot. Fine seat, that man, and a fine shot as well."

"Oh?" I asked. "Do you hunt, then?"

"I did, out on Long Island. Used to go with the farrier, Ned. Fine tracker, Ned. Well, he'd have to be, knowing hooves."

I felt distinctly out of my depth in this conversation of masculine pursuits, and so nodded absently as I tried to compose a way of turning the subject. My misgivings must have shown in my face, for Mr. Vandeman smiled broadly and said, "Ah, but I am certain you must have ventured over for something other than a tale of Ned Walton's tracking skills. May I assist you, Miss Ballard?"

"You are good, Mr. Vandeman," I said, "to divine that I am indeed in need of aid."

"You have but to ask," Mr. Vandeman said. "Though I must warn you that while I'm a fair hand with a currycomb, I know little of hairdressing."

"Then permit me to be blunt—perhaps even indelicate," I said, plunging forward. "Surely it has not escaped your notice that Miss Walden is being courted earnestly by Mr. Dawson."

"I'd be a purblind fool not to have noticed," he said, mirth playing at the corners of his mouth.

"And I could not help but wonder, if, knowing Mr. Dawson as well as you do, you might have some . . . insights that would benefit my mistress?"

"Well, I can see your dilemma plain. May I be blunt in return?"

"You may," I said, relieved he had grasped the situation so quickly.

"Then I can offer you this," Mr. Vandeman said. "Mr. Dawson was never one to do a thing in haste. If he was hunting, he would lie in wait until he was certain beyond a doubt he'd have a clear shot and assured of his success. I've never been courting, but for a man like Mr. Dawson, I would reckon he might take that approach to it, see?"

"I do see," I said. "He must be assured that the way is clear. I believe I can help Miss Walden to give that impression. Thank you, Mr. Vandeman. You have been most helpful."

"And one thing more," Mr. Vandeman said. "Mr. Dawson might prefer to hunt game, but more often than not, you'd find him shooting grouse for his grandmother's table. He's devoted to old Mrs. Dawson."

"I'm grateful, Mr. Vandeman," I said, filing that away. "Truly."

"I'm simply glad I could oblige you, Miss Ballard. Are you returning to the kitchen? Perhaps you could tell Young Frank he's wanted out here."

I assured him I would do so, and, thanking him again, went back to the house.

Grace Porter, happily, was in the kitchen, and after I had let Young Frank know he was wanted, I turned my attention to her. Mr. Vandeman's information would do little for Charlotte—Mrs. Walden was my target now.

I allowed Grace to pour me a cup of the tea she and Mrs. Harrison had brewed, and sat to wait for my opening. It didn't take long; Grace was eager to discuss the next evening's dinner, at which Mr. Dawson would be in attendance.

"Do you think it might be tomorrow?" she asked. "Perhaps he will arrive early and ask her then."

"I have wondered," I said very slowly, "if perhaps it is the choice of company that has deterred him."

"What on earth can you mean?" Grace asked. "Who could object to dining with the Astors?"

"Certainly that is not what I wanted to imply," I assured her. "But an invitation to the Astors always includes Miss Emily Astor and young Mr. John Astor, and I must wonder if another young man at the table might give Mr. Dawson reason to pause in his suit."

"Why, Mr. John is still at college—he is practically a child," Grace scoffed. "Certainly Mr. Dawson cannot see him as a rival?"

"But what of Mr. Ward, who sometimes comes with Miss Astor?" I pressed.

"He is Miss Astor's beau. Mr. Dawson must have eyes in his head to see that," Grace said. "Mrs. Walden only invites him when young Mr. Astor cannot make up the party."

"But do you agree that Mr. Dawson sees it that way? He has been such a careful suitor, and perhaps he supposes that Miss Walden's affections are not secure."

"Gracious, what a queer thought," Grace said. "If I were him, I should be quicker to secure them, if I suspected that there might be other admirers. And why shouldn't there be, I ask you, with a young lady like our Miss Walden?"

"I couldn't say," I relented. "But I am so fully in agreement that this courtship is becoming tedious that I am casting about for any reason I can think of for delay."

I could see the gears churning in Grace's head and said no more: the seed was planted. Either she would find a way to speak to Mrs. Walden or no; there was nothing more I could do in the matter. Still, the weeks crept by and I was rewarded to see that the Waldens' table was more frequently occupied with married couples.

At last, in early May, there came the invitation for Mrs. Walden and Charlotte to spend the weekend at the Dawsons' estate. Geraldine Dawson had not left the grounds in nearly twenty years, and it was not to be expected that she would do so now, even to approve her grandson's choice of bride. Mrs. Walden directed Grace and me in the packing herself, forcefully asserting which gowns she felt showed Charlotte to her best advantage while the object of all this fuss sat in her tufted chair by the fire, her eyes downcast.

Augusta Walden was not fond of visiting, and I had only rarely been required to travel outside the city since I'd arrived. There had been only the yearly sojourn the Walden and Graham ladies had taken to Saratoga Springs in imitation of the trips Augusta Graham and Sabrina Clemons had taken during their debutante years. On those occasions, Charlotte and Prudence had spent much of their time perched on the bench of the Grand Union's pianoforte, strolling the grounds, or attending one of the salons organized by Madame Eliza Jumel and her daughter, Mary Chase. Packing for those occasions had been a simple affair, and Grace, familiar with the journey after years of accompanying them, had directed things with a steady hand. Now, as we prepared to visit the Dawsons' estate, I thought back on Mr. Vandeman's observation about Mr. Dawson's devotion to his grandmother. I tried to consider every possible item that I might need to attend to Charlotte whilst we were away. I remembered parties of Mrs. Boyle's cousins coming up from Dublin to summer in Donegal, and tried to recall what the young ladies had done. The gentlemen had gone shooting, and the ladies had done a great deal of walking out. I had never been to Long Island—did the gentry go out walking there? Unresolved, I packed Charlotte's sturdiest boots and spare traveling gown anyway. Grace Porter and I oversaw the loading of our mistresses' trunks onto the back of the coach before Mr. Vandeman and Young Frank handed us up and we were off.

The day was bright and brisk, a light breeze wafting off the river as we passed the docks. I'd had no occasion to come down to this district since the first time I'd been there. The shouts of sailors, the bustle of porters, and the mingled smell of brackish water and fish reminded me of that first fateful day I stepped from the *Peregrine*. I looked about, wondering how Johnny and I, ragged and dazed, had navigated our way out of the press—more people crowded together than we had ever seen before in one place—and made our way through the narrow, twisting streets. Above the box, looking down on the jumble below, I felt worlds away from the bewildered lass who'd clutched her brother's hand. It must have been a lifetime ago.

It was impossible, then, not to wonder where he was now, my brother. I tried to picture him as we stumbled through New York's winding streets from the harbor, the way his arm curled protectively around mine, but the image was almost immediately replaced by the baleful look of hatred as he'd glared at me from his reddened eyes before cursing us, Charlotte and me, for what we'd done. My stomach lurched, and my carefully schooled features must have slipped, for Grace Porter patted my arm awkwardly and assured me that we'd be away from the dockside stench of fish soon enough. I smiled weakly at her, banishing Johnny from my thoughts with a flicker of anger.

The ferry crossing was blessedly smooth, though I was grateful to reach the Brooklyn side. From the way Grace had gone on, echoing Mrs. Walden's opinion that Long Island was a barren wilderness, I had expected a lonely, winding path through great, untamed forests. I was instead surprised by the neatly laid out fields, the tidy hamlets and villages we passed through on well-tended macadam roads. The farmhouses were of fieldstone and timbered, with a solid, patrician look to them, and I was impressed by the air of quiet, unassuming cultivation. The smell of freshly tilled fields and the warbling birdsong reminded me of Donegal, and I thought how strange and familiar it was to be in the country again after so long. I had closed the door so thoroughly on my old life, and, for the first time, homesickness welled up in me.

We rested the horses at an inn while the ladies dined. Grace, Mr. Vandeman, and I took our places at the end of a bare wooden table in the back of the courtyard, and the innkeeper's daughter brought us mugs of small beer, followed by a platter piled high with bread, cheeses, and cold meats: jellied tongue, sausages, and cured pork. She left it in the center of the table with a pot of mustard and a jar of gooseberry jam. Mr. Vandeman tucked in while Grace stared at the heap in bewilderment. There were neither plates nor utensils, save a knife stuck in one of the cheeses. Dismayed, she picked at a slice of bread, eyeing Mr. Vandeman's show of good appetite with mild distaste.

The groom in question suddenly seemed to realize he was the sole member of our trio enjoying the repast and looked up at us on the other side of the table. "Tuck in, if you're minded to eat," he said, gesturing with the knife he had excavated from the cheese. "It'll be three or four hours yet before we reach the Park, see."

I eyed the half-chewed mass of bread and meat in his hand before reaching for a slice, daubing the bread with mustard, wrapping the results around a sausage, and taking as delicate a bite as could be managed. Grace's eyebrows shot into her bonnet.

"Here, Miss Porter, allow me," Mr. Vandeman said, placing his makeshift sandwich directly onto the bare table and brushing his hand off on his trousers. He smeared some jam onto a slice of bread, speared a piece of tongue with the knife, and deposited it on the bread, bits of jelly still clinging to it. He wiped the knife off on a clean slice of bread and then proceeded to shave a few bits of cheese off one of the hunks. These he sprinkled atop the tongue and covered it over with the second piece of bread before presenting it to Grace with a marked show of gallantry that was utterly lost upon the poor woman in her horror of the comestibles being offered to her. She inclined her head graciously and took the proffered sandwich, taking a small bite and smiling fixedly as she chewed under Mr. Vandeman's eye. Satisfied that his efforts were appreciated, Mr. Vandeman retrieved his abandoned refreshment from the table and resumed cramming it in his mouth.

I suppressed a smile as I chewed my own meal, wondering where on earth Grace Porter went on her nights off. I, certainly, was used to such fare, though I might ape at gentility for Grace's benefit. But this, as every other aspect of the façade I employed in the Waldens' house, was as cultivated and studied as the accent I put on whenever I opened my mouth. Grace, though. She was the genuine article. She never stayed out on Thursday nights, I knew, but returned punctually at eleven to her own room below the attic. I tried to picture her tapping her feet at a music hall, or raising a pint in a pub, and the image nearly choked me laughing.

Covering my amusement, I turned to Mr. Vandeman. "I suppose you will be glad to return to Salisbury Park again?" I inquired.

He smiled, pleased to be addressed. "I am at that. Mr. Gregory, that's the head groom there, see? He taught me all I know, but it's a bold man that would think to fill Ignatius Gregory's shoes." He chuckled. "It'll be fine to see the old man. He's been like a father to me, see, and I'd be lying if I said I didn't suffer a bit of the sin of pride coming back now, head groom in my own right."

"Well," I said warmly. "I must say, I think it seems likely that we might have more frequent occasion to make this journey, and it is well we have so familiar a driver as yourself to take us."

I kicked Grace gently under the table, and she chimed in, "Oh, indeed!" before pausing to consider the food in her hand. "This is . . . not unpleasant fare. My thanks, Mr. Vandeman."

The remainder of our repast passed pleasantly enough as I plied Mr. Vandeman with questions about Salisbury Park and received, for my pains, such details about the property and household as minded me that an estate on Long Island was probably run no differently than an estate in Donegal after all. When the innkeeper's daughter returned to tell us that the ladies were ready to continue their journey and inquire if the horses were sufficiently rested, I felt satisfied that I should be able to acquit myself credibly in Mr. Dawson's home.

As Grace and I settled onto our seat, Grace leaned over and said, "Do you know, Miss Ballard, I do believe I find Mr. Vandeman to be quite a civil sort of man. Yes, quite civil indeed."

"Tell me, Miss Porter," I asked. "Where do you go on your nights off?" And the remainder of the trip was filled with an enlightening portrait of the Episcopal Ladies' Missionary Society.

We turned off the main road two hours before sunset, making our way up the drive, overhung with trees, to Salisbury Park. The stately redbrick manor house appeared at last from behind the trees, and I took in the sight with mingled appreciation and apprehension. Should Charlotte Walden secure a proposal from Elijah Dawson, I thought, this was my first sight of my new home.

I never met a housekeeper who wasn't imposing—no woman rises to such a state in the world without that quality—but Mrs. Crenshaw wore the dignity of her office more subtly than most. She greeted Grace and me cordially, escorting us to the room we were to share, giving quiet direction to a chambermaid we passed in the winding corridor. Her voice never rose above a murmur, nor needed it to, for her staff listened attentively and obeyed her in an instant. The butler, it transpired, was Mr. Crenshaw, and between this equally taciturn specimen and his wife there seemed genuine affection. Much later that night, in the blessing over the meal, I saw him squeeze her hand, and she allowed herself a small smile. It was a shock, after the stony but civil relations of Mrs. Harrison and Mr. Buckley, and, back at Ballyboyle, Mrs. Morgan and Mr. Noonan had seemed to be two halves of the same stern beast.

As I dressed Charlotte for the evening in a brocade silk of celestial blue, it was clear I felt more nerves than did my mistress. Charlotte sat motionless, still as her own reflection in the mirror, as I twined up her hair in a neat braided coil atop her head. I fixed her pearls about her neck and held out the earbobs to her. She stared at the pair of pearls resting in my hand, her eyes unmoving for so long I cleared my throat nervously. She plucked each pearl from my palm, moving deliberately, and fastened them to each ear. I extended my arm and helped her to rise, and she smiled wanly at me. I smiled back, bobbing a curtsy, and left her to prepare to meet Geraldine Dawson.

I was not to meet Mrs. Dawson during our visit to her home, although I did catch sight of her that evening as I left Charlotte's room. She was a small woman, straight-backed, who wore her age with dignity. Her crisp, white curls fell from a black lace cap to lie against her papery cheeks. Her black moiré dress had the tiered gigot sleeves that had grown so popular when the English princess wore them, which I though very modish, though she wore the style so gracefully that one might think it had been the vogue her whole life. Her only ornament was a large cameo. I gave her a little curtsy before scuttling from her view.

Down in the hall, Mrs. Crenshaw introduced me to a bland-faced man who transpired to be Mr. Lindeman, Mr. Dawson's valet. Mr. Lindeman might have been anywhere between forty and sixty, and was possessed of a soft voice and a bright eye. Crisp of trouser break, spotless of cuffs, he was possessed of those qualities that spoke of a confirmed bachelorhood, which put me greatly at ease. I knew, of course, in many households, that between a lady's maid and the master's valet there were "expectations," and reflected that it was good fortune to be thrown in with one who was as ill-disposed to women as I was to men. I exchanged a few pleasantries with him, recalling how I'd wondered about the subservient creature responsible for Mr. Dawson's cravats, and regretfully excused myself from the conversation as Grace plucked at my sleeve. If all went as planned, I would have time enough to get to know Mr. Lindeman in the years ahead.

There is much one can glean about the temperament of the master in the observation of his servants. Though Mr. Dawson spent much of his time at his Great Jones Street address, his influence and that of his grandmother were clear in their choice of staff. Unlike the eclectic jumble of voices in the Waldens' kitchen—drawling southern accents and brown skin mingling with clipped British English and the squashed vowels of those born in New York, the servants of Salisbury Park reminded me of Ballyboyle. Here, not only were the distinctive Long Island accents uniform, but the same prominent nose or blond curls might be seen on multiple members of the same family, all living and working under one roof. Estate life here, as in Ireland, appeared to be a multigenerational affair, and I filed this knowledge away to discuss with Charlotte later. If she were to become the mistress of Salisbury Park, she must understand the traditions and hierarchies in order to command her domestics' respect.

It seemed an age I sat with Grace in the servants' hall, the young maids watching the footmen play at cards, and I wondered, looking at the wistful, attentive faces of the maids, how different my life might have been if I had ever been the sort inclined to fancy one of the footmen over one of the chambermaids. What must it be like to wear one's want and need so baldly on one's face, advertising one's intentions for all to see—indeed, hoping for them to be seen, and recognized, and returned. I was too used to schooling my features to blush or become otherwise moved by such a thought, but I spared a moment to wonder if Charlotte, too, was schooling her features in a different way. Smiling when she would rather not. Forcing a light she did not feel into her eyes. Advertising that interest, that desire, which every human creature hopes one day to see in eyes riveted to his or herself, though she felt it not. That first night, when she rang for me, I undressed her in a silence tinged with mutual relief.

It was not until I was unpinning her hair that her eye caught mine in the mirror, and my heart near broke at the sadness I read there. Wetting my lips nervously, I strove to divert her.

"I say, Miss Charlotte," I began, attempting to keep my tone light. "If I'm to judge the cookery of Salisbury Park by that jugged hare, I shall have to let out both of our gowns by this time next year." She was silent after this observation, and I tried again. "Why, Porter had two portions, and she eats like a bird, it was that rich. No offense meant to Mrs. Freedman's cooking, of course," I added when she did not respond. "Of course, we do not have game as often," I ended weakly.

"There is always a game course at Salisbury Park," said Charlotte bitterly. "Mr. Dawson insists upon it, and provisions the table himself whenever he may."

"Indeed, miss?"

"And there are always tea roses, white ones, in memory of Mr. Dawson's father and brothers," she said, almost angrily.

"What a nice tradition," I said, still lightly.

"And when I am Mrs. Dawson," she said, her voice shaking, "I shall take my place at the table, wearing the blue gown he insists upon, and become another tradition in this place—another windup figure in this clockwork house!" Tears had begun leaking from the corners of her eyes, and I moved to put my hand on her shoulder, but she batted me away.

"My role is already written for me," she said, after a moment. "All I have to do is parrot back the lines he expects me to speak and my place is secure." She shuddered, straightening her back and dashing her tears away. "Forgive me, Ballard, for my momentary weakness. I made my choice when I drank that tea. Let us speak no more of this."

I murmured my assent and helped her into the canopied bed. Later, when I lay awake staring at the ceiling, I wondered if she, too, was gazing up at the hangings on her bed, too fretful for sleep to take her.

Salisbury Park boasted a maze, in which Grace and I distracted ourselves as the visit drew on. Grace was unusually silent as we took the turnings, our arms linked in an unaccustomed show of camaraderie, for we were both consumed by a sense of tense anticipation to which neither of us felt able to give voice. Instead, we ambled through the shrubberies, taking each dead end or through way in stride, neither heartened nor discouraged as we made our way. It was a warm day, and shady in the maze, with melodies of birdsong ringing pleasantly, though all felicity went unappreciated by either of us.

In the afternoon, oppressed by the tension of Grace's company, I inquired as to the direction of the stables, hoping that, as usual, the familiar sights and scents there would soothe me. It had been an age since I had seen the inside of a stable larger than the Waldens' small outbuilding in the mews, and, knowing from Charlotte's apathetic chatter that Mr. Dawson was an accomplished horseman, I looked forward to visiting a stable like the one back at Ballyboyle.

I made my way across the back courtyard and let myself into the stables. The wide central aisle was paved in fieldstone, a layer of fresh straw spread over top. On either side were the neat rows of stalls, over which a few of the horses were peering, made curious by the sound of my unfamiliar bootheels. There were three Thoroughbreds, Mr. Dawson's hunters, I assumed: two bays, one of them dark, and a gray yearling. The names on their boxes were Diligence, Dignity, and Divinity. I snorted, and Dignity, the dark bay, snorted back. Johnny had always said you could tell a great deal about a man by how he names his horses. They craned their long necks at me, young Divinity tossing his mane at my unfamiliar scent.

I passed by four Cleveland bays so perfectly matched I could barely tell them apart. Placid, as carriage horses often are, they paid me little attention as I passed their stalls. At the end of the row were the Waldens' Friesians, Onyx and Obsidian, who came nickering eagerly as I approached. I rubbed their long noses before offering them some of the sugar lumps I had pilfered from the morning's tea tray.

The aisle opened into the paddock behind the stable. As I busied myself with the Friesians, from the corner of my eye I could see three figures approaching the stable entrance, talking amongst themselves.

"You've done well, the both of you," Mr. Dawson was saying in much warmer tones than I'd had occasion to hear him use in the parlor or ballroom. "I am pleased to see she is not too high-spirited, but I trust, Ignatius, if she were, it is nothing she could not be broken of?"

"No, sir, Mr. Dawson," came a voice tinged with gravel. "With training, she'll be a lamb, though she'll still step lively enough. She shows a pretty leg."

"So with wives as with horses," Mr. Dawson said, and I heard the sound of laughter. "Well, I shall leave you to it. Have her ready to be presented tomorrow morning."

He did not wait for a response, but watching from under my lashes, I saw him move toward the entrance to the stables, and pressed myself further in the direction of Obsidian's stall. There was nowhere out of his line of sight, however, and, as he crossed under the shadow of the lintel and spied me, he gave a curt nod. I curtsied back, but he neither slowed his gait nor paid me further heed as he made his way down the aisle back to the big house. I waited until he had gone before making my way out in the opposite direction.

Mr. Vandeman and a steel-haired man I presumed to be the much-vaunted Mr. Gregory were leaning against the stable wall, observing the paddock, as I approached. A lad of fifteen or sixteen was leading round a lanky yearling filly, her copper coat curried bright as a new penny. I stood transfixed. The little horse was daintier than any beast I'd seen, with a graceful, curving neck and straight, narrow shanks. Her tail perked, and her eyes were bright and alert as she high-stepped into the paddock. Her coat was the same color as Charlotte's hair.

"Beautiful animal," I said, and Mr. Vandeman turned, smiling warmly.

"Ah, Miss Ballard!" he said. "Permit me to introduce you to Mr. Gregory. Miss Ballard is Miss Walden's maid."

"Ah, pleasure, pleasure," Mr. Gregory said gruffly, taking my proffered hand into his callused one. He was in his shirtsleeves, wearing braces and a tweed cap, and I was reminded so acutely of my da that my heart constricted. He grinned, cocking his head toward the little horse. "Pretty creature, isn't she?"

"Indeed," I said, genuinely impressed. "I've never seen such a delicately built animal before. What breed is she, please?"

Mr. Gregory smiled broadly. "Ah, know something about horseflesh, do you?"

"Some," I said. "But her . . ." I trailed off. The horse was beautiful.

"Pure Arabian," Mr. Gregory said proudly. "And a fair bit of work it took to find her, bloodlines and that coloring and what all. What do you make of her, missy? Think she's fit to be a lady's palfrey?"

"She's perfect," I breathed, aching to run my hands along her coppery flanks. "Oh, might I?"

Mr. Gregory nodded assent, and in a trice the boy had led her over as I beckoned and whickered to the lovely creature in the most appealing tones I could muster. She pranced to where I stood, tossing her mane, and before I could lament not having brought a treat, Mr. Gregory was offering me a carrot for her. She even ate daintily—Angelica's eager nibblings seemed grotesque by comparison—and she nuzzled my palm sweetly when she was done. Every part of her was pure velvet, and the sweet, grassy scent of her minded me so strongly of sitting on the paddock fences next to Seanin that I began to come over quite misty. It was everything to pet and make much of this little horse, and I would have quite willingly launched myself atop her back and galloped off, as Da had let me so many times in my youth. It was a wrench to remain on the other side of the fence, petting her decorously and doing no more.

"She's a gift," Mr. Vandeman explained, as the silence deepened. "For Miss Walden."

"Well." I laughed. "They'll cut a striking figure, certainly. A matched pair, was that what Mr. Dawson had in mind?" For the slim, ruddy horse was Charlotte in equine form, if such a thing could be. As if echoing my thoughts, the little mare tossed her finely made head.

Mr. Vandeman and Mr. Gregory chuckled at my quip. "You can keep a secret, can't you?" Mr. Vandeman asked. "Mr. Dawson will be greatly disappointed, see, if we've spoiled the surprise."

I smiled tightly. "Oh yes," I assured them. "I can keep a secret. Has she a name?"

"Mr. Dawson thought perhaps Felicity—do you suppose that will serve?"

"I can think of no greater Felicity than to ride such a pretty beast as she," I said. "Yes, I imagine Miss Walden will be greatly pleased. You have my assurances that I will keep this secret."

I excused myself and turned back to the house, uncomforted by having visited the stables after all. No gentleman would give so intimate or extravagant a gift to a lady to whom he was not engaged. The message was clear; the greatest felicity Mr. Dawson could imagine was beneath Charlotte's nethers. There would be time enough for me to visit the stables after they were married.

That night, dressing Charlotte, daubing buttermilk against her creamy skin, I felt the same lackluster heaviness of anticipation, taking no joy in the simple tasks for which I lived. The routine, devoid of comfort, had become oppressive. Though the previous evening's rage had passed, Charlotte herself seemed weighted down with anticipation, her shoulders slumping. I smiled wanly at her in the mirror, but she did not smile back. We both knew that tonight would be the night; I sent her down to supper as though she were going to her doom. It took me a full ten minutes to compose myself before I felt I could go belowstairs. Grace, who was in no better state than I, chewed her nails nervously in the hall all evening, but I was too agitated myself to find any real fault with the behavior.

Tonight, any curiosity I might have had about the servants of Salisbury Park—my future companions—was overshadowed by a strange, pricking anxiety as I watched the smooth workings of the house. The domestic staff appeared to go about their tasks so seamlessly that Charlotte's words echoed in my head, and I was put to mind of clockwork figures. The same maids smiled at the same serving men, while Mr. Lindeman engaged me in the same pleasantries as he had the evening prior before darting off to black Mr. Dawson's riding boots. The sameness and the uniformity weighed heavily on me, and I began to feel the familiar flutter I had felt that morning in the Waldens' kitchen, smothered in the fear that my brief life would be snuffed out in such dull routines before I had really lived it. I kept my mouth closed, frightened that I would scream in frustration if I allowed my lips to part.

Twice or thrice, Grace made as though to speak to me, then left off in agitation. Her discomposure rattled me even more than Charlotte's spiritlessness had. I was more than a little startled to find a sudden spot of blood on my apron where I had picked at the cuticle of my little finger until it bled—a habit of which Mrs. Morgan had broken me nearly a decade earlier, and sucked the bit of raw skin clean of blood. The coppery taste called to mind the Boyles' housekeeper's scolding, and though I knew not if that venerable woman was still living or dead, I felt a sudden pang of guilt. Everything was wrong, and everything that had led me to be here, so far away from the place that I was born, so utterly bereft of allies, and so distant from my brother, left me feeling queasy with guilt. This pass we were in, Charlotte and I, felt like my fault. I wished heartily for the first time that I had never met Charlotte Walden. And then, I thought, why not wish I had never had cause to leave Ireland? Why not simply wish never to have been born? And thus, in misery, I passed the dinner hour.

When I answered Charlotte's bell, I found her sitting fully clothed on the bed. Her face looked worn and weary, her eyes red-rimmed. She glanced up as I came through the door, smiling grimly.

"Congratulate me, Ballard. I'm to be married."

I stood still a moment, struggling to quiet my racing pulse and school my rebellious features. I took a breath, and, when I spoke, my voice was calm. "Congratulations, miss."

She choked back a sob. "For Christ's sake, Ballard," she said, her voice trembling. "Don't be a bigger fool than I am."

"No, miss."

"Come here."

I was beside her in a moment, her arms winding about my neck like a drowning man reaching for succor. She sobbed silently onto my shoulder, great, racking shudders heaving through her frame. My skin grew damp where her tears soaked through my dress, and I stroked her hair, holding her tight. She pulled me onto the bed, her arms still viselike about my neck, and I lay down with her, letting her muffle her sobs against my neck and throat until she had cried herself to sleep.

Da used to say that there are moments in your life that show you who and what you are, and that those moments, however rarely they may come, define your character and the course of your history. I wanted so badly, with Charlotte in my arms, to take hold of her face and kiss her tears away, for I knew in my soul I should not be unwelcome to do so. How I ached with the wanting of her, and the wanting to comfort her! There were two things that held me back, and the first—the knowledge that Charlotte's tears came from mourning the life she could not share with Johnny—might not have been enough to dissuade me had not then the memory of another night, another girl clinging to me in tears, froze me cold.

I would remember that night later, remember it all my life. How we lay face-to-face upon the same pillow, Charlotte's breath slow and heavy at last, and her tears drying upon her cheeks. The candles had burned low, guttered, and gone out, and I watched her sleeping, knowing that the smooth veneer of peace spread over her features belied the turmoil within. I lay beside her, at war with myself, going mad for wanting her, for knowing—perhaps only for this night—I might have her. But even the temptation of that bliss was not enough to overcome my fear of the morning, of what lay beyond. I was no longer one who could act without thinking what came next, and neither was Charlotte. I could not face what might follow—her coldness, her regret, her spurning of me. For here was a girl, a woman, who had loved my brother to madness, to distraction, beyond reason or propriety, and had given him up wholly rather than risk her position. What could a single night with the likes of me be when compared to that overthrown love?

I lay beside her, and, as her cheeks grew dry, mine grew wet, for this knowledge that held me back tortured me all the same, and that was the night I began to give up Charlotte Walden.

> Reflect, then, seriously, before temptation lead you astray: reflect that when once you break through the barrier of good principle, it is difficult, if not impossible for you, ever to return.
>
> —*The Duties of a Lady's Maid*

It had been months now since I'd heard tell of Johnny Prior, or Seanin O'Farren either. In the wake of our rupture, he had come by to Dermot's a few times at first, to make arrangements and collect the wages he had banked there from the past three years, and then he had simply disappeared. He and nearly a third of the regular patrons at the Hibernian had stopped coming around, a loss of business that might have troubled Dermot had Liddie not taken rapid steps to fill the void.

When Seanin had cleared out of the Hibernian, Quigley had left off coming around to Liddie's, and suddenly her wages, such as they were, were her own again. I say such as they were, for, in the wake of the rupture, she had noticed a distinct drop-off in custom and clientele. She had given up wearing the Order's medal, and her life returned to what it had been before the fiery night that Johnny Prior had stepped into it.

There were now but few secrets between Dermot and me, and I lost no time in bringing Liddie around to the Hibernian on my nights off. Now it was I who took my pleasure after seeing Charlotte to bed, meeting Liddie in whatever alley or convenient place we could find before tripping merrily into the Hibernian together, smelling faintly of our mingled sweat and hair oil, calling for rounds to slake our thirst.

Dermot, it must be confessed, did not, at first, take this new development in stride. He bore Liddie's initial few visits with uncharacteristic ill grace, muttering churlish and cutting remarks pertaining to both Liddie and myself until, after the second night of half-spoken slanders reddened our ears, I slapped my hand impatiently on the bar and asked him to declare once and for all what, exactly, he objected to.

"It's not that she's a stargazer," he said, once half a bottle of whiskey had begun to loosen his tongue. We were all down in the basement, slung about on the pillows and blankets in various stages of undress, passing the bottle amongst the three of us. Dermot and I were the ones conversing, while Liddie was attending to her toilette and mine in a languid if somewhat theatrical manner.

"It's not that she's a stargazer," I prompted him, for he had trailed off as Liddie, clad now only in her corset, boots, and stockings, began unpinning my hair.

"Sure and who hasn't needed a friendly hand now and again?" he agreed. "Why, it's practically charity work, what she's doing."

"My gratitude is endless," I said, looking over my shoulder at Liddie, who had seated herself splay-legged behind me in order to unbutton my frock at her ease.

"And it's not that she's one of the Order's molls, for I know she isn't any longer."

"Indeed I am not," murmured Liddie, easing the dress from my shoulders and sliding my arms from the sleeves.

"And it isn't even that she's colored, though I've never known a colored lassie before," Dermot said, taking another swig directly from the bottle.

"Oh, indeed?" Liddie said lightly. "If you're not opposed, I could introduce you to a few. I promise you we taste just the same." By now, her nimble fingers had made short work of my stays and I was clad in only my thin shift.

"It's only," Dermot said, shifting uncomfortably, "that I've never in all my born days seen the English treat the Irish well, and it'll be a cold day in hell when an Irishman or woman gets any comfort from a London accent like hers."

"Why, my dear Mr. O'Brien," Liddie said, her face now inches from mine. "If you only knew what comfort I intend to provide your friend Miss O'Farren, I think you might be convinced of my devotion."

The last thing I remember before Liddie's kiss was the sound of Dermot swallowing audibly. Then her lips were on mine, and the whiskey we'd been drinking gushed hot through my veins and I no longer cared if Dermot O'Brien watched or approved, and his muted groans seemed to come from very far away to penetrate the haze of my pleasure.

In the morning, Liddie and I awoke alone in the basement and found breakfast for three laid on the potbellied stove in the back of the bar. Dermot was just returning from the pump with fresh water for coffee, whistling merrily as we sat ourselves at the bar to tuck in. Chatter over breakfast was pleasant, and, as we departed, he kissed each of our hands quite formally and bade us each a good week.

Within a fortnight, Liddie had flattered, cajoled, and charmed Dermot from a grudging tolerance of her presence to admiration and respect, which only deepened as she took over the ordering of his account books—a task he detested—and set his records neatly with her carefully printed hand. By the end of the month, they'd together hired carpenters to make over the second floor of his establishment—empty since the departure of his tenants from the Order—and, a few weeks later, Liddie installed herself and four other girls whom she had recruited into the new apartments. In a magnanimous move, she allowed the other light-skirts who had infrequently worked the fringes of the Hibernian to remain on the premises, and, in a more calculated move, she began tithing them for the privilege. She closed up the house on Chambers Street, and my Thursday nights were now spent in her fine linen sheets instead of in a pallet on the cellar floor.

"Come up in the world, haven't we?" Dermot asked, grinning, a month or two into the arrangement. It was a balmy night, a thin band of sunset reddening the sky, a riot of flowers blossoming in the park. It had been a pleasure to walk down to Mulberry Street, the trees from which it took its name coming back to life after the bitter, snowy winter. After my laboring each day over Charlotte's trousseau, pausing only to ready her for this ball or that dinner in honor of her pending nuptials, my Thursdays began to come as a relief, and I found myself ready to forget Charlotte for a few hours in Dermot's ale and Liddie's arms. It was something to see my own sort of people prosperous and successful in their own right, and not at the beck and call of those who'd call themselves their betters. I was in a fine mood for the first time in I couldn't remember when, and the grin I returned Dermot was genuine.

"Sure and I thought it wouldn't do to be whoring," I said, jerking my chin toward the ceiling. "And with a col—"

"Ah, and they aren't such bad lasses after all," he interrupted, filling his dudeen. "The care I've seen her lavish on you, and sometime when you're too fashed to care much o'er yourself. You could do worse than that Liddie of yours."

"What makes you think I haven't?"

He spread his free palm toward me, a gesture of warding, of retreat. "Christ, lass. You keep your own counsel, but what hints you do drop fall like hailstones, and just as welcome."

I laughed at this. "Now and here I was thinking you'd no need of my counsel, for you always seem to know all my secrets anyway."

He shrugged, the pipe between his lips, the lit lucifer igniting the contents of the packed bowl. The sweet, peaty aroma of the lighted tobacco curled up in plumes around his face as he puffed rapidly a few times to start it smoldering. He took a long draw, regarding me soberly before he answered.

"I'll be free with you, Mar. I don't know as I've ever quite had your measure. Lass as clever as you, as ambitious as they come, with only ever an eye on working in service. Why's that now, I've always wondered."

"I'll have some service out of her," Liddie said, sliding up beside me at the bar, and wrapping her arms about my waist. "What do you think, Miss Maire O'Farren? Can I press you into my service?" I could feel her small, high bosoms pushed up against my back, straining over the top of her corset. Dermot leaned back behind the bar, regarding us with mirth.

"You'll not mind then, Dermot, if I take her off your hands now? There's a service I think she owes me." And winking pertly at him over my shoulder, she led me quite willingly up the stairs.

Afterwards, my flaxen locks mingling with her stiff black curls on the pillow, we lay together as Liddie traced patterns on my stomach with a feather.

"He's right, you know," she said. "You could do better than service."

"Like whoring?" I asked, and, when she sat up, indignant, I

pulled her back down, pressing myself to her lips. "I'm no more cut out for that than you are for service. You have your way, Liddie. You convinced me of that some time past. And I've mine."

She shrugged, settling herself back down into the crook of my arm. "Were you always a lady's maid? Back in Ireland, I mean?"

"I was never a lady's maid in Ireland. I never maided for a lady proper till this cut Dermot found me. Before that—back in Donegal, I mean—I was a scullion."

Liddie laughed. "What, like blacking grates and hauling water? You?"

"I'd just worked my way up to housemaid there, when I left. I would have got to lady's maid, eventually."

"So what stopped you?"

I nestled her closer to me, as though the heat of her body next to mine, the slick, sweaty places where our skin pressed together, had the power to dispel the chill I still felt speaking of it. "I was dismissed."

"Wicked thing." She was still laughing good-naturedly. "For making love to your lady, I suppose."

"No," I said. "To one of her maids."

It is owing, indeed, to this single mistake, of trusting some one person, that the breaches of faith and divulging of secrets have disturbed the quiet of so many families.

—*The Duties of a Lady's Maid*

Nuala Begley was fifteen to my sixteen, and had never seen the world outside of her Donegal parish before, but I could tell from the way she kissed me, knowing and sure of herself, that I wasn't her first. She arrived at Michaelmas, fresh as the autumn air, and presented herself in the kitchens of Ballyboyle Manor, confident with expectations of a warm welcome. She had come with a single set of clothes plus the one on her back, a small banded box, and an excellent character from the rectory in Glencolumbkille. Mrs. Boyle had come to the estate from Dublin only two years before. A young wife, anxious over her first child, and priest-ridden to boot, she took in Nuala with good grace. A year as a maid of all work under her, with her eager, winning ways, she started off as a housemaid straightaway.

The first time I saw her, she was making up the bed we were given to share, shaking out the sheets as a few dark tendrils spilled from under her cap. The bed, only recently vacated and open to the likes of us, I regarded with trepidation, and the bedmate too, for I had been used to roosting with Seanin in the loft above the stables. I tugged nervously at my first new dress, jealous of the way the strange girl snapped the linens efficiently and comfortably, realizing that, in her last home, she probably had sheets every day. She looked up at me and smiled.

"You'll be Maire, I suppose. I can tell by the carpetbag, for Missus said you'd be coming up to share with me. Who shares the other bed, d'you know?" She spoke softly, in the leisurely, rolling lilt of the more desolate parts of Donegal. I brightened considerably at the friendly note in her voice, but was still too nervous to converse properly.

"Them's Katie and Rosie."

"Rosie!" Nuala smiled wryly. "I've a sister called Rosie. Roisin, really. And Mrs. Boyle, she's just had a baby called Rosalie, hasn't she? Sure and it seems roses'll bloom where'er I go." She was still smiling at her own joke with a mirth that didn't match the unease in her eyes. It occurred to me then that this was probably the farthest she'd ever been from home, and though I might feel out of place sleeping in a different part of the estate where I'd spent my entire life, it must be nothing to packing up and moving away from everyone and everything you know. I cleared my throat, but the bells began then.

"Is that the dinner bell?" she asked, seeming grateful for something to say. I nodded, leading the way to the back stairs, gathering the courage to speak, and racking my brain for a topic of conversation.

"Where're you from, then?" I asked.

"Glencolumbkille."

"Oh." I wasn't quite sure where that was—far to the west, clearly, by the rustic note in her voice. We took two landings in perfect silence as I strained for further topics of polite conversation.

"Was it long?" I asked, at last. "The journey, I mean?"

"Twelve hours, hoofing it by the shore road. I stopped in Killybegs midday."

"What, by yourself?"

She snorted. "No one to spare taking me, was there? I didn't mind. I'm used to being by myself."

I shivered, thinking of the lonely stretches along the cliffs where Seanin and I would go sometimes with Da in the trap, imagining tramping along them with no sound but the breakers on the rocks below, and the high bleating of the sheep in the pastures above. There were old heathen monuments there, and the ruins of castles, and the wide, arching sky. I much preferred the ringing cobbles and salty, bustling quays of Donegal Town. I confessed, "I'd've been scared, going it alone like that."

"Are you ever alone, then? Big house like this, all them queer corners and twisting halls?" she asked.

I shrugged. "Here, there's always someone by. And down in the town—oh, have you been to the town yet?"

She shook her head. "No, well, yes, Roisin says they brought us once, when we were very young, but I can't remember it."

"In the town, a good, proper town like Donegal, you're never alone, for there's always a face you've seen before waiting around the corner. Sure, though," I said, smiling ruefully. "For us, it's more like a face I've seen that Da's drunk with that remembers us in hippings."

"Us?" We had reached the servants' hall now, and the household staff were arranging themselves along the table, according to station.

"My brother, Seanin, and me." I pointed covertly to where Seanin stood, down with the other grooms, conversing with the new stableboy. "Him, just there. Me twin."

"Is that your brother then?" she whispered, with a note of admiration. "Aye, I see the likeness." She peeked at me sidelong, smiling.

I felt a sudden twinge just then, as she spoke of Seanin: an anxious pain I attributed to the worry of no longer sharing his pallet in the hayloft. No one much cared where I slept when Da was alive, but I had had my courses for two years now, and with my new station, Mrs. Morgan, the housekeeper, said it wasn't fitting for me to be the only skirt in the stables. That veritable lady was rapping the table for order, and, with her command, the lot of us grew quiet while the butler said grace, and then there was no more opportunity to talk with Nuala.

It was uncomfortable that first night, lying next to a stranger when I was used to huddling close to Seanin, breathing in scents of hay and sweat and leather and horse coming off him. Nuala smelled of lye soap and lavender, of a delicately musky sweat so different from my brother's. She slept uneasily, tossing her head about the pillow, where Seanin was still as a stone. From the next bed, Katie's nose whistled and Rosie's nose rumbled, and between the noise and the bustle, I scarce slept a wink.

In the morning, I awoke to find Nuala out of bed before me, stirring the fire. The late September mornings were growing chill, and the warm hearth was gratifying. She looked up from the grate and smiled at me, looking pleased with herself.

I smiled back. "That's kind of you."

She shrugged one shoulder. "'Twas always my task back home."

I would learn later that this was Nuala's cheerful, matter-of-fact way of winning people: hard work, modesty, and the willingness to go above and beyond. She never shirked, Nuala, and, when she was praised for her gumption, she simply smiled and shrugged and went on to do something to further impress, with equal nonchalance. As we scrubbed the marble in the hall, she was like an illustration of "Industry," her graceful form curved, her face intent on her work, one stray curl edging out from under her cap.

Eager to live up to both my new role and the new housemaid's zeal, I threw myself into the work with a vigor to match Nuala's own. I was determined to impress her as much as anything, and to prove I was her equal. Each day, Nuala and I worked side by side, dusting the mantels, polishing the furniture, sweeping the floors, doing the laundry, and worn to the bone as we collapsed into our shared bed every night, ready for the oblivion of sleep.

On the third twitchy night, jerking again in her sleep, she tossed an arm over me, curving her body around mine, and finally lay still, pressing me close to her chest. I lay stiffly at first, afraid to move a hair, but her steady breathing soothed me. I began to relax into the rhythm of her breaths, until I at last took comfort in lying cradled by her, as I was wont to be by Seanin.

There is a thing that happens when you are often in another's company. There develops at first a certain sympathy of beings engaged in the same work, sharing the same frustrations at the same odious tasks. A camaraderie forms, and an understanding, as you learn to anticipate one another in your shared duties. I grew to know her moods, to read the significance of her silences, to plumb the deeper meanings in her chatter. I could tell when she was merry, and I could tell when she was restless, and I could tell when she was homesick.

We began to share our histories with one another, in moments stolen and carved out from the workaday bustle. Out in the back court together, taking turns beating a rug. Or bent together at the pantry table, polishing the silver. Or whispered in the last few moments before we slept. I learned about her sisters, with whom she'd shared a bed their entire lives: proud, imperious Roisin and sweet, timid Briana. Then there was her da, who pottered over his poitín stills and fiddled down the pub. I learned how her mam had gone mad and run off with the babby, Aideen, and how Nuala had hired herself out as a maid of all work at the parish house to help keep the porridge pot full.

I told her how Da had worked in the stables on the estate ever since he was a lad, and how he met Mam when Old Mrs. Boyle brought her lady's maid up from Wexford when she married. I told her how Seanin and I came into the world, hand in hand, awash in the blood that took our mother out of it. And I told her of the gelding that kicked Da in the head while he was shoeing it, killing him stone dead in an instant.

We wept over one another's tragedies, and comforted one another in sharing the sorrows of our young lives. My entire life, there had been nobody but Seanin to talk to, Seanin to confide in, for there were no other young girls on the estate in service but me. I told Nuala of the games we used to play, the tricks we'd get up to, driving Da to distraction. Living with her sisters, she was unused to the brusque displays of a brother's affection, and delighted in hearing of the time he trapped me under an overturned keg, or the time he tore my best apron when he lost a wager and dressed up in my clothes.

Ballyboyle was an isolated place. Situated on an isthmus jutting out from the south of Donegal into the Atlantic, it was only three quarters of an hour's walk into Donegal Town, though it might have been at the end of the world. The Boyles did not go much out into society, for there was but little society. A Catholic family of an ancient lineage, they would but rarely mix with the Protestant gentry to be found in the county, entertaining only when cousins came up from the south to stay for monthlong holidays on the northern coast. We servants felt their isolation acutely, mingling only with our own kind on nights off or Sunday afternoons if we made the trek into town. In such environs, closenesses and alliances form. You are forced to camaraderie that blends on into intimacy, and you make your own amusements, or you find you have none at all.

It was with Nuala that I first discovered my talent for putting on voices. We were in the kitchen one day when Mrs. Boyle made her way down the stair, one white arm half-aloft, lifting her skirts out of the nonexistent dirt of the servants' quarters. It escapes me now what slight, essential thing she had to say to Cook, but I can still hear her tone: the pealing Dublin lilt, the way she held her clipped consonants in the front of her mouth, like a horse teething its bit. She was the only one on the estate who talked that way, Mr. Boyle's posh diction still unmistakably Donegal in tone. I knew, of course, that she was laced within an inch of her life—pregnancy had not been kind to her once-lithe figure—but was all the same impressed with the ramrod straightness of her posture, her lofty carriage. She gave her directions over dinner with the same genteel dignity that Father Broderick gave his sermons every Sunday, with equal assurance of her authority, and then left, secure in the knowledge that, her word being law, dinner would meet her expectations.

Nor can I now recall to mind what expression of exasperation Cook invoked, the mistress now being out of earshot, but, at Nuala's stifled laughter, I was encouraged to exhibition, rising to stand. Arranging myself where Mrs. Boyle had been, I turned out my toes, straightened my posture, and clasped my hands in perfect imitation of the lady of the house. Nuala tittered at the haughty, affected look I took on, and I arched my brows at her.

"Indeed, Miss Begley," I said, forcing my consonants to the front of my mouth and looking down my nose at her. "I find it most indecorous, most indecorous *indeed* to take on in such a manner, for I can think of nothing humorous in the proper directions for dinner."

Nuala howled gratifyingly at this display, and Cook wheeled about, a curse for the meddling Mrs. Boyle dying on her lips as she turned, all color drained from her mien, to face me.

"Laird above, Maire," she cried, clasping one hand to her bosom. "And you did give me a turn! I thought it was herself!" She brandished her spoon at me, recovering both her composure and her quick temper. "Christ, lassie," she said, waving the utensil at me, "and don't think you're too grown to be thrashed now for playing tricks like that!"

I took a step back, oozing dignified affront, and pushed the spoon from where Cook had leveled it at my chest with one disdainful finger. "I do hope, madam, that you do not presume to dictate to me?" I froze momentarily, as though I heard something, and then, allowing my posture to melt a trifle, looked around conspiratorially at my audience. "Ah, I fancied I heard the cooing of my precious Miss Rosalie, but no matter, for Nurse will attend to her darling snotty nose and her dearest soiled bottom!"

Cook was laughing outright now as well. "Aye, that's the mistress to her shadow, it is! Where'd you learn the likes of that, you wee hussy?"

I held a hand theatrically to my temple, looking pained. "Have I not eyes in my head, nor ears as well, that I cannot see clearly in the example of my betters the model on which my own behavior must be formed?" But my mimicry of Mrs. Boyle proved too much, even for me, and I joined my compatriots as we dissolved into gales of laughter. It was only at the sound of boots on the stair that we collected ourselves, hurrying back to our work lest our mockery be discovered.

Later, as we lounged on the sun-warmed stones, our arms aching from beating the feather ticks, Nuala expressed her admiration for my performance. "I wish I could talk like that," she said, frank and unassuming in her jealousy. "You sound just like her, you know."

I shrugged, affecting modesty and muscling down my considerable pride. "Isn't so hard. You just push your words up against your teeth-like."

She shook her head. "If it's so simple, why don't you do it all the time? You sound so posh."

I shrugged again, discomfited by the prospect. "Isn't me, then, is it? I mean, I don't talk that way natural. You don't think I sound strained after a bit?"

"Nay indeed!" Nuala smiled, rising and stretching. "You should do it more. Practice, you know, till it comes quite natural."

"Ah, go on," I said, smiling back and taking her proffered hand. "Where's the profit in it?"

"Well," she said. "I do fancy it."

Thereafter, when we were alone, I would amuse Nuala by narrating our more onerous tasks in Mrs. Boyle's Dublin accent: "Gracious, Miss Begley, is it not beastly scrubbing the flags?" Or "I must say, I have never seen blacking so neatly applied—very game!" Or "Do have the goodness to empty those kitchen slops *directly* into the pig trough, Miss Begley, for we must ensure our swine are properly fed!" These performances were met with great enthusiasm, and I hitherto took greater note when Mrs. Boyle was speaking in order to perfect my imitation.

Mere diversion was not Nuala's sole interest in my newfound ability. Indeed, she worked tirelessly to perfect her own diction and smooth the edges of her accent. Intent on improving her station in life, Nuala aimed to become a lady's maid. This coveted position at Ballyboyle was currently held by a redoubtable personage by the name of Bathsheba Kirk. Miss Kirk—stern, proper, imported from Edinburgh—associated solely with Mrs. Morgan, the housekeeper, and Miss Timmons, the nurse. Small-boned, with nimble fingers that were always busy in tatting lace or embroidering edging, she was some five or six years older than her mistress, in whose employ she had been since the latter's coming out. It was said she was half-French, for she spoke that language fluently, and subscribed to two different Parisian fashion magazines. It was also said that she had a shelf devoted entirely to the back numbers of these coveted periodicals, a fact that no one had confirmed, given her private room, until Nuala, with more nerve than I would have given her credit for, approached Miss Kirk and asked to borrow them.

It was an absurd request. One did not simply ask Miss Kirk for things any more than one juggled full pint glasses, and I fully expected the attempt to be equally disastrous. It was therefore with a measure of awe that I later regarded Nuala, who, poring over back numbers of *La Belle Assemblée,* recounted that Miss Kirk had been extremely gracious in the loan, and had promised to teach Nuala the broderie anglaise Mrs. Boyle favored on her pantalets. It soon became our custom to inspect minutely the pages of these magazines before bed, Nuala quizzing me mercilessly on the lengths of trains for court occasions that neither of us would ever attend, and debating the merits of different types of fur to line a pelisse.

Nuala was indeed adept at ingratiating herself with the diverse members of the estate. The same ease with which she had approached Miss Kirk was evident in her exchanges with the grooms. Naturally, my having introduced her to Seanin, she accompanied me on my many trips to the stables. Perched primly atop the neatly stacked bales of hay, she conversed freely, acknowledging Seanin's teasing as the form of acceptance it was.

On Thursday nights, she began to join Seanin and myself on our outings down to Colleen O'Brien's pub in town, where the three of us would chat merrily. When Seanin went to refill our mugs, I would take on the accents of those around us to amuse her, mimicking Colleen's rolling lilt, or the listing Galway patter that sailors up from the bay spoke, dissolving into laughter when Seanin returned. On the way home, she would drop back, lagging as we walked in the ditch along the ring road back to Ballyboyle, until I lagged too to keep pace with her. We would link arms in the dark, the stars bright above in the crisp winter air, the moon's watery reflection in the waves just offshore, and the smell of salt and turf fire carried on the wind. We would hum scraps of old tunes, and giggle, sometimes, at nothing, but march on without speaking. Seanin would call back to us, teasing us for being so slow, and we would catch hands, racing up to him. Then we would crawl into bed, and I would wait, lying stiff and still beside Nuala, who'd take me in her arms as soon as she was asleep.

Months spun by this way. By now, I knew from all the stories we had shared that she sought me in her sleep as she was wont to seek her sisters. But one night even this was not enough to soothe her, and I woke to feel her silent, shuddering sobs against my back. I rolled over, taking her hands in mine. I brushed the tears from her cheeks, stroking her hair.

"What ails you?" I whispered. From the other bed came Katie's and Rosie's mingled snores.

She whispered back, "It all seems so far away here."

"What does?"

"Home. Sometimes I feel so alone here."

I caressed her cheek. "But I'm here. I'm here, Nuala."

Nuala sighed, shook her head, and, pressing herself against me, kissed me hard on the mouth. She wrapped her arms about my neck, her kisses urgent and desperate, and something within me suddenly fell into place as I realized I wanted her. I had never felt that sense of wanting before, never known—quite—that craving and that need. But Nuala's kisses wakened something in me. Her hands, now sliding down my legs to draw up my nightdress, felt right, and that I should be stricken with a slick tightening between my legs was natural to me.

She was drawing up her own nightdress now, then pressing her skin to mine, one knee slipping between my legs, and I ground myself into her, kissing her hungrily. She guided my fingers down past the wiry tangle of hair and into her soft, wet folds. I felt moved by a force larger than myself, knowing with sudden surety what to do, and we swayed as one in the bed, a silent frenzy of hands and lips and—finally—release. It was release more than pleasure, that first time. A giving way into each other. There were still tears on Nuala's face. I licked tenderly at the salt. She wrapped her arms around me, pillowing her head on my bosom, and, thus embraced, we fell asleep.

We said nothing in the morning. Our hands brushed as we passed one another buckets, and the touch sent shivers through me. We hardly spoke a word all day—what could be said under the yoke of so many duties, under so many watchful eyes? But whenever our eyes met, a current ran through me, and that night, as soon as we were assured the other maids were sleeping, we fell upon one another greedily. I savored the taste of her on my lips, and slept deeply in her arms.

By Sunday, Seanin could not stop smiling at me as we walked from St. Patrick's down to Colleen O'Brien's pub on Castle Street. Nuala had gone back to Glencolumbkille that morning, hitching a ride an hour before dawn, and we were walking alone. Every few paces, it seemed, he would glance over at me and break out into a foolish grin.

"What's that you're grinning at then?" I finally asked him, exasperated.

"Yourself," he said, doing it again. "I like to see a lass in love. Puts roses in her cheeks, and you're too pale without 'em, Maire."

"Ah, go on then," I said, with an ill-concealed waver in my voice. "Who'd I be in love with anyway?"

"Mar, if I was half as thick as you take me for, I'd be, well, as thick as your bein' now."

I said nothing, my face going hot. My bootheels ringing on the cobbles, the crying gulls above seemed to swell to an unnatural volume in the silence when I should have said something. I swallowed nervously. My tongue felt thick.

Seanin drew my hand through his arm. "I'll not say a word, Mar. You know that, sure? Not a word to a soul. I'll not mention it again if you'd rather I didn't." He paused, waiting for me to respond. When I didn't, he said, "I'm happy for you, Mar, is all. Can I not be happy for you?"

We had reached the open door of the pub by now, and I unhooked my arm from his. "Come on now, Seanin," I said. "Let me stand you a pint."

In the cool of the pub, a stoneware pint sweating before me, Seanin laughing at some quip of Colleen's as she read aloud her latest letter from her son, Dermot, in America, I thought how grand it would be, next week, to bring Nuala around again. We would sit side by side, arms at each other's waists, and Colleen would call her a pretty thing, and wink at me for my good luck. As I sat wrapped in my daydream, the swell of noise in the bar fell away, and the clink of glasses, the peals of laughter, the rumble and the roar dimmed to a faint hum. In my daydream, Nuala was smiling at me over the rim of her mug. There in the bar, I smiled back, idiotically, at nothing.

Thinking back years later, I could not have said what my intentions with Nuala were. If it had been a lad I was walking out with, I might have dreamed of marriage, perhaps a cottage, or a child on my knee. With Charlotte, of course, I could never dare to dream. I think now that, back then, I was too young and too stupid to think past the next kiss, the next embrace, the next night in Nuala's arms.

There would be entire nights running, when, too wearied from the day's labors, there was nothing for us but sleep. The day after such a night, Nuala would be irritable and fidgety. She would go out of her way, in the course of our work, to caress my hand, or tuck my hair under my cap, once even rubbing my bottom as I knelt over the hearth I was sweeping. I would playfully bat her wandering hands away, making her laugh, her eyes twinkling with mischief.

It was Nuala, in one such fey mood, who hit upon the guest rooms. A finger to her lips, she took me by the hand and led me up the back stairs to the hall from which the guest rooms branched. The first door she tried was open, and she ushered me in, closing it silently behind us. The room was unaired, and smelled of must. A fine layer of dust lay over the furniture.

"What are we doing here?" I hissed. "It'll be hell to pay if the missus finds us up here."

"Hush now, Maire," she said. "Sure and there's none as ever comes up here unless there's company." She sat me in a stiff-backed chair, facing the bed, and whispered in my ear, "Close your eyes until I say."

When she told me to, I opened them to find her lying naked on the bed. Many a night I had lain with her in my arms, running my hands and lips over her body, but never had I seen her fully undressed. I drank in the sight of her. Her skin was taut over her wiry frame, her limbs corded from hard work. She lay with her legs spread, and I climbed up onto the bed to kneel between them, kissing the moistened petals there. She tasted of earth and salt, and she raised her hips to meet me, moaning softly as I felt her tense, arching up one last time before going slack on the bed. I crawled up beside her and took her in my arms, but she was atop me, shimmying up my skirts with questing, eager fingers as she kissed me. I was all ready for her, and it was over far too quickly.

Nuala was never one to be satisfied with the things she had; once she had accomplished a thing, she set about striving for more of it. It was Katie who caught us, in the end. Opened the door, bold as brass, and hollered loud enough to bring up Mrs. Morgan at a run. We were having a tumble in the guest room, our third that week, for the wet little minx could never have enough, and Katie was sore tired after months of us slipping off with our work half-done. I never knew if she'd had an inkling of what she'd find when she opened the door.

I remember Mrs. Morgan's face well enough. We were standing before her in the guest room, still half-clothed. I remember my shift kept slipping down one of my shoulders, and I kept tugging it back up impatiently. I don't remember what she said, or what accusation she made. But suddenly there was Nuala, weeping at her feet. Her voice sounded so far away as she sobbed, "She made me, Missus, she made me." The last thing I saw was the hard look in her watery eye as Katie led me from the room by my ear.

I remember thinking absurdly that I had never realized that Katie, a woman I'd known nearly my whole life, was so damn strong as she dragged me down the back stairs and shoved me out the kitchen door. I tried to speak, to say something in my own defense, but she slammed the door in my face with a look of pure hatred twisting her features. The yard was empty, the grounds of Ballyboyle spread before me, and, compelled by some primal impulse, I took off toward the fields at a run.

I lay in the tall grass, my back damp through, the smell of sheep heavy around me. Above, pendulous clouds hung like gathered draperies. I closed my eyes. The earth had warmed beneath my body, cooler in places when I shifted my weight. A breeze played over my face, the cloying sheep scent cut by the sharp smell of the coming rain. I could hear Seanin's voice on the wind, my name borne faintly across the meadow. I closed my eyes tighter. He had news. Or he didn't.

I had been lying in the grass for hours, my heartbroken sobs ebbing as I began to grow numb. I had retched every tender feeling I had ever had, and was now empty of all, save my great love of this land, of this pasture where we had spent so many afternoons watching Da break the yearling colts. I could close my eyes then and still see his face, the way he looked when he took each of us by the hand, his expression as he said, *You are so like your mother* as he reached out to tuck a strand of hair behind my ear.

As I lay there, thinking back on my father, what came to me, as it always does, if not his face, was the smell of him. And when, if you take my meaning, I could capture the impression of that smell in my mind, one perfect memory that I have of him always stirred and rose to the surface of my mind.

It was the hour just after dawn, pale light slanting down through the slatted windows of the stables. The horses nickered from the cool shadows of their stalls. Hand in hand, we moved down the aisle between them, just Da and me. He told over their names to me, his voice a great, low rumble, echoing quietly through the high rafters. All around us was the smell of sweet hay, saddle oil, leather, and polished brass, and the heady musk of so many horses close together. It was a warm, clean animal scent, which clung to Da's whiskers and clothes at night when we sat before the fire together. To me, it was the smell of steadiness and calm.

Da swung me up to settle on his hip, though I was a great big lass then, too grown to be held like a wee babby. He held me high so I could see over the door of the stall to the new roan foal, asleep at its dam's side. I watched the foal breathe, fascinated by the steady intake of breath and exhalation, by the way the ribs rose and fell so deeply. Da whispered to me, and though I could clearly recall the tickle of his whiskers against my ear and the deep timbre of his voice, his words were lost. I could only ever recall that moment and think, though he must not have said the words then—he said them rarely, if at all—that this was his way of showing he loved me.

That love was there, welling up in me, filling the empty place where I had retched away all the shame and pain that Nuala Begley had burst in me. That love of my father, of the land, of this corner of this island where I was born and he had died, and in the intervening years, bookended by sorrows, where there had been something like joy.

The sound of my name, rising and falling with the breeze, became one with the sheep scent, became one with my great, welling love of the land. The empty, hashed-away place was overwhelmed with this love. Tears wound their way down my cheeks, and I felt, for one golden moment, healed.

By the time Seanin reached me, my tears had all fallen and dried, the hot, welling love hardened, and myself prepared for whatever he would say. For a brief, glorious moment, I had been one with that island on which I had been born, and now I wore the memory like a pendant, hanging just above the void where once lay my heart.

I could hear the grasses rustle as he came to lie beside me. I turned my head and opened my eyes to meet his. His lids were red-rimmed. When he spoke, his voice was raw.

"There's a ship," he said. "It sails from Skibbereen in a week."

I nodded.

"I spoke to Colleen O'Brien. She says she'll write Dermot for us."

I closed my eyes.

"It's better this way," he said, pleading.

I nodded.

"Just answer me one thing," he said. "One thing, and I swear I'll never trouble you over it again. Did you love her?"

"Love her?" I repeated stupidly. "Love her? I wanted her. I wanted . . . what it was I did with her. But did I love her? I don't know. She hurt me deep. My heart's near broke, and no mistaking, but in the end I'll get on. Without her. I'll get on without her. No, I don't suppose I loved her. I don't think I did. No."

He shrugged, sitting up, rubbing his eyes with the backs of his reddened knuckles. "Just as well. I popped the wee bitch one in the mouth for that trick she played you."

The thought of Seanin's fist connecting with Nuala's jaw did not move me in the least. I sighed. "You shouldn't have done that, Seanin. I expect the wee chit'll have told, and there's no going back for you after that."

"Fuck going back, Mar," he said, rising, offering me both his hands. "Are you not my sister, my only flesh? Where you go, I go."

> If you are dishonest to your employers, and it be discovered, you cannot expect either to have a character, or to be retained.
>
> —*The Duties of a Lady's Maid*

Liddie stubbed out her third cigarette with far more malice than the task strictly required. "So they turned you out with nothing more than the clothes on your back? And they kept that lying little cunt on?" She sniffed with an aggrieved air. "I like that. And you born on the estate, no less. Oh, I like that fine."

Objectively, I rather enjoyed the fact that my misfortunes seemed always to move Liddie to a passion of some sort. Practically, however, I was frequently far too heartsore to derive much sympathy for the offense she took at my ill-treatment. I drew her close to me, as much to hide my face as to take comfort in the nearness of her.

"Must sound absurd to one brothel-born. All that to-do over the goings on under the sheets."

She pulled back to regard me, brushing a stray lock from my face, cupping my cheek with her hand. "It's always a to-do, isn't it? That's why brothels exist, after all."

"I never thought about it like that before," I said.

"I can assure you my virginity was just as closely guarded as any debutante's, being just as valuable, in its way," she said drily, settling her head against my shoulder. "Men will pay a mint to be the first to plow your field, whether it's in the form of a house on Bond Street and a family name or fifty pounds directly to the Abbess's hand. The only difference is that the light-skirt doesn't have to look him in the face over the breakfast table every day for the rest of her life, and the debutante does."

"How old were you?" I asked quietly.

Liddie turned her neck sharply, the vertebrae popping satisfactorily. "Fourteen. Mama wanted to wait until I was fifteen—that's how old she was—but the Lady Abbess had a . . . request. An offer. More considerable than my mother's objections. And I knew it was only a matter of time. So."

"Was he . . . did you . . ." I trailed off, cheeks aflame, unsure of what it was I was asking, or if I even wanted to know the answer. I'd heard of girls who were forced, naturally. It happened all the time, in Donegal Town. There'd be words whispered of landlords who had taken daughters and sisters to their ruin when the rent was short, of masters who considered every female on the estate their rightful property. Even at Ballyboyle, everyone knew that the old master had been a stag in rut—there were rumors of housemaids sent suddenly away. Da had spoken darkly about the way old Mr. Boyle had looked at my mother when she came to the estate. But none of that was anything like being raised to know that one day your maidenhead would be sold to the highest bidder. I wondered at the cold-blooded mind that sent a fourteen-year-old girl off to be deflowered for a price, and more so at the sanguine mind of the fourteen-year-old girl who went about it as the start of her career.

"I always knew I would do it, someday," Liddie said quietly. "Growing up as I did, I knew what to expect. I knew it would hurt, but I knew there was pleasure to be had. The Abbess never suffered brutes. It wasn't that sort of establishment. I came away bleeding and bruised, and she gave me a fortnight to recover myself to see if I wanted to go on about it."

"What if you hadn't?"

"Well, I didn't really, you see," she said slowly. "I wanted to be on the stage. Oh, I know," she said, waving away my look before it could blossom into a full-blown objection. "There's no company of players in the world for the likes of me. When they need someone of my complexion, why, that's what cosmetics are for after all. But after all, you'll never see a dusky Juliet."

I took her hand. "I've seen a dusky Olivia, and, being dusky, I do find her fair."

Liddie drew my hand to her lips, kissing it and squeezing my fingers tightly before letting it go.

"The lady doth protest too much," she said ruefully. "It was a dream, and one I gave up on long ago. So it was always to be brothel work for me. And it takes more than light-skirts to run a brothel of that caliber, you know," she said, smirking. "They employ a terrible lot of laundresses, they keep a cook. Someone's got to sweep the hearths. There's never any shortage of work to be done." She shouldered me gently. "But I was happier on my back playing the courtesan than I was at the thought of blacking grates or lighting the lamps. I told you before I wasn't cut out for service."

"You talk overmuch, Liddie Lawrence," I said, wearied with the well-trod lines of our old argument. "Just now's the time for silence."

"Maire, my dear," she murmured before covering my mouth with her own, "I could not agree more."

> Such marriages have taken place, but they are seldom, if ever, happy ones.
>
> —*The Duties of a Lady's Maid*

Charlotte Walden was to marry Elijah Dawson at St. Bartholomew's Episcopal Church on Wednesday the twenty-seventh of September, in the year of our Lord 1837. The date and location were secured only after protracted negotiations between Geraldine Dawson, Augusta Walden, and Thaddeus Graham, the first feeling it crucial that the nuptials take place at Salisbury Park, while the latter two insisted on the fashionable Great Jones Street congregation that the Graham diamond mines had helped to endow. Thaddeus Graham had contributed quite handsomely to the new parish, and, in the two years since its massive carved doors had opened, that gentleman's family had not had occasion to patronize the establishment with a wedding, baptism, or funeral. To miss the first opportunity for such an honor was not to be borne, and even the stately and stationary Geraldine Dawson could see the impropriety of the bride marrying elsewhere than the church her grandfather's wealth had made possible.

This concession to locale was tempered by Mrs. Dawson's insistence on selecting the date. A coveted June date would be far too soon for Charlotte to make the necessary preparations, and, upon reluctantly agreeing to make the remove to the City to witness her grandson and only heir's marriage, Mrs. Dawson was adamant in her refusal to subject herself to either the stink of the City's miasma in full summer or the chill of winter travel. As she could not be persuaded to depend upon her living to see another June, it was agreed that an auspicious autumn day should be chosen, and Charlotte conveyed to me as I unlaced her one evening that her future grandmama held with the old rhyme "Married in September's golden glow, smooth and serene your life will go," and with Wednesday being "the best day of all."

Naturally, I was not consulted, but I held with the notion that Charlotte might as well bow to the old lady's wishes now, as it would be good practice for her married life. I could not see the appeal in shackling myself to a man who was wholly his grandmother's creature, but then I never saw much to appeal in any man, and, without Johnny in her life, one flavor of domestic tranquillity would be much like the next to Charlotte.

Augusta Walden, who had herself been married on an auspiciously chosen Monday in February, held with no such superstitions. She had enjoyed neither Monday's promised health nor February's assurance of a solid mate for life, and she sniffed loudly that anyone who put so much stock in a pack of absurd old peasant rhymes was a delusional fool. Grace Porter, over tea in Mrs. Harrison's closet, whispered that her mistress was often privately in tears over the preparations for her daughter's marriage. Mrs. Walden began choosing gowns of deeper purple hues, and Grace was kept busy stitching black edging on her more colorful frocks. She wore Mr. Walden's cameo every day now, and could often be seen running her fingers over the smooth, carven features fastened at her throat.

Charlotte's intended made his opinions known less vocally. The week after the announcement ran in the *Post,* there arrived from

Mr. Dawson twenty yards of the palest Columbia blue silk and four packets of seed pearls, the meaning of which could not be mistook. It was just the hue to complement Charlotte's coloring: soft, fine-woven stuff that draped liked water running. Charlotte brushed a delicate finger over the material and sighed, "Blue again," but made no other comment. It was decided that Grace and I both would convey the heavy parcel to Miss Marguerite's, for the job could be entrusted to no one else. Claire rubbed the fabric between her thumb and forefinger with delight, exclaiming something to her employer in French, and we left the two women in raptures over the beautiful material. In the coming weeks, I escorted Charlotte to the boutique and watched as she was measured and draped while the hasty sketches Miss Marguerite had tacked about the walls of the shop began to take shape on Charlotte's form.

Prudence Graham was to be Charlotte's only bridesmaid. Faithfully, she sat many hours in the Waldens' parlor, playing melancholy airs on the pianoforte while Charlotte embroidered the handkerchiefs of her trousseau so thoroughly I didn't doubt her nose would be chafed every time she blew it. Prudence spoke but little, sang not at all, and played too loudly and too intently to facilitate much conversation. Had Charlotte been a more eager bride, her selections might have been troubling. During the lengthy periods of silence between the two young ladies, she indulged herself expressively in her beloved Beethoven, hammering the keys to his Sonata Pathétique, or his Poco moto Bagatelle in A minor. When Charlotte seemed more intent on conversation, Prudence ran through any number of shorter, if doleful, hymns, sprinkled with sentimental parlor songs. But most often she played "Binnorie," which made my blood run cold.

O sister, reach me but your glove,
Binnorie, O Binnorie
And sweet William shall be your love.
By the bonny mill-dams of Binnorie.

Sink on, nor hope for hand or glove,
Binnorie, O Binnorie
And sweet William shall better be my love.
By the bonny mill-dams of Binnorie.

Looking at them, dark Prudence and fair Charlotte, I felt chilled, thinking of the lyrics that Prudence left unsung. Charlotte, who played and sang with proficiency and obligation but little emotion, seemed outwardly unmoved by her aunt's displays of wordless and bitter passion, but later, as I was pressing and folding the fine linen that she had worked, I could see her agitation told in the unevenness of her stitches.

Charlotte's engagement secure, the Grahams began once again to appear at the Waldens' table. More often than not, invitations were filled by Mr. Thaddeus and Mrs. Sabrina Graham, as any engagement at which Mr. Dawson would be present began suddenly to conflict with Prudence Graham's musical obligations. She began accepting invitations for a great many salons, though she often complained afterwards that she found the playing uninspired and insipid. She became a permanent fixture in her family's box at the symphony, often importuning her grandmama Clemons as a kindly but thoroughly deaf chaperone when she could find no one else to accompany her. When she could be persuaded to conversation, it was often to engage her half sister in increasingly acrimonious debates about the appropriateness of playing nocturnes at an afternoon salon. When she did consent to dine at Washington Square, she descended aggressively upon the pianoforte immediately after coffee was served, drowning out conversation.

Charlotte bore her aunt's behavior first with patience, then with weariness, and finally with annoyance. One evening, as Mrs. Sabrina Graham inquired as to whether Charlotte intended to wear the Walden family veil, Prudence launched into a Chopin ballade that was decidedly more forte than piano, prompting her niece to slam her teacup down in agitation, the amber liquid splashing onto the lemon-colored brocade of her frock. Later, as I sprinkled the stain with soda ash in preparation for blotting it out, Charlotte relayed to me the rancorous scene.

With the clatter of the bone china cup, Prudence's flying fingers faltered, and Charlotte clamped her hands over her ears at the resulting discords. "Will you have done?" she cried, and silence fell upon the room. "Your poor opinion of my engagement is duly noted, Prudence. For pity's sake, have done!"

"Opinion?" Prudence. "I have voiced no opinions, poor or otherwise."

"Yet you have made them plain enough without vocalizing," Charlotte said, whilst her step-grandmama and mother interjected simultaneously with "My dear girls!" and "What can have come over the both of you?"

"Then I shall have done," Prudence said, rising from the pianoforte. "Mama? Papa? I find I am quite unwell and must retire." And, bobbing to Augusta, she swept from the room, her baffled parents scrambling in her wake.

Friendships, you should recollect also, are, for the most part, very frail . . . and sometimes broken without provocation.

—*The Duties of a Lady's Maid*

A few months before her niece's wedding, Prudence Graham ran away. It was a sticky night in early July, and I tossed on my bed, a sheen of humid sweat plastering my night rail to my skin. Sleep, which, in the heat, had evaded me, was just beginning to take hold when the muffled sound of footfalls on the stair outside my door propelled me to wakefulness. I could hear a heavy breathing from the far side of my door, and I froze, paralyzed in sudden fear for a moment before a timid knock came. I bolted from my bed and cracked the door. Agnes stared back up at me, her eyes wide, her lower lip trembling.

I glowered at her. "Well?" I hissed.

She swallowed. "You told me never to come into your room again."

"And so I did."

"So I knocked."

"You did."

The girl stared back at me silently. I tried to recall that Agnes was an orphan, like myself. I tried to remember that she had great skill in starching pinafores, was an excellent baker of pastries, and that no one was kinder to Young Frank than she. I counted to ten and held my breath, and at last I let it out with a sigh and a resolution to be charitable to her.

"Agnes," I said, trying to adopt a gentle tone, but unable to keep the flint wholly from my voice. "Why? Why did you knock?"

"She's back. She gave me this. It's not for you. It's for her. Miss Walden, I mean." She thrust an envelope into my hand. It bore the name "Charlotte" in a hand I recognized as Prudence Graham's. I pursed my lips.

"Agnes, listen to me. This is important." I rested my hands on her shoulders. "Agnes, did you leave her at the bottom of the stairs again?" The girl shook her head. "Good girl, Agnes. Where is she now?"

Agnes shrugged. "Gone. She didn't wait around."

I took a deep breath. "Agnes, you are going to follow me back down the stairs to the kitchen, and then I am going out into the mews to look for Miss Graham. Did you see which way she went?" Agnes shook her head. "Very well. Stay by the door to let me back in, you hear?" She nodded, but I was already pushing past her and tripping lightly down the stairs.

Prudence Graham was just reaching the east end of the mews as I dashed out the kitchen door. Barefoot, in only my night rail, I flew across the cobbles, the stones still radiating heat in the thick night air. Overhead, the sky rumbled, and a brief flash of light illuminated the retreating figure as I reached for her.

"Ballard," she said, smiling thinly as I overtook her. "My apologies for having woken you. I'd rather hoped my missive would be delivered in the morning." She looked pointedly over my shoulder, as if expecting Charlotte to appear at the kitchen door, but I shook my head.

"I will deliver your letter to my mistress when she rises, of course, Miss Graham. I wanted to see . . ." I trailed off, suddenly uncertain. "That is, I wanted to ensure that there was nothing . . . no service I might render you?"

She let out a breath, smiling more naturally this time. "No indeed, Ballard. I thank you. You have always been most solicitous." She held out her hand, and I took it, tentatively. She squeezed my fingers. The first few fat drops began to fall. "Good-bye, Ballard. You'll take care of her, won't you?"

"Of course, Miss Graham." She released my hand and turned, striding off into the starless night. I was overcome by the sudden, rushing aroma of rain before the sky opened up and I was pelted with hard beads of warm summer shower.

There is scarcely a family whose most secret affairs do not come to be known in their neighbourhood, though it be ever so improper that they should be so.

—*The Duties of a Lady's Maid*

The ensuing riot was no more than I expected. Thaddeus and Sabrina Graham arrived early, their raised voices mingling with Augusta Walden's from behind the parlor's closed doors. Trays of tea, rung for and then left to cool untasted, were trundled up and down from the kitchen all morning. Mr. Buckley collected visiting cards on a silver salver, his courteous protestations that the Waldens were not at home belied by the bellowing down the hall.

Charlotte sat pale and silent amidst the thundering around her, Prudence's letter wedged tightly between the feather tick and the bed boards above stairs. I had delivered the letter when my mistress woke, watching her lips grow thin and white as she read her aunt's parting words before folding the sheets of paper away and feigning ignorance of Prudence's flight as the Grahams descended upon the house.

Naturally, when the uproar became obvious, I retrieved the envelope from where Charlotte had secreted it. Inside was Prudence Graham's card, the lower left corner neatly and deliberately bent inward, the letters "p.p.c." scripted neatly in blue ink below and to the left of her engraved name. I raised my brows at the redundancy of these formal gestures—surely Prudence did not need to specify twice on her card that she was announcing her departure?—and turned to the letter the envelope also contained.

My Dear Lottie,

You will have ascertained that I am taking my leave—of yourself, of New York, and of our dear family—and I write you now to say farewell. Certainly, you must find this to be a most unsuitable manner in which to express such sentiments, and I do assure you that I should have preferred to bid you a more personal adieu face-to-face, however, as the contents of this missive will reveal, I could not take the risk that my reasons would be heard unchallenged, and that my plan might succeed had you stood before me, hearing all this.

I will not burden you by detailing the rift that we have suffered between us of late, nor with a litany of those occasions wherein I could not secure your confidence, with which you were once so free with me. For since your affections have been engaged by an unknown admirer, you have become untowardly closed to your most bosom companion. I state this only as a matter of fact, and not in reproach, for I too have hidden my heart, and cannot fault you for my own sin.

It is a simple matter—you are to marry the only man I have ever cared for, and I shall not, my dear Lottie, be able to bear it when you are wed. I have known my desires to be in vain, for even if he had not given me every proof of being most ardently in love with you, he has avowed it to me as well, and in such plain words that I could neither mistake his meaning nor continue to cherish even the faintest hope. It is therefore unthinkable to me that I should remain to see you unhappily married to one who loves you to distraction, the object of my own abortive affections.

There will be such things that you might come to hear of me, and

I pray that you will think well of my actions. My heart sunk, my affections thwarted, and my love blighted, I will find such solace as my music may offer me. Once, I might have told you all my hopes for the place where I am going, but I find now I have not the heart, nor the inclination, as I cannot but fear you will try to stop me. Therefore, Lottie, be contented to know that I am going away, far away, to become one with the pianoforte, and should you hear tell of where I have gone, it will only be because I have realized my dearest ambitions in music.

But you, my Lottie, will have no such solace, for you have contracted to wed one man when it is plain you love another. I cannot think of what circumstances you are in to have brought you to such a pass, but I grieve for you. You have always been as a sister to me—more so than Augusta—and all my natural sympathies are yours. Our lives till now have been entwined, we have always been by for each other, and daily I will lament that I will not have you by my side. If, perhaps, one or the other of us might have had the courage to open her heart and mind to the other, perhaps an understanding of some sort might have been reached, but as I remain in ignorance of your tribulations, it is folly to conjecture.

But now you have him. I commend him to your care, and pray that one day your heart might open to him, that you might find the worth in being beloved of such a man.

With everlasting and deepest affection,

Prue

Frowning, I folded the letter away, two rather uncharitable thoughts warring at the forefront of my mind. The first was that I could hardly see what in the sedate, taciturn Mr. Dawson could possibly elicit such an outpouring of emotion, culminating in such an extravagant act. The second was that Prudence Graham, accustomed all her life to extravagance, would have been unlikely to behave in any other way.

As I sat later in the kitchen, making a pretense of mending one of Charlotte's lace collars, the uncharitable thoughts continued. I tried to pinpoint exactly why it was that Prudence's flight so angered me, for, as the hours following her vanishment lengthened, I found myself becoming unreasonably enraged at the girl. My color mounting, I poked at the lace, fuming at Prudence's foolish weakness. For had she any self-pride or moral character, she might have set her cap herself at Elijah Dawson, or made her feelings known to Charlotte. Certainly her niece, out of the great love the two ladies shared, would never have allowed the object of her aunt's desire to pay her court. It was unreasonable of Prudence to suspect that Charlotte knew of her unspoken love, despite Prudence's keen insight that Charlotte's affections were elsewhere engaged. This flying into a rage at Charlotte without ever troubling to tell her niece of her feelings was ridiculous! It was worse than ridiculous, it was pathetic! It was . . . it was precisely what I had done with Seanin, a small voice whispered in my head.

I shook my head. No. This was completely different. Two young women, born of good society, being paid court by an eligible gentleman was the natural order of things. It was commonplace. Expected. And candor between two such women—kinswomen, no less!—should be expected as well. To shrink from such candor was cowardly on Prudence's part. And even had the circumstances been the same, it was cowardly and weak for her to flee. Had I not stayed and watched Seanin woo and bed the girl I loved? Had I not helped each of them in their clandestine meetings? Had I not raged and wept, and did I not bury my nails in Seanin's face, in the end? the voice whispered.

No. No.

Perhaps, the voice said, very gently now, perhaps to leave one's world behind is not weakness. I knew firsthand how much bravery was needed to wipe the slate clean and start anew. Hot, angry tears welled in my eyes, and I brushed them away hastily. My fury unabated, the tears multiplied, spilling over my lids, and I wept silently, my shoulders shaking.

Grace Porter laid a hand on my back, and I looked up, startled to find tears staining the older woman's cheeks as well.

"There, there Miss Ballard," she said, her mouth quavering. "They'll find her. They'll bring her home soon."

And I found myself sobbing quite openly on Grace Porter's shoulder.

> Take care, therefore, never to brood over resentment which may, perhaps, be from the first ill-grounded, and which is always inflamed by reflecting upon an injury, real or supposed.
>
> —*The Duties of a Lady's Maid*

The Grahams' agents in Calais had sent report of Prudence's landing in mid-August, and she had been missed when she slipped through Paris. The last the family had heard, she had boarded a stage bound for Lyon, but she never arrived in Lyon and there the trail went cold.

It was impossible for the family to imagine where she might have gone. Mrs. Graham had been adamant in her faith that Prudence had returned to Paris, where the family had spent a happy season before her coming out, and was shaken when her daughter passed through that city without stopping. Augusta Walden, always critical of Prudence's French, maintained that the stage to Lyon was a canard, and that a search should be conducted in London. Charlotte offered no opinions, silently holding her grandfather's hand as they sat side by side on the sofa, her mother and step-grandmother a frenetic whirl of skirts and volley of conjectures. She had maintained the secrecy of the letter, tearfully repeating when asked that she had no notion of Prudence's whereabouts.

For myself, as I thought on it, combing out my hair before I climbed into bed, the best clue lay in her letter, that she was going to pursue her music and seek solace in the pianoforte—a nicety that, easily observed by a lady's maid, would likely be overlooked by her family, Charlotte notwithstanding. Had I the charge of finding her, I would have sought her in Bonn or Vienna or any other city where Beethoven had ever set foot. I suspected that Charlotte, too late acquainted with the secrets of Prudence's heart, might have thought similarly, but she kept confident the details she might have gleaned.

The gentle tock of an acorn hitting my window broke my reverie, and in the dark of my room, I blinked, unsure if I had dreamed the noise. I lay there in the moonlight, still and listening, and, after a time, the noise, now unmistakable, came again.

I went to the window and looked out onto the mews. The doorway of the carriage house was shadowed and silent. I strained my eyes, peering into the darkness, and, yes, peeking out from the gloom below the eaves, barely visible against the cobbles, was the toe of a man's boot.

I caught my breath. My heard raced as I weighed my options. By now, surely, he had seen my shadow against the glass. My mouth was dry as dust. Since Liddie and Dermot had told me about Johnny Prior and his position in the Order, I'd felt my footsteps dogged. Perhaps I had imagined this, but still, perhaps not. I resigned myself to finding out, pulling on my wrapper, and opening the door to the servants' stair.

His face was gaunt and unshaved. The beginnings of a beard marked his jaw.

"Christ, you look like hell," I said, a nervous smile twisting my lips as I said it.

He laughed, a bitter sound. "You're no beauty yourself, Mar," he replied, brushing the loose strands of hair back from my face.

I laughed too, at this, and shook free from his grasp. "What is it you want, Seanin?"

"Is it true?" he asked hoarsely. "That she's to be married? Is it true?"

I snorted. "I'm a born fool. Should have known it was her you've come about."

"You're thick," he said, but reached out for my hand and grabbed it tightly as I scoffed and tried to turn and go. "Now, Mar," he said. "You know well enough why I've kept from you."

"Aye, I'd not have thought it of you."

"Sure and they're not bad lads," he said ruefully.

"Not bad with a shillelagh is what I hear."

"Only when it's needful."

"And from what I've heard of you, it's been needful often enough."

His grip tightened. "I'd asked Dermot never to speak of it to you. Goddamn the man."

"I'll hear naught against him!" I said fiercely. "He's been a true friend to me, Seanin O'Farren, and if you'd asked him not to speak of it to me, sure and it's that you knew I'd not take well the news my brother had turned so rough."

"And what if I did?" Seanin said, dropping my hand. "'Tis a rough city. Christ, it's a rough world, rougher still for us Irish, and if I wished to get ahead, there was naught for it but to rise up and meet the path before me."

"You once said," I began slowly, "that, as we were kin, the only kin we have now, you'd not be parted from my side. And after all we did to come here, to stay together, I come to find I barely knew the lad I was so desperate to stay beside. The things I've heard you'd done . . ." I trailed off, shaking my head. "I'd not believe it, at first.

And it's queer to think you've held yourself apart from me all this time. That I knew we were growing distant with each other and I never thought you had this . . . this other life."

He made a face. "Sure, and it weren't I alone with something to hide. You never said a word to me about her. That it was about . . . how you cared for her."

"Never needed to, did I?" I said. "And didn't the truth shine out of my face? I thought you liked to see a lass in love, but only if you're not in love with the same person?" I looked down. "You knew."

He swallowed. "Might have done."

"Ah, go on. You knew."

He sighed, exasperated. "And what if I did? It was me she wanted, Mar. She wanted me. There was never any contest between us for her. What was I to do?"

"You could have said!" I looked up, eyes blazing. "You might have told me you knew how things stood. I'd have borne it better, maybe."

"Maybe. And maybe no. You never did see her for a person. Christ, you made an idol out of her, and, as far as you were concerned, she was always just a prize I didn't deserve to have won. I've always loved her for the woman she is, not the lady you're paid to make her seem. But at least I've always known her for flesh and blood, Mar. What's it she's been to you?"

I froze, stung. There was nothing bitter or sharp or reproachful in his words, the way there ought to have been. There was only curiosity, the naked question that I could not answer, for answering it made me no better than the baron or Mr. Dawson, and I could not bear to throw my lot in with such as them. And so when it finally came to me to open my mouth, I said something else altogether.

"Was it," I asked tentatively, "was it because I pushed you away, loving her like I did, that you joined the Order?"

He took hold of my hands again, but gently this time. "No. Christ, Mar. You'd grown so close with her, so wrapped in everything she does, you can't remember anymore it's a role you play. That if they knew you were Irish, and Catholic to boot, you'd not be welcome in that house. The nights you stayed away from the Hibernian, when I talked with the other men there, I come to realize how bad it's growing. And then I was out there in the thick of it, and, ah, well," he said as I went pale. "Best not to dwell on that. I did what I had to. To protect myself and my countrymen. There are thousands of our people in this city, and more coming all the time, and the folks've been here before us don't like it any too well."

I shifted uncomfortably. "The lads at Dermot's place seem to do all right. Sure, look at Dermot himself—does he not prosper? He's thick with that Tammany lot."

"Aye, the lads have prospered, in their place. And those who've the backing of Tammany do well enough. But there's nativist gangs who'd not see us prosper further, and would take away what footholds we have here. Or are we to be content to be their servants all our lives?"

"But you'd been in service all your life! So'd our da. So'd our mam, come to it. And I didn't see you complaining about the hours you spent in Charlotte Walden's carriage house."

"Aye, and I'm expected to be content with that after I've shared her bed? I couldn't court her. I wasn't fit. But if this is supposed to be a land of opportunity, why shouldn't I rise? Why shouldn't I have something better here than I did back home? If I left everything behind, should it not be for a better life? Mar," he said, "I want a better life. I'm planning for a better life."

We stood silent there for a moment, and the silence between us grew until it seemed a living thing.

"Well, and out with it," I said finally.

He ran a hand nervously through his hair. "There's a ship," he said.

I shook my head. "Sure, and I've heard that one before."

"To Dublin," he said. "This one is on its way to Dublin."

"And who would you know in Dublin?" I asked.

"Where'd you think I've been these months? And there are some there," he said, "as think that a man's worth ought not to be judged by the church he sings in on Sundays. That we should have the same sorts of rights as other men do, and are helping our people to rise."

"You sound like a right Republican," I said.

"So what if I am?" he shot back, and I stared at him, taking in his frank, earnest face, and once more feeling the waves of jealousy at him rise up and overwhelm me, and I shook his hand from mine in disgust.

"And how will life in Dublin serve her?" I asked. "And till that day that you have all those rights, what will you have her do while you're plotting treason? Live on scraps, make her work to survive, take on the service you're so keen to shed? Or will you turn to 'protection' over there to keep her in style, and let her spend her days making calls on your other Republican friends' wives? Drop her card for every Hibernian's dam? Embroider St. Brigit's cross on your hankies? What name will she whisper to you at night—Johnny or Seanin? What manner of life would she have, your Mrs. O'Farren-Prior, while you're fighting for your *equality* with a fecking brickbat?"

"It needn't be that," he said sullenly. "I've a fair deal saved by. You have too, if you're of a mind to it. There's no cause for us to stay in service, when we could start over. Nobody knows us in Dublin, except my contacts in the Order—I could be anyone there. I could set up as a merchant, or a horse trader—and I know the right people now to make it happen. It wouldn't be so grand as here, but she could still live well. As the Tredwells or the Melvills do."

I tossed my head. "I've never seen her dance a waltz with Gansevoort Melvill, or taken tea with Elizabeth Tredwell. Don't move in quite the same circles, do they?"

"Said it wouldn't be as grand," he muttered. "But it could be respectable, and it could be in style, and no one would need to know that I was born in service, and she was born to riches. And we could be together."

"Well, then," I said, crossing my arms. "I supposed you'd better shimmy up to that window and get down on one knee to ask her."

Seanin gave a short, hoarse laugh. "Christ, you really are a bitch, Mar. I'm offering a new life, a new start, for all of us."

"All of us," I said. "For me to do what? Go on every day plaiting her hair and doing up her buttons? A new life for the two of you, maybe."

"What care I who's doing her buttons or plaiting her hair? You'll ne'er be happy unless she's by, so come with us, aye, but have pity on a man, Mar, and ask her for me?"

"Come again now?" I asked, shaking my head. "Are you not man enough to ask her yourself?"

"You know 'tisn't that. Jesus, I'd give up my eye just to see her again, Mar." He held up a paper, folded into a crisp, neat square and sealed with a blob of red wax. "Please, Mar. I'm begging you. Please."

I snatched it from his hands and marched back to the house without another word.

There are things I saw, from the way she held that paper, that Seanin had written there, but I'll be damned if I ever tell them to another living soul, for every stolen word burned into my heart like a brand, and there are some secret things, written with the heat of love, that burn too brightly to be shared. I never knew he had it in him. I suppose I never really understood until then.

But Charlotte knew him, and now, seeing his heart laid bare on the page like that, she ran to the window overlooking the mews. She pushed the curtain aside, and, with the candles blazing brightly behind her, her red hair flaming, I knew she must look like a beacon from below. She gasped, putting her hand to the glass a moment before touching her fingers to her lips and to her heart. The sight of her doing it in profile from where I stood in the corner of her room nearly slayed me. I dare not think of what it did to Seanin waiting in the dark below.

> It will neither be required nor expected of you to speak with the elegance and polish of an accomplished and highly educated lady, nor with the accuracy of a professed governess; but it will add much to your respectability.
>
> —*The Duties of a Lady's Maid*

The first time I clapped eyes on Charlotte Walden, I loved her in the same moment. Mrs. Harrison had shown me into the parlor, where I sat on the stiff horsehair sofa, my back ramrod straight, smoothing my skirts for the third time, waiting. It was early autumn then, and from the vantage of the front windows, I could see the trees in the park turning, branches of crimson and gold breaking out amidst the paling green. There were so many trees there, and I was thinking how unlike home it was when I heard a rustle of skirts in the passage, and I rose as Charlotte Walden appeared framed in the door. She wore a morning dress of celadon muslin, her hair arranged in a few curls that fell along her cheeks and a simple knot at the nape of her neck. At her throat she had a cameo, but, aside from the ivory combs in her hair, she wore no ornament. I dropped a curtsy, and she bade me sit, taking the chair opposite. In her hand, I recognized the letter of introduction Dermot had written for me, imitating a lady's mincing hand. A born forger, Dermot. An odd talent for a publican, but a useful skill for one who did a steady side trade as a one-man registry office and labor agent.

Charlotte smiled, dimpling prettily, and I smiled back as demurely as I might. My heart, which I had felt so recently broken by

Nuala Begley, thumped rapidly and loudly against my ribs, attesting suddenly to its wholeness.

"You are Mary Ballard, I think?" It was less of a question than a statement, but I nodded my assent. "I am Charlotte Walden, but you will know that, of course."

"I do indeed, miss," I said in my best impersonation of Bathsheba Kirk's soft and cultured Edinburgh burr. Dermot had coached me thoroughly, forcing me to practice for days on end, not allowing me to speak a syllable in my own voice until he felt the timbre of my words was perfect. "It is a great pleasure to make your acquaintance, and I am most gratified for the opportunity to present myself in your employ."

Charlotte nodded graciously. "How long have you been in New York, Miss Ballard?"

"I am but new arrived."

"From . . . Yorkshire, is it?" Charlotte asked, glancing at the letter.

"Indeed, miss."

"But you are not English?" Again, though it was not exactly a question, it invited an answer.

"No, miss. I came over from Scotland when my mistress, who was Miss Lillian Campbell, married and became Mrs. Burke."

"As her lady's maid?" Charlotte inquired.

"No, miss, as my mother's daughter, for I was no more than eight at the time. It was my mother who was her maid. My father, God rest him, had been the Campbells' head groom." The story Dermot and I had concocted stuck as closely to the truth of my life as possible.

"Oh, I see. And when did you become Mrs. Burke's maid?"

"When my mother passed out of this world, miss. She had trained me, you see, and I had the benefit of working all my life in the Burkes' employ."

"What were you, then, before you became Mrs. Burke's maid?"

I pressed my lips together. Dermot and I had not anticipated this particular question, but I decided that, when in doubt, it was probably best to stick to the truth. "I was a housemaid," I began, and then, seeing her eyebrows shoot up, quickly amended, "But only for a year before I became a chambermaid, and then Mrs. Burke's youngest was weaned and I became a nursemaid." Charlotte nodded expectantly, and I plunged on. "And all the while, of course, my mother trained me up, for it was always expected I should follow in her profession. When ladies came visiting and did not bring their own maids with them, it was I who served them."

Charlotte's eyebrows had lowered considerably, but there was still, on her face, a slight air of surprise or disbelief. "That is a great confidence shown in the abilities of one still so young. Pray, what is your age now?"

"I am four and twenty," I lied, adding three years to my life. "And have spent the past four years as Mrs. Burke's maid."

"Yes, that is in accord with her letter." Charlotte glanced at the document again, though it was clear she was quite familiar with the contents. Her long fingers fiddled with a corner of the paper. "And you quitted her service because she was removing to Dublin?"

"Yes, miss. When Mr. Burke passed, God rest his soul, Mrs. Burke was resolved to go to her sister in Dublin, but I having no wish to go to that city, my mistress was kind enough to book my passage over the Atlantic." This part of the story was vital. With no address for the fictional Mrs. Burke, save one in Dublin, there would be no surprise should a potential employer write and find the letter returned.

"Why not stay with your mistress and go to Dublin?" Charlotte inquired. "Since you had been with the family for so long?" And, as I had practiced with Dermot, I bit my lip, as though wondering how much to reveal before taking a deep breath and diving in.

"May I be quite frank with you, miss?" I inquired, and, at her nod, went on. "I am a Presbyterian, miss, as my mother was before me, and the Burkes were. And you will know, of course, miss, that Dublin is rife with popery, and I did not wish to go to that city. My aunt, my mother's sister, came out to New York two years past, and wrote to me that there were many *respectable* opportunities here." I suppressed a shudder delicately. It was crucial, Dermot had drilled into me, that I leave no doubt about my religious sympathies. It would be a rare family that would hire a Catholic lady's maid. A housemaid or a maid of all work, perhaps, but certainly not a lady's maid. Dermot had told us that we must never cross ourselves, or invoke the saints or the Blessed Virgin, or else our positions would be forfeit.

Charlotte nodded sympathetically, and I smiled at her, pleased the gambit had worked. "Well," she said almost apologetically, "this is an Episcopalian house, but I assure you that, on your Sundays off, you might worship as you choose. There is a congregation in Wall Street, I believe."

"It is a hard thing, miss," I said slowly, "to be born in one country and raised in another. It is difficult to feel that one quite fits in, you see. That is why I took my aunt's advice to come to New York, miss. Here, I can begin again, seen not as Scottish or English, but on my own merits, as myself."

Charlotte dimpled again. "Of your merits, Mrs. Burke is most effusive. I understand you are quite skilled at the dressing of hair?" Her smile turned momentarily wry as she touched a hand self-consciously to the plain coil atop her head. "Porter, my mother's maid, you know, has had the goodness to contend with"—she gestured helplessly—"all this. But I will require someone with great skill in the dressing of curls."

"Oh, indeed, miss!" I said, and launched into a well-rehearsed soliloquy juxtaposing the virtues of papering, hot tongs, and sugared curls.

There were many questions testing my knowledge of style, of course, but I had spent long enough poring over fashion magazines with Nuala to be able to speak fluently about the plunge of the season's necklines, the correct measure of fabric for a visiting gown, and the best types of lace to use for a pelerine.

In all, we chatted quite freely for the better part of the hour before Charlotte announced that I might have the position and inquired as to when I might begin.

I had come to the business with my heart sore, but I went away from our first interview smitten and smiling. I expected nothing, certainly, nor cherished any hopes that she might come to fancy me as Nuala had. That had been folly, of course, and it was rare—impossibly rare, I thought—that I should ever meet another girl with inclinations such as mine. I was content simply to worship Charlotte, to adore her as an idol, and to bask in her presence. And so it was to be for the first two years I had in her employ. I was happy, blissfully happy to be her maid, and to love her quietly, and to have my brother by.

> You must not only be particular about the respectability of those with whom you live, but you must try to gain their good-will and esteem, that if through any cause you have to leave, you may obtain the best recommendation from them.
>
> —*The Duties of a Lady's Maid*

Seanin's plan, as he explained it to me, was a simple one, made smoother by the fact that Charlotte's maid was one of the confederacy. The contents of Charlotte's trousseau—her new gowns, her lace caps, her lacy petticoats, and her eyelet drawers—were replaced in twos and threes each Thursday and alternate Sundays with bolts of canvas to make up the weight, while the originals were secreted to Seanin in St. Patrick's Church on my way down to the Hibernian. Already packed and provisioned by Seanin, Charlotte would therefore be able to slip unburdened from the house, simply and economically clad in one of my gowns, carrying nothing that might betray her purpose. I would guide her to the quay where Seanin would be waiting for her to board the SS *Cortona.* They would be married immediately in their stateroom by the captain, and the ship was scheduled to depart on the dawn tide. By the time Charlotte would be missed, she would be somewhere in the Atlantic out past Long Island, enjoying her first morning as a married woman. When the newlywed couple arrived in Dublin, two months later, they would be greeted by Seanin's brothers in the Order and escorted to the modest town house he had commissioned them to purchase in his name. Installed immediately as the lady of the house, Mrs.

O'Farren would be supplied an ample purse to equip and plenish the place—culled from Seanin's earnings and my own for the past three years, augmented by Seanin's cut of the protection money and the sale of Charlotte's jewels, which would be pawned by a trusted member of the Order upon her arrival. The entire plan was neat as two pins, requiring nothing of Charlotte but her compliance, and a great deal of work on my part, to say nothing of what amounted to my life savings.

It was the acquisition of my own wages, which I had been turning over to Dermot for safekeeping, that troubled me. The problem in all of this was twofold, and lay in the fact that not only was I loath to tell Dermot about the venture, but I was not, in fact, sure I wanted to go at all. Turning the matter over in my mind, I could not say what stung more: the fact that Seanin expected me to fork out three years of my wages without demure to keep Charlotte in style, or the fact that it took me several days to realize that I had a choice in the matter.

Again and again, I played out what would happen if I went. What I had told Seanin that night in the mews had been the truth. It would be a new start for him and for Charlotte, but I could not fathom what my own role in such an arrangement would be. Would Charlotte expect me to go on dressing her hair and helping her to robe? Or would we sit companionably together in the parlor—as she and Prudence once had done—receiving callers, attended to by a maid of our own? Such a thought—that I might sit before the glass while some girl twisted my hair into braids, or raise my arms so she could do up my laces—was a welcome absurdity, and I laughed outright at the notion. Did Seanin truly think he could support his unmarried sister, as well as his fashionable young wife? If so, his connections through the Order and the Order's influence in Dublin must run far higher than I had expected. But support me in what? Making calls to the ladies of other such households? What was it that Charlotte, an unmarried lady herself, did? The answer to that, of course, was make herself marriageable, and I was certainly not inclined to do that. My life, then, would be lived out as a guest in my brother's household, and a hostage witness to the love between him and Charlotte.

I felt ill as I began to play out what life in that house would be like. Charlotte, who had conceived once before, would surely get with child again, and there would be a succession of little O'Farrens before long. And I, the doting sister-in-law and auntie, would likely aid in their birthing and rearing, all the while watching their parents' adoration of one another exhibited daily. It would be inescapable, the thing that Seanin had said to me that night he came back for Charlotte. That it was him she wanted. Him she loved. And if I went with them, I should have to watch them live their love every day.

But what life was there for me here, if they left without me? My livelihood was in Charlotte's keeping. I had been my entire life in service, and certainly could find another position as a lady's maid if I wanted to continue such a thing. But the thought was not an appealing one. I was not such a fool as to think that my experience as Charlotte's maid would be typical of the next cut I might find. If I could find another cut—the thought suddenly struck me. Who would write my character, if Charlotte was gone, and what would a character written by a society girl who'd taken to her heels count for, at any rate? Most of the housekeepers of Manhattan's ton knew me on sight. Would anyone hire the maid left behind by a disgraced mistress? Would I be blamed for not stopping her? I paused in my ruminations to curse Charlotte, who, for the sake of her family, would not stoop to bear Seanin's child for fear of ruin, but who would now cheerfully flee with him, ruining me.

For now, however unfairly, I had begun to resent Charlotte. How simple it all would have been if she had swallowed her pride and married Seanin when she had been pregnant with his child! Where was that hauteur now? Or perhaps, having been contracted to another man and forced to contemplate the realities of a loveless marriage, she had reconsidered the priorities of her own heart. Or perhaps now, in the wake of Prudence's departure, Charlotte's prior reluctance to sacrifice her family's position in society had evaporated. Certainly, she did not share her reasons for accepting Seanin's mad proposal with me. In our moments alone, she talked only of her love for him, her longing to be with him, her impatience until the day of our flight—for she, as Seanin did, could not but assume I would simply do as they did, and go where they went. She talked as though Prudence Graham and Elijah Dawson did not exist, and perhaps, removed, as they were, from her state of joy, it no longer mattered to her that they did. Certainly I, who was there before her, folding up her chemise into the bundle I would take to Seanin, mattered very little, and Charlotte could not seem to contemplate that I might have an opinion that differed materially from her own.

I held my tongue. She had the right to love whomever it was she loved, be it Seanin or Mr. Dawson, or . . . I could not finish the thought. It was of no consequence. She loved Seanin. She would never have been able to love me.

It is not to be imagined that I gave no consideration to Liddie

Lawrence as I contemplated my position. Indeed, I gave great consideration to her, for if I could not reconcile myself to what I was to Charlotte—maid or sister—I was on unsure footing indeed where Liddie was concerned. I had known from the first that Liddie was a distraction to me, albeit a welcome one, but beyond that I could not have said what we were to one another. My mind kept wandering back to that first night, kissing her on the hogsheads, her breath fiery with ale and smoke. She hadn't been caging me, or sizing me up as she would a cully. She had wanted me simply for the sake of it. It was a mystery to me that she should keep taking me to her bed without pay, or forgo accepting paying clients on Thursdays in order to spend them with me. The terms of our arrangement, such as they were, remained unspoken, and I wondered greatly if she would give me another thought if one Thursday I should not arrive. I thought, perhaps, in her practical way, she would give a little shrug and write me off as a bad investment of her time, turning her attentions to more profitable prospects.

I lay in bed beside her, my chin resting upon her brow, wondering if I could be anybody—or any body—at all, and would her hand rest as easily on someone else's chest? Or would her leg curl around someone else's knee? In the sticky heat of an early September night, the places where our bodies touched were slick with sweat, bare skin plastered to bare skin. Her breathing was soft and even. I thought she was asleep before she kissed the hollow of my throat and murmured, "Sing the one about the last glass."

"What's that now?"

"The lilty one about having one more drink before you're off."

I hummed a few notes, and she nodded sleepily. "Mmm. That one. Sing it for me, Mar?"

If I had money enough to spend
And leisure time to sit awhile
There is a fair maiden in this town
Who sorely has my heart beguiled.
Her rosy cheek, her ruby lip
I own she has me in her thrall
So fill to me the parting glass
Good night and joy be to you all.

"Mmm, that's you all over, Mar," she whispered, and I held her tighter, shivering though I was not in the least cold.

Unable to make up my mind in the matter, I sought her at Dermot's each week, making love to her quickly and abstractedly and desperately, saying as little as possible and holding her tight in her sleep. I don't think, in all that undecided time, I ever once could look her in the eye. I was too afraid of what I might find there.

She who trusts another with a secret, makes herself a slave; but all who are so bound are impatient to redeem their lost liberty.

—*The Duties of a Lady's Maid*

On the eighteenth of September, the *Cortona* came into port to take on cargo and make repairs before its scheduled departure on the twenty-third. Seanin had sent word upon the vessel's arrival, and I had taken myself down to the docks on my way to the milliner's to see it. It looked more or less exactly like a steamship. Its bare masts rose from the harbor as stevedores swarmed up and down the gangplank, shouting raucously while they unloaded crates and casks. It was in all ways indistinguishable to me from the many other ships docked, and I turned my steps toward the milliner in disgust. There were no answers for me there. It was a ship, like any other. It would take me somewhere or it wouldn't. It was for me to do the choosing.

The following Thursday, misery dogged my steps down Mulberry Street.

The Hibernian was quieter than I'd seen it in some time. I approached the bar, where Dermot handed me my pint and a package that looked like a brick done up in brown paper. I hefted the compact parcel and cocked an eyebrow at him.

"What's this then?"

He cleared his throat unnecessarily and said, "Your wages," in an undertone, then chuckled mirthlessly. "Figured you'd never get around to asking me for them, so I thought I'd take the sting out of it, like."

I raised my pint. "I'm obliged to you."

"Ah, go on," he said softly. "They're your wages, aren't they?"

"You know that's not what I was on about."

"Aye, I know it well enough, lass." He smiled sadly.

I took a sip, thinking things over. "I won't ask how you knew, but only how long."

He shrugged. "Long enough. Does it matter?"

"What you think matters a great deal to me," I said.

"Does it? I wonder," he said ruefully. "You never do confide in me. Your Liddie, now, she's always telling me this or that, and half the time she's talking Shakespeare and I can't understand the whole of it, but at least she's confiding in me, which is more than I can say for you all these years."

"Sure and how can I, with you always knowing my mind without me saying a word?" I put my pint down heavily, the amber liquid streaming frothily along the sides. "Christ, is there a thing I've done since I first met you that's been without your knowing of it? What of it you haven't orchestrated yourself, that is?"

"Didn't tell you to go mooning over that wee baggage's meant to be your mistress, did I? Sure and I'd not orchestrate the mizzle you're thinking of running."

Comprehension dawned. "He was here, was he now?" I asked, already knowing the answer.

"Aye," Dermot said. "Came by for a chat, he did, two days ago. I had the whole of it from him. I may be part of the Order, and Tammany still has me doing my share for them, but, at the end of the day, I'm the moneyman." He shrugged. "Easy to funnel money in and out of a pub, and I'm not opposed to what they're after, then, am I? Anyway, that's neither here nor there. He came by for the money, the Order's share of the take, and I found out where he'd been these months. No notion of how far he'd gone into their inner circle. He's done well for himself, has Seanin, and all on his own. You're two of a kind there, keeping your own counsel. He's had plans for a while to go back to Dublin and join the cause there. Seems yourself and your lady are just the most recent additions to the plan."

I set my jaw. "Kept his own counsel, sure, but free enough with mine, it seems, if you had the entire story from him."

He shrugged again. "It did explain a fair bit, didn't it? Christ, lass, you're one for the books, aren't you? I've heard o' brothers tearing each other to bits o'er the same lass, but you're a first and no mistaking."

I snorted. "I've heard that phrase before. That's what Liddie said. 'Bout something else, come to it, but you know what I'm on about."

"I expect I do." He paused, pursing his lips. "But does Liddie?"

"I don't know what Liddie thinks."

He refilled my glass. "Might help if you asked her."

"It might at that," I said, "if I knew what to ask."

Dermot was silent for a moment, scratching the back of his head. "Well, now, Mar," he said. "I never knew you for a fool before. Don't become one now. Sometimes there're no words needed for a thing the entire world's got eyes to see, so?"

Liddie was slow with me that night. She teased, she hesitated, she held back and took her time, kissing me with a languid passion, her limbs melting against mine. We neither of us spoke, being otherwise occupied, and, when it was over, she lay with her head on my chest, tracing patterns along my abdomen. I lay, stroking her head, aware of her hand becoming slower and heavier against my skin before her fingers stopped moving altogether and her hand lay still. Her face hidden from me, her shoulders rose and fell gently with her breath, and I watched her in the dimming light as the lone candle in the room guttered and went out.

She stirred then, with the change of light, and moved herself up to lie on the pillow beside me, kissing me absently as she settled herself back down. “Don’t wake me,” she said, her voice thick with sleep. “Just kiss me when you go.”

> If you cannot otherwise avoid the evil which will certainly await you by rashly listening to the importunities of passion, leave the situation at once, without disclosing to any one the reason of your conduct.
>
> —*The Duties of a Lady's Maid*

Bidding good night to Grace Porter as we parted on the stairs, I wondered perhaps if my composure were a form of madness. Surely, I thought, I should not be able to so calmly and dispassionately bid good night to her—to Cook, to Mrs. Harrison—knowing that, one way or another, I was never going to see any of them ever again. Never mind that our enterprise rode upon my sangfroid, never mind that my entire life with these people was a complete fiction. My heart beat regularly as I gave my usual evening pleasantries whilst my mind reeled against the normality of my actions.

Charlotte sat in silence, flushed with pleasure as I took the pins out of her hair, brushing the locks and rebraiding them into a single plait down her back. I wondered what her own good evening to her mother had been like. It was not, I knew, Charlotte's intention to part permanently from her family, but, after a suitable period, to break the news of her elopement and by and by reconcile her family to her new circumstances. While I was of the opinion that "by and by" might be a period of years where Augusta Walden was concerned, Charlotte, with the simple naïve privilege of being an heiress and an only child, seemed unfazed by the prospect of estrangement from her mother for very long. In the weeks since we had been planning her flight, I had learned that her portion from her grandfather would come upon her marriage, and that this largesse was dependent not upon parental approval but upon grandpaternal approval of her choice of spouse. While Augusta Walden might choose to spurn her daughter upon the occasion of her marriage, Charlotte felt confident that, in consequence of Prudence Graham's flight, old Thaddeus Graham would reconcile himself quickly enough to his granddaughter's elopement rather than be parted from another of his descendants.

Augusta Walden's qualms, Charlotte had assured me, would be laid to rest upon the receipt of her, Charlotte's, marriage portion. Mrs. Walden had long depended upon her daughter's share of the Graham diamond mines. By cutting her daughter completely, she stood to lose any allocation Charlotte might appropriate her mother. Certainly, Charlotte reasoned, her mother's wrath would be great indeed, but sheer mercenary logic would triumph in the end.

I had listened to her think aloud over the ramifications of her actions for weeks now, wondering, not for the first time, what it must be like to live a life that could be measured in dollars. Where one kept a ledger of family affections, to be reconciled and balanced like a bankbook. I wondered if it was preferable to a life where you fought your family tooth and nail, literally sinking your fingernails into your brother's face when you disagreed with him.

Having helped Charlotte dress in one of my old traveling frocks—hers, incidentally, from three seasons ago—I left her sitting impatiently in the tufted chair by the cold fireplace while I checked the small leather bag containing her jewels one final time before our departure. We were to wait until the clock struck three before making our way down to the harbor. I enjoined Charlotte to rest, if she could. For myself, I sat bolt upright on my bed, staring, for the last time, at the laurel wreath on the ceiling, lit dimly in the moonlight.

The house had been silent for hours when the appointed time came. Softly, the small bag in one hand, our boots in the other, I came to stand in the doorway between our rooms. In the gloom I could just make out Charlotte, her cheek resting on her hand, her face pointed toward the empty grate. She was so still I thought perhaps she had indeed fallen asleep, but, when I stepped into the room, she turned to me, and I saw her eyes were bright.

"Is it time?" she asked, her voice so soft I barely caught the words, and I nodded. She smiled, rising, and glided shoeless toward me. At the bottom of the stairs, I held up a hand, motioning her to pause, before stepping forward to inspect the kitchen. The room was silent and empty. I motioned to Charlotte, we moved on stockinged feet across the flagstone floor, and I handed her our boots so I could silently slip the latch to let us out into the mews. We laced up our shoes and walked on tiptoe to keep our heels from ringing on the cobbles.

Charlotte gripped my hand nervously as we made our way down the Bowery. Even so late, on a Friday the pubs and music halls were still open, and I counted on the light foot traffic to mask our progress, should anyone follow us. It was a ridiculous notion—no one could possibly have missed us at this hour—but it was a precaution I was unwilling to forgo. The route, however, alarmed my mistress, who shrunk from the entrances of bars as we passed, starting at the raucous cries issuing from inside. I squeezed her hand reassuringly, and she smiled back.

The walk to the quays would have taken me no more than forty minutes on my own, but, with Charlotte in tow, it was over an hour before we arrived. Out of a surfeit of caution, I might have doubled back or led a false trail, but Charlotte was unaccustomed to walking so far, and I was wary of exhausting her, so it was after four by the time we arrived at the quieter streets by the docks. The light and din of the Bowery long behind us, we moved as softly as we might, keeping to the shadows of the narrow buildings.

He was waiting for us, alone on the empty quay. The briny-brackish smells of the dockyards seemed unromantic to me, but Charlotte let drop my hand and flew into Seanin's waiting arms.

It was something of a shock, I think, seeing them together like that. I had imagined it so many times, tortured myself with the image, in fact, but it was nothing to the lurch I felt in my stomach actually seeing it before me. Her lips on his, heedless of their surroundings, the sheer passion—taking it all in, I felt something cold clawing at my heart. I felt ill and angry and shamed all at once, and I think I knew then, I hope, now, looking back, that I knew then, I could not bear the sight of them so every day of my life. I want so badly to believe that I chose not to go with them in that moment, but I will never know, for so lost was I in my grief that I never heard the footfalls behind me, nor any other thing until the hammer of a gun cocked against the back of my head.

A heavy hand came to rest upon my shoulder: unnecessary, as, in fact, I was frozen with fear. "That's quite enough of that, Paddy," said Mr. Vandeman from behind me, severing Charlotte and Seanin's warm embrace with the chill in his voice. They sprang apart, and Charlotte shrieked at the sight of Mr. Vandeman and the pistol he was holding to my head.

Seanin raised his hands warily. "Right now," he said, taking a tentative step toward us. "There's no call for that. Just let the lassie be, so?"

Mr. Vandeman snorted. "I will if you will." He inclined his head toward Charlotte. "Good evening, Miss Walden. If you will come with me, I will escort you home."

Seanin took another step toward us, his hands held out, showing his palms. "Easy, easy. Let's talk this out like friends."

"Friends?" Mr. Vandeman spat. "As if I'd ever be friends with Papist scum like you. Come now, Miss Walden. Let me take you away from this heathen."

Charlotte shook her head, trembling where she stood. "You mistake the situation, Mr. Vandeman," she said, her voice unsteady. "I am not in need of your assistance. Please," she said, her voice cracking. "Please. Have the goodness to depart."

I felt the muzzle of the pistol shake with Mr. Vandeman's laughter. His fingers tightened painfully on my shoulder. "Do you hear her, Miss Ballard? 'The goodness to depart.' As if she could dismiss me so easily! This isn't your parlor, Miss Walden, and I don't answer to you anymore."

"What is it you want now?" Seanin asked. "Just put the pistol down. We've no quarrel with you."

"But I've one with you, see?" Mr. Vandeman said. "And if you take one step closer, I will blow this little bitch's brains out the front of her face."

Seanin stopped cold, raising his hand higher. "Right now, I'm stopped, see? Let the lassie go. She's naught to do with this."

"No, I don't think I will," Mr. Vandeman said. "I require your cooperation, and quickly, and if I don't have the assurance of the little bitch's life, well . . ." He shrugged. "It makes no difference to me if she lives or dies, see, and it's certainly worth more than her sorry life for me to ensure Miss Walden gets back home."

"Please," Charlotte said. "Oh, please let her go, only I can't go back with you! I'm marrying Seanin and I'm leaving, and there's nothing you can say that will change my mind."

Mr. Vandeman laughed nastily, and tears began to dribble down my cheeks. My eyes met Seanin's, and he held my gaze. "You're coming with me and you're marrying my master on Wednesday, and he's had enough of indulging you while you defile yourself with this scum, Miss Walden. Frankly, I don't see that you're worth the effort, on his part or mine, but I'm not paid to consider the niceties, see? I'm paid to make sure you get to the altar."

"Your master?" Charlotte asked. "Mr. Dawson?"

"Well, he couldn't very well have you fucking another groom, could he?" Mr. Vandeman sneered. "It wasn't hard for him to puzzle out, all the hints the Graham girl kept dropping. Only reason I've stayed in this cesspit city is to keep an eye on you."

Charlotte blinked, her terror melting to fury. "How dare you use such language to me? Remove your hands from my sister-in-law and go back and tell your master that I will never have him."

"Your sister-in-law?" Mr. Vandeman asked. "That's rich. I knew this cunt here." He jabbed me hard in the back of the head with the gun. "I knew she was part of it, see, but I never figured on her being Prior's sister. Think he'd thank you if I split her skull?"

"You leave my sister alone, you bloody bastard," Seanin shouted, charging at us, and I felt the muzzle of the gun scrape against the back of my head as Mr. Vandeman turned the pistol on Seanin and fired.

The cry was Charlotte's and mine, screamed out with one voice as Seanin fell to the cobbles. Freed of Mr. Vandeman's grasp, I reached Seanin first, grabbing his torso and rolling him to face me.

Dark blood blossomed against the crisp white of his shirt; my hands were sticky and wet. I heard Charlotte's footsteps as she ran toward us, intercepted suddenly by Mr. Vandeman.

"No you don't, miss," he said, wrapping strong arms around her. "You'll forget all about this, and you'll come back with me."

"Let go of me!" Charlotte shrieked, struggling wildly. "Seanin! Seanin! Oh, god no! Take your hands off me!"

I ran to her, grappling at Mr. Vandeman's hands, clawing desperately. He backhanded me with the pistol, sending me reeling. I clamored to my feet, my ears ringing from the blow, and saw, blurred before me, Mr. Vandeman taking aim and Charlotte grabbing suddenly at his arm. The pistol fired.

My left foot was exploding in pain. I looked down stupidly at the hole in the top of my boot and back up at Mr. Vandeman, who, having expended both bullets, flipped the pistol deftly with one hand and struck me neatly over the head with the pommel. I crumpled to my knees, my eyes refusing to focus on my fingers gripping the cobbles, my stomach heaving. From somewhere very far away, I heard Charlotte's voice crying out, growing fainter and fainter. I vomited violently, pissing myself in the process.

Somewhere, someone was calling my name. I blinked slowly, my vision swimming, blood from my split forehead dripping into my eyes. Fingers closed over my wrist. I turned to see Seanin grasping for me, and I pivoted to face him, forcing my eyes to focus.

"Maire."

My tongue felt thick in my mouth. I swallowed, tasting bile. "I'm here, Seanin."

"Maire." His voice was wet and gurgling. His chest heaved, making his wound gush.

"Hush, now, Seanin," I said, choking. "I'm here. I'll care for you. I'm sorry, *mo chroí.* I'm so sorry."

His mouth moved, a rivulet of blood oozing from his lips, but he made no sound. I held his hand in mine, my eyes on his. There were so many things I wished to say. I wanted to ask forgiveness. I wanted to tell him that all would be well. I wanted to say something that would make him feel that healing, welling love I'd felt lying in the grass in Donegal, but all I could think was that it was wrong, terribly wrong for him to be lying in the street, his blood mingling with the filth between the cobbles. And so I said nothing at all. I held his hand tightly in my own and I stared into his eyes and I tried so hard through the force of my gaze to keep him fixed here on this earth for just a moment more. He was looking right at me, and then suddenly he wasn't. His gaze went glassy and his chest went still. I kissed his forehead, closed his eyes, sobbing brokenly for my brother.

> But always be patient, and remember that hasty words will rankle a wound, while soft language will soothe it; forgiveness will heal it, and oblivion will take away the scar.
>
> —*The Duties of a Lady's Maid*

The dark sky was growing pale, but light still streamed from the Hibernian, the sounds of raucous laughter spilling onto the street. I limped through the door, making directly for the bar, my mangled foot dragging behind me. Dermot, busy with pouring ale, did not note my approach at first, but when my legs buckled and the cry went up, I saw him vault over the top of the bar to be at my side at once. My vision was blurring badly just then, from more than the sweat and blood that streamed into my eyes. The last thing I remember before the darkness that played against the edge of my vision rose to swallow me was realizing I could no longer feel my face as I heard Liddie's voice, shrill with worry, calling out my name.

When I came to in the basement of the Hibernian, she was sponging my brow, lips pursed grimly, her face lined with worry. She dipped the cloth in a basin beside her, and I saw it streaming reddened water. Liddie held a cool hand to my cheek, twisting her lips into a forced smile. "Back again, are you?" she asked.

"Liddie—" My voice was cracked and harsh.

"You've a nice gash on the edge of your hairline, and I'm quite sure what's left of your foot is broken to bits," she said, stiff and businesslike, her smile fixed. "Dermot's gone for the nick to stitch you up and set your foot. We'll see you righted soon enough."

"Liddie—"

"Here, can you sit up a bit? Drink this." She was propping me up, putting a pint glass in my hand. I took a sip, realizing it was whiskey. "Best to finish it, I'd think," she said apologetically. "Dermot said the nick'll likely have a devil of a time setting that foot, for it's nearly pulp."

"Liddie—"

"You should have at least two pints in you before they attempt it, I think. It's going to hurt a considerable lot, and you're far too steady in your cups for just the one to have much effect."

"Liddie, good Christ, will you not let me speak?"

"What's that now?" she said, looking at me properly for the first time. I met her eyes, taking her hand.

"I'm sorry, Liddie. I'm so terribly sorry."

She snatched her hand away. "None of that, now, Maire O'Farren. We'll have a devil of a time ahead of us, patching you up, and damned if I've the constitution to hear you out at the moment."

I reached for her imploringly. "Please, Liddie, please. You've every right to be cross."

"Cross, she says!" replied Liddie. "I'm many things at this moment, but of all of them she lands on cross!"

"You've a right to be cross, Liddie, I know that you do, and I'm that sorry for it."

She took my outstretched hand then, holding it stiffly in her own and looking down at the floor. "What's it you're sorry for, Maire?"

"For leaving." I stroked the back of her hand with my thumb. "For not saying anything to you."

"What on earth should you have said?" Liddie said, still looking down. "You don't owe me anything."

"I owe you a great deal, Lid. I can't even—"

"You don't owe me anything," she repeated, her voice hard.

"I owe you an explanation."

"What's to explain?" She snatched her hand away in exasperation. "You love her, don't you? You've told me so a thousand times or more. And I'm not such a fool to expect you to stay if she was going. And, anyway, I told you not to say good-bye. Lord! You're hurt now. This is entirely the wrong time for such a scene. Why can't you just leave it be?"

"You knew I was going?"

She made a gesture of impatience. "I knew something was happening. Out of the ordinary. You didn't say anything, you see, about what would happen after she married the Dawson fellow. If they'd settle out on the Island, or if they'd keep a house in town, and if you'd stay her maid or no. So I knew she wasn't really going to marry him after all, or you'd have said something about it. There were a hundred ordinary, commonplace things you could have said, and you kept mum." She rolled her neck to release the tension, and I heard the faint crackle and pop that accompanied the motion. "And then I'd heard a scrap here and there about Johnny Prior back in town."

"And you're no fool," I said.

She snorted. "Well, that remains to be seen, doesn't it? Seeing as how I'm still down here in this fucking cellar with you."

I shook my head, a mistake, for it nearly blinded me with pain. "It's I who's the fool. I never really decided if I was going or no."

She furrowed her brow. "But you're here, now, if somewhat worse for the wear. You must have decided on something."

I leaned back, closing my eyes. "She didn't go. Seanin's dead. She went back and she'll marry Mr. Dawson. And Seanin's gone."

"Dead!" Liddie's eyes widened in shock. "Good lord! What happened?"

"It was that bastard Vandeman. He was Dawson's man all along. He must've followed us to the docks."

"To the docks?"

"There was a ship. To Dublin. Seanin and Charlotte . . ." The thought of what should have been nearly broke me. I was shaking. Liddie wrapped her arms around me, and I sobbed freely, too overcome to go on for some time.

"He shot Seanin. Dawson had him watching Charlotte. He shot Seanin and he took her back to Dawson," I said.

"And yet, you're here."

I shrugged one shoulder, swallowing, my throat tight. "Nowhere else to go, I figure."

"You could have gone on to Dublin without Johnny. You're Irish, after all, and isn't Ireland home? His people there—"

"Stop it, Liddie. I never properly decided, and then suddenly I didn't have a choice. I won't have you making me out to be nobler than I am."

She picked up my hand, holding it lightly in her own. "But surely your brother's people—"

"I didn't even think to come here, Liddie. I just came. It's all I have left, now. This place. Dermot. You."

She squeezed my hand, and I opened my eyes. Tears glistened on her cheeks. "I'm not her, Mar. I can never be. I can't replace her. And I've no thought to offer you . . . whatever it was you hoped to have with her." She smiled tightly. "But I thought, whatever it was we had, you might like to go on in such a way. Even though I'm not her. Even if I'm only me. I should have said, ages ago, how much it means to me. All this, whatever it is we have. But I was afraid you'd tell me you were going. How's that for stupid? You think too much about being noble, or what it means that you came here. But you're here, all the same, and perhaps it doesn't matter why. Perhaps we have time, now, to figure out what it means that you did. Together." She wiped her eyes roughly with the back of her free hand. "For Christ's sake, say something, Mar!"

"Liddie? You want me to stay?"

"Oh, you bloody stupid bitch!" she cried, tears running freely now. "Yes, goddamn you. Stay. Tell me you'll stay!"

I reached up, cupping her cheek, wiping the tears away with my thumb. "I'll stay."

> I shall leave you to perfect yourself in these indispensible acquirements, by careful observation and daily practice.
>
> —*The Duties of a Lady's Maid*

EPILOGUE

MULBERRY STREET, 1845

I unlocked the front door of the Hibernian Queen, opening it wide into the late morning sunshine and propping it open with an overturned bucket. Turning back in to the public house, I took up my broom and swept the stale sawdust out into the street, where the light breeze running up from the harbor whirled it away. I stood for a moment in the doorway, looking down the block. The flowers were beginning to fall from the mulberry trees, the white petals already turning brown in the gutters; soon they would begin to fruit. I would have to remember to look in the mornings for the red berries and start collecting them. The cordials I distilled always sold well. Overhead, the crowned raven on the pub's sign swayed, creaking gently in the morning breeze.

I shut the door, leaning the broom in the corner behind the bar and fetching a pail of water where it had been warming on the stove, replacing it with a kettle. Liddie always liked to take her coffee when she returned from her errands, and I expected her back in half an hour. There was a ship come into the harbor this morning from

Dublin—it seemed there were more coming all the time—and Liddie was bound to bring a packet from one of our agents at the docks. Best to have the chores finished before she returned so that I could join her in a leisurely cup and talk over affairs. Dermot would be by later in the morning, if business at Tammany did not keep him. With more starving Irish pouring into the city every day, we were never short on news or recruits to the Order, and, so long as Dermot kept palms greased at Tammany, City Hall turned a blind eye.

I poured vinegar and lemon oil into the bucket of water, dipped a rag in the mixture, and began to wipe down the surface of the bar, the pleasant, lemony smell of the warm vinegar rising up from the damp cloth in my hand. Rubbing methodically, my head bent to my work, I did not look up as I heard the front door open.

"We're closed," I said, focused on the concentric circles of the cloth against the wood.

"Hello, Ballard," she said.

I snapped my head up. She stood in the doorway, a vision in cornflower and navy paisley silk.

She smiled nervously. "It has been quite a long time."

I swallowed nervously. "It has, yes, Mrs. Dawson."

She smiled. "And you seem to have done well for yourself." She gestured vaguely to the door as she moved into the room. "I saw the sign. 'The Hibernian Queen: O'Farren and Lawrence, Proprietors.' I thought . . . I'd hoped it might be you. You own this place, do you?"

I wiped my hands on my apron. "I'm a partner, aye. The ownership is something of a collective, you might call it."

"My!" Her smile was growing fixed. I wondered if hearing me speak in my own accent was upsetting her. I felt naked, exposing myself so finally before her, and the sensation was unnerving. It had been the better part of a decade since I'd seen that crease between her brows, but I knew well enough it bespoke her discomfort. "So you have done well for yourself. I'd often wondered, you know."

"Did you, now? And yourself, Mrs. Dawson?" I asked.

Her smile was a mask. She was pressing her lips together so tightly that they were growing white. I could see now the circles below her eyes. "I am well," she said, smiling wider to bare her teeth. "Mr. Dawson is good to me. He is . . . a generous man." There were crow's-feet around her eyes. Her skin was so pale that she was luminous.

I plucked a bottle of my best whiskey and two glasses down from the shelf and came out from behind the bar, doing my best to hide the permanent limp I'd acquired the last time I had seen her. I pulled out a stool and motioned for her to sit as I took a seat and poured out two generous glasses of amber liquid.

"Oh, no, I couldn't," she protested. "I never take spirits."

I regarded her carefully. "Well, Mrs. Dawson," I said in a gentle tone. "It seems to me you've done a great many things in your life that you never imagined you'd do." I held a glass out to her. "When we knew each other before, I held myself to the rules of your way of life. Sit with me a moment and try playing by the rules of mine."

Her eyes went wide, but she sat, her wide skirts bobbing and rustling as she wordlessly took the proffered glass. In my time as a publican, I've seen enough green lads choke on their first sip of whiskey to recognize when someone has a fair mouth for spirits, and it cut me deep to see, after all this time, how casually she'd lied.

My heart was beating faster by the moment as I cast about, trying to recall the benign pleasantries ladies exchanged during morning calls. “And what brings you to Mulberry Street this morning, Mrs. Dawson?” I inquired, cringing inwardly as I spoke the words. It had once been my entire life to put her at ease, to smooth the way for her, and it struck me now how hollow I sounded.

She colored. “I did more than wonder about you. I . . . that is . . . I looked for you, you know.”

I inclined my head. “I wasn’t hiding. I’ve given up on hiding, you see.”

“I know. I see, that is.”

I looked down at her narrow hands, in which she played with a pair of kid gloves. Her fidgeting bothered me. Her nails had not been pared evenly, and I thought, with a pang, that it was no longer any of my concern whether her nails were pared well or pared ill. A dull ache curdled my stomach. She was waiting for me to speak. I wanted to ask if she still thought about my brother. To know if she looked at her husband every day and hated him for the way his man had shot Seanin dead. I wanted to ask her why, if she had looked for me, had she not come sooner. Was she ashamed, after everything? The silence lengthened. She took a nervous swallow of the contents of her glass, and went back to playing with her gloves.

I realized then that none of my questions mattered. She was ill at ease because she wanted absolution and didn’t know how to ask for it. It made no difference what she thought or felt about that horrible night and all the nights that had led up to it because the answers wouldn’t change anything at all. After this moment had passed, she would go back to her mansion on Fifth Avenue, and I would go back to wiping down my bar, and I was suddenly filled with a great desire to hasten the end of our mutual disquiet.

I took her hands into my own, meeting her eyes steadily. “It is good to see you, Mrs. Dawson, after so many years. It was a lifetime ago, I saw you last." I took a deep breath. Once I said the next words, it would be over and there would be no way to cross the breach again.

So I said them.

"But I have another life now. It was good of you to stop by."

She let out a breath. "Yes. Of course. I . . . of course. Thank you, Ballard. For everything." She made a small bow to me. "Good day to you." She squeezed my hands and withdrew her fingers from my grasp. The door shut behind her with a solid click.

And she was gone. Slipped through my hands, gone from my life, and the smell of her faded from the place where she had been standing and there was nothing left to remember her by. And my heart, which I had thought healed long ago, was a wordless ache, beating out her name, a silent tattoo she would never hear. And the void that she left still holds her shape, never to be filled. There are times when, entering a room, I catch something like her smell—a hint of lavender, a shade of verbena, and something more, something unnameable, unless that name be hers—and the memory of her, full and complete, comes rushing once more to the surface of my mind, the loss every bit as keen, my heart every bit as broken as it was the night I lost her, so many years ago. My mistress. My love. My Charlotte.

AUTHOR'S NOTE

When I first arrived on Washington Square, in 1999, it was to submit my application to New York University in person. I remember walking up the steps of the Federal-style town house and hoping that, as a future student, I would one day be able to explore more of these stately buildings. Twenty years later, I am privileged still to be a part of the NYU community, spending five days a week in the red—not ivory—tower of Bobst Library, overlooking the Square. I have been inside many of those town houses that I once longed to explore, and today, from my office window, I can look out over the fountain and the arch, right to the Waldens' door at number 17 Washington Square North.

Of course, it doesn't exist anymore. Perhaps it never did. For the primary setting of *The Parting Glass,* I chose a building that had been demolished decades before I was born. As a writer of historical fiction, I strive to ensure that the world I have constructed on the page is as accurate as research can make it, embellished by the imagination only when sources fail. While the house in which Maire and Seanin fall in love with Charlotte Walden is as fictional as the characters who populate it, the structure I have described is an amalgamation of my favorite features of those Federal town houses still standing today. If it seems a little larger and a little grander than those still extant, blame it on that wide-eyed seventeen-year-old girl who was so excited to hand-deliver her college application.

While my younger self was captivated by the Charlottes and Prudences who glided through the drawing rooms, silk and taffeta skirts swishing over thick-piled rugs, crystal chandeliers illuminating gilt-leaf furniture and flocked wallpaper, I've grown to have a greater appreciation and affinity for the domestics whose efforts made such lavish lifestyles possible. Prior to the twentieth century, the vast majority of women in the workforce were employed as servants. Besides various types of needlework, there were few other trades available to women. A household such as the Waldens' would employ a small army to keep itself functioning: a housekeeper, a butler, a cook, two ladies' maids, two footmen, three housemaids, a stable master, a stableboy, and a scullion. All to serve two women of leisure. Presumably, had Mr. Walden lived, a valet and additional stable staff would have been employed as well. I have done my best to represent the diversity of the New York servant class in the microcosm of the Waldens' household. Some, like Maire and Seanin, would have been immigrants. Others, like Mrs. Freedman, Young Frank, and Agnes, would have been former slaves, freed in New York in 1827, who remained in paid domestic positions after abolition. Many would be working-class descendants of the Dutch and Anglo immigrants who had lived in New York for generations, or who had come to the city from the surrounding countryside in search of economic opportunities. By the time the story ends, in 1845, the Great Hunger had begun in Ireland and thousands more immigrants were pouring into New York from there, from Germany, and from other parts of western

Europe. Freed and escaped slaves began to make their way north during the antebellum period as well, further contributing to New York's melting pot reputation.

The city's nineteenth-century population surge would correspond with an abundance of cheap labor. Average wages, particularly for women, fell as the labor pool grew. While Liddie and Maire's repeated debate over the benefits and drawbacks of service over prostitution is of course imaginary, in the years before sex work was criminalized and routinely prosecuted, a small number of women were able to own their own brothels or be their own mistresses. It should, of course, be noted that most sex workers never attained Liddie's autonomy or professional success. Few had any sort of protection at all, and those who did were beholden to procurers or brothel owners. However, for a short period in the early nineteenth century, it was possible for sex workers to achieve a level of affluence equal to or surpassing that of their high society counterparts, while enjoying a degree of liberty that other women rarely did.

Although none of the on-page characters are modeled on historic figures, a few of the people they reference and the events they experience are based in fact. Liddie's presumed father, Edmund Kean, was, indeed, the premiere Shakespearean actor of his day, known for many of the backstage antics described in this book. Madame Eliza Jumel, grande dame of the Saratoga spa scene, lived and is said to still haunt her mansion in Washington Heights. As I live within walking distance and am a regular visitor to her beautiful home, I would have been remiss not to include some small reference to a woman whose name was infamous in New York's wealthiest drawing rooms during the period. The Jays and Astors, casually mentioned as the Waldens' friends, have gone on to spawn dynasties whose names are now woven into New York's landscape. The Tredwell family home is now the Merchant's House Museum.

This novel also takes place at a curious moment in the prehistory of the Fire Department of New York, when fire brigades, according to contemporary accounts, seemed to spend just as much time clashing with one another as they spent fighting fires. Massive street brawls over control of the water pumps would end only with the formation of a paid fire department, in 1865. Until that point, it was not uncommon for buildings to burn as fire companies and street gangs engaged in melees as violent as the blazes they'd come to quell.

The attack on Old St. Patrick's Cathedral, after which Seanin becomes a prominent member of the Hibernians, is, sadly, all too true. The mid-1830s saw a number of riots as members of the anti-Catholic Know-Nothing party incited violence, attacking churches and Catholic-owned businesses. Indeed, the anti-Irish and anti-Catholic sentiment I have described here is well documented, only increasing as the century wore on. And while the Ancient Order of Hibernians did emerge as a powerful force to protect Irish interests in 1836, and certainly had ties to Irish Nationalist movements, I have taken some artistic license in embellishing those links. Many members of the AOH were anti-Unionists who were in favor of an independent Ireland, but the international conspiracy I have described, while based on many historic Irish secret societies, is my own creation.

Likewise, the Hibernian, that stronghold of the Order, though similar in many ways to several of my favorite Manhattan drinking establishments, is an invention. The layout described is typical of the timber structures that made up a great deal of the area south of Houston, none of which remain standing today. It might be considered a hybrid of McSorley's Old Ale House, Swift Hibernian Lounge, and the late, lamented Grassroots Tavern for all the reasons one might expect of an author who came of age in the East Village. Dermot's position as publican and ward boss would have been a common one, for who else would have known the neighbors so well as the person serving their drinks?

The research, therefore, that made this work of fiction possible was conducted in various university libraries (namely Bobst at NYU and Butler at Columbia), and on-site, in and around the myriad locations named in this book. For the reader who wishes to delve further into Maire's world, I have provided a collection of source texts consulted in writing *The Parting Glass*. For those who wish to go further, well, I can recommend nothing so heartily as a walk through Washington Square Park.

ACKNOWLEDGMENTS

Writing tends to be a rather solitary occupation, but bringing a book into the world is not. I am therefore indebted to a number of individuals without whom the volume in your hands would not exist. Foremost amongst them are my parents, Denise and John Guadagnino, who, upon discovering early my knack for making up stories, encouraged me to keep at it. I cannot honestly apologize to them for the amount of profanity used in this novel, for "You taught me language, and my profit on it is, I know how to curse." My thanks as well to my grandmother Gloria Pane, for her early cultivation of my grammatical pedantry.

To the various teachers and professors with whom I've honed my writing over the years, particularly Keith Young, who stressed authenticity of voice; Nancy Bucklew, who encouraged my earliest efforts in historical fiction; Shelley Jackson, for her inspiration in nonlinear narrative; and Zia Jaffrey, for exhorting me to write something with "Sapphic overtones."

I am deeply grateful to an incredible group of readers for their assistance in researching and workshopping various drafts, including Michael Robertson, Gil Varod, Jennifer Jordan, Jennifer Lobasz, and Amanda Ripley. Most especially, I would like to thank Stephen

Danay, my meander scout, who read multiple drafts, gave feedback over countless sessions, and patiently endured endless conversations on the subject of this book.

Hands-on research for this novel was conducted with the assistance of the knowledgeable and informative curators and docents of the Merchant's House Museum and Morris-Jumel Mansion. I would also like to thank the staff at 60 Morningside Drive for teaching me how to walk quietly on the servants' stair.

As it is a truth universally acknowledged that one cannot write without a room of her own, I wish to thank Teresa Davanzo for providing one, from which the bulk of the first draft was composed. Similarly, Evelyn and the rest of the team at Kopi Kopi kept me fueled with the positively criminal amounts of caffeine that allow my synapses to fire properly. My colleagues on the twelfth floor of Bobst Library were incredibly supportive of this endeavor, and, without their insistence that I actually leave my desk once in a while, the editorial process could not have been completed so swiftly.

This book would have languished as a file on my laptop had not Alexandra Machinist, agent extraordinaire, plucked me from the obscurity of her slush pile. I am deeply indebted to her faith in my writing, and her commitment to this novel. Likewise, I am grateful that *The Parting Glass* found a home in Trish Todd's capable and highly supportive editorial hands. She and the tremendous team at Atria Books have made my lifelong dream a reality.

I would like to offer a tribute to the memory of the original Dermot John O'Brien: friend, mentor, pub trivia champion, professor, drinking companion, and relentless supporter of my writing, right up till the end. Not a day goes by when I don't miss him, and I hope he will forgive me the sentimental gesture of having stolen his name for use in this volume.

Finally, my deep and abiding gratitude to my husband, Aaron Zwintscher, for his support and encouragement, day after day, year after year. *Sláinte* to you and to our Finnegan.

SELECTED BIBLIOGRAPHY

Adams, Peter. *The Bowery Boys: Street Corner Radicals and the Politics of Rebellion*. Westport, CT: Praeger Publishers, 2005.

Anbinder, Tyler. *Five Points: The 19th-Century New York City Neighborhood That Invited Tap Dance, Stole Elections, and Became the World's Most Notorious Slum*. New York: Free Press, 2001.

Asbury, Herbert. *Gangs of New York: An Informal History of the Underworld.* 1927. Reprint, New York: Vintage Books, 2008.

Brekke-Aloise, Linzy. "'A Very Pretty Business': Fashion and Consumer Culture in Antebellum American Prints." *Winterthur Portfolio* 48, no. 2–3, (Summer–Autumn 2014): 191–212.

Burrows, Edwin G., and Mike Wallace. *Gotham: A History of New York City to 1898*. New York: Oxford University Press, 1999.

Byrd, Ayana D., and Lori L. Tharps. *Hair Story: Untangling the Roots of Black Hair in America*. New York: St. Martin's Press, 2001.

Carpenter, Theresa, ed. *New York Diaries: 1609 to 2009.* New York: Modern Library, 2012.

Diner, Hasia A. *Erin's Daughters in America: Irish Women in the Nineteenth Century.* Baltimore: Johns Hopkins University Press, 1983.

Dunne, Robert. *Antebellum Irish Immigration and Emerging Ideolo-*

gies of America: A Protestant Backlash. Lewiston, NY: Edwin Mellen Press, 2002.

The Duties of a Lady's Maid; with Directions for Conduct, and Numerous Receipts for the Toilette. London: James Bulcock, 1825.

Hill, Marilynn Wood. *Their Sisters' Keepers: Prostitution in New York City, 1830–1870*. Berkeley: University of California Press, 1993.

Knapp, Mary L. *An Old Merchant's House: Life at Home in New York City, 1835–65*. New York: Girandole Books, 2012.

Matsell, George W. *Vocabulum; or, the Rogue's Lexicon*. New York: George W. Matsell & Co., 1859.

Morgan, Jack. *New World Irish: Notes on One Hundred Years of Lives and Letters in American Culture*. New York: Palgrave MacMillan, 2011.

Parker, John, ed. *Who's Who in the Theatre: A Biographical Record of the Contemporary Stage*. Boston: Small, Maynard, 1922.

Pollard, H. B. S. *Secret Societies of Ireland: Their Rise and Progress*. London: Philip Allan, 1898.

Richardson, R. C. *Household Servants in Early Modern England*. Manchester, UK: Manchester University Press, 2010.

Yamin, Rebecca. "Wealthy, Free, and Female: Prostitution in Nineteenth-Century New York." *Historical Archaeology* 39, no. 1, (2005): 4–18.